Wizard or Witch?

A Magical World Awaits You
Read

THE
SECRETS
OF
DROON

Wizard or Witch?

by Tony Abbott

Illustrated by David Merrell

Cover illustration by Tim Jessell

A
LITTLE APPLE
PAPERBACK

SCHOLASTIC INC.

New York Toronto London Auckland Sydney
Mexico City New Delhi Hong Kong Buenos Aires

ISBN 0-439-56049-7

12 11 10 9   9/0

Printed in the U.S.A.   40
First printing, January 2004

For Janie and Lucy,
my amazing and magical daughters

Contents

Contents

Wizard or Witch?

One

This Magic Moment

It was the sound of words that woke me.

At first, they seemed strange and beautiful, like mysterious fish weaving around a swimmer.

Then the shouts came, and the running of feet, and the voices, full of fear, calling me. . . .

No. Wait. That's not right.

I need to begin this story properly.

It isn't every day a person gets to write in her Wizardbook. This is far too important to get wrong. The story I set down on these pages — every single word of it — has to be right.

It has to be perfect.

Perfect? Yes. That's part of the story, too.

Okay, then.

My name is Keeah. I live in Jaffa City, the royal capital of the land of Droon. King Zello is Droon's ruler and the leader of its people. He's also my father.

Queen Relna is my very beautiful and kind mother. She's a wizard of incredible power.

Since I'm their daughter, I'm a princess.

And a wizard.

The more I practice all my charms and spells — and the bright blue wizard sparks shooting from my fingertips have been getting stronger each day — the better it is for Droon.

That's because not all of Droon is good.

And *that*'s because of Lord Sparr.

I shiver even writing his name in my Wizardbook. Sparr is a sorcerer of great power. He wants to control not only his Dark Lands — the smelly, smoke-filled countries east of Jaffa City — but every single inch of Droon itself.

And not just Droon, either.

A long time ago, Sparr created the Three Powers — the Red Eye of Dawn, the Golden Wasp, and the Coiled Viper.

For ages and ages, these magical objects were lost.

Then, Sparr found his Powers — one after the other — until only the Red Eye remained hidden from him.

Of course, my parents and I aren't

the only ones trying to stop Sparr from ruling Droon.

The great wizard, Galen Longbeard, has fought the sorcerer and his army of Ninns forever, trying to keep them from taking over.

Or, he used to.

A very mysterious genie named Anusa took the wizard away from us on a long journey. Where Galen is now and when his quest will end, nobody really knows.

But Max, his trusty spider troll friend, is here to help us, along with many friendly people and creatures in every corner of Droon. They're part of this story, too.

Best of all are my friends Eric Hinkle, Julie Rubin, and Neal Kroger.

Ever since they discovered a magical staircase between us and the Upper World where they live, they've been helping me keep Droon safe.

Eric has even become a wizard with his own really strong magic. Julie now has the ability to fly. And Neal . . . well, Neal is Neal.

Droon can be pretty dangerous, but my friends are always here when I need them most.

I needed them today.

Which brings me to the beginning. I'll start my story with the very first thing I remember.

Morning . . .

The sun was just below the eastern hills. I was in my royal bed, asleep and dreaming . . . dreaming . . . dreaming . . . deep dreams. . . .

Krooth-ka . . . meshti . . . pah-la . . . Neffu!

"What?" I bolted up in bed thinking that someone had called out to me. Strange words I'd never heard before swam in my head for a moment, then faded.

Looking around, I saw hazy pink light beginning to streak the floor of my room.

"Who's there?" I said. "Mother? Father —"

Thump! Thump! The sound of running feet filled the corridors of the palace.

"Stop, you! Stop!" someone yelled.

Pushing aside the book lying next to me, I jumped up from my bed, only to find that I had fallen asleep in my clothes — blue tunic, leggings, and belt. My gold crown lay resting on my pillow. I put it on.

"Max? Max!" I called. He didn't answer. His tiny bed was all rumpled and empty in the corner.

A sudden cry came through the halls.

"It is mine . . . *mine*!"

A chill ran through me. The voice, part

hissing, part snarling, sounded like *his*. It sounded like the voice of Lord Sparr.

"Him? Here? Never!" I whispered.

Long ago, Galen had cast a spell against Sparr. He could never enter Jaffa City unless he was invited in. *And he never would be.*

I looked up at the ceiling. Objects I had levitated the night before — two clocks, a bucket, five pencils — still hung where I'd charmed them. Levitating things was my latest skill. Among the hovering objects was a glass ball that I always use to call my friends.

"Princess!" cried a fearful voice from below. It came from my parents' throne room.

"Coming!" I shouted. I glanced back at the floating ball. "Sorry, friends, I'll call you later. Right now, I'm needed!"

I knew going over the rooftops would

be even quicker than running through the palace halls, which I wasn't supposed to do anyway. So, I flung open the far door and dashed onto the stones of my balcony.

Above me, the sky was turning from deep violet to the pink of morning. The sun just peeped over the eastern horizon. I breathed it all in.

"Okay, Keeah," I said to myself. "It's magic time. Mother, Father, here I come!"

Trembling, I sprang off the balcony and darted up across the roof tiles to the peak. I skipped along the top, then leaped off.

Whoosh! I glided through the air and came down running on the next peak. Speeding across, I jumped to a low tower, then to a little dome.

Fwit-fwit-fwit! From one roof to the next, I flitted and danced, twirling in midair, flying across the tiles for a moment, then leaping onto the next rooftop.

This power had just come to me, too.

Quickening my pace, I jumped one last time, landed on the giant dome of the main palace, slid down, and dropped to its large balcony. It overlooked the city square and the sea beyond.

I saw people running in the courtyard below, calling out wildly. Shaggy six-legged pilkas clomped in every direction. And there, in the middle of it all, was something that chilled me to the bone.

A car.

With a long yellow body, eight fat tires, twin silver horns on either side, and a glass bubble on top, it was a car I had seen before.

My stomach tightened.

"Sparr's car!" I gasped. "He *is* here!"

Already my hands were hot. I didn't know how Sparr had gotten into the city, but I knew I'd have to join my parents to battle him out again. I only hoped that when my sparks flared, we would all be a match for him.

Gritting my teeth, I turned, crossed the balcony, slammed through the giant doors, and strode into the throne room.

"Sparr —" I shouted. I stopped.

Against the bright silver and green banners, the evil sorcerer stood alone in a circle of dark light.

One of his hands was raised high, clasped tightly in a fist. A sizzling spray of red sparks shot from it.

"Where are my parents?" I demanded.

Slowly, Sparr turned his head. His face was thin, his nose sharp, his eyes flashing like black flames. But it was the dark red fin behind each ear that proved he was not like the rest of us.

"Your parents are . . . sleeping in," he said softly, pointing to the end of the throne room.

My heart nearly stopped. There, inside a large crystal box, standing silent and unmoving, were my mother and father.

I ran to the box. "What did you do to them?" My parents' eyes were shut as if they were in a deep sleep. "Sparr, answer me!"

"They were in my way," said the sorcerer. "Or, I should say . . . *our* way."

"Our way?" I turned back to Sparr. "You can't be in the city. How did you even get in here?"

A cold smile crossed his lips. "Why, Keeah . . . don't you remember?"

I trembled. "Remember what?"

"How you kindly opened the gates for me!"

Red light sizzled from his closed hand.

"What? I'd never do that. I couldn't do that. I'm a wizard —"

"Oh?" he said. "And do wizards turn their palace guards into . . . *toads*?"

He motioned behind him. Several helmets on the floor toppled over. Under each was a big brown lump. They croaked one after the other, then hopped away.

"I didn't!" I said. "I was sleeping —"

"How nice, then, that *my* dreams came true!" said Sparr. "Because you gave me — this."

He opened his gloved fist and lifted his palm to me. In it sat a large crimson jewel, lighting up his face with a bright red glow.

I shivered. "The Red Eye of Dawn! But who — how did you — that's impossible —"

Turning, I saw the large iron door behind my father's throne hanging open. The small room inside was empty.

My head throbbed. My mouth felt dry.

"Sparr, I don't know what tricks you're playing here, but you won't get away with this!"

"I'm *not* getting away," he said calmly. "I'm staying right here. With your parents no longer a problem, Jaffa City is mine. You are mine. Oh, now look —"

Wham! The doors flew open.

Max charged in, his orange hair wild and standing straight up, his eyes wide and afraid. "Princess, creatures are pouring out of the Dark Lands. Ninns are sailing to the city right now. Sparr is taking over! We must fight —"

Without wanting to, I felt my hands moving up from my sides, growing hot. "Max, I . . ."

The spider troll stumbled to a halt. "Princess?"

Poooom! — a flash of sparks left my fingers. Max flew across the floor, blasting out the doors and over the balcony as if he were dragged away by an invisible rope.

A second later, he vanished out to sea.

"Max, no, no! My gosh, what have I done?!" I looked at the sparks spitting from the tips of my fingers.

They were jagged and hot and . . . red.

"Witch powers!" I gasped.

Sparr howled with laughter. "Ninns *are* coming here. Creatures from the Dark Lands *are* on the move. I *am* taking over. And all because of you, Keeah. Your dark powers — your *witch* powers — have finally come out! There's no one to stop me anymore. What a perfect moment. *Perfect!*"

I could barely speak. "Perfect? It's not perfect. It's the opposite of perfect. . . . It's . . . it's . . ."

Sparr turned to my parents' empty thrones and offered me his hand. "Now that you are a witch, Keeah, let's rule Droon as I had always hoped — *together*!"

Two

Ninth Orbit, Second Moon

I felt as cold as ice. I stared at my fingers. They sprayed red-hot sparks in the air.

"I didn't mean to do this. I *can't* do this!"

Sparr smiled, still waiting for me to take his hand. "But you did do it, Keeah. I have waited so long for your dark side to rise up and take over! Now, tell me. Jaffa City sounds so old-fashioned. What do you think of *Sparrville* —"

"Sparrville?!"

I couldn't believe it. Here I was, standing inches from the worst sorcerer in Droon, all black clothes and red fire, but instead of blasting him, I had just zapped away my dearest friend!

"No. No! NO!" I yelled.

Sparr smirked. "Oh, I see. I suppose you like *Keeahport* better? Or perhaps . . . *Princesstown?*"

I backed away.

I knew what I had to do.

Keeping my arms at my sides and closing my eyes, I saw my parents' faces before me, as gentle and kind as they were last night.

I spoke the words my mother had taught me.

"Blibby . . . blobby . . . snoo!"

Sparr's face twisted. "Eh? I thought you were done with those silly spells — oh!"

Kkkkrrreeeekkkk! Everything in the

room, in the palace, in the whole city, stopped moving.

Everything went still.

Sparr stood there as motionless as a statue. His black eyes stared ahead. One of his hands still clasped the jewel while the other reached for me. His fins burned a deep red.

"You . . . horrible . . . *thing*!" I shouted.

Wiping my cheeks, I faced my parents, asleep in their crystal box. "Mother, you taught me this halting charm. Father, I have twelve hours before everything moves again in Jaffa City. Twelve hours to figure out how I let Sparr in, to find Max, to wake you both, to save Droon! My friends will come. Together, we'll fix this. We will!"

The sound of my footsteps echoed down the hall as I left the throne room.

Up the main staircase I ran, pounding up the marble steps two at a time. I raced through my father's library, up the final set of stairs, and into the corridor outside my room.

I paused to catch my breath.

In the stillness around me, I heard only the sound of my heart beating.

I felt so completely alone.

Peering for a moment out a small window, I saw the vast sea where I had sent Max. Its dark, booming waves suddenly brought up a name I hadn't thought of since last night.

"Demither!"

Demither was my mother's sister and the ruler of a powerful sea empire.

Demither was also a witch.

"Is it true, then? Am I becoming like her?"

Oooo — oooo. A low sound drifted up from the stairs. It was as if the wind were moaning through every silent room and open door of the palace.

I shook my head to clear it. "It's only the wind. And I have only twelve hours. Come on!"

I rushed into my room and quickly bolted the door behind me. Turning, I reached for the glass ball hanging in the air and pulled it down.

My heart leaped to remember how many times Eric, Julie, and Neal had dropped what they were doing to come and help me.

"Friends," I said, shaking, "my parents are under a spell. Sparr is here. I cursed poor Max! I need you now. Please hurry!"

I rolled my hand over the ball, and it lit up as if there were a fire inside it. Taking a feather pen, I formed a letter on the ball.

I nearly laughed to think how Galen
would scold me if he saw how shaky my
writing was.

"Wizards should have excellent handwriting," he told me once. "Power comes
from words, both spoken *and* written. Remember that!"

Lifting my pen to the ball again, I wrote
the letters slowly, starting from the end of
the word and finishing at the beginning.

ε . . . m . . . o . . . c

I paused, then added a second word.

ε . . . s . . . a . . . e . . . l . . . p

I'm not sure I needed it, but my father
always taught me to be polite. His Rules
for the Kingly Art of Combat flashed
through my mind.

1. Straighten your tunic before entering battle.

2. Always say, "May Droon be with you!" if your opponent sneezes.

3. No matter who wins, don't forget to offer your enemy a ride home.

I swallowed hard as I remembered his gruff voice reciting those rules. I set down the pen.

After a moment or two, the letters faded. The ball went clear.

"Okay," I said. "Now I wait —"

But right then, I saw a purple object sticking out from under my bed.

"My Wizardbook."

I picked it up and opened it. A lump formed in my throat as I remembered the first time I had ever seen the book.

Last night . . .

*   *   *

Fwoosh! Blam! Whizzz! Bright blue sparks were whizzing around my room in the twilight air. I spun near the ceiling for minutes at a time, sending objects flying wildly around me.

Knock, knock! I jumped to my bed as the door opened. My mother stepped in, wearing a long white gown. Behind her was my father in full armor, his twin-horned helmet on his head.

Between them was tiny Max. His wild hair was combed flat, and he was wiggling as if ready to burst into song.

"What is it?" I asked.

"Keeah, do you know what tomorrow is?" asked my father.

I thought for a moment. "Is it my turn to walk the pilkas again?"

He laughed. "No, dear! Max, if you please."

"Ahem!" The spider troll cleared his throat and unrolled a small scroll.

In a voice as deep as he could make it, Max began, "My dear princess, tomorrow is the first day of the seventh month before the last week nearest the fourth hour of the third season following the ninth orbit of the second moon!"

I think I must have frowned.

"In other words," said my mother, laughing as she brought out a package from behind her gown, "open it!"

I gasped. "A present? For me? I knew I liked the ninth orbit of the second moon!"

I tore off the paper. Inside, I found a small book covered in rich purple leather. Gold designs coiled across its shiny finish. A hazy silver stone set right in the center of the cover shone with threads of red and blue light twisting deeply within it.

"It's so beautiful," I said. "Thank you!"

"Keeah, this is not just any book," my mother said, sitting on my bed. "It is your Wizardbook. A moment comes to every wizard when your magic becomes greater than it has ever been —"

"It's like a growth spurt!" said Max.

I gazed at the objects floating above us.

"That moment is coming," my mother said. "Your Wizardbook is your story of how you become a *droomar* wizard."

"*Droomar!*" I whispered.

"Yes, *droomar!*" boomed my father. "Even before Galen, the mysterious *droomar* were living in caves, keeping alive the ancient wisdom of Droon. They are a magical elfin sort of folk —"

"But I'm not an elf," I said. "How can I become a *droomar*?"

My mother smiled. "Elfin Sight," she said. "It is a power given to you at the moment you need it most. With the Sight, you see our world as you never have before."

"It is a wizard's secret weapon," said my father. "Elfin Sight is the true mark of a *droomar*."

"And a sign of great love," my mother said.

Max patted my shoulder. "The queen traveled a thousand miles in a single day to find her deepest magic," he said. "An old *droomar* was her guide. That was a dangerous journey!"

"At every step I was tempted by the darker ways," she said. "I had many friends with me, including your aunt, my sister. Finally, I was alone —"

She paused, looking out my window to the sea beyond the city walls.

My aunt. Her sister. Demither.

The Sea Witch.

I shivered to remember how, like my mother, Demither was born to do great magic — *droomar* magic — until Sparr tempted her to join him.

From the moment she became his servant, she couldn't rebel against him. She had to help in his plans to take over Droon.

I remembered, too, how once, when I was very young and far from home, Demither shared her powers with me. I remembered how her red sparks flowed into me, and how happy I was when those dark powers seemed to go away.

"Is Demither a *droomar*?" I asked.

My father shook his head. "The day she turned away from her family was the day she lost her Elfin Sight."

My mother looked at me again. "Keeah, let your Wizardbook inspire you. You alone can tell your story. When you come to write it, I know you will fill these pages with the wonderful language of your soul!"

It was true — the blank white pages seemed to call out to be filled with magical words.

"Thank you," I said.

"Soon you'll be a true *droomar* like your mother," said my father proudly. "Keeah, your moment is nearly here!"

Nearly here.

I remember the thrill of hearing that.

Now, as the memory of their late-night visit faded, and the wind howled in the halls again, I couldn't deny it anymore.

"I might be a wizard," I murmured, "but so was Demither once. When my big moment comes, maybe it won't be like anyone expects. Maybe my true powers *are* coming out. And they're not *droomar* powers. Maybe I'm a —"

Ooooo — The sound echoed up the stairs.

I felt a chill on my neck.

"That's not the wind," I said. "It's a voice. . . ."

"*Oooo* —" The moan sounded closer.

"It's the voice of . . . a ghost!"

Without saying a word or thinking a thought — *zzzz!* — my hands flashed red, and the bucket I had flown the night before was hovering before me, brimming with cold water.

"*Oooo* —" The sound came closer still.

I gulped down my fear and grabbed the bucket. "So there's a ghost, is there? Well, witch powers or not, if it comes here, it'll get a wet head!"

Leaping to a chair, I carefully balanced

the bucket on the edge of the door frame.

"If ghosts even *have* heads!"

I braced myself, staring at the door, both hands sprinkling bright red sparks.

Suddenly — *shooom!* — the little fireplace behind me exploded with a giant cloud of smoke.

I whirled around to see legs and arms and sneakers shooting straight at me.

I gasped. "Eric?"

"Out — of — the — way!" he cried.

Three

Chitchat with a Hat

Blam! Wump! Oooof! Eric flew like a shot across the room, hurtling me back to the bed.

"Sorry!" he yelled. "We — uh — fell!"

Julie thudded down the fireplace shaft, leaped to her feet, then collapsed to the floor. "*Owww!*"

"Way to be in the way!" said Neal. He tumbled over Julie, struck my bookcase, rolled back, flipped once, slammed against the wall, then stopped.

Dazed, he looked up. "Oh, Keeah . . . hi!"

"I'm so glad you're here!" I said, rushing to help them up.

Eric stared at the fireplace, wobbling back and forth. "Lucky you didn't have a fire!"

"Neal would have put it out anyway," said Julie. She stepped over the puddle at Neal's feet. He was soaking wet.

Neal laughed. "Water balloons!" he said. "When you called us, I was filling them to throw at Julie and Eric. But they kept exploding."

"The water balloons kept exploding," said Eric. "The magic word being *water*. Neal was drenched —" He stopped. "Keeah, you look worried. What's happening? Why did you call us here?"

There were so many things to tell. But when I opened my mouth, I couldn't make myself say any of them. I just pointed out to my balcony.

They saw the square full of people and animals, all silent and still.

"Holy cow!" gasped Neal. "Everyone has become statues? What's going on?"

"It's a halting spell," I said. "Every person and creature in Jaffa City has stopped moving for twelve hours. I had to do it. Because of Sparr. Because . . . he's here. . . ."

Julie's jaw dropped. "Sparr's here? How did he even get this far? Who let him into the city? What does he want?"

I swallowed hard. There was only one answer.

"Me, me, and, I guess, me . . ."

Holding back the tears as best I could, I told them everything. That Sparr had put my parents under a spell, that he said I let him through the gates and gave him the Red Eye of Dawn, and that I cursed Max far away across the sea.

"It's all because," I said, forcing myself to say it, "I'm turning into a witch. Just like Demither did. The dark powers she gave me once are coming back. They're growing in me."

To show them, I opened my hands. Red sparks glowed from the tips of my fingers.

"To make things worse, a huge army of Ninns is on its way," I said finally. "And creatures from the Dark Lands. It's happening. Sparr is taking over —"

Eric stared at me for a second, then shook his head. "I don't believe it. Somebody's playing tricks here. Maybe even Demither, trying to win you over. This must be some weirdo evil plan."

"Besides," said Julie, "you used a wizard spell to halt things, right? And you called us to come. So you're not totally a — you know."

Neal frowned. "Plus, letting Sparr just stroll right into your home? I don't think so —"

"*Oooooo!*" came the sound from the hall.

Everyone went quiet.

"And there's that," I whispered.

Neal gulped. "*That?* What exactly *is* that?"

"A ghost, I think," I said. "It's haunting me."

"A ghost! Why didn't you tell us?" said Eric. Bright silver sparks began to sprinkle from his fingers. "Stand back, everyone. We'll stop it where it stands. Or hovers. Or whatever!"

"*Oooo — oooo — eeeee — kkkk — ohhh!*"

As we watched, something big and brown and rumpled pushed itself right through the wall and into the room with us.

It floated three feet above the floor.

It had a wide, floppy brim.

It was a hat.

"*Oooo-oooo-oooo!*" said a voice from a few inches below where the hat was floating.

Julie blinked. "The ghost is . . . a *hat*?"

"Thum!" said the space under the hat. "Augustus Rudolphus Septimus Thum! At your service. Yes, yes, I know. Big name, tiny body —"

"We don't see a body," said Neal.

"Of course you don't see a . . . What did you say?"

"All we see is a hat," said Julie.

"All you see is — oh, dear, I'm so forgetful!" The hat wiggled, twirled once, and dipped backward.

Plooop! In the space below it appeared a small, white, four-footed creature, standing upright. He had a stubby snout, bushy whiskers, green eyes, and pointed ears. He was wearing blue spectacles tied on a ribbon. He bowed with a flourish.

When he did, I saw through him slightly.

"There!" said the creature. He cleared his throat. "Now then. I'm not a ghost, no, but a *droomar*. That's a *drrr*, and an *oooo*, and a *marrrrr* —"

I gasped. "My mother is a *droomar* wizard!"

"*Oooo*, I know," said the creature, wiggling his nose. "And I am your guide. Well, sort of. I've come to give you a message. Now then, what was it? Oh, yes. *Booooooo* —"

"Now, stop that!" said Julie, her hands on her hips. "Why are you haunting poor Keeah?"

The creature let out a big gasp. "Haunting? Goodness, no! *Booo* was just the first part of what I have to say. The rest of the message is . . . is . . . oh. Oh, now I've forgotten. Wait. *Boogie dune!*"

We looked at him.

"Or, no," he said. "That's not it. *Beagle drum!* No, no . . . *Baggy dome . . . ?*"

"*Bagel Town!*" said Neal, lighting up.

"That doesn't sound right," said Thum.

"Could it be . . . *Bangledorn?*" I asked.

"THAT'S IT!" Thum shouted. "Bangledorn! The Bangledorn Forest! Where the Bangledorn monkeys live! You must go there at once!"

Julie frowned. "Go to Bangledorn? But Sparr is right here in the palace. The Bangledorn Forest is a long way away. Why should we go there?"

Thum grumbled. "Yes, well, you would have to ask me that. . . ."

I clasped the Wizardbook. "I know! My mother's wizard journey took her a long way. Maybe this is part of my *droomar* journey —"

The elfin creature jumped. "Mother's journey? Wizardbook? Now I remember!"

He waved a little paw over my book's silvery stone. An instant later, the haze cleared and it showed the image of a thick green forest.

Neal gasped. "It's like a tiny TV!"

Eeeee — eeee! A high-pitched shriek rang out from the stone. Then we saw dozens of tiny green monkeys fleeing through the trees.

"Something's happening," said Eric.

A moment later, we saw a mass of black wings. Finally, we saw the red fur, rusty armor, and glinting claws of an army flying into the forest.

"Oh, my gosh!" gasped Julie. "Wing-wolves!"

We knew wingwolves. We had battled one before. It was a terrifying creature from an ancient tribe that Galen called the Hakoth-Mal.

"So, it's true," I said. "Sparr's creatures *are* coming from the Dark Lands. If this is part of my journey, it's up to me to stop them!"

"It's up to *us*," said Eric. "Together."

Thum grinned. "Yes, yes, that's the message! Go! And remember this — Droon's future lies with the one who has the biggest head!"

"The biggest head?" said Julie. "What does that mean? You know, Thum, for someone who can be invisible, you're not very clear —"

"I am now!" said the *droomar*.

A moment later — *pooomf!* — he was gone.

Neal stared at the empty spot. "Could the guy have *been* any weirder? Wait. Let me answer that. No, he could not."

Eric laughed. "But he showed us that Bangledorn's in trouble. We need to go. Come on!"

For the first time since I woke up, I felt myself smile.

I had just remembered my mother's words.

I had many friends with me.

"Okay, then," I said, tucking my Wizardbook into a leather pouch and hooking it on my belt. "Maybe we *can* change things. To the forest, everybody. And Sparr will take us there!"

I pointed down from my balcony to the yellow car. Its fat tires pointed to the city gate.

Neal grinned. "We are gonna travel in style! And I wanna drive!"

He charged over to the door. That's when I remembered the bucket. "Neal, wait, no —"

Splooooosh! A gallon of icy cold water dropped over him, soaking him completely.

"I am so sorry!" I said, trying not to laugh.

Neal stood there, dripping onto the floor and staring at us. "Just when I was starting to dry out, too," he said. "Nice. Very nice. . . ."

Four

Flight of the Wingy Wolves

Racing outside, we dashed across the square to the long yellow car.

"It looks super fast," said Eric, lifting the bubble top. "There's a map here, but no steering wheel. How does it work?"

"It's magical," I said. "Galen told me it goes where Sparr commands it to go. And it goes fast."

"That's why *I* should drive," said Neal. Eric turned. "You? Why you?"

"Because I love fast cars," said Neal. "Besides, I'm pretty sure I'm the tallest." He brushed his wet hair up on his forehead.

"But I'm a week older," said Eric.

"We're all getting older!" said Julie, leaping into the driver's seat. "And we're wasting time. Car, to the Bangledorn Forest!"

The moment we jumped in — *ooga!* — the horns blared, and we screeched out the courtyard gates and away from the silent palace.

"The journey begins," I said. "Mother, Father, I'll do everything I can to stop Sparr. I promise."

"We promise," said Eric. "Droon is important to us, too."

Neal nodded. "Plus, how often do you get to freeze Old Fishfins and stop his creepy plans?"

"And we *will* stop him," said Julie.

"Thanks," I said.

But as the car leaped away from Jaffa City, bumping and twisting toward the plains of middle Droon, I saw black clouds forming on the distant horizon.

What Sparr had said was already happening.

Creatures were coming from the Dark Lands.

He was taking over.

I only hoped I wasn't helping him.

We zigzagged through the countryside, with Julie driving first, then Neal. We raced faster and faster. Sparr's car seemed to know which roads to take.

Finally, we wove through the plains and rose over the crest of a giant hill. We slowed.

"There it is," I said.

In front of us stood the huge mass of

the Bangledorn Forest. It stretched all the way to the border of the smoky Dark Lands.

Neal drove up and stopped where two giant oak trees soared over a path leading inside.

"It looks peaceful," said Julie. "And magical."

"Except it's neither," said Eric. "Wing-wolves are in there. Plus, we can't use our powers here."

For ages, the Bangledorn Forest has been one of the few places in Droon where no magic is allowed. Luckily, my fingers weren't sparking.

"I'll try my best," I said. "Julie?"

She looked at a small scar on her hand. It was where a wingwolf had scratched her, giving her the power to fly. "No flying. I promise."

"I guess we can't use magical cars, either," said Neal. "We'll have to go in on foot."

We all got out and entered the forest slowly. It was hushed and cool around us, but the birds that usually greeted us were silent. And the sky above was getting darker by the minute.

"Bangledorn City is this way," I said.

But the moment I took a step — *fwish-fwish!* — a thick net of vines swept around us. It pulled us instantly into the high branches.

"Hey! We're trapped!" said Neal, struggling.

"Magic or not," said Eric, "I'll blast us out —"

"Oh!" hissed a voice. "It's Princess Keeah!"

As we dangled upside down, we saw

two furry green faces peering down through the leaves.

I gasped. "Wait, Twee, is that you?"

"And Woot?" said Julie.

It was the tiny brother and sister monkeys we had met on an earlier adventure. They jumped with surprise and hurried down to us.

"Forgive us!" chirped Twee, quickly untying the net and leading us out to a thick branch. "We thought you were the enemy. Wingwolves have invaded our forest!"

"And chased us from our homes," said Woot.

"They're moving in," added a third voice.

We looked up. A tall figure in a blue cape swung down silently from above. She wore a crown of purple leaves on her head.

"Queen Ortha," I said, bowing. "We

came as soon as we heard —" In the leaves beyond her, I saw the faces of hundreds of monkeys, their eyes huge with fear.

Ortha put a finger to her lips. "Follow me!"

Grabbing a thick vine, she slipped away quietly. We followed, swinging on vine after vine, until we landed on a branch overlooking Bangledorn City.

Houses of all sizes were built among the curling branches around us. Vine bridges dangled between them. And in the center, largest of all, was the many-leveled palace of the queen.

But crawling over every inch of the city, leaping from house to house, flying among the trees, were furry red warriors with long claws.

"We are not a fighting people," whispered Ortha. "But to see them take over our homes . . ."

Neal grumbled. "No kidding. One wing-wolf is bad enough. They brought the whole family!"

From the moment I saw the terrible creatures, I felt my hands growing hot. Words began swimming in my head, like the ones that woke me that morning.

My eyelids felt heavy. I closed my eyes. "*Pen-ga . . . zo . . .*"

Zzzzz! My eyes shot open, and I saw my fingertips spark suddenly.

So did Ortha. "Keeah . . . those words. They sound like the ancient language of Goll. How do you know them?"

I looked around. Twee and Woot were staring, too. "I'm sorry . . . this morning . . . I . . ."

I explained everything that had happened, and how I was acting so strangely.

"I must have let Sparr into the city," I

said. "I don't really remember. He told me his creatures would come. I think my new powers are behind it all."

Ortha frowned. "When Queen Relna took her wizard journey, it was also a dangerous time."

"But what are we going to do?" asked Eric.

I looked out at the wingwolves, then at the distant forest, then at my sparking hands. I knew I wouldn't be able to control them for long.

"Maybe there's a way. . . ." I said.

Ortha nodded. A small smile came to her lips. "First, the wingwolves need to know they aren't welcome here."

Twee glanced at his sister. "How about some nuts?" He chuckled.

Neal blinked. "A snack before fighting? Cool phase one. I like how you guys think."

"Not a snack," said Twee. Giggling, he and Woot leaped away with all the other monkeys.

A moment later, they were back, carrying mounds of small, shiny nuts.

"These nuts are only good for one thing," said Woot.

"To make a wingwolf think twice about trying to move in!" Twee added.

My hands were growing hotter by the second. "Phase two is up to me," I said.

While everyone took nuts and quietly surrounded the city, I moved carefully out to the edge of a long branch.

When we were in position, Ortha gave a loud shout. *"O — lee — lee!"*

Thonk! Flang! Whizzz! The hard nuts rained down on the wingwolves.

"Gaaaakkkk!" The creatures roared as the nuts struck their big furry heads and their giant clawed feet. They leaped for

cover, bumping into one another, catching their wings, and falling.

"Take that!" yelled Eric.

"Nuts for the nuts!" cried Julie.

"Now phase two," I said. "This is my job —"

I leaped from the end of the branch and grabbed a vine. While my friends kept hurling nuts, I swung away through the trees.

As I had hoped, the Hakoth-Mal saw my sparks. More and more of them flitted through the air after me. When I swung to the ground, I dashed between the trees until I flew out of the forest.

I turned to the Hakoth-Mal. "I can use magic here!" I aimed my hands, my sparks flaring.

Then I spoke. *"Pen-ga . . . zo . . . thool!"*

The air rang suddenly with shrieks and howls.

But instead of diving at me, the creatures flashed their claws and flew higher, then higher.

I didn't understand the words that I heard in my head, but I knew what they meant to the wingwolves. "Go away!"

The creatures howled again and again even as the sound of their flapping wings grew faint.

I searched the sky until I couldn't see them anymore.

They were lost in the dark air.

The wingwolves were gone.

"*O — lee — lee!*" A cheer rose from the forest. A crowd of monkeys came running out to us, led by Eric, Neal, and Julie.

"You beat them," said Eric. "They're gone."

I couldn't stop trembling. "The wingwolves are gone. But I didn't beat them. I think . . . I just . . . sent them away. And the journey isn't over. I heard them talking."

"You heard them?" said Eric. "All they do is grunt and growl — when they're not attacking!"

"Don't ask me how, but I understood their words," I said. "More monsters are coming from the Dark Lands. To a place called Rivertangle."

"Let me guess," said Julie. "It's not a cool water park, is it?"

"Please don't mention water," said Neal.

Ortha smiled. "No. Rivertangle is a place where five rivers come together. It is near the deserts of Lumpland. Keeah, I told you your mother's journey was dangerous. You helped our forest. Perhaps now I can help you. I will come."

"Our queen will go with Keeah!" yelled Twee. "I will come, too. And Woot, too!"

"But my powers," I said. "The red sparks —"

"Red sparks. Blue sparks," said Woot. "We love green most of all!"

Eric grinned. "It looks like our troop is growing. Good thing we have a big car!"

It turned out to be even bigger than we thought. When Ortha, Woot, and Twee climbed in, the long yellow car amazingly stretched out even longer, adding another whole row of seats.

"Car — to Rivertangle!" yelled Eric.

Together there were seven of us as we roared away from the forest.

Mile after mile, we rumbled south across the plains. It wasn't long before I heard words in my head again.

But this time I wasn't the only one who heard them.

"Keeah, your pouch!" said Woot. "Look!"

The Wizardbook's stone was glowing.

I pulled out the book. In the stone, we saw what looked like waves moving wildly on a vast blue sea.

Crouching closer, we spied an enormous ship, its dirty sails billowing with wind. It sailed along a rocky shore ahead of many smaller ships.

On the side of the hull was a single word:

Stinkenpoop

"Oh, my gosh," I said. "That's a Ninn ship —"

"And I know that coastline," said Ortha. "They're sailing north . . . to Jaffa City."

"Sparr really is trying to take over!" said Eric.

The image on the stone closed in on a

fat barrel lashed to the main mast. As the ship drove over the waves, the barrel's top wobbled slightly, and a head popped up from inside.

A head covered with messy orange hair.

I jumped. "It's Max! He's all right!"

My heart beat wildly to see Max again. He glanced around the ship carefully, then stopped. His mouth hung open. His eyes widened.

Then we saw what he was looking at.

The crew of chubby Ninns was leaning close together.

They slung their big arms around one another.

And they began to sing.

Five

On the Bad Ship Stinkenpoop

Yo-ho-ho! Yo-ho-ho!
We grunt and pull the heavy oar
across the seas that splash and spill!
We sail and sail and sail some more
to our new home in Spa-arrville!

We listened in shock as the warriors grunted and growled their song.

"Sparrville?" Neal snorted. "Yeah, I don't think so! Not with Max standing in your way. Well, okay, he's hiding in a barrel, but still!"

As Eric followed the map, zooming the yellow car through the grassy plains, the Wizardbook's stone showed us what was happening on the ship.

Ninns lurched across the deck, some dragging ropes, some hauling giant cartons, still others clambering up the rigging to trim the ship's sails.

As they did, Max turned carefully around in the barrel, spying everything.

"Well, well," we heard him whisper. "Of all the places I could have been sent, it had to be here."

"I'm so sorry, Max!" I whispered, wishing he could hear me.

A cluster of Ninns plodded by the barrel and climbed to a crooked wheel on an upper deck.

A smile crossed Max's lips. He blinked

his eyes and twitched his nose. "One spider troll, lots of Ninns? Seems about right!"

Looking both ways, he gripped the sides of the barrel and was out in a flash. Leaning back in for a moment, he came out with four of his eight paws clutching plump yellow bananas.

Neal grumbled as we raced along. "Why do I never eat before I come to Droon? I can practically smell those bananas."

Max chuckled. "Ninns may like to sail, but they also like fruit! Let's see how much!"

"He's got a plan," said Julie. "Go, Max!"

Peeling one of the bananas, Max darted behind a bundle of furniture — bedposts, a mattress, an armchair, a twisted lamp, and a cradle.

"They really want to set up shop in Jaffa City," said Eric. "Don't worry, Keeah. They won't."

Max looked around. "Spider trolls," he whispered. "Orange hair, people think. Big noses, people think. Furry and cuddly, people think!"

He giggled suddenly. "True enough. But when we are pushed to the limit, watch out. I'll stop this ship. And the whole Ninn army, too!"

"Yay, Max!" Twee cheered. "But be careful!"

Max tossed the empty peel near the barrel. Opening another banana, he tossed its peel not far away.

"And here they come!" he whispered.

Two large Ninns stomped heavily up to the barrel and popped it open.

They blinked.

"Empty!" the first one growled. "Sparr said treats. How do we sail with no treats?"

Max giggled, peeling and eating a third

banana. "What can I say? When I'm hungry — I eat!"

"I wish I could," whispered Neal.

The second Ninn kept staring into the barrel, frowning. "I only came for treats. And to help Sparr fight the baddies and take over."

The first Ninn snorted. "*We're* the baddies."

"Well, *you* are!" said the second Ninn.

"No, you."

"Nuh-uh, YOU!" He pushed hard, sending the other Ninn back onto one of the banana peels.

Wump! The red warrior thundered to the deck in a heap. "I get you!" he roared.

He kicked out, and the second Ninn slipped on the other peel and landed faceup.

"*Owww!*"

That's when a dozen more Ninns stumbled up from below. They spotted Max's hiding place and began shouting. "Get the furry rat!"

"Rat? Rat!" said Max. "Well, I never ever heard such a thing. . . . Rat? Well, follow this rat!"

He leaped to the mattress, bounced once, and flung himself into the rigging. Then he clambered up to the very tip of the giant mast.

"Get him!" shouted the Ninns.

The warriors on the upper deck charged up after him, leaving the ship's wheel spinning.

The thick ropes sagged under the Ninns' weight. The ship began to wobble on the waves.

Even as the Ninns followed, Max scampered across the rigging as if it were a spiderweb.

"I must get to the wheel!" he shouted.

"Must help Keeah! Turn — ship — from Jaffa City!"

"He's amazing!" said Julie. "Even against all those Ninns, he can do anything!"

"And he hasn't lost faith in me," I said.

"Of course not!" said Twee.

"Who could ever?" said Eric.

My heart raced to hear them say that.

Max sprayed a stream of spider silk at the Ninns, snaring them in a thick web.

More red warriors climbed up from below. They followed Max over the rigging until he had all of them tangled in his spidery goop!

The Ninns howled. They shouted. They shook their fists. But they were stuck to the rigging.

"Yahoo!" cried Eric. "Take *that*, Sparr!"

Max laughed at the tangled Ninns. "I was going to ask for help sailing the ship, but I see you are all tied up! Now, watch this!"

Clutching the top of the mainsail, Max dug his paws into it and slid down to the deck, tearing the sail in two all the way down.

"Hey! Way to go!" shouted Neal.

"He is a great little warrior," said Ortha.

With its sail ripped and its wheel spinning, the giant ship twisted in the wind. The smaller ships behind it began to follow it in circles.

Max stormed up to the ship's wheel. "Galen always told me of the power of words! Well, here's a word you Ninns won't forget — Max! That's me! How's that for a *yo-ho-ho* — oh!"

Suddenly, the hull rose on a wave and the ship went careening toward the shore. It lurched straight at the rocks that lined the coast.

"Oh, dear, dear!" cried the spider troll. "I fibbed! I can't really sail a ship! Someone, please help! Oh, Galen! Oh, Keeah! Oh, help!"

"He's in trouble!" shouted Woot. "Max!"

"Don't they have a brake on that thing?" said Neal.

The ship began spinning quickly. Giant waves broke over the deck, driving the ship right at the jagged rocks.

Max pulled the wheel. "Keeah — good thing you taught me to swim — oh!"

"Max!" I shouted.

Krrkk! The hull struck the rocks and cracked.

"*Stinkenpoop* sinking!" cried one Ninn.

"Ninns — wet!" boomed a second.

As wave upon wave crashed over the ship, they seemed to splash against the inside of the Wizardbook's stone, washing away the scene.

"Max! Max!" I said. "This is all my fault —"

"He'll be okay," said Julie. "He has to be. He's . . . Max."

Eric nodded. "If anyone can escape a shipwreck and a bunch of Ninns, he can. I know he will."

"I know it, too," said Ortha. "But right now, look. We're here!"

In a valley just ahead were the blue waters of several rivers, twisting and splashing together.

"Rivertangle," said Twee. "We found it —"

"We found them, too," said Neal, pointing up.

Three dark shapes swooped down from the massing clouds and flew over Rivertangle.

As we raced closer we saw their scaly skin and giant heads. We saw their pointed red noses, whiskers, long gray hair, blazing eyes, and broken teeth. We'd seen the creepy creatures before.

"Haggons!" I whispered. "Hag dragons fresh from the Dark Lands. What do they want here?"

Twee jumped straight up. "Look in the river!"

Bobbing in the wild water was a boat. Inside, flailing wildly with a tiny oar, was what looked like a small purple pillow.

"Khan!" I said. "It's the King of the Lumpies!"

The haggons pointed their claws at the boat, and the largest one cackled, "I smell lunch!"

"Our last meal was hours ago!" growled the second.

"And I need my beauty snack!" said the third.

"No, you don't!" said Eric. "Car! Go! Now!"

But as we roared to the river, the ugly sisters dived at Khan, shrieking their own terrible call.

"Haggons! Attack! Now!"

Six

Follow the Leader

Ooga! The car's eight tires shot waves of dust behind us, and we raced even faster.

"They're almost at the river!" yelled Julie.

"Haggons, get lost!" shouted Eric. Silver sparks burst from his fingers. He fired. *Blam!*

The hag sisters ducked the blast and clacked their jaws angrily, but kept diving for Khan.

Angrily, I pounded the dashboard. "Faster!"

As if the car heard me — *floink!* — a small panel flipped down from the dashboard. On it were two buttons, one green, one yellow.

Suddenly, my fingers sparked red. The hag sisters must have seen it. They slowed their dive.

"Keeeeeahhhh!" gargled the lead haggon.

"Never mind her," cried Julie. "Press one!"

"Okay, but —" I pressed the yellow button.

Vrrr-rrrt! Two giant webbed fins, like Sparr's own, jutted from the back of the car. A second later, we shot straight up from the road.

"*Weeee!*" shouted Twee. "I like this!"

"Me, too," said Eric. "But we're on the

haggons' turf now. And they know how to fly!"

"Let me try —" I said.

Right, left, up, and down, I flew us away from the river into a range of hills. The haggons followed, but every time we thought we'd lost them, they swooped from behind another hill.

"Wherever we go, they're there!" cried Julie.

I drove the car straight up into the clouds. The haggons followed us. Then I circled around and around, but they stayed on our tail.

Faster and faster I drove, until the haggons' eyes began to spin around in their heads.

"Yes!" said Eric. "Keep doing that! Make them dizzy!"

I kept flying the car around until, finally, the three sisters pulled up short and began coughing. Their heads wobbled, and their wings drooped.

"Good, Keeah!" said Ortha. "Now, to Khan!"

I dipped the car below the clouds. Khan's boat was hurtling into the worst part of the river.

The crashing of giant waves nearly drowned out his calls for help.

"Press the green button!" cried Woot. "We love green!"

Vrrrrt! The fins on the back flipped in, and the car dived. Right into the water.

Sploosh! The tires became fatter, and long hulls slid out from under the car. We splashed down onto the lurching waters and raced to where Khan's boat was sinking under the waves.

"Oh, dear, help!" cried the little Lumpy king.

"Grab on!" I shouted. As we pulled up,

Khan jumped from his boat, landing softly in the car.

"Keeeeeaaaahh —" the haggons shrieked from beyond the clouds.

It was a sound that made me shiver. "Oh, no."

"Hey, I saw a movie once where people who were being chased hid in a tunnel," said Neal.

"Good idea, Neal!" said Khan. "There are tunnels all along Rivertangle!" He pointed to a cavern on the riverbank, hollowed out by the waves.

"So let's get out of here!" said Eric.

With the haggons still in the clouds, we raced to the tunnel and drove in. We stopped.

The tunnel was dark and quiet.

"Khan, are you okay?" whispered Julie.

"Only because of you!" he said, still huffing and puffing. "The hags attacked

Lumpland and chased me into Rivertangle. What is going on?"

"The dark powers are rising," I said. "Starting with me."

"It's happening all over Droon," said Twee.

"Hush now," said Ortha. "The haggons are close. Let them pass by."

We heard the flap of leathery wings.

And I heard words again. When I glanced at my fingertips, they were sprinkling red sparks. That's when it came to me.

"We can't hide," I said. "The haggons know where we are. Someone's telling them."

"Who?" asked Julie.

I breathed deeply. "Me."

"Princess, no!" Khan cried.

"I hear words in my head," I said. "Strange words of old magic. I don't know where they're coming from, but the haggons understand. It's like with the wing-wolves. Wait here."

I jumped from the car to a path running down the side of the tunnel.

"Keeah, where are you going?" asked Eric.

I didn't answer. When I got to the entrance, the three haggons were already there, flapping down over the water, flashing their claws.

I heard everyone gasp when I spoke.

"Plah — no — thloom."

Still hovering, the haggons bowed.

Then the largest of the three spoke. "What would you have us do . . . our princess?"

"Leave us alone," I said, my sparks flaring.

The three winged sisters grinned wide, toothless grins. Then they nodded their gray heads.

I finally understood what was going on. The haggons followed us because . . . I was their leader.

I could command them to do anything.

The sisters clustered together. Then they flapped their wings and leaped away into the air. A moment later, they were gone.

"That was awesome!" said Neal, running to me. "They didn't eat us. Not even a single bite!"

"Keeah, you saved us again!" said Twee.

I shook my head. "I only sent them away. I —"

My heart fluttered to see something appear three feet above the water.

It was a wrinkled brown hat.

"Thum!" I said, running to the hat. "It's Thum, everybody! Show yourself. Do you have a message for me?"

"Oooo, I do!" The *droomar*'s little face appeared under the hat. "And here it is. Oooo!"

"Thum, please!" said Julie. "What's the rest?"

". . . bja," he said, dangling his toes in the water. "*Oooo* first, *bja* second. Oooo . . . bja!"

Eric blinked. "Oobja? You mean the Oobja mole people ruled by Batamogi?"

"Who live in the Dust Hills of Panjibarrh?" asked Neal.

"Exactly!" said Thum. "The Panjibarrh of Batamogi ruled by the Dust Hills of Oobja. Or, rather, what you said. You need to go there."

"Why must Keeah go to Panjibarrh?" asked Ortha.

"Are more of Sparr's creatures attacking there?" I asked.

Thum splashed his toes and grinned.

"This time I know the answer. You must go there because the Oobja know what you need to know. Only, they don't know that they know what you need to know. Do you know what I mean?"

Julie frowned. "No."

Thum shrugged. "Then let me be as clear as possible. Like this —" *Pooomf!* He vanished in a big spray of water that splashed into the cave.

And right onto Neal.

He stared at the empty spot and grumbled.

"Even so, he told us where to go," said Ortha.

"And we only have a little time left," I said. "The halting spell is half over."

"Then let's go to Panjibarrh to see what the Oobja know," said Woot.

"And when you say us," added Khan, "I

certainly hope you mean me, too. For I am coming!"

"The pillow king will come!" said Woot.

"It will probably be dangerous," said Eric.

Khan fluffed his tassels. "I expected no less!"

I gave Khan a hug. "Thank you."

Moments later, the eight of us drove Sparr's even longer car out of the tunnel, splashing water high on both sides. Twee and Woot sat in the driver's seat with Ortha as we raced over the plains to Panjibarrh.

Panjibarrh. The Land of the Dust Hills.

The country that gets its name from the giant dust storms that rise suddenly out of nowhere.

Like the one that just then began to spin around our car.

And lift us off the ground.

Seven

What the Oobja Know

Whoosh-sh-sh! A giant funnel of dust whirled around us, lifting the car high in the air.

"Hold on tight!" shouted Ortha. "We're going up!"

Blam! Blam! I blasted the air with red sparks, but the dust storm just whirled faster and faster.

Eric sent a bright shower of silver light

from his hands. The wind only swept it away.

"We're doomed!" yelled Khan.

A moment later, the car jerked upside down. The glass dome flipped open, and we were thrown out while the car kept rising.

And we fell.

"Now we're *really* doomed!" Neal shouted.

"Grab one another!" cried Ortha. "Stay together!"

Julie clutched Eric's feet while Neal whirled upside down in the dust, clinging to Twee and Woot. Ortha, Khan, and I held one another tight.

"Brace yourselves!" I yelled.

A moment later — *plop! plop! plop!* — Eric, Julie, and I went slamming down into a hedge of brown bushes. Ortha, Khan,

Twee, and Woot landed in a soft mound of dust.

Neal missed the bushes and the dust.

He landed in a fountain.

Splash! Neal was drenched — again.

Jumping up, he shook himself, then looked at us.

"Don't even say it."

The storm whirled away as quickly as it had come. When it did, we could see that we were in a village of small mud homes. They were stacked one on top of another up the sides of big brown hills.

"Well, we're in Panjibarrh," Julie whispered. "I remember this village from the last time."

In the center of the village was a giant wheel made of thick planks of wood and lying flat on the ground like a big plate. A long wooden lever stuck up from its middle. The Oobja mole people used the wheel to make dust storms to protect against enemies.

Looking at my red sparks, I wondered if they would think *I* was an enemy.

"My princess!" called a voice.

We turned to see a small head with a large crown on it pop out from one of the huts.

"Batamogi?" I asked.

A short creature jumped from the door and ran to us. He had curling whiskers and pointy ears. He wore a green cape and a gold crown.

"Princess Keeah!" he shouted. Instantly, doors in the other mud huts opened and the village square filled with the furry folk called Oobja.

"We were so afraid," said Batamogi. "We sent the dust storm because of the yellow car. We thought you were the evil one, Lord Sparr himself!"

"We just borrowed his car," said Neal, looking up in the clouds. "It's still spinning around up there somewhere."

Batamogi took us into his small hut. Huddling by a fire, we told him everything that had happened since morning. Even about my powers.

"A *droomar* told you to come here?" said Batamogi, his eyes wide. "But I don't know anything. All I've seen are black clouds moving over the plains and getting thicker all the time!"

"The *droomar* said you know something," I said. "But you don't know that you know."

Batamogi frowned. "Not knowing there is a secret is the most secret kind of secret. Let me see. . . . Sometimes I get tired of all the dust. No one knows that. . . . I broke my brother's wagon when I was three. . . . And then there's — what's *that?*"

A glow shone from the pouch on my belt.

"My Wizardbook!" I said, taking it out to show him.

In the glowing stone, we made out a stretch of brown dusty earth. Crowding around the book, we watched a tiny figure running down a hill, a plume of red dust billowing up behind him.

"It's Max again!" cried Eric. "He's okay. I knew he would be —"

Batamogi gasped. "That red dust means he's in Panjibarrh. He must be nearby!"

As Max ran, we could see a band of Ninns charge over the top of the hill behind him.

"We catch you, furry thing!" cried the

lead Ninn, shaking his fist at Max. All the Ninns' ears were droopy. The warriors were drenched.

"Get over it!" Max yelled. "It was just a boat!"

Then he giggled. "Well, a boat that led a bunch of other boats. All of which are . . . sunk!"

"Way to go, Max," said Neal. "He stopped the Ninns from invading Jaffa City!"

Max scurried to the top of the next hill, slipping and sliding on the dust, then climbed over the ridge. We saw him stop and gasp. "Oh, yes. Ha-ha! Come on, Ninns. Try to follow me — there!"

He ran with all his might to an enormous rock sticking up in the center of the dusty foothills.

Batamogi jumped suddenly. "Bump-alump!"

"Excuse you," said Neal.

"No," he said. "Bumpalump, the big rock that Max is running to. It's been here forever. I can lead you there!"

My heart began to race. "Of course. That's why Thum told us to come here. To find Max!"

"We must get there now," said Ortha.

Batamogi nodded. "Bumpalump is just two hills away. Our dust wheel can take us."

"We'd better hurry," said Eric. "Those Ninns look really mad — as usual!"

As the scene in the Wizardbook stone faded, we ran to the giant wheel in the village center. Everyone crowded around, and we clasped hands as Batamogi and Julie pulled the lever together.

Whrrrr! The giant wheel began to turn faster and faster. A funnel of dust spun up from the ground. It lifted us into the air.

"Here we go again," shouted Neal. "I

hope we don't meet Sparr's car flying around up here —"

Whoo-ooo-osh! The dust storm whirled us around and around, up and over one hill, then another. Finally, we were set down on the very top of the giant rock called Bumpalump.

As the dust storm faded away, we saw that the surface was rough and uneven.

Twee looked around. "Max is not here!"

"But the Ninns are," said Julie, peering down. "They're coming fast. If only we had some banana peels."

"We have something better," I said. "Look!"

Near my feet was a hole in the rock. Below it, a narrow passage carved its way underground.

"I bet that's where Max went," said Eric. "There's something down there. Let's go!"

"Something down there . . ." I whispered.

Seeing my friends jump one by one into the rock, I remembered my mother's words again. Khan, Eric, Ortha, Neal, Woot, Julie, Twee, and Batamogi were with me. So many friends!

But as they slid away inside the rock, I remembered other words.

I was tempted by the darker ways.

I turned and saw the Ninns charge over the top. I watched them slow down when they saw me. I began to speak.

"Kleth . . . nara . . . toom . . ."

They put down their swords and started to bow.

"Nooooo!" I cried as I leaped into the darkness.

Eight

A Face from the Shadows

I shot quickly into a smooth narrow passage.

Everything went dark. The tunnel looped around and up and over, tumbling me down faster and faster. Finally, it leveled out.

Plunk! Oooof! Ayeee! Whoa! Plooop!

I was thrown from the end and landed in a heap. When I stumbled to my feet, I was surprised to find that the floor was flat. "Hello?"

"Everyone's here," Khan said with a cough.

"Except Max," said Batamogi. "He's not here."

"And neither are my sneakers," moaned Neal. "I think I left them about halfway up the passage."

The Ninns were grunting and shouting as they tried to jam themselves into the narrow entrance.

"They'll have a hard time getting down here," said Ortha.

"Somehow, I don't think the Ninns are our biggest worry right now," said Eric. "This Bumpalump is not just any rock. It's sort of . . ."

"Sort of . . . unbelievable!" whispered Julie.

Our eyes had finally gotten used to the

bright light twinkling in from above. And as we looked around, we couldn't believe what we saw.

We were in a room.

High walls. Doorways along one side. A staircase curving down. Tiles on the floor. And in the center of the room, two dark thrones.

"Oh, my gosh —" I whispered.

"Keeah, this is impossible!" said Ortha.

I stared at every part of the room — walls, ceiling, floor, thrones — and I knew.

I had seen this room before.

"It's your parents' throne room in Jaffa City," said Eric. "It's an exact duplicate, except —"

"Except that it's exactly wrong," I said. "Those stairs should be on the wall behind me. At home they lead up, not down. And the thrones —"

The two thrones — the seats of the

king and queen — were made of rough black stone instead of glistening white pearl.

"It's like Jaffa City in reverse," said Khan.

The walls were even draped with banners, but not like the bright silver and green ones at home. Black cloths, tattered, torn, and ragged, waved slowly in the damp air.

"But this isn't possible!" said Batamogi. "Bumpalump has been here forever. How did all this get inside the rock?"

"I think someone is living here," I said, moving ahead. "Let's stay close. With all of us together, maybe we'll be okay. Maybe *I'll* be okay —"

I wanted to tell them about what the Ninns did just before I jumped into the rock.

But the moment I opened my mouth — *vrrrt-vrrrt!* — the floor beneath us began to move. The black tiles shifted, leaving open spaces right under our feet.

"Julie!" said Ortha, trying to pull her away from a moving tile. "Watch out — oh!"

In an instant, the floor opened up under them. When the tiles slid back into place, Julie and Ortha were gone.

Eric jumped. "Where are they? Julie — hey!"

The floor opened up beneath him next. Eric clutched the air wildly, and Batamogi grabbed for him. Together they flew down a tilted shaft.

Fooom! The floor closed back over them.

"Twee!" I shouted. "Woot, look behind you!"

"Help!" the two monkeys screamed together.

They leaped to Khan but all three fell down through the floor in the center of the room. Tiles moved back over them, leaving only Neal and me together on the floor.

"I hear them yelling," said Neal. He stamped on the tiles. "They're down below. Eric! Julie!"

"Stay close," I said. "Give me your hand —"

Wrong move. Neal reached for me, but when he stepped on the tile between us, it slid away and he fell.

"Noooo!" he cried, clutching at the floor.

I jumped to grab him, but he was gone. My Wizardbook went sliding across the stone floor.

"Neal!" I cried. "Neal? Don't leave me here!"

The only sound I heard was a distant *splash*.

I remembered that in Droon, all waters connect. Lakes, pools, rivers, and streams are joined with one another and with the sea.

I also remembered something else my mother had said about her journey.

Finally, I was alone.

I got to my feet. For a second, everything was still, except my heart. It was thundering loudly.

Then — *fwoosh!* — the torches flared up suddenly and gave off a weak orange glow.

"This place does look like Jaffa City," I said. "Just much uglier!"

"What? Don't you like it?" whispered a voice from the shadows. "I call it . . . *Princesstown.*"

So I wasn't alone.

Sparks shot from my hands. "Who's there?"

From the distant corner, lit by a drooping torch's flame, I saw the face of a young girl.

My blood ran cold.

On her head was a crown encircling her long blond hair. When she stepped toward me, I saw that she was dressed in a red tunic and leggings. Around her waist she wore a thick leather belt with a golden buckle.

My mouth opened. "You look like . . ."

"I know," she said. "I look like you. My name is Neffu."

I gasped. "Neffu —"

I remembered the words of my dream. *Krooth-ka . . . meshti . . . pah-la . . . Neffu!*

My red sparks sprinkled into the darkness.

"Neffu," I said. The girl looked so much like me. *Too* much like me. "But are you even . . . real?"

"Real enough," she said in a sharp voice. "I am you . . . as a witch."

I felt my knees go weak. Her face was exactly like the one I saw each day in the mirror.

A witch.

"You probably want to know all about me," she said. "I know everything about you."

"No, you don't," I said.

I listened for the sound of my friends. I could barely hear them somewhere in the rock below me. I felt lucky to have so many of them with me. They would help me. They would. If I could find them.

Neffu moved closer, laughing. "Demither gave you dark powers as a child. I know that."

My heart jumped. The girl took another step.

"I was born the day she gave you those

powers," she said. "Right here in this rock. In a little room. I guess you could say those powers *made* me. Over the years, I've been building myself a little palace —"

I looked around. "Playing princess?"

"Practicing my powers," she said sharply.

"I think maybe you've been in this rock a little too long," I said.

She gave a cold laugh. "I agree! Now that your wizard powers have grown, your witch ones have, too. So I'm ready to come out. Actually, I already started. This morning. With you."

My breath caught in my throat. "You made me open the gates for Sparr?"

She smiled.

"You made me turn the guards into toads! You made me steal the Red Eye —"

"Me, me, and, I guess, me!" she said. "I

whispered words to you magically. You heard me."

"The wingwolves," I said. "And the haggons. The Ninns! Every single word that came to me came from you —"

She grinned. "You're welcome! I whispered the old magic of Goll and you used it. There's only one more thing I need to take you over completely."

She reached her hand out to me. It was the color of ice. "Touch me. And I'll be really real!"

"So, you're getting stronger, huh?" I said.

"Every minute!"

Then my wizard powers must be getting stronger, too.

Neffu stood before one of the thrones. "The moment we join hands, I'll take your place. The dark powers will win. Droon

will be mine! You know, all that good stuff. So, come on."

I noticed the Wizardbook on the floor. The stone was glowing. In it, I could see Max again. He was climbing up the wall in a small stone room, trying to escape.

But he wasn't alone.

My heart leaped to see everyone else there, too. Neal, Julie, and Batamogi were with him. Ortha, Twee, Woot, Eric, and Khan, too.

"Oh, yes, your little friends," said Neffu, glancing at the book. "It was nice that Sparr got your parents out of the way. With your friends gone, it will just be us. *Thep-na . . . fo-koosh* —"

As she spoke, the walls rumbled. I could hear Neal and Batamogi call out. The sudden smell of damp air filled my nose. It rose from under the floor. It was the smell of water.

Seawater.

"Say good-bye to your friends," she said.

My hands glowed brighter and brighter. Jagged red sparks scattered and hissed on the floor. "I'll save my friends," I whispered.

"Save yourself instead," she said, holding her hand out to me. *"Poolah . . . no . . . mem —"*

I heard more calls from below.

"Mumble all you want," I said. "You can't tempt me!"

Snatching my Wizardbook, I grabbed a rock from the floor and shot it at the wall next to her.

"What —!" Neffu fired at the noise. *Blam!*

I dived to the stairs and out of the room.

"Get back here!" she cried.

"Yell all you want — I'm outta here!" Feeling my way, I rushed into the passages ahead — down, down, down. The stones were damp and slippery beneath my feet.

But I knew where I was going.

If Neffu's palace was the opposite of Jaffa City, her room — *my room!* — wouldn't be at the top of the palace. It would be buried at the bottom.

It would be like a dungeon!

Neffu said that's where she was born.

That's where it all began.

And that's where it would have to end.

One more hallway, then quickly down the wet steps to her room. I rushed through the door and stopped.

My heart swelled. The floor of the room was a pool as dark as the walls. It smelled of the ocean.

I hoped the waters in this dark palace

connected with all the others in Droon. I spoke the name of the only one who could help me.

One second . . . two seconds . . .

The surface of the pool splashed and a mass of green hair rose from the water.

A face appeared from the depths of the pool.

She had answered my call.

"Demither!"

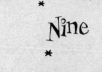

Nine

Royal Family

The serpent witch arched up to the ceiling of the small room.

Her tail slapped up from the pool, swished through the air once, then slithered under the water again.

"Keeah," said Demither.

Her voice echoed sharply against the stones. Her lips were black, her skin paler than ever.

I was afraid of her, but I knew I had to speak.

"Long ago," I said, "you shared your dark powers with me. Why?"

She stared at me with deep eyes. "To fight Sparr. You needed them then —"

"Those powers are taking over now."

The Sea Witch nodded. "I did not know it, but Neffu was born that day. As your wizard magic has grown, the dark magic I gave you has also. And with it, *she* has grown. While you slept, she told you words, charms, spells. . . ."

"She made me let Sparr into our city!" I said.

The witch's head moved from side to side like a snake watching me. "Neffu wants to take you over. Then you'll truly be a witch, as Sparr wants."

"I won't let it happen to me," I said.

"You won't let it?" cried Demither. "I was a wizard like your mother — it happened to me!"

Her shiny skin flashed in the light, making the room glow green.

It was then that I saw a black medal nearly hidden by the scales on her neck.

Carved deeply on the medal was a shape I knew. A triangle pointing down, sharp horns curving up from the upper angles, and a lightning bolt driving straight down the middle.

It was an ancient symbol, from the earliest language of Droon.

It was a name.

Sparr.

Demither twisted and writhed in the pool, knowing I had seen the amulet. "It would take more power than you have to remove this curse!" she said. "I am Sparr's servant. I turned away from my family, from you, from everything —"

Booom-ooom! Neffu was blasting in the halls, yelling, coming closer.

"Keeah, listen!" said Demither, her eyes flashing. "I answered your call for a reason. One day, sorcerers and wizards will meet in a great struggle."

I shuddered. "I hoped it would never happen —"

"It will. And when that day comes, Sparr will call on me, even against my will, to help him."

My heart pounded. I couldn't take my eyes off the black medal.

Demither's eyes grew large. A red glow seemed to burst from them, then she looked away. "Do not let Neffu win! One becomes a *droomar*, but one chooses to be a witch. The dark powers are strong, but remember — until she becomes real, Neffu is magic, just magic. Nothing more!"

With that, she dived under the surface of the pool.

"Demither, wait!" I shouted.

Her tail slid away under the water.

I stared at the pool. She was gone.

"Demither," I whispered, "if I ever get the chance, I will set you free!"

Suddenly, the room lit up with a red glow.

Neffu ran in, breathing hard. "So, you found my little room. Not bad, huh? But I think I'm ready for a change. A new room in Jaffa City. In the palace. Like your room, perhaps?"

But I had already decided.

"Sorry, Neffy," I said. "I think living here has made you a bit wacky. Dark powers and all."

"Dark powers?" she said. "Do you want to see what dark powers can do? Take a look!"

She murmured under her breath, *"Pleth-ku . . . mala . . . tengo . . . hoo . . ."*

All of a sudden, the damp air swirled with moving shapes. I saw wheels creaking and thousands of pilka hooves thundering toward us from a hazy distance.

"Is this some kind of vision?" I asked.

"I want you to see what could be ours!"

Then came chariots. I saw dozens of green groggles harnessed to golden cars, Ninn warriors inside, grunting and cheering. They raced right through the room and vanished.

Next came rivers of gold. They seemed to flow around the room's dark walls, then fade away.

"All this will be ours for the asking!" she said.

A sudden blare of trumpets sounded, and I saw myself enthroned in the court-yard of Jaffa City, surrounded by Ninns blurting out a song.

Keeah here! Keeah there!
She's our princess everywhere!

Neffu laughed. "You like?" She laughed again, and her face became as hard and cruel as Sparr's face. And from behind her ears, beginning to sprout and grow, came burning red fins.

"It's time!" she snarled. "Any last words?"

That's when it came to me.

Words.

Galen always says power comes from words.

I closed my eyes, and words filled my head, thousands of them. But of all of them, one word sounded the loudest.

From the moment I heard it, I knew it was a word of great magic and power. But it wasn't strange-sounding or from an ancient language.

It was a common word.

An everyday word.

A word I heard all the time.

And in my mind, I heard only one voice speaking it. My own.

I breathed in and opened my eyes.

All of a sudden, the dark room seemed to go still. And for an instant, I saw . . . *everything.*

The sights and sounds of Neffu's magic visions were gone. Flooding my ears instead was the murmur of a million voices.

And a million hearts beating all over Droon.

On the wall in front of me, I saw a bead of water trickle down the stones as if it were a diamond, leaving a thin silver trail behind it.

I heard the whisper of the tattered black banners above and of the green and silver cloths hanging at home in Jaffa City.

The air itself seemed not dim and damp but tingling and alive with thousands of points of sparkling light.

It was beautiful!

And I knew what it was.

The Elfin Sight!

That's when I knew I could defeat Neffu.

"So, are you ready?" she asked coldly.

I looked at the witch. "In a second," I said.

Then I leaned over the pool and twisted my belt in the reflection, first one way, then another.

"There. Perfect."

"What was that all about?" Neffu asked.

"My father always says you should straighten your tunic before battle."

"Battle?" Her face turned hard. The fins behind her ears turned black. "So, you're not joining me?"

"It's the red tunic," I said. "It's not really my color."

BLAMMM! I sent a blast at her feet — a bright blue blast of wizard sparks. It sent her back to the wall.

"I'll get you —" she howled. "You — *you!*"

"Now you sound like a Ninn!" I snapped. "No offense to the Ninns! Oh, and since you like words so much — *snippity-ippity-plum-jumm!*"

Instantly, the vision of a chariot roared into the room. Ninns urged the groggles to go faster.

"You're nothing but magic?" I said. "Well, here's your magic ride!"

With one more blast — *whoom!* — I sent her into the passing chariot. "Bye now!"

"I'll come back!" she screamed. "I'll barge into that pink room of yours and I'll — ohhhh!"

Just before she went speeding away, I yanked the gold crown from her head. An instant later, the chariot drove straight through the ceiling and was gone. When the vision faded, the crown fell through my fingers, nothing more than dust.

"I figured," I said. "Just magic."

The rock rumbled again.

I dashed back into the hall and shot up the stairs. "Eric! Max! Ortha! Julie!"

My friends shouted back from somewhere above me. More stairs, more halls. The rock began to crumble. "I'm coming!"

"Keeah —" called Eric.

BLAMMM! I blasted the wall in front of me.

All my friends came tumbling out. And from across the room, a furry little shape ran to me.

Max leaped into my arms. "Oh, my princess!"

I hugged him tight. "Max! I'm so sorry for blasting you out to sea!"

"But no!" he chirped. "You sent me away from Jaffa City for a reason. If you hadn't, I never would have been able to scuttle the Ninn boats. They never would have chased me here. It all led me back to you! Now *that* is true wizardry!"

Boom! Krrrackkkk! Thunnnk! The giant rock quaked all around us.

"With Neffu gone," I said, "her palace is crumbling."

"We'd better get out of here!" said Neal.

The ceiling began to fall in giant chunks.

"Booby trap!" yelled Julie.

"Bumpalump booby trap!" shouted Batamogi.

Ten

The Nose Knows

Huge pieces of ceiling shattered on every side. Neffu's home was crumbling around us. The Bumpalump was cracking apart.

"The ugly palace is coming down!" cried Twee. "We'll be squished!"

Whammm! A wall tumbled down at our feet.

Suddenly, Julie pointed to a hole breaking open in the floor. "Daylight. A way out —"

We rushed toward the light, but two walls were sliding together in front of it.

"We won't make it!" cried Batamogi.

"I can!" said Neal. He ran, then dropped to the floor, his wet clothes helping him slide between the closing walls. He stopped in the gap and jammed a stone between the walls.

"I hate being wet," he crowed, "but the slippery thing works for me! Everyone out of here — fast!"

We jumped between the walls and down through the floor, where we found another rock slide. Daylight glinted below.

"Here we go again!" I cried.

Whooosh! Down and around and up and down we flew. In passage after passage, we twisted and tumbled, thrown together and split apart.

"Wheeee!" Khan shouted, bumping Twee into Woot and Max into Batamogi.

Finally — *whoomp! whoomp!* — we flew out of the stone and tumbled away from the quaking Bumpalump.

A gang of Ninns were also running away from the crumbling rock. "Get away!" they yelled. "Keeah not lead us!"

We rolled to safety while more and more rocks tumbled down around us. After what seemed like a long time, the quaking stopped. The dust cleared.

And we stared.

"Oh, my goodness," Ortha whispered.

Julie gasped. "Um . . . whoa."

"Pretty much me, too," said Eric.

Batamogi gulped. "The Bumpalump — is not the Bumpalump!"

The enormous stone was no longer a mass of jagged rock. It was now a giant head, looking east toward the Dark Lands.

"It's like what Thum told us," said Eric.

"Droon's future lies in the one with the biggest head."

"And that's the biggest head ever," said Julie. "Keeah, it's you. The face is you!"

It was me. My face. My eyes. My hair and crown.

And no fins growing behind the ears.

My heart soared to see the stone sculpture.

"It's a sign," said Ortha.

"A sign?" said Neal, looking up at the head. "It's nice and everything, but I think we just fell out of the nose!"

Plop-plop! Neal's two sneakers came down from the nose and struck him on the head.

"Things are looking up," he mumbled.

"Speaking of looking up," gasped Batamogi. "Look there — haggons!"

We turned to see the three hag sisters

circling overhead. *"Keeeeeeaahhh!"* they shrieked.

I raised my hands in the air. Blue sparks sprinkled from them.

"Attack-k-k-k-k!" the haggons howled.

"Guys," I said, "I think they figured out I'm not their leader anymore. This time they *will* attack."

"But maybe we can choose the place," said Batamogi. He turned to Julie. "Can you take us back to our village right now?"

Julie's eyes sparkled. "I think I can!" she said. "Everybody grab hold of one another. Keeah, Ortha, you take my hands. Here we *gooooo!*"

We held hands tightly — all ten of us — and Julie lifted into the air. Together we flew up and soared back to the village.

The haggons flapped noisily behind us, shrieking and snarling at my bright blue sparks.

"So," the first one said, grinding her two teeth together. "Keeah is our enemy again?"

"She always was a goody-goody," snarled the second. "And we are the baddy-baddies!"

"Plus, I never did like *blue*!" the third one howled. "Are you ready to attack, sisters?"

They began to circle the little village.

"Should we use our magic?" asked Eric.

"Maybe there's a better idea." I looked over at the dust wheel. "Batamogi?"

"Just what I was thinking," he said. "Oobja!"

"Dive, sisters — dive," shrieked the haggons.

Batamogi and everyone from the village raced to the big wooden wheel in the square.

"Now!" he said. They pulled the lever hard.

Whrr-whrr-whrr! The wheel turned faster and faster, and more and more dust whirled around until — *whoosh!* — a funnel shot up at the haggons.

Dust spun in their faces, and they sneezed — *aaaa-chooo!* — over and over again. The force of the sneezes threw them to the ground. They sat up sneezing even more.

Finally, the largest one grunted. "This is just too hard. Come, sisters. Let's go back to the Dark Lands. Sparr is on his own!"

The three hag dragons flew up over the dust hills, sneezed some more, and were gone.

"May Droon be with you!" I called.

The Oobja cheered loudly. And my friends joined in, too.

I looked around. Everyone was with me. Three friends from the Upper World.

Three from the Bangledorn Forest. My trusted spider troll friend. The leader of the Lumpies. The Oobja king and all his people.

My heart lifted as if it had wings.

"To Jaffa City!" I cried.

Using my mother's words again, I waved my hands, and together we flew back across Droon in a tube of spinning blue light.

We raced over the ground, passing the great Rivertangle, the deserts of Lumpland, the giant Bangledorn Forest.

"My beautiful Droon is almost safe," I whispered.

"Thanks to you," said Eric, smiling.

But I knew that the most dangerous part of the journey was still to come.

We would have to face Lord Sparr himself.

By the time we got in sight of the city

walls, there were only a few minutes left before the halting spell ended. Soon the city would be alive again.

Whoosh! We soared over the palace and into the courtyard. It had been nearly twelve hours since that morning. Already, the sun was setting over the western sea. The ocean's dark waves flashed gold in the last of the light.

"It's nearly time," said Julie.

We charged into the palace together.

We raced right to the throne room.

I stopped. My parents were still trapped in their crystal box, their eyes closed in sleep.

"Soon," I said.

In the center of the room, Sparr stood silent, a gloating smile fixed on his face.

"Children, hide behind the banner," said Max. "I'll climb to the rafters. Khan, would you care to come?"

"And us, too!" said Twee.

"Certainly," said the Lumpy king.

All together, Khan, Max, and the three Bangledorn monkeys climbed to the ceiling.

I took my place, stepping up to Lord Sparr.

As he moved behind the curtain with Neal, Julie, and Batamogi, Eric turned to me. "This is your moment, Keeah. Good luck."

I smiled. "Thanks."

The room went silent.

Three seconds . . . two seconds . . .

Then I heard the soft scratch of the sorcerer's cloak moving over the stones.

It was time.

Eleven

Just Magic

Whooosh! The spell ended. Everything came alive at once.

My heart trembled as I saw Sparr move.

He noticed me instantly, narrowing his gaze. "You stopped everything."

Closing my eyes for a moment, I sensed Max and Ortha scampering across the ceiling, as stealthy as mice.

I heard my father's slow breathing in

the crystal box, my mother's heart beating in her sleep. I felt Eric, Julie, and Neal waiting behind the curtain.

It was the Elfin Sight.

I saw and heard everything.

I opened my eyes. "I needed time to think."

"And¿" said Sparr.

"I've made my choice," I said.

Sparr stepped forward. "And¿"

I smiled. "Show me the power we'll use to rule. Show me . . . the Red Eye of Dawn!"

Keeah — Eric said silently.

Wait . . . I answered, also silently. I told him we needed to use our powers at just the right moment.

Okay, said Eric.

The sorcerer paused, his eyes glinting. Then he grinned. "Why not¿ Look there. The day is nearly over. The sun is almost under the horizon. Time for sleep? But no! See what the Red Eye can do. See what power is ours!"

He stepped to the doorway and out onto the balcony, overlooking the vast ocean of Droon. He opened his hand.

WHOOOOM! A blast of red lightning exploded from the crimson jewel.

It shot across the waves. It struck the sun.

Then, as Sparr slowly drew the jewel up in the air, the sun itself rose back up, inch by inch, until streaks of pink light slanted over the balcony stones.

Staring at the rising sun, I remembered what my father had said last night.

The day Demither turned away from her family was the day she lost her Elfin Sight.

I vowed that would never happen to me. But I also knew that Demither was my mother's sister. She was my family. We were bound together. I knew it in Neffu's room when, above all the others, I heard that one word.

The word of greatest magic.

Love.

Closing my eyes, I used my Elfin Sight to search the watery passages under our world.

I found her.

Demither! I called across the miles.

When I opened my eyes — *splash!* — the waves broke open and her giant serpent's form burst up, coiling and twisting in the air.

Sparr, still holding the jewel aloft, laughed suddenly. "Demither? Of course. Keeah, Demither, and me. The three dark powers of Droon are all here as we take over. How *perfect*!"

I shuddered to hear the word.

Demither had to be free of Sparr, if only so she could choose for herself. *That* would be perfect.

"You like?" asked Sparr, drawing the sun higher, casting its glow over the white floor tiles.

My fingers heated up. I looked down. A blue beam of light shot from my hands. As I watched, the sparks turned red, and finally violet.

It was time. I turned to the curtains.

One . . . two . . . three . . .

Blammm! I blasted the crystal box. It shattered into a thousand shards of glass and blue sparks. My parents opened their eyes and rushed out.

"Mother!" I shouted. "Get ready —"

"What?" cried Sparr, turning.

"I'll tell you *what*," said Eric, bursting from the curtain. "You're on our turf now, Sparr!"

Everyone jumped out from behind the curtain. Max and the others leaped from the ceiling.

Sparr's fins flashed a burning red. "What's all this?"

"Keeah has a big family!" said Julie.

"Now!" I shouted. "A single beam of light!"

My mother and Eric turned to the sea. We shot beams out over the water.

Violet. Blue. Silver. Our blasts joined.

"What?" cried Sparr. "No —"

KKKKK! The sky lit up with a brilliant, many-colored blast. It met the ray from the Red Eye and turned it away from the sun.

And right onto Demither. The blast struck her with a bright flash. Shrieking, she rose like a monster over the bay.

"No! No!" howled Sparr, closing his fist. But by the time the light went dim, it was too late.

Something tiny whizzed through the air.

Plink! A small black medal dropped to the stones at Sparr's feet. He picked it up.

I laughed. "Your amulet fell off, Sparr. You don't have Demither's power. She isn't your servant anymore. She's . . . free!"

Demither stared at me with her yellow eyes. She dived and burst up near the city walls, arching high over all of us. Then, flipping her tail hard, she sent a spray of seawater over Sparr.

She drenched him completely.

"Hey, I know what that's like!" said Neal.

An instant later, she was gone.

Max jumped. "Look at that! I know *them!*"

A tiny rowboat swayed into the harbor. A handful of Ninns stumbled toward the palace. They waved at Sparr.

The sorcerer's fins turned black and rimmed with fire. He stared at me.

"KEEAH, YOU SHALL PAY FOR THIS!"

Everyone rushed to my side. Eric and my mother had their hands ready. My father wielded a giant wooden club. Julie, Ortha, and the others were ready to charge. Neal even had a bucket of water ready to throw.

"This just isn't your day," said Julie.

"Call it quits," added Eric.

Quivering, Sparr raised his hands to me. "Why — you!" He sent a blast at me.

Don't fire! I said. *I have a better idea.*

Even as his bolt came at me, I jumped at him.

I spun around in the air, not touching down. It was as if everything slowed while I alone moved. I dodged his lightning bolt, then everything sped up again.

My foot met his shoulder.

Whump! He was pushed back ten feet. His shot went wild, and he teetered on the edge of the balcony.

"Sorry, Sparr," I said, coming down. "These new wizard powers are *soooo* tricky!"

He swayed back, then finally fell from the balcony. "Ninns!" he cried out. "Catch me —"

We ran to the edge.

The red warriors hustled across the grass, holding out their hands for him. Then they suddenly jerked back, as if afraid of being hurt.

"What — no —" Sparr cried out.

Blumffff! He thudded to the ground.

He lay there on the grass, his dark eyes rolling in his head.

Finally, he wobbled to his feet. "I still have the Red Eye of Dawn! You will see its great power — *my* great power — as you never have before. The Empire of Shadows begins now!"

As I watched Sparr limp to the sea, his hands clasped over the red jewel, I realized something.

The great magical *things* he might discover or create didn't seem to matter so much.

They were . . . just magic.

"Take the Eye," I said. "The Golden Wasp, the Coiled Viper. Take them all. Together, we're more than a match for you."

Right at that exact moment — *ka-whoooom!* — something large and heavy crashed to the earth in a crumpled heap next to Sparr. He gasped, his mouth hanging open.

"Oh, my gosh," said Batamogi. "So that's where that went. It traveled a long way!"

It was Sparr's yellow car.

It had finally come down.

Completely smashed.

"Oh, yeah," said Eric. "We borrowed the car. It got pretty wrecked, though. Sorry."

My father boomed a loud laugh. "Can we offer you a ride home?"

Saying nothing, Sparr turned away. His Ninns crowded around and helped him into what was left of their great fleet of ships. We watched as the little rowboat splashed away from the city and was gone.

"Yahoo!" cried Neal.

"Yay, Keeah!" shouted Julie.

Eric smiled. "We won today."

"Keeah!" my father boomed, rushing to me and swinging me around.

My mother kissed me, then looked into my eyes. "The Elfin Sight. You have it —"

"And not a minute too soon!" I said.

Surrounding me were Ortha, Woot,

Twee, Batamogi, Khan, Max, Eric, Julie, Neal, and my parents.

My family.

After all that had happened, it was amazing to have them all here for this moment.

It was perfect.

"The *droomar* would be so proud of you today," said my mother.

"Oh, we are!" said a familiar voice.

Twelve

The Soul's Language

I turned and saw the old brown hat hovering on the balcony. The little elf appeared below it.

"Thum!" I said, running to him. "I'm glad you remembered to come!"

"I almost didn't," he said as he drifted across the stones to us. My mother hugged him.

"You really helped us today," said Julie.

"You helped Keeah most of all," said my mother. "Thank you!"

The little creature bowed. "Oooo, yes. But really Keeah helped us. She was inspired by what she saw in the stone of her Wizardbook."

I held the book close to me. It seemed to call out to me to begin writing in it.

"Bring the tea," my father boomed. "This calls for a great feast. Keeah is a *droomar* today!"

Almost instantly, dozens of kitchen workers brought out pot after pot of Droon tea and huge platters of food to go with it.

"Talk about magic," said Neal, "it's like they can read my mind."

"Talk about magic," I said, "look at this." I sprayed a narrow stream of blue sparks from my right hand and red ones from my left.

"That is so cool," said Eric. "When did you learn you could do that?"

"In Neffu's palace," I said. "The Elfin Sight showed me how even the dark powers can be used for good! Look at this, too."

I lightly touched the tips of my thumbs together and sprayed out a glowing stream of blue and red sparks together.

"Violet sparks," gasped Julie. "So awesome!"

But the most awesome part was how all my friends stayed to party with me for hours.

Lights went on all over the city. People began dancing through the streets. The great palace fountain bubbled softly with the fresh, sweet water of summer.

When twilight came, my father stood over the courtyard and yelled.

"To the newest *droomar* wizard!"

"*O — lee — lee!*" yelled Ortha, Twee, and Woot together.

A great cheer went up all over town. The guards, not toads anymore, waved the bright green and silver banners high.

Finally, my father unscrewed the horns from his helmet and blew a big blast of air through both of them. *Woooo-hoooo!*

They made the sweetest music.

Until the moon came up, my mother sang harp songs and Max danced. His eight legs flew around as if there were two of him!

All evening, we knew Droon was safe.

Neal chuckled. "Sparr is too tired to try anything now."

Finally — *whoosh!* — the rainbow staircase appeared over the courtyard.

As my friends stepped onto the glistening steps, Eric paused and turned.

"We went a long way today," he said.

"We saw a lot of stuff," said Neal. "And found out a lot of things."

"We did," I said.

"But some things we knew all along," said Julie, giving me a hug.

Eric laughed. "You took the words right out of my mouth. Keeah, you'll always be a wizard to us. And we'll be back before you know it."

"Yeah," said Neal. "I have a feeling there are a lot of things to get done!"

Laughing, my three friends ran up the staircase and away into the clouds.

I closed my eyes and heard a faint squeak, then a click, as the door at the top of the stairs closed. Then the stairs faded.

"See you soon," I whispered.

Five minutes later, I was sitting cross-legged under the stars on the little balcony outside my room.

I could just hear the sounds of my father singing and my mother's bright laughter as they made their way through the halls of the palace below.

I had more power than ever before. With my mother's help, I would learn to use every bit of it to make sure Droon was always safe.

And when Galen came back — and I knew he would return to us soon — there would be nothing we couldn't do together.

Besides, everywhere I looked, I found people who loved me. People who I loved.

I remembered that simple word again.

Love.

"*Snkk-grrr-snkk!* Yes, yes! In a moment!"

I turned to see Max curled up like a ball of fur, muttering and snoring in his little bed.

Yes, everywhere I looked there was love.

I pointed a finger to the small rose-colored candle on my nightstand and whispered words Galen had taught me.

"*Sepp-o-bah . . .*"

Fwishh! The candle stand wobbled, then whisked itself up off the table. It set itself down with a soft *plonk* on the tiles in front of me.

I winked, and the candle flared into life.

Moving the Wizardbook to my lap, I looked at the stone on its cover.

This time, it showed nothing but my own face.

I opened the book to where the very first page gazed up at me, blank, white, clean, and ready.

Looking up, I saw that the moon was full.

In its glow, the sky was wide and blue and streaked with violet.

Violet. The color of my powers.

So.

Midnight.

The candle flickered its warm flame over the blank page. I thought of the wonderful, magical words I would write.

I looked around and listened to the quiet sounds of Droon at night.

Everything was perfect.

Dipping my pen in ink, I set it on the page, breathed once, and began to write.

It was the sound of words that woke me. . . .

About the Author

Tony Abbott is the author of more than fifty funny novels for young readers, including the popular *Danger Guys* books and *The Weird Zone* series. Since childhood he has been drawn to stories that challenge the imagination, and, like Eric, Julie, and Neal, he often dreamed of finding doors that open to other worlds. Now that he is older — though not quite as old as Galen Longbeard — he believes he may have found some of those doors. They are called books. Tony Abbott was born in Ohio and now lives with his wife and two daughters in Connecticut.

For more information about Tony Abbott and the continuing saga of Droon, visit www.tonyabbottbooks.com.

THE SECRETS OF DROON

by

by Tony Abbott

Under the stairs, a magical world awaits you!

MEET Geronimo Stilton

A REPORTER WITH A NOSE FOR GREAT STORIES

Who is Geronimo Stilton? Why, that's me! I run a newspaper, but my true passion is writing tales of adventure. Here on Mouse Island, my books are all bestsellers! What's that? You've never read one? Well, my books are full of fun. They are whisker-licking-good stories, and that's a promise!

www.scholastic.com/kids

■SCHOLASTIC

GERSTT

MORE SERIES YOU'LL LOVE

For fun, magic, and mystery, say...

Abracadabra!

The members of the Abracadabra Club
have a few tricks up their sleeves—
and a few tricks you can
learn to do yourself!

™ Jigsaw and his partner, Mila
know that mysteries are like
jigsaw puzzles—you've got to loo
at all the pieces to solve the case!

Hey L'il D!

L'il Dobber has two thin
with him at all times—hi
basketball and his friends.
Together, they are a great team. And they
are always looking for adventure and fun—
on and off the b'ball court!

The Author
and His Publisher

Lectures Delivered in Mainz and Austin

Siegfried Unseld

The Author
and His Publisher

Translated by
Hunter Hannum and Hildegarde Hannum

The University of Chicago Press

CHICAGO AND LONDON

SIEGFRIED UNSELD, who holds a doctorate in
German literature, is the head of Suhrkamp Verlag
in Frankfurt, Federal Republic of Germany.

Originally published as *Der Autor und sein Verleger:
Vorlesungen in Mainz und Austin*
by Suhrkamp Verlag, Frankfurt am Main, 1978

The University of Chicago Press, Chicago 60637
The University of Chicago Press, Ltd., London
© 1980 by The University of Chicago

87 8y 85 84 83 82 81 80   5 4 3 2 1

Library of Congress Cataloging in Publication Data

Unseld, Siegfried.
The author and his publisher.

Translation of Der Autor und sein Verleger.
Includes bibliographical references.
1. German literature—20th century—History and
criticism.   2. Authors and publishers—Germany.
I. Title.
PT405.U513   070.5'2   79-26021
ISBN 0-226-84189-8

FOR JOACHIM

Contents

Preface

The five chapters of this book were written at different times and for different occasions; they have been revised for publication.

The chapter "The Responsibility of the Literary Publisher" is based on the lecture "How are Literary Books Made?" which the Bremen Literary Society invited me to give on November 6, 1968. This talk gave rise in turn to a lecture entitled "Publishing Today," which I delivered in Tübingen on November 12, 1971—the occasion was the three hundred seventy-fifth anniversary of Osiander's Bookstore—in the main auditorium of the university, where I had earned my doctoral degree twenty years earlier. A new version of this lecture was presented when the Vienna Literary Society invited me to speak about "The Responsibilities of the Literary Publisher" on May 15, 1975. As time went by, I continued to work on this unpublished speech whose topic is of paramount importance to me. I expanded it, adding this or that insight, and it gradually turned into a more comprehensive treatment of the subject matter. The resulting essay also remained unpublished, with the exception of short passages that appeared as contributions to the festschriften for my honored colleagues Joseph Caspar Witsch and Heinrich Maria Ledig-Rowohlt. I went over the text of this essay again before it was published here, adding a few nuances, but I had no wish to make any changes in the content or form of my credo. It is only natural that one's attitude toward one's tasks changes in the course of the years, that one's sense of priorities changes as well as the way one sees and describes them. The first chapter of this book is thus both a definitive statement and a record of my thoughts about my own profession.

The other four chapters are lectures I had the honor of delivering at various universities. I gave the two speeches "Hermann Hesse and His Publishers" and "Bertolt Brecht and His Publishers" at the Johannes Gutenberg University in Mainz, where Professor Dr. Hans Widmann had invited me to lecture and take part in his seminar investigating the history of publishing. The Hesse material was prepared specifically for the lecture in Mainz. The Brecht lecture is based on earlier studies of Brecht's reception. In one of these, on the occasion of the seventy-fifth anniversary of his birth, I had described his method of working and his publishing history. Excerpts from this study have been published and were also presented as a lecture at the 1974 meeting of the International Brecht Society in Toronto. The text is published here in its entirety for the first time.

In 1976, Professor A. Leslie Willson invited me to be guest professor at the University of Texas at Austin. The two lectures "Rainer Maria Rilke and His Publishers" and "Robert Walser and His Publishers" were prepared for that occasion. I delivered a section of the Rilke lecture at the Vienna symposium "Rilke Today" in 1976. The Robert Walser lecture was given for the first time in Austin, and I shall never forget my surprise at the number of readers and admirers Walser turned out to have at this Texas university. An excerpt from this lecture became an address I gave at the Herzog August Library in Wolfenbüttel in May 1977.

These studies, written as they were at different times, were thus conceived as speeches, not as written essays. The tone of oral delivery has not been basically altered. Occasional repetition was unavoidable if each individual section was to retain its own integrity. The studies also differ in approach, for each of the four authors is viewed from a different standpoint; the relationship of each of these writers with his publishers was unique, and this had to be brought out.

Special thanks are due Elisabeth Borchers and Jürgen Becker for encouraging me to publish these studies.

It is my hope that the five chapters of this book may be a contribution to a field that has not yet been adequately investigated—the social history of literature.

S. U.

The Responsibilities
of a Literary Publisher

It is the same for literature as for deeds; if we speak of them
without loving sympathy, without a certain partisan enthusiasm, then there is so little value in our utterance that it is
not worth making at all. Pleasure, delight, sympathy with
things is what alone is real and what in turn creates reality; all
else is worthless and only detracts from the worth of things.
Goethe to Schiller, letter of June 14, 1796

I was grateful to have a publisher, happy to live in a world in
which there are publishers.
Wolfgang Koeppen about the publisher Henry Goverts, 1977

THE CONFLICT BETWEEN
AUTHOR AND PUBLISHER

One of the signs of Napoleon's greatness—according to
a sociologist who recently wrote to our publishing
house—is the fact that he once had a publisher shot.
Goethe was notorious for the anger he directed against
booksellers (and he meant publishers): "Booksellers are
all cohorts of the devil; there must be a special hell for
them somewhere." Friedrich Hebbel, the nineteenth-
century German dramatist, said, "It is easier to walk on
the waters with Christ than to get along with a publisher." This is the way classical authors felt about publishers. (It would still seem that publishers of the past

I

had an easier time of it, for we publish contemporary authors, whereas they published classical ones!) Max Frisch, the Swiss author of our own time, made the following entry in the second volume of his diaries about his impressions of the Frankfurt Book Fair: "The difference between an author and a horse is that the horse doesn't understand the horse dealer's language." Just a few years ago, the great English publisher Frederic Warburg entitled his memoirs *An Occupation for Gentlemen?* Today, no publisher would dare to give his autobiography such a title, not even with a question mark. Today, the image of a publisher is automatically associated with such labels as rich, elitist, conservative, authoritarian; he is accused of practicing censorship and of being a capitalistic exploiter and profiteer.

As it happened, the publisher whom Napoleon had shot was hardly on the side of the establishment. Johann Philipp Palm of Nuremberg was condemned to death by a French military court at the age of forty after he had been apprehended "as the author, printer, and distributor of libelous works threatening the respect that is due crowned heads." We would be unlikely to judge Palm's publishing activity as harshly as the French military court of that time.[1] Goethe's anger must also be understood in its historical context. He himself had little trouble in getting the better of his publishers: Christian Dietrich Grabbe, one of the major exponents of realistic drama in nineteenth-century Germany, described Goethe's negotiations with his publisher, Cotta, for the publication of his correspondence with Schiller as "stealing the shirt off his back." Yet Goethe was justifiably annoyed with the publishers of pirated editions. Since they did not pay royalties, they could offer larger editions of books that sold at reduced prices but contained distorting misprints; their books thus provided considerable and damaging competition for the authorized editions.

Whatever the facts in a given situation, we always find a lurking reproach that publishers exploit the intellectual work of their authors, that they "drink champagne from bowls made out of the skulls of authors who have been slowly starved to death." Authors have made repeated attempts throughout the history of literature to protect themselves against such "exploitation" and to avoid conflict with publishers by establishing their own publishing houses. We know about Leibnitz's plans in the year 1716 for a Societas subscriptoria. Then there was the Scholars' Bookstore of Dessau in 1781, the German Union, an authors' publishing house, in 1787, and, finally, the publishing house set up by Friedrich Klopstock to bring out *Die Gelehrtenrepublik* [The scholars' republic], a venture that turned out to be, in Goethe's words, an "unsuccessful undertaking." These efforts all failed dismally, creating large losses for the authors. The same fate was accorded a publishing house and press undertaken jointly by Gotthold Ephraim Lessing and the diplomat and printer Johann Joachim Christian Bode in Hamburg in 1767. Lessing wrote to his family (on December 12, 1767) that he had invested his last cent in this business, which was supposed to publish his main work, *Die Hamburgische Dramaturgie* [*The Hamburg Dramaturgy*]. When the venture failed, he wrote his brother (on January 4, 1770), "Here I am, in debt up to my ears, and I simply don't see how I can get out of it honorably." He had to leave Hamburg literally under cover of darkness, and neither his salary as a librarian in Wolfenbüttel nor the proceeds from the sale of his entire personal library was sufficient to free him of these debts.[2]

It was because of such experiences that Schopenhauer rejected the idea of founding his own publishing house eighty years later. His publisher, Brockhaus, had turned down his *Vermischte philosophische Schriften* [Miscellaneous philosophical writings] and recommended that the author have them printed privately. In his reply (July 8, 1850), Schopenhauer refused to follow this suggestion, "because I have such a horror of private printing that I would prefer to leave my manuscript in a drawer until it has become posthumous, at which time the publishers will fight tooth and nail over it."[3]

Karl Marx and Friedrich Engels had great difficulty trying to get their *Deutsche Ideologie* [*The German Ideology*] into print. For years they were involved with publishing houses or with attempting to establish new ones. On October 26, 1847, Marx wrote Georg Herwegh in Paris: "Since it is impossible under present conditions in Germany to make use of the book trade, I have ... taken it upon myself to establish a monthly review, with financial support from stock subscriptions. If the volume of stock sales should permit, we would set up our own printing company, which we could then use to print our works." But like so many other attempts, this one failed, too, and with it the hope of publishing *Die deutsche Ideologie.* From then on, Marx and Engels left the manuscript "to the gnawing criticism of the mice," as Marx put it; and, indeed, when finally printed, twelve years later, the manuscript *had* been nibbled on by mice.[4]

With the rise of increasingly mechanized and thus more expensive methods of book production, experiments in author-run publishing houses are becoming increasingly rare. Today there are only two examples in Europe, De Bezige Bij [The busy bee] in Amsterdam and the Författer Förlaget [Authors' press] in Stockholm; although these houses are owned by authors, neither provides a model for firms with a different structure. Here in Germany, at least since the first Writers' Conference in November 1970, held in Stuttgart, writers have been proclaiming "an end to modesty." They have founded the Verband Deutscher Schriftsteller (Association of German writers) to represent their interests, but there are no plans thus far for an author-run publishing house.

The discontent that rises to the surface from time to time in the relationship between author and publisher is due to the strange, Janus-headed nature of the publisher's activity. He must both produce and sell the book, that "sacred commodity," as Brecht called it. That is, he must combine intellectual stature with business acumen so that the person who writes literature can make a living and the one who publishes it can remain in a position to publish it. Alfred Döblin put it this way in 1913: "The publisher casts one eye at the writer, the other at the public. But the third eye, the eye of wisdom, gazes unflinchingly at the cash register."[5]

The formula "intellectual stature plus business acumen" is, however, too simplistic. The publisher, according to Ralf Dahrendorf, occupies a "position in society"; his work in the personal as well as the economic sphere has a public function. Everyone who occupies a position in society must fulfill certain expectations. Dahrendorf speaks of expectations in terms of "must," "ought," and "can." The publisher is especially subject to these expectations, since his work is expressed in books, i.e., publicly. He wants to produce literature, and for this purpose he needs an economically oriented enterprise. Depending on the publisher's character and individual nature (whether he is more interested, for example, in the artistic, technical, economic, or purely literary aspect of his profession), he will unequivocally identify himself with one of these categories. Peter Meyer-Dohm, who has attempted the first typology of publishers, comes to this conclusion: "In setting up a typology of publishers, the phenomenon of group identification offers a heuristic principle that can give a better account of the various motives involved than can the formula 'Commerce/Culture,' which in any case is misapplied here."[6]

The publisher's position is an unusual one because he bears the intellectual as well as the financial responsibility for the activities of his house and because he alone must answer personally for his books and his enterprise—not only in a political, moral, intellectual, and legal sense but also with all the material resources he has at his disposal. This is the way things are and the way they will have to remain as long as books possess the character of a commodity—in other words, as long as author and publisher, the producers of this commodity, are inescapably involved in the total economy of our society. Only if the structure of society should change could this aspect of the book—that it is a commodity— also change. But it is very doubtful whether this would be desirable, for we see what price authors in present-day socialist countries must pay for such a change: sometimes the price of not being published, often of censorship, self-censorship, or even of complete silence. And here we touch upon a second problem: to what extent can a publishing house, like all other enterprises in our society a capitalistic organization that must produce profits, publish literature which frequently takes the side of the weak and oppressed, even explicitly political literature which speaks out against maximizing profits, against indiscriminate growth, against the exploitation of the environment by our technological civilization and *for* new basic rights of the individual? The publisher promotes literature that strengthens these rights, that encourages the individual's concern for his neighbor, and that also proposes other, new forms and theories of our society and economy. And yet, at the same time, he heads an enterprise that must be directed, on the economic level, toward profit. He publishes books that defend man's unceasing struggle for liberation from social restraints, and yet, as employer, he must insist on performance and disciplined work habits on the part of his employees. Is this that "role-conflict" which Dieter E. Zimmer says publishers "can hardly bear"?[7]

THE PUBLISHER'S "ROLE-CONFLICT"

I believe that publishers have always had to play these two roles, at least those literary publishers who have mirrored or given a new direction to the literary or cultural history of their times. The history of literature teaches us that it is almost a law that decades of rich poetic production are followed by lean and poor ones and that, during these latter periods, writing of a secondary, more reflective, nature comes to the fore. There were and still are times in which writers feel the necessity of political commitment and times in which they must undertake "the journey to the interior." The era of romanticism was followed in German literature after 1830 by the political commitment of the revolutionary writers of Young Germany. Then came another era of an inward direction, which in turn gave way to the storms of naturalism.

A similar rhythm can be observed in the history of Swiss literature. I shall never forget what Pestalozzi wrote in his preface to *Lienhard und Gertrud* (1781): "These pages represent an historical attempt to tell the people some important truths in a manner intended to speak to their hearts and minds." Seven decades later, the young Gottfried Keller made the following entry in his diary: "Woe to everyone who does not link his own fate to that of the community, for not only will he find no peace but in addition will lose all his inner security and be exposed to public contempt, like a weed by the roadside." Again, seven decades later—on December

14, 1914, to be precise—in the hall of a Zurich guild house, Carl Spitteler made an important political speech that gave rise to manifestos and declarations in which many key political formulations and humanitarian ideas were expressed; we find one of the finest of these in Leonhard Ragaz's book *Die neue Schweiz* [The new Switzerland], where he speaks of the "rights of the world citizen," which, transcending all national civil rights, must be established. Six decades later, Max Frisch, in his turn, becomes politically engagé, reexamines Swiss myths, and submits the Swiss self-image to continually renewed analysis.

After the chaos of 1945, after the shock and trauma suffered by the generation that was to begin Germany's reconstruction, the first literature to appear was of a purely literary nature. It began with a drama by Wolfgang Borchert, *Draußen vor der Tür* [*The Man Outside*], stories by Heinrich Böll, and poems by Günter Eich and Paul Celan. Only gradually did authors and literature become politicized, both anticipating and accompanying the worldwide youth movement.

A contemporary publishing house must reflect such developments. The publisher must be aware of the limits of the debate; we Germans in particular have a penchant for the radical and the extreme in all areas, and we do not succeed in attaining what Hermann Broch once called "the radicality of the middle." But because we do affirm our society, because we do want to encourage its possibilities and its chances for reform and progress, we must publish books in which progressive theories are disseminated so that they can be discussed. We see in our own times that such discussion cannot take place in some of the socialist countries, for example; not a day goes by that we do not hear of an author's freedom being curtailed and his works suppressed. Solzhenitsyn is a world-renowned example. There are many others, such as the Romanian author Paul Goma, who stressed in an interview that he hoped his books could appear again in Romania, although he had no idea when this would be or in how large a printing or which of his books would be released. The situation of writers in Czechoslovakia should arouse us to daily protest. And in East Germany, where a law was passed enabling the state to take charge of Brecht's posthumous writings, not all the Brecht works published in Suhrkamp editions had appeared as late as 1977.

Many publishers started out with the intention of dealing exclusively with literary works and then, influenced by their authors' commitment, saw themselves becoming actively involved in the political arena. The publishers of the past, whether their name was Palm or Göschen or Cotta, invariably experienced a similar conflict. Anyone taking a stand on the side of social progress finds himself in an avant garde or at least in a minority.

Traditionally, culture has been a matter not of the majority but of a minority, a matter of wealth, often a matter of accidental good fortune. Whoever proposes a change in this situation, whoever thinks that culture ought to become democratic, seeing it as a process of humanization of daily life, almost unavoidably comes into conflict with his times. This is especially true of the publisher who does not take part in the race for mere best-sellers but who brings out books intended to support what can and should be, in other words, what is progressive as opposed to what merely *is*. It is not a contradiction to be part of a capitalistic organization and yet to publish progressive literature. For surely this is a valid consideration: if a modern capitalistic publishing house takes part with heart and soul in throwing light on the psychogenic structure of the individual and on the sociogenic structure of society and, thereby, also on the very ground it is standing on, it is making a greater contribution to progress than if it were to desert this ground that makes its influence possible for the sake of a "progressive" label. It is this very ability to exert influence that can one day be expected to change the individual human being and thus bring about an organic change in society itself. "What else is our metier for," Rilke wrote in a letter of June 28, 1915—and this will come as a surprise only to those not familiar with Rilke's works—"if not to provide the motivation for change in a pure and grand and free manner?" The desire for change is the impetus behind all great literature: its intention is to make readers stronger by making them uneasy. It tells what was, what is, but also what will be, what ought to be.

THE SICK BOOK
AND THE DISPENSABLE PUBLISHER

Another problem must be addressed here: the author Peter Härtling, himself the head of a publishing house at the time he made this observation, referred to the "sick book," in other words, the book as a decrepit and untimely medium. Publishers, he went on, at one time proud of their prestige as makers of books, are today nothing but slaves to the demand for quick profits. Still others view publishing as a superfluous and obsolete profession. In the opinion of Jobst Siedler of Ullstein Verlag, today in 1977 we have not even begun to see the death throes of the publishing business! Are the publishing houses indeed dying? Is the book sick and the publisher dispensable?

When books were first produced by machines, thanks to Gutenberg's invention, the scribes of the time who copied manuscripts by hand spoke of the impending death of beautiful books. In the place of a single copy of a manuscript there appeared editions of from one hundred and fifty to two hundred copies which were thorough-going imitations of the hand-copied ones. When sweeping technical innovations—the high-speed cylinder press (1812) and the typesetting machine (invented by Mergenthaler in 1884)—were introduced, there was again talk of the death of the beautiful book; it turned out, however, that the art of the book reached a high point at the end of the nineteenth and the beginning of the twentieth century.

Then came the silent film, the sound film, records, radio, and television; each time, the doom of the book was prophesied. Today audiovisual multimedia, home video and film cassettes, video records and, most recently, the magnetic disk recorder provide the background for a new lament about the end of the book. A decade ago, Marshall McLuhan spoke of the book's demise as a fact. (By the way, how little we hear about McLuhan nowadays.) But now we hear talk of the end even of paper as a bearer of information. "Information," wrote Karl Steinbuch, "is liberating itself from paper and becoming mobile, like electricity." A new audiovisual system is certainly on its way, whether in the form of cassettes or video records or magnetic records—the multinational corporations have not yet agreed on a standard system—but, just as certainly, it too will be an entirely different development from the one today's propagandists expect.

I should like to mention only two of these propagandists of the early seventies, Hans-J. Liese and Hans Altenheim. In one of the many superfluous articles in the *Börsenblatt für den Deutschen Buchhandel* [Journal for the German book trade] Liese reported on the changing nature of publishing.[8] He too spoke of the death of the book but had scarcely anything new to report, merely citing the head of the Deutsche Gesellschaft für Zukunftsforschung [German society for futurological research]: "Vital information no longer needs to be transmitted in a time-consuming way from person to person by means of written reports but can be processed much more quickly by computer." The American, E. B. Weiss, took this as his point of departure and developed—quite consistently, in Liese's view—the concept of the "Home Communication Center," the communication medium of the future, which was supposed to have become a part of every household by 1978. A central console in every home would, he thought, receive television, record teleprint, have access to data centers, have a radio, stereo, and a new type of telephone with visual screen and push buttons. Then, according to Weiss, there would not be any more books. Liese therefore called upon publishers to "draw the consequences." "It took over 2000 years for Plato's ideas to become the intellectual possession of mankind. In ten or fifteen years ... with the help of the computer it will be possible to transfer every brilliant idea instantaneously ... into the brain." On the basis of this misconception, Liese drew the conclusion that a "readjustment" will be required of publishers: "The future of publishing has already begun—but only for those publishers who have recognized the signs of the times sufficiently early."

I do not believe that Liese's arguments are valid. One hardly needs to argue about why it took two thousand years for Plato to become the intellectual possession of mankind or how it could be possible for a "brilliant idea" (such as Einstein's seemingly simple but actually complicated equation, $E = mc^2$) to be transferred instantaneously to the brain by means of computer and television. Liese cited, as the star witness for his prophecy, the founding of the Deutscher Studienverlag (German press for study materials), which was to make use of new media, such as McLuhan's "magic canals," "to produce and disseminate practical and modern study materials and instructional aids." During the publishers' meeting at the Frankfurt Book Fair in 1970, the head of this firm, Hans Altenheim, did in fact proclaim the demise of the "old-fashioned" publisher. He also expanded on the new publisher, an engineer who is in charge of the central office of an information network, his electronic "desk"—free of paper and manuscripts—the focal point of all means of communication. But Deutscher Studienverlag no longer exists, and Herr Altenheim has returned to the management of a publishing house that uses the old methods.

The myth of the book's demise has itself met its demise. The book is certain to occupy a secure place in our world in future decades. I should even like to predict an ever-growing scale of book production during the coming years. Of course there will be changes in form and presentation. Just as books have an impact on the development of society, so too does social development have an influence on the book's form, production, and distribution. Given the democratic process that characterizes our society, the eagerness for education at all levels, and the knowledge that only if mature attitudes are developed can we face and cope with a world increasingly dominated by technology and political totalitarianism, the book will undoubtedly serve as the primary source of enlightenment for a long time to come.

Publishers who recognize this situation and proceed accordingly need not be concerned for their future; however, they must focus more clearly on their specific responsibilities than they have in the past. In view of rising costs in every area, the rate of inflation, a possible paper shortage (called to our attention by the oil crisis), and the fact that the low-priced book is more in demand than ever and that cost increases cannot be passed on to the consumer entirely, publishers are more than ever obliged to concentrate their attention on what is uniquely their domain: the publication of books. The peaceful days when it was easy to publish books, especially with the aid of rich patrons of literature, are over; the difficulties that reputable publishers have had in our day are an indication of this. It is certainly no longer possible for one individual to oversee the entire scope of a publishing conglomerate.

Reinhard Mohn, the head of the Bertelsmann conglomerate, a "giant publishing house," has some interesting ideas about this.[9] In his view, such a firm has three tasks: to give information, to transmit knowledge, and to offer entertainment. He envisions the publisher turning out new products in addition to those associated with his traditional "book business": newspapers, periodicals, records, films, and—in the future—video cassettes, television productions, and data banks. In a giant publishing company, Mohn contends, it is not only methods of distribution or production that have changed but "program initiatives" as well. The earlier union, in one person, of head of the firm and program initiator can no longer be maintained. The demands on the individual have increased too much, and no one person has enough energy to meet them all.

Reinhold Mohn is thinking exclusively in terms of large profits, and when he speaks of "giants," he means the "five largest German publishing houses," which are, in order of size: Axel Springer, Bertelsmann, Gruner & Jahr, Bauer, and Burda. It is perfectly clear that these giants no longer resemble traditional literary publishing houses. They do not produce, or at least not solely, the "sacred commodity, the book" but exist primarily by publishing newspapers and periodicals—in other words, they exist by the proceeds of advertising. For this purpose, they need a management with an economic orientation more than they need a publisher with literary inclinations. As far as I am concerned, Mohn's giants lack the stature of true publishing firms. Completely excluded from his description (as from others, including Altenheim's) is the person for whose sake publishing houses and publishers are supposed to exist: the author.

THE PUBLISHER'S ASSOCIATION
WITH AUTHORS

A literary publishing house is defined by the nature of its association with its authors. Ideally, a give-and-take occurs, leading to mutual benefit. An impressive example, in my opinion, is the growth of S. Fischer Verlag, described in detail in Peter de Mendelssohn's interesting book, *S. Fischer und sein Verlag* [S. Fischer and his publishing house]. In the beginning, Samuel Fischer could not have foretold that he would someday become a publisher, and a great one at that. It was when the firm of Steinitz & Fischer was founded that the name Fischer first appeared in the German publishing world. One of the first publications of this house was a family almanac that came out in November 1884 with the title *Souvenir*. After founding his own firm (on October 22, 1886), Fischer published books by Ibsen, Tolstoy, Zola, Dostoyevsky, Gerhart Hauptmann, Hermann Bahr, Jens Peter Jacobsen, and Knut Hamsun; at the same time, however, he also brought out *Die Kunst, eine Zigarre anzubieten* [The right way to offer a cigar], *Jour fixe bei Muckenich* [*Jour fixe* at the Muckeniches], and the illustrated monthly *Das humoristische Deutschland* [Comic Germany]. In addition, the firm had a technical section that published two handbooks in the second year of its existence: *Das Färben und Imitieren von Holz, Horn, der Knochen und des Elfenbeins* [Staining and imitating wood, horn, bone, and ivory] and *Die Fabrikation von schwefelsaurer Tonerde* [The manufacture of aluminum sulfate].

The 1901 catalog lists two periodicals as well: *Zeitschrift für Beleuchtungswesen* [Journal of the lighting industry] and *Zeitschrift für Werkzeugmaschinen und Werkzeuge* [Journal of tool machinery and tools]. Fischer had learned from the experience of another publisher, Wilhelm Friedrich, who had published a thousand literary works in fifteen years, including those by the German realists and naturalists of his day. It was he who gave a militant flair to German literature at the end of the nineteenth century, but he met with failure before he was forty-five because, in the last analysis, he was no longer up to dealing with the constant financial problems of his authors: he paid Detlev von Liliencron's debts, paid Hermann Conradi's burial costs, paid his authors' fines in the notorious "realists'" trial. In 1895 he went out of business and "his authors disappeared like fleeting clouds," as Walter Hasenclever remarked. Max Dauthendey reported in his memoirs: "The career of the Leipzig publisher Friedrich, who had been the first one to lend vital support to the growth of the modern movement, was destroyed by his modern authors, for the book-buying public had as always lagged many a year behind the new literary figures and did not want to understand them or buy them. In place of the Friedrich Verlag, however, Berlin's S. Fischer Verlag blossomed for all Germany."

Fischer had all this in mind when he embarked on his own career. In 1890 he took over the journal *Die freie Bühne für modernes Leben* [The free stage for modern life], whose editor was Otto Brahm; in the third year of publication it was given the sub-title, *Für den Entwicklungskampf der Zeit* [For the progressive struggle of the times]. Julius Hart and Otto Julius Bierbaum were among its later editors and, in 1894, it became the *Neue Deutsche Rundschau* [New German review],[10] a periodical with a long and honorable history that still exists as *Die Neue Rundschau*. In its pages appeared examples of the work of a literary school now known to us as naturalism. Later, S. Fischer was called "the Cotta of naturalism," a description that was hailed by Thomas Mann, one of his most prominent authors.[11]

Fischer was influenced by this literary movement, by this journal, by the authors of his day, and above all by his editor, Moritz Heimann. He ran his firm in such a way that its history paralleled the literary history of his day. This seems to me a decisive criterion by which to gauge the importance of a literary publishing house. Samuel Fischer grew with his task. He wrote, in a fragmentary autobiographical sketch:

> At an early age I learned from my surroundings and my relationships with others to regard the rise to higher social levels of existence as the goal of all work. And so, with this goal alone in view, I was a man obsessed only with profit. Little by little, a process of broadening and enlightenment took place in me. I know today that there were good tendencies in me which never reached maturity because they were awakened too late.[12]

Later, Fischer described this process of "broadening and enlightenment" in these words: "The poet does not write in order to fulfill the needs of the public. The more personal...the way in which he expresses his nature, the more difficult it will be for him to make himself clearly understood....The publisher's most important and beautiful mission is to force upon the public new values it doesn't want."[13]

In his description of Fischer's first encounter with Hermann Hesse, Hugo Ball—author, critic, essayist, and Hesse's biographer—defined the possibilities and function of a publisher, who "lends the work reality and a social stamp even before it has been written" and who can give an author "that sense of meaningfulness in his actions and that abundance of expectation" without which his works might not come into being.

A publisher's list of authors gives each individual author support, security, and a basis for communication. Of course, this is true only if the authors have something in common, only if their association represents a kind of totality and not simply a random collection.

Peter Suhrkamp was another person who could not have foretold the way his life's career as publisher would turn out. He too was influenced by his work, by his need to protest the course of events, and by his authors, who were—or else became—his friends. Still, Suhrkamp had his own, quite specific, conception of the publisher's relationship to his authors. An anecdote dating from the nearly eight years during which I worked closely with him is in order here. It involved the statement of one of his guiding principles, one of those statements that illuminated a situation like a flash of lightning and betrayed the earnestness of an educator and the irony of someone who was himself a creative personality. It was in January 1953, and we were discussing a manuscript, the first novel of a young writer. We were not in agreement about it, and so Suhrkamp decided to ask the young man to come to Frankfurt. On the day before he was to arrive, Suhrkamp, his editor Friedrich Podszus, and I were considering how best to handle the young author. Suhrkamp energetically rejected my suggestion that we get right down to business. No, he was to be given only the most discreet criticism, and we received strict orders to talk only about the weather, family matters, and the like until Suhrkamp arrived. And then came these words: "I want you to remember one thing. Every author, no matter how young he is, in his capacity as a creative personality towers above the three of us sitting here." Suhrkamp meant what he said; he was sixty-two years old and experienced in dealing with authors.

His "towering" respect for the creative personality did not, however, mean that Suhrkamp sent out only acceptances. Uwe Johnson discovered this when he met Suhrkamp for the first time in Berlin (in July 1957). Johnson knew by heart a sentence Suhrkamp had written him a month previously: "I am itching to make a book out of it, and the book should appear by fall if at all possible." How Suhrkamp subsequently altered his intention was "instructive" for Johnson. "The old gentleman, who greeted his visitor with a special politeness no longer in general use, immediately urged the author to participate in the rejection of his own manuscript." The manuscript, "Ingrid Barbendererde," never appeared.[14]

I have often told my own authors the anecdote about Suhrkamp, but they don't want to hear about the towering creative personality. We are living in a world in which, to quote Walter Benjamin, the work of art is losing—and should lose—its special aura, so that "something higher" may become "something useful" that will reach and transform the largest possible number of us. Writers are dispensing increasingly with "messages." Max Frisch is one example: he states that even when successful he cannot feel "any sense of mission," that he has chosen writing as a career because he is "more successful at writing than at living and because there is not sufficient leisure time [if he were to pursue another profession] for this attempt to come to terms with life by writing about it."[15]

Samuel Beckett issued a warning in the last sentence of his novel *Watt:* "No symbols where none intended." And in an earlier work he wrote: "I have the feeling that there is nothing to express, nothing with which one could express it. No force of expression either, no desire to express anything along with the obligation to express it."

Martin Walser described writers as "students of behavior. They themselves are the object of their research." In the same passage he recalled a statement by Robert Walser: "It will be all over for me the moment I stop writing, and I am glad of that. Good night."[16]

Writing without a message: another example is Wolfgang Hildesheimer, who saw writing "as a process of repeated trial, of feeling one's way." But these trials, as Robert Musil once said, should be pursued only as long as they are really experienced by the writer: "I shouldn't feign completion [of a work] when I haven't attained it myself."

It is certainly not possible to define exactly what it is that motivates writers. In the last analysis, the source of creativity will remain a secret; the writer obeys a secret command. The only formulation I shall venture is that a great writer is not basically seeking *truth per se,* but *his own truth.* He attempts to give perfect form to his personal experience in the imaginary world of his work. He may renounce a message, but he gives expression to his longings. His reality begins beyond the commonplace world. The reality he finds around him is transformed by the power and magic of language into a fabricated, poetic reality, an extreme reality created by extreme art, into that "second world within this one" of which Jean Paul spoke.

In Hans Erich Nossack's novel *Die gestohlene Melodie* [The stolen melody] there is mention of a "strict obligation" to be inconspicuous, to remain apart and not betray "the only thing we have in common, loneliness." The passage goes on: "We must not offer ourselves as guides, but if someone who is a stranger in town asks us

ends with the words, "and how he kissed me under the Moorish wall and I thought well as well him as another and then I asked him with my eyes to ask again yes and then he asked me would I yes to say yes my mountain flower and first I put my arms around him yes and drew him down to me so he could feel my breasts all perfume and yes and his heart was going like mad and yes I said yes I will Yes."[21]

Joyce's letter to Frank Budgen (August 16, 1921) provides us with some insight into this final passage: "'Penelope' is the clou of the book. The first sentence contains 2500 words. There are eight sentences in the episode. It begins and ends with the female word *yes* . . . . Though probably more obscene than any preceding episode it seems to me to be perfectly sane full amoral fertilisable untrustworthy engaging shrewd limited prudent indifferent *Weib. Ich bin der* [sic] *Fleisch der stets bejaht.*"[22] (Note Joyce's use of German and his error in gender: it should be "das Fleisch.")

I have never read a more extreme formulation of a writer's longing.

For someone like a publisher, who stands at a point of intersection between inner and outer demands, who is conscious of the literary as well as material aims of authors, and who observes the tremendous social and economic difficulties burdening the life and work of a writer, it is often difficult to see the work and its creator without a special aura and to judge them objectively. But whoever has sat before an empty sheet of white paper (Ödön von Horváth once said, "And the empty paper is so terribly white"[23]), wanting to write down what he has experienced or learned, comes to respect productivity, to respect the demands placed upon those who produce. And he will even contradict Martin Walser, who considered the word "creative" a "shopworn metaphor."

This respect should be reflected in the publisher's faithfulness to his authors. Literary publishers have demonstrated this respect by placing their hopes not so much on the individual book that may bear promise of success as on the oeuvre, the author's total production. The publication of these oeuvres then contributes to the firm's growth. The individual titles are like the growth rings of a tree, and in the course of time what we call the character of a publishing house emerges organically.

This is not as easy as it sounds. We need only remember that Franz Kafka's two publishers—Ernst Rowohlt and Kurt Wolff, both significant figures whom I respect highly—were unable to bind Kafka to their firm, neither when they were in business together nor later when they were developing their own great houses separately. On November 15, 1912, Max Brod wrote to Kafka's fiancée Felice Bauer (the letter appears in Kafka's only really completed "novel," *Briefe an Felice* [*Letters to Felice*]): "Franz suffers greatly from having to stay in the office every day until two o'clock. In the afternoon he is worn out and so there remains only the night for the 'fullness of his visions.' It's a shame! And yet there he is writing a novel that stands out above all the literature I know. Just think what he could accomplish if he were free and in good hands!" Brod assessed the situation correctly: Kafka's life revolved around his writing, and he wrote to Felice that he had no literary interests; rather, he himself was made of literature. Brod knew that Kafka needed a quiet place if he was to write: "For his whole nature cries out for a peaceful life free from care and dedicated to his writing. Under present circumstances, his life is more or less a process of vegetating, with a few more fortunate bright moments."[24]

Brod had started looking for a publishing contact for Kafka at an early date. On June 29, 1912, on a trip to

Weimar, he took Kafka to Ernst Rowohlt and Kurt Wolff, who were then jointly heading Rowohlt Verlag. Kafka took leave of Wolff with a highly unusual sentence: "I shall always be far more grateful to you for returning my manuscripts than for publishing them."[25] Such was the nature of this author, who always remained shy about submitting manuscripts. Kafka was favorably impressed by Rowohlt; after meeting him, he urged his friend Brod: "Leave, Max, leave Juncker [then Brod's publisher], take everything or as much as you can with you. He has held you back, not in terms of yourself . . . but certainly in terms of your career."[26]

Finally, on August 14, 1912, Kafka sent Rowohlt his *Kleine Prosa* [Short prose pieces]:

> While I was putting the pieces together for this purpose, I sometimes had to make a choice between giving in to my feeling of responsibility or to my eagerness to have a book of mine among your beautiful books. Certainly I did not always reach an entirely faultless decision, but now I would of course be happy if you should like the things just enough to print them. After all, even with the greatest training and the greatest perception what is bad in things isn't always apparent at first glance. The most common form of a writer's individuality is his ability to hide (each in his own special way) what is bad about himself.[27]

Rowohlt accepted the manuscript and Kafka gladly agreed to the conditions set forth; "the conditions that reduce your risk as much as possible will also be the ones most preferable for me." But he requested "the largest type possible, given the restrictions" and he hoped for a dark paperback binding with tinted paper, something like the kind of paper used for Kleist's anecdotes, which Rowohlt had published.[28]

The association between Rowohlt and Wolff did not work out. On November 1, 1912, Rowohlt left the firm, which became known (in February 1913) as the Kurt Wolff Verlag. Kafka's first book, *Betrachtung* [*Meditation*], appeared there in 1913 (with the imprint November 1912) in a single printing of 800 copies. With the exception of his short story "Ein Hungerkünstler" ["A Hunger Artist"], all of Kafka's works published during his lifetime appeared with Kurt Wolff. Initially, the relationship was a close and good one; as late as July 27, 1917, Kafka wrote Wolff that he now had hopes of giving up his salaried position. He would like to go to Berlin; to be sure, he wouldn't be entirely dependent on his literary work then either, "in spite of which, however, I—or the bureaucrat deep within me, which is the same thing—have an oppressive fear of that moment; I only hope that you, my dear Herr Wolff, will not abandon me entirely then, assuming of course that I halfway deserve your support. One word from you now on this subject would mean so much to me and help me over all the uncertainties of the present and the future."[29]

Wolff was willing to give him financial assistance on a continuing basis. On November 3, 1921, Wolff wrote again, with the feeling of having to apologize for the poor sales and give Kafka encouragement: "I can assure you with the greatest sincerity that there are scarcely two or three authors whom we represent and have the honor of placing before the public with whom I personally have such a deep and heartfelt relationship as with you and your work."[30] But these comforting words came too late; Kafka could not bring himself to complete even one of his three novels or to give his publisher the opportunity of examining the manuscripts for possible publication. Sales of *Betrachtung* were minimal:

in the first year, 258 copies were sold; then 102, then 69 (the printing of 800 copies was not sold out until 1924). In the end, the firm was actually embarrassed to remit such insignificant royalties. On July 1, 1922, it closed its Kafka account, marking the dissolution of the relationship. As an "expression of our good intentions," the firm offered to send him a shipment of books as compensation. Kafka wanted to have a say in the selection, and he chose Hölderlin's *Gedichte* (Poems), Eichendorff's *Gedichte,* Chamisso's *Peter Schlemihl,* and others. The last piece of correspondence was a postcard from Kafka to the "very honored publishing house," postmarked December 31, 1923, a half year before his death; he complained that the books had still not arrived. "Would you be so kind as to find out what has happened to the shipment. Respectfully, F. Kafka."[31]

We can hardly imagine the result for literature and for intellectual history if Kurt Wolff had succeeded in giving Kafka the assurance, the security, and the possibilities for further development that, according to Hugo Ball, S. Fischer gave to Hesse. Kafka's pronouncement, "One word from you ... would mean so much to me and help me over all the uncertainties of the present and the future," touches directly upon the theme treated in these pages: what are the responsibilities of that man whose word means so much?

AN OUTLINE OF THE
PUBLISHER'S RESPONSIBILITIES

When an author decides upon a publishing house, he is choosing the total character of that house and its publisher. The following factors influence his decision: the list of authors whose books are published by the house; the format in which the house will present his books; the efficiency of the house in producing those books and projects entrusted to it—in other words, the efficiency of the staff; and the publisher himself, the author's primary partner, who has "managerial" responsibility for the preceding three criteria. Something should be said about each of these factors.

The List of Authors

The reputation of a literary publishing house is determined by the quality of its authors and the recognition they win, and by the influence their books have and the level of discussion they produce. A literary publishing house does not build its reputation on individual books, especially not on best-sellers, for today's best-seller lists are often tomorrow's obituary columns. The publishing program, as well as that program's scope, grows in accordance with the growth of its authors. The right admixture in the program is, of course, a matter of importance. This is an age-old publishing secret—the mixture, the combination, the blend of young and old authors, of salable books and those with little or no salability, of authors who follow the political currents of the day and those ("Don't talk to me about politics"— Joyce) who fanatically follow only the demands of their own work; of authors who are delighted to present themselves to the public every day and those who refuse such publicity all their lives; of authors who make excessively high, sometimes even absurd, financial demands in advance (in his comedy, *Die Macht der Gewohnheit* [The force of habit], the contemporary Austrian writer Thomas Bernhard writes, "Even genius has delusions of grandeur *once more* when it comes to money") and those who would rather not mention financial matters at all. Not to make a hodge-podge out of such a mixture but to create a synthesis out of the disparate parts, to form a unity, a single program, a totality, out of what is nearly unreconcilable—this constitutes the publisher's task and results in that special "stamp" of which Hugo Ball speaks in reference to S. Fischer.

We can now see why a publishing house that is not subsidized by public funds nevertheless furthers culture for the public benefit by taking on "the young author" year after year, a venture that is usually unpromising from a financial point of view. The prestige of the famous authors of a publishing house is useful to the newly published writer; young authors are often drawn to a house by the example of a great model. On the other hand, the older author who is beginning to fall into neglect needs a publisher in whose catalog there appears, along with his own works, new literature, literature of an innovative character, with new and provocative ideas, new impulses, new forms, and new language. Therefore, a literary publisher who is serious about his responsibilities will never, not even in hard times, stop publishing the latest literature, no matter how difficult it is to find buyers and readers for it. Young and new, as well as older and passé, authors always "live" to a certain extent off those who are at the peak of their potentiality and popularity. The history of literature and the literature of our own day prove that there are exceptions and that older authors sometimes enjoy a renaissance; I need only mention here the recent renewal of interest in the works of Hermann Hesse.

The literary publishing house also "lives" off the variety of receptions accorded its authors. When Peter Suhrkamp started up his firm again after the war, it was the rising popularity of Hesse's works that helped him build up his firm and made it possible for him to publish Brecht's works (more of which he exported to Scandinavia than he sold in the Federal Republic over the years) and devote himself to such young authors as Max Frisch. When the demand for Hesse's works declined, the works of Brecht and Frisch were flourishing, and this in turn enabled the firm to consider works by Proust and Walter Benjamin, which at first were unsalable (today we are seeing a growing interest in Walter Benjamin). Only Brecht's popularity made possible the publication of the collected works of Ödön von Horváth, and the popularity of both Brecht and Horváth, in turn, made feasible the publication of the collected works of Marieluise Fleißer, a disciple of Brecht.

Thus, if there is a discernible program in a publishing house's list of authors, it did not merely happen by chance. It is an organic program, originally put together by the publisher, that develops a character of its own. It has an external impact in the form of a public image as well as an internal one that affects the authors themselves and those who work for the firm and who try to realize this program in their daily work.

The Format

When an author decides upon a publisher, he is also choosing the way this particular house will present his books and defend his rights. This means, for example, that the modernity of an author's technique must be matched by modernity of the book's appearance. Each individual step in the production of a book is important: the treatment of the manuscript, the watchful care along the way of transformation from manuscript to book, the book's exterior, its jacket, its typography, and the words used to announce the book. A book's exterior is an expression of its interior. Difficulties often arise because the exterior must not only do justice to the interior, it must also be effective advertising, i.e., make the buyer decide to buy the book. In addition, it must please the author, do justice to his expectations, and yet at the same time be successful in the marketplace.

The character of a publishing house can best be inferred from its series. Here it can express its own ideas. This explains why new series keep appearing and others are discontinued. These series have significance. They can be influential when they are read by specific groups. A series can follow a tendency of the times or give rise to it.

The image of a publishing house is determined not only by the content of its books but also by their appearance. Here too we should not look for uniformity but rather for a unity in multiplicity. The most important factor is the appropriateness of the book's format.[32] Suhrkamp Verlag initiated the so-called Werkausgaben (popular complete editions in paperback) for the works of Proust and Brecht and continued this format for the works of Beckett, Bloch, Frisch, Hesse, and Horváth. The impact of these editions is evident when we note all the imitations at home and abroad and when we consider that experts discussing the plans of other publishing houses publicly recommend the issue of a popular edition "à la Suhrkamp."[33]

The Efficiency of the Staff

The author with a manuscript will choose the house he believes capable of doing the most for his future book. By this choice he is also voicing his confidence in the firm's staff. Although some firms have customarily published literature on the side while their main business was the production of technical books, it seems to me that this will not be possible in the future. Publishing houses must increasingly concentrate on the interests of the great majority of their authors, and this means, in turn, that the house and all its staff must be en rapport with the character of the majority of its books. For a literary publisher, this means five things.

To begin with, it means first-rate editors who are experts in their fields and disciplines, who can advise authors, and who are in the position of guaranteeing foreign authors a faithful translation of their works.

Second, it means good craftsmen, i.e., those persons responsible for turning the manuscript into a book.

Third, it means good advertising, public relations, and distribution staff who can present the author to the public and who can sell his book.

Fourth, it means specialists in the copyright department who are able to manage the author's subsidiary rights to his own best advantage as well as the firm's and to protect the author's rights in general. The copyright department at Suhrkamp is responsible for releasing the firm's books to approximately two hundred foreign publishers, agents, and translators. The more native literary works a firm publishes, the more intensive these contacts are; this is also true of its relations with book clubs and paperback publishers at home and abroad. The subsidiary rights which the firm attempts to manage as profitably as possible for its authors and, naturally, for itself as well involve advance publications; reprints; translations; adaptations; radio, television, and film rights; stage rights; microfilm editions; recordings; tapes; rights for paperback, book-club, and reprint editions; rights for popular, special, and school editions and for anthologies; the commercial and noncommercial lending of books; photocopies; musical settings; and future multimedia rights. The firm also provides basic copyright protection.

For instance, Suhrkamp successfully defended Heinar Kipphardt's rights to his *In der Sache J. Robert Oppenheimer* [*In the Matter of J. Robert Oppenheimer*] in a plagiarism case in Paris against the celebrated director Jean Vilar. In another case involving Suhrkamp, Rudolf Noelte's suit, in which he claimed to be a co-author of

Max Frisch's *Biografie* [*Biography*] as a result of his having directed the play, was finally dismissed by the Federal Court in Karlsruhe. The firm takes care of entry visas and residence permits and provides expert legal opinion in complicated questions—for example, when copyright laws are different in different countries—and sees that its authors' titles are protected.

Finally, the efficiency of the staff involves organization, which is of primary importance. More than ever, a publishing house needs to be well organized; it has to meet the highest expectations. I often think of T. S. Eliot's remark that to write poetry it is just as necessary to have organization as imagination.

Important, in this connection, is cooperation among all the departments, which is needed to solve problems of delivery, storage, and inventory. These items are becoming increasingly costly, and the accounting department must be able to make an overview of all the firm's transactions readily available. Also of importance is the electronic data-processing equipment, to which is being delegated more and more responsibility for billing, statistics, information about sales, royalty payments, and decisions about printings and reprintings.

The Publisher

The role of the publisher is easily described here. He is the author's primary partner in giving an opinion of the manuscript and perhaps working with him on it to obtain the utmost substance and quality of which the author is capable. He is the primary partner in judging the chances for the financial success of a book, a play, or a film; he is the partner in arranging the possible financing of a book. As a rule, an author likes to know whom he has to deal with in the publishing world; it is remarkable that the ever-expanding book conglomerates, which are swallowing up individual publishing houses these days, have not yet demonstrated that they can "make" new authors.

An author's confidence in a publishing house is concentrated in the person who is responsible for the firm both intellectually and financially, who can give him a feeling of security, and who often must give him the courage to finish a work already begun, to begin a new one, or—in the case of a fiasco, a total failure, a negative review, or a failure of nerve—the courage to start all over again. The author centers his confidence in the person who respects creativity but who also knows that a source of that creativity often lies in illness, in neurosis. For when the author succeeds in neutralizing his libidinous and aggressive energies through the act of writing, with the result that his experiences become Word, he often pays for this in everyday life by being asocial, set apart from what is normal, an outsider.[34]

To be sure, this kind of publishing partnership cannot be sustained by every publisher or with all authors; in a large house, other members of the staff also assume this function. It is easy to understand that these activities we have described are often hindered by a generation gap. Literary publishing houses today must be of a certain size in order to be independent, to be able to follow their authors' wishes, to remain competitive, and not to be at the mercy of the book trade in general or competitors in the other media. In the future, there will always be the small one-man publishing house and the large literary one, which may have to grow to meet changing circumstances. But the limits to such a firm's growth will be determined by the fact that the publisher must still be able to perform his traditional functions for the house's most important authors and, in addition, be able to oversee the individual relationships between the staff and the authors. It has been my frequent experience that an author is interested only in his own work; basically, he wants the firm to publish only *his* book. To return to the example of James Joyce: after first meeting him in 1921, the young T. S. Eliot described him as a bundle of nerves who had the conviction of a die-hard fanatic that the whole world was obliged to foster his work. And Richard Ellmann, Joyce's biographer, reports that in the Paris of the early twenties Joyce concealed himself behind a wall of silence concerning literary matters but spoke with unabashed openness about his personal problems, specifically money, his children, and his health. What else could matter to Joyce besides his superhuman work? In order to survive, he had to concentrate exclusively on his own affairs.

In the works, in the attitude, and in the letters of Thomas Bernhard, a similarly cold despair about a writer's ability to survive prevails. In his story "Am Ortler" [At Mt. Ortler] he talks about writing:

> What one writes, he said, is basically there only to be destroyed . . . what one writes is meant to be destroyed . . . The difficulty of showing or publishing . . . the intellectual product without having to commit suicide on the spot, going through this frightful and embarrassing process without killing oneself, to show what one is, to make public what one is, he said . . . to go through the hell of publication, to be able to go through this hell . . . to have to go through this hell of publication, ruthlessly to go through this most frightful of all hells.[35]

And then Bernhard writes to his publisher, "At the moment, I wish for nothing more than to walk up and down with you clarifying unclear ideas, to uncomplicate the complicated, and to reestablish with openness, honesty, and circumspection what is obvious and necessary for our mutual long-term future."[36]

An author may even want his publisher to issue a writing ban for other authors so that his book can be the only one to receive attention. One author writes to his publisher: "Besides, I am constantly fluctuating between elation and depression. Would like so terribly to make a real start on my next opus, but for the present my hands are still tied . . . damn it! Actually, I am counting on you to stand by me while I take this all-important step, march, leap, *salto* (the most important and decisive of my career)."[37]

This is what the publisher's responsibility involves: to instill courage, to set energies in motion. In the festschrift for Anton Kippenberg I found an essay by Karl Scheffler on professional idealism:

> The peculiar thing about the publisher's profession is that he has the urge to give form to something of an intellectual–spiritual nature, that he wants to be productive but lacks the means to carry out his will directly. He must set in motion others who have these means: poets, artists, writers; he is a person with the liveliest of interests, with the liveliest urge to express himself, but one who can speak only through others, being mute himself . . . to his profession belong vitality on the one hand and renunciation on the other. It is his business to assert himself by taking the part of others.[38]

The publisher seeks out people for his staff and attempts to integrate them into the total organization and to coordinate the efforts of the individual departments.

The publisher must provide a sound financial basis for the firm, enabling it to remunerate its authors adequately and to sell ever larger numbers of books, which is the only way to offset increasing costs; he must also see that there are sufficient funds to provide the staff with suitable working quarters and to give them appropriate salaries and social benefits. We need a strong financial basis primarily in order to be able to remain independent and to assure our authors as much independence as possible. We wish to continue to retain the capacity to produce the books we want to.

Since the publisher is responsible for the entire undertaking, it is also he who, in the last analysis, determines which books the firm publishes and the amount of capital the firm invests in a given project. This can be accomplished only by teamwork with the staff: with the production and distribution personnel and with the editors with whom he discusses individual manuscripts as well as overall planning. Even though the publisher may be more inclined by temperament to say yes than to say no, his decisions will always require a no more often than a yes. In this connection Hermann Hesse was of great help to me. When Peter Suhrkamp died and I became his successor, Hesse wrote: "The publisher must move 'with the times,' as people say, yet he should not simply follow the fashions of the times but also be able to resist them when they are undesirable. The function, the very breathing in and out, of a good publisher consists of accommodation and critical resistance. This is the kind you should be."[39]

The publisher is responsible not only for the job security of his employees, for pensions, insurance, and other social benefits. In his hands there frequently also lies the material well-being of the authors, translators, editors and, often, of the descendants and heirs of these authors, translators, and editors.

The publisher's personal relationship with the authors is crucial. Since they know that for the publisher there is no division between working hours and leisure time, he must be available at all times for personal matters. Thus, he has to be something of a literary midwife, a psychoanalyst, a businessman, and a patron of the arts. The closer the publisher's contacts with his authors, the greater is their influence on the publishing house. They can be antennae for the house; they can send and receive, sending messages of their own and often receiving reports or signs of new and coming literary trends.

The publisher is not so intent on satisfying needs *with* his books; what he wants is to awaken new needs *for* his books. Insofar as he is interested in persuasion, education, and molding public taste, he is a kind of pedagogue; he must at least have a certain love for pedagogy. As a lover of detail, he is mindful of the words of Pestalozzi concerning the necessity for a certain pettiness in grand matters and a certain grandeur in petty ones. The main thing, however, is that the publisher must be thinking continually and creatively about his firm. He must think for others. His innovative powers constantly prepare him for what is new; on the other hand, he remains faithful to tradition. He must continually keep the creative potentiality of his authors and the productive potentiality of his firm in sight, in mind, and in his heart. He must have a large heart and should always see that it receives proper sustenance.

WHICH BOOKS DOES A PUBLISHER LIKE TO PUBLISH?

The question most frequently asked of a publisher is, What is the guiding principle in the selection of books? At one time, my answer was that I liked to publish books that were enjoyable to do. Later, my answer was books that the firm can best produce, books that the firm, as an entity, with all its staff and authors, is attuned to. I like to publish books that have some impact, and in this connection I must always think of Kafka's words, "A book must be the ax for the frozen sea within us." Or as Marcel Proust wrote at the end of *A la recherche du temps perdu:*

> Mais pour en revenir à moi-même, je pensais plus modestement à mon livre, et ce serait même exact

que de dire en pensant à ceux qui le liraient, à mes lecteurs. Car ils ne seraient pas, selon moi, mes lecteurs, mais les propres lecteurs d'eux-mêmes, mon livre n'étant qu'une sorte de ces verres grossissants comme ceux que tendait à un acheteur l'opticien de Combray; mon livre, grâce auquel je leur fournirais le moyen de lire en eux-mêmes.

These are the books that the publisher would like to publish. The criteria are substance and quality, and the criteria must be tested again and again against each individual manuscript. The publisher wants to bring out literature that penetrates the readers' consciousness and attempts to alter it, literature which provides readers with sustenance at the same time that it disquiets them.

Literature is always what authors make of it, and the publisher strives to follow the author's inner rhythm. We have already noted that richly endowed literary epochs can be followed by more meager ones. It can also happen that literature in a given language relinquishes its leadership and significance to literature in another. In the eighteenth and early nineteenth centuries, German literature was dominant; then came the great Russians; then, in the beginning of our century, the Americans, the great Irish, and the French. In the literary concert of European nations, the German-speaking voice is at present quite audible, and within this German-speaking realm, Swiss and Austrian writers are playing a growing role. Today we realize that German literature at the beginning of this century was in crisis, but this crisis was by no means limited to German literature. Writing became difficult for many authors. Some of the best remained silent for a long time. The old problem of how to reconcile one's conception of reality with reality itself is growing more complicated; for example, the contemporary writer's favorable conception of socialism has quite often been destroyed by the socialist reality with which he is presented. For a time, it was erroneously believed that writers ought to work out and propagate concrete remedies for present-day problems. In addition to this, there arose, and still exists, a difficulty of a completely different nature, brought about by our tremendously rapid, worldwide communication systems: our minds find it difficult to absorb and withstand the onslaughts of a constant barrage of news, facts, and figures produced by computers, communication satellites, and all the other paraphernalia of a technological society.

In his *Versuch, die Welt besser zu bestehen* [An attempt to cope with the world more successfully], the social psychologist Alexander Mitscherlich comes to the conclusion that in the face of an increasingly bureaucratized and computer-controlled world, we must encourage a strengthening of the "ego forces" and of a new cultivation of basic human rights. Max Frisch's words from the year 1945, "It's up to mankind . . . the Deluge can be manufactured," have become timely again. For many centuries people strove to perfect themselves; our century is directing its energies toward the perfecting of objects—of everyday computer-controlled objects, from data bank to space capsule. Erhart Kästner spoke of the "revolt of objects." It is perfectly conceivable, Mitscherlich deduces, "that the responsibility for a tolerable life for the human species will lie with that group which can arouse a passion for self-awareness as well as a passion for perfecting objects."[40] I am firmly convinced that the process of developing self-awareness can best be accomplished through literature.

Again: literature is always what authors make of it. And we are often blind to the true contours of the literature of our own day. We should be cautious about predicting future literary trends; nevertheless, I think it is safe to say that the tendency toward a growing de-

mocratization of literature, toward a rationalistic literature, written in an easily understood style, that shows
mankind in terms of the constraints and inter-
relationships of prevailing social conditions will become
stronger. Then we will have literature that demonstrates
a more intensive and intimate relationship with language, a relationship based on the recognition that
altered content can be adequately rendered only by
altered linguistic forms. And I am sure of literature's
ability to apportion greater significance to the play principle again, to our imagination, which has become sur-
feited with reality. Such literature does not contain a
direct message; it speaks to the reader's sense of freedom, urging him to give free rein to his imagination.
Peter Handke expects novelty from a literary work, "a
new way of seeing, of speaking, of thinking, of existing."
In his essay "Die Literatur ist romantisch" [Literature is
romantic], he says:

> The person who is engagé concerns himself with the
> way things ought to be in a purposeful, not a playful,
> manner . . . There is no such thing as engagé lit-
> erature; the concept is a contradiction in terms. There
> are engagé people but not engagé writers . . . En-
> gagement emphasizes the goal of changing social
> reality, whereas a goal for art would be monstrous.
> It is not serious and not direct, i.e., directed to-
> ward something, but a form and, as such, not di-
> rected toward anything, at most an earnest game.[41]

In this process, in the readiness for phantasy and play,
there will be ever new possibilities for literature, for
poetry, for drama, and especially for the old forms of
the novel, the story, the novella. To transcend reality in
the free play of imagination and in an earnest game
seems to me to be one of literature's important possibilities. Transcending was an important ideal of the

late Brecht, who wrote, "Real progress is not having progressed, but progressing" and who spoke of "transcending, not transcendence." A favorite saying of the aging Josef Knecht in Hermann Hesse's *Das Glasperlenspiel* [*The Glass Bead Game*] is, "My life should be a process of transcending, of progressing from stage to stage."

This emphasis on progressing, on imagination, and on the capacity for play does not appear to me to be an accidental one nor one that is reactionary, but rather an objective sign of future literary possibilities. Only a short while ago, literature was declared dead; at first this pronouncement was made only about bourgeois literature, then about literature as a whole. Even Kafka and Beckett, in whose works mutilation and capitulation in the face of the social forces of alienation were depicted, were included in this judgment. I see it differently: by describing this alienation in his works, the writer places it on a conscious level, and I consider this to be a first step in overcoming it.

Those who insist that literary works must be politically and socially relevant and who regard the author as a mere "agent of the masses" are assigning literature an ersatz function. They would be astonished to learn that Lenin's brother had a copy of Heinrich Heine's poems in his pocket when he went to his execution. They would also be astonished at this entry in Brecht's diary: "When a person's feeling for literature fades, he is lost."[42] People who for the present reject pleasure and a delight in beauty, in other words, the fulfillment of the desires of the libido, who reject imagination and playfulness as well, reserving all these things for a future classless society, are only impeding its realization. Actually, we should not take offense at critics who insist on "social relevance," not even those all-too-familiar preachers of the death of literature; they too have performed a service. Sociology is now making fiction possible again. This literature, with its capacity for imagination and play, will bring about a new growth of human potentiality. It is a literature that proceeds from the actual and points to the possible. This is how Theodor W. Adorno put it in his posthumously published *Ästhetische Theorie* [Aesthetic theory]: "Imagination is also, and essentially, the unlimited command of the possibilities of resolution that crystalize within a work of art ... solely by passing through being does art transcend into non-being."[43]

To publish such literature strikes me as a goal worth striving for. I too would like to do my work without having a specific identifiable ideology, without giving in to the German tendency toward extremes and excess, but definitely with the courage to make compromises with all the imagination I can muster and, whenever possible, in the spirit of an "earnest game." I am firmly convinced that books, especially the kind our house publishes, will continue to maintain their position in our society, a society with increasing time for leisure on the one hand and the clear goal of the maturation of the individual on the other. The marketplace as well as the media will be dominated more and more by economic factors, thereby increasing the chances that substance and quality will make their impact felt in contrast.

Many changes are being made in the manner of book production owing to far-reaching, even revolutionary technological innovation; this will help us to make books that are as practical as they are beautiful. We know that writing has become more difficult in our time, and for many demonstrable reasons. It is in the individual self, wrote Max Frisch, that human life transpires. The individual who, today, is attempting to free himself from authoritarian structures, who dares to be himself, to be different, to go his own way in thought and deed, a way leading from a strong "I" to a sociable "Thou," from a reinforced individuality to a more just society—is not this individual the source of a new challenge for literature, for those who write it? We have found that knowledge, that theories, have grown more difficult to deal with because it is more difficult for increasingly complex societies to develop individuals with rational identities. Are not these difficulties a challenge to learn, for those who pursue learning?

Literature is always what authors make of it. The responsibilities of the literary publisher may have changed slightly in the process of streamlining literary communication, but basically they remain the same: to be receptive to the author and the new elements in his work and to help to win him readers.

Hermann Hesse
and His Publishers

The function, the very breathing in and out, of the good publisher consists of accommodation and critical resistance.
Hermann Hesse to Siegfried Unseld, April 1959

Today, as so often in reporting on my work, I shall speak about teachers I have had.

Authors—when what is peculiar to them, the measure of what they have experienced, thought, and described, reaches the level of the exemplary—are also teachers. Late in his life, Bertolt Brecht said to a woman who wanted to write about him, "Simply describe me as what I am, as a teacher." The publisher Samuel Fischer was also making a pedagogic confession when he said that "the publisher's finest and most important mission is to force upon the public new values it doesn't want." My teacher Peter Suhrkamp was a pedagog of the first water. The profession of schoolteacher, which he pursued for only a short time and which he described in his story "Munderloh," left an indelible stamp on him. His publishing house was a kind of teaching center, his publishing a kind of teaching. Karl Korn, who had a long personal association with Suhrkamp, called him "a publisher, a writer, a schoolmaster." And Hermann Hesse told, in his eulogy, how much Suhrkamp's whole life had oscillated "between the two poles of venturesome activity, of the desire to be effective in a creative and educational way, and the longing for escape from the world, for peace and seclusion."[1] The urge to educate was, without a doubt, the basic element in Suhrkamp's existence.

Do you still remember the first thing you read that made a lasting impression on you? In my case it was a book entitled *Der Löwe von St. Markus* [*The Lion of St. Mark*]. I didn't know then, nor do I know today (the book was destroyed when our home was bombed out during the war), who the publisher of this volume was.[2] In 1946, my German teacher, Eugen Zeller, told me about Hermann Hesse. Zeller was another teacher, a great one, who had three favorite German writers: Goethe, Mörike, and Hesse. He was, moreover, a true progressive because he didn't make us write essays about these authors and because he was against grades. He introduced me to Hesse's work and lent me Hesse's books, which I read one after the other. A young man of twenty-two in those troubled days immediately after the war, I experienced a sense of direction for the first time, for I read these books as if I were reading about myself. Although I did notice their physical appearance—the blue linen, the black spine label with the gold lettering—I didn't notice the line on the title page reading "S. Fischer Verlag, Berlin" or "Suhrkamp Verlag, formerly S. Fischer Verlag, Berlin." I believe many people don't notice the publisher's name, and I think this is all right.

Today, I am a publisher attempting to produce books of literary quality and substance, books in which an individual can find himself and which, at the same time, further an interest in a rational society. Since this is what I am trying to do, it is my wish that a new young reader be convinced, first of all, of the *author's* importance, of what the author can mean to him. He ought to make up his own mind independently of the publisher's imprint. This reader who won't allow himself to be manipulated but follows his own interests exclusively is a constant challenge to a publisher. Günter Eich once made some relevant observations about the reader's responsibility. Eich had criticized and "in a certain sense" rejected Hesse's *Morgenlandfahrt* [*Journey to the East*]; Hesse wrote him a reply about the "sin of criticism." Eich, struck by the cordiality as well as by the harshness of Hesse's response, wrote (I am quoting an unpublished letter from Eich to Hesse, dated October 30, 1932): "But for someone who, in the midst of a practical world, is helplessly addicted to the pointlessness of writing— for him there is always, in addition to sad doubts about what he is doing, the other, torturous question of whether at each moment and in each word his sense of responsibility and his conscience were strong enough." It is just this question about responsibility and conscience that every reader of a book must ask—without regard to the publisher's imprint.

How does an author view this question of a publisher's imprint? Why does he choose to associate himself with a given house? Hesse's relations with his publishers seem exemplary to me, exemplary in regard to his strategy in having his own works published, in regard to his financial and moral independence, and in regard to his loyalty.

The history of Hesse's relations with his publishers and with publishers in general is rich, varied, and not without surprises. He knew, unlike many other authors, that such beings as publishers exist. "Of the many realms," Hesse wrote in 1930 in his important essay "Magie des Buches" [The magic of the book], "that man did not receive as a gift of nature but created out of his own spirit, the realm of books is the greatest."[3] Hesse became acquainted with the world of books at an early age—in his parents' home; in his education, which was self-education, self-education through books; but above all through his occupation as bookseller. In October 1895, Hesse became an apprentice in Heckenhauer's Bookstore in Tübingen, learning his trade in hard ten-to-twelve-hour days. His apprenticeship ended on July 31, 1899, and from September 15th of that year until January 31, 1901, he worked as bookseller and rare book dealer in the R. Reich Bookstore in Basel. Writing about this occupation in 1899, he stated: "It is interesting, but I don't like it. My fellow workers above all are responsible for this; two-thirds of them are completely uneducated and unrefined. Also, I am without doubt an expert but a poor salesman."[4]

We shall see that Hesse nevertheless became an accomplished defender of his interests so far as the economic aspect of his writing was concerned. At the time, to be sure, he viewed publishers only as businessmen. His first book of poetry *Romantische Lieder* [Romantic songs], written in Tübingen, appeared with E. Pierson in Dresden only after Hesse had agreed to share the costs of production, with the prospect of royalties. He paid 175 marks, which, considering the pocket money he was getting as an apprentice at the time, was a considerable sum. (Many a famous author on S. Fischer's list made his debut with E. Pierson by contributing to the printing costs.) The first printing of *Romantische Lieder* numbered six hundred copies; in the first year, forty-three softbound and eleven hardbound copies were sold—a total of fifty-four copies. Hesse's royalties amounted to 35.10 marks.

Hesse was corresponding at that time with Helene Voigt. The young lady (she was twenty-two) had read his poetry in the magazine *Dichterheim* and expressed her admiration in a letter of November 22, 1897. In spite of Hesse's slightly condescending answer (he was then already "tired of his work") to the "honored Fräulein," there developed a cordial correspondence in which two people confided their first poetic attempts to each other, each trying to inspire the other to further efforts. Hesse, who never met the "fascinating and beautiful" budding "young North German poetess," learned that she had married a publisher by the name of Diederichs in the course of the year that they began writing to each other. Soon thereafter, the bride offered to recommend *Romantische Lieder* to her husband. Hesse reacted in a way already characteristic of him: "I am pleased and honored that you should come up with the idea of my submitting my manuscripts to your husband's publishing house. And if you ask me again someday, I would like to take you up on it if possible. But to be honest, it seems to me that I should try to have something published *this first time* without your help, I mean entirely on my own. Do you understand?"[5]

Hesse's second book, consisting of nine prose studies entitled *Eine Stunde hinter Mitternacht* [An hour beyond midnight] was in fact published by Diederichs in Leipzig. Eugen Diederichs certainly did this for his wife's sake, for he knew nothing about Hesse and the book really didn't fit in well with his publishing program, which was not devoted to contemporary literature. He missed "a liberating impulse" in these sketches, as he wrote to Hesse. "Frankly, though I have little faith in the commercial success of the book, I am all the more convinced of its literary merit. . . . I do not count on selling even six hundred [copies], but I am hoping that the physical look alone will attract notice and make up for the author's unknown name."[6]

Also typical of Hesse were his remarks in a letter to Diederichs: "I shall always have the warmest regard for you and be grateful for your helpfulness. But I also thank you for describing so honestly the impression you have of me." Hesse asked to see exact samples of the book's typography and paper. He wished "to be permitted a few questions" about the terms of the contract suggested by Diederichs:

> I am completely in agreement with them and should like only to have a few things explained as a matter of interest. You write: "1. ten free copies. 2. the rights to all editions. 3. possibly new editions with honorarium based on the practice of the publisher." How am I to understand point 2? That you have the copyright forever or that I am to receive ten free copies of each new edition? Also, practice of the publisher. Does that mean what the publisher deems proper from case to case or an amount based on some norm? I am asking purely out of curiosity and in order to understand these terms once and for all. You already have my approval.[7]

It is clear from this that Hesse would resist what is called "the practice of publishers" for the rest of his life if it placed restrictions on what he considered his own rights.

Meticulously printed by W. Drugulin, *Eine Stunde hinter Mitternacht* appeared in July 1899. In the first year, fifty-three copies were sold (Pierson had sold fifty-four copies of *Romantische Lieder*). But whereas *Romantische Lieder* had gone unnoticed by the critics, this book, no doubt because of the publisher's imprint, found an important reviewer, Rainer Maria Rilke: "The words are as though forged out of metal and must be read slowly and with effort. Yet the book is very unliterary. Its best passages have an air of inevitability and strangeness. Its tone of reverence is sincere and deep. It conveys great love and all the feelings expressed are pious ones: it stands at the edge of art."[8] When *Eine*

Stunde hinter Mitternacht appeared, the work was also already standing at the edge of the author's consciousness because of the disappointment it had brought him. Hesse reviewed books published by Diederichs "in order to reduce the losses my poor book has incurred for the firm."[9] He was doubly upset: the public took little notice of the volume and his parents in Calw were offended by it. In a bitter letter to his mother (dated June 16, 1899) that he never sent, he defended himself against her reproach that he had written "a godless book":

> I can't write any more. . . . You speak of "thinking it over ahead of time." I fear I weighed and thought over my book "ahead of time" as much as you did your kind letter. Unfortunately, there is nothing to smooth over or apologize for. I don't believe my book hurt you half as much as your interpretation of it has hurt me. But talking about it doesn't do any good. You both must know the saying, "for him who is pure, everything is pure," and accordingly you have both relegated me to the ranks of the impure.[10]

Years later, when the book was out of print, Hesse withdrew *Eine Stunde hinter Mitternacht* and did not permit a new edition. Not until 1941 did a facsimile edition appear in Zurich, and then as a historical document. In the preface to that new edition, Hesse gave "biographical reasons" for its disappearance for decades from the list of his books. He had "created for himself an artist's dream realm, an island of beauty, whose artistry was a retreat from the storms and depressions of the daylight world into night, dreams, and beautiful solitude; the book was not without its overly 'aesthetic' qualities."[11] But the most important reasons for his negative reaction to the book were its commercial failure, its lack of popularity, and the protests from his mother and other relatives.

Hesse's next "publication" was twenty handwritten copies of a manuscript entitled "Notturni," which he offered to a small circle of friends in the fall of 1900 for the price of 20 francs ("orders will be accepted only by invitation"[12]). He had submitted another manuscript to Diederichs on August 16, 1900, from Basel ("Prinzessin Lilia," which was to be the "Lulu" chapter of his next book *Hermann Lauscher*), and he offered to share the publishing costs if it appeared as part of a collection to be called "Schwäbische Erzählungen" [Swabian tales]. But then he changed his mind, not only about the title and the publisher but also about the author's name, and he hid behind the mask of editor. In late 1900 (with the imprint 1901), R. Reich in Basel published *Hinterlassene Schriften und Gedichte von Hermann Lauscher: Herausgegeben von Hermann Hesse* [Posthumous writings and poetry by Hermann Lauscher: edited by Hermann Hesse]. The book was not distributed to bookstores; "it was meant only for Basel."[13] These intimate publications gave him the advantage "of knowing that my writing, kept from commercial speculation and the gossip of the press, is being read only by friends and well-disposed people."[14]

One must not take this stand-offish attitude toward publicity too seriously; it was only a phase. But whatever attitude Hesse took, he took it decisively and consistently. Gradually, despite his first experiences, he developed a different image of the publisher. Later, when he made the acquaintance of Eugen Diederichs, he listened "with astonishment and pleasure to a man who spoke of his business and his plans as though they were matters touching his heart."[15] He was soon to repeat this experience with Samuel Fischer.

Books have a fate of their own. *Lauscher,* appearing in a very small edition, had been intended only for Basel, and except for a small circle of Swiss literary friends, hardly anyone knew it. However, the Swiss regional author, Paul Ilg, took the unusual step of sending the book to Samuel Fischer even though he had no personal or business connections with that publisher. *Lauscher's* prose and poetry were not lost on Fischer, and it is likely that his editor Moritz Heimann also read the book and recommended its author. Fischer wrote to Hesse, probably early in 1903: "Dear Sir: We have read with great pleasure the posthumous poems and writings of Hermann Lauscher; in these few pages there is great beauty that arouses considerable hope. We would be pleased if you would care to send us some of your more recent works."[16] Hesse answered (on February 2, 1903) that Fischer's letter had pleased him; he couldn't send him anything at the moment but he promised to send "a little prose work" he had been working on for years. This he did on May 9th, and, on the 18th, Fischer wrote him about the new manuscript, "Peter Camenzind":

> Just in time for Pentecost I should like to send you my warm gratitude for your wonderful work. It's not so much the subject matter as the manner in which experiences, not significant in themselves, are communicated to us by way of a poet's nature—this is what lends the work fullness and splendor. Elisabeth, Richard, Frau Nardini, the cabinetmaker's child, Boppi the cripple have become dear to me by virtue of the directness of what is experienced. I congratulate you upon this first book of yours; I shall be delighted if you permit me to publish it.[17]

On June 9th, Fischer sent Hesse a contract guaranteeing him 20 percent of the store price of the soft-cover edition. The first edition numbered a

53

thousand copies, and Hesse granted the publisher "first option on the publication of any books he wrote in the next five years." Fischer was not completely convinced of *Camenzind*'s prospects. This is clear from two letters to Hesse (June 9, 1903, and February 15, 1904) in which he predicted that *Camenzind* would not be a commercial success. In the first letter, accompanying the contract, Fischer showed where his real hopes and aspirations lay: "I very much hope that even if your *Peter* is not an instant commercial success it still will find very many friends and admirers and especially that it may be a good indication of what can be expected of you in the future. I have the feeling that you are well on the way to a good prose style. You are a neighbor of Emil Strauß, whom I consider our best hope."[18] It is still hard for me to understand how Fischer, a publisher who was experienced about authors, could refer, in one of his first letters to an author, to a second author as "our best hope" and call the first author only "well on the way to a good prose style."

Fischer wanted to present the novel to the readers of his *Neue Rundschau,* and Hesse agreed to an abridgement by one-fifth. Thus, the appearance of the book had to be postponed until the beginning of 1904. Oscar Bie, editor of the *Rundschau,* published the advance version in three issues from September to November 1903. Hesse received an honorarium of 487.50 marks. Then, on February 15, 1904, *Peter Camenzind* appeared, similar in its format, paper, and type to Emil Strauß's *Freund Hein* [*Death the Comforter*]. Contrary to all the publisher's expectations, *Camenzind* became a success. Two years after publication, the book had sold thirty-six thousand copies. By 1908, it had sold fifty thousand copies.

Hesse wrote about this episode in his *Biographische Notizen* [Biographical notes] of 1923: "At the time I had begun *Camenzind,* and Fischer's invitation gave me great encouragement. I finished it; it was accepted immediately; the publisher wrote in a warm, even cordial way; there was an advance printing in the *Neue Rundschau;* the book received recognition from Emil Strauß and other men I admired; I had arrived."[19] "And not only arrived," wrote Hesse's biographer, Hugo Ball. *Camenzind* had with one stroke made Hesse's name famous throughout Germany, and Hesse

> now was where he belonged: in a forum where he could be heard from far and wide. And this connection [with Fischer] was significant for him in another sense as well. Even during the worst years Fischer managed to sustain a kind of community and intellectual élite, a circle that lends the work reality and a social stamp even before it has been written. The publisher's firmness, Hesse's keen awareness of his publisher's sense of direction and his dignity were perhaps just what Hesse needed for his steady development. It is very possible that only this publishing house could provide the writer with that sense of meaningfulness in his actions and that abundance of expectation without which Hesse's work as we know it today would perhaps not exist.[20]

I cite this observation of Hermann Ball's again and again because it is such a felicitous description of the function of a literary publisher.

Hesse first met S. Fischer in Munich, in the early days of April 1904, and it was then that Fischer introduced him to Thomas Mann. A businesslike but friendly relationship developed between author and publisher. The association with Hesse was not always easy. *Camenzind*'s great success had, it is true, made possible a new independence. He gave up his career as bookseller, traveled, and bought a house in Gaienhofen, on Lake Constance—but the highly sensitive and nervous Hesse, subject to inner tensions, was not an easy partner for the publisher. When Fischer inquired (in November 1904) about how Hesse's new work was progressing, Hesse took offense at his "feverish commercialism." In 1906, *Unterm Rad* [*Beneath the Wheel*] appeared; in 1907, *Diesseits* [In this world]; in 1908 *Nachbarn* [Neighbors].

Then, as Peter de Mendelssohn writes, something "strange" happened. In the contract for *Camenzind* (dated June 10, 1903), Hesse had promised Fischer options on the books he wrote during the next five years. This right of option was to be extended "automatically for another five years" if not specifically terminated. Hesse did terminate the clause. His success with *Camenzind* had given him a name not only with the public but among publishers as well. As early as November 4, 1904, Fischer had expressed his concern in a letter to Hesse: "it is only natural that after *Camenzind*'s success you will receive offers from all sides, also that a certain type of publisher, who sees his profession exclusively in terms of pursuing successful authors with tempting offers, will start pestering you, and that this external pressure will cause you agitation that can be just as dangerous for you as it is exciting." Indeed, in the wake of Hesse's frequent visits to Munich and his work for the magazines *März* and *Simplicissimus,* he had established contact with the publishers Albert Langen and Georg Müller, who made a strong play for him. The wooing by the publishers or, in other words, the capitalistic system of competition, strengthened Hesse's drive for independence. He succeeded in securing a contract with Samuel Fischer that no other author before him had obtained from that company.

On February 1, 1908, two supplementary clauses were added to the 1903 contract. Hesse promised to give S. Fischer three of his next four works and retained the right to submit one of the four to Albert Langen. That was one stipulation; the other one was just as amazing. Hesse demanded something in return for the rights of option reserved for S. Fischer, and thus the firm had to promise "to pay the total sum of 5400 marks over the next three years in monthly instalments of 150 marks. This amount will not be deducted from the royalties."[21] This kind of remuneration was highly unusual at the time. It went against Fischer's grain, but he was finally able to see Hesse's point. Hesse wanted to remain free and independent, and if he gave up his freedom to negotiate each book as he finished it, then the publisher had to grant him something in return. When this contract expired, it was renewed on March 31, 1912, with a "second supplement"; Hesse agreed to submit to S. Fischer whatever he produced in the next six years and received in return "the total sum of 9,000 marks, to be paid in quarterly instalments of 375 marks; this sum is not to be deducted from what the publisher pays for the books themselves." These monthly and then quarterly payments were not so high in themselves; still, by October 1913, the amount Fischer had to pay Hesse, according to Mendelssohn, came to 18,000 marks. This was no small sum, especially for a publisher who always had to watch every penny.

Hesse held strictly and literally to the contracts. In 1910, after he had given S. Fischer three books, he did in fact send a fourth, *Gertrud,* a novel about a musician, to Albert Langen. This minor "infidelity," although agreed upon in the contract, was preceded by a heated correspondence with S. Fischer, who fought to the end against the submission to Langen. In the draft of a letter to Fischer (January 29, 1910), which he did not send but which was published in his collected letters, Hesse expressed his displeasure at Fischer's position:

Since you take pains to present the matter as if you were doing me a favor with your suggestions, I would rather forego future agreements since you are already trying to hold me forcibly to my letters and contracts. I have a contract with you according to which I have the clear right to send Langen any book I please. In spite of that, you now act as if I were committing a crime by sending him *Gertrud* and as if I ought to offer you something in return. . . . I can no longer put up with this tone that presents you as the donor, me as the one who must be grateful. My last letter was still as loyal as possible. In it, I promised you to forego all negotiations with other publishers this year. You are not content with that. You use every expression of my devotion and loyalty as a string with which you want to bind me contractually. I don't feel like continuing this completely unnecessary correspondence. I have letters from the four most important German publishers offering me 25 percent without my having to commit myself in any way for the future. If you are not content with me and simply will not leave me in peace, then I too will take the commercial point of view and declare that I have fulfilled all stipulations of my contracts with you and wish to be left in peace in the future. That I may give Langen a book is no favor on your part but simply a point in our agreement. Therefore, the idea that I should compensate you now for this long-agreed-upon little escapade with Langen by means of new contracts that are of benefit only to you is one that I must reject. I certainly appreciate your publishing house and its significance, but you are not the only one in Germany and I have no reason to make myself more and more dependent on you.[22]

This is—even though the letter was not sent off—a

definite position indeed. In the letter he actually sent, Hesse took a more friendly but still unyielding tone about the business at hand.

For a long time, until Fischer left the firm, Hesse's relationship with his publisher remained businesslike and friendly. His brief tribute on Fischer's seventieth birthday is indicative:

> I don't think that my publisher and I have many traits of character in common. It would be too bad if we did. We have after all such different functions. But I do have something in common with him after all: stubborn tenacity, a sense of thoroughness, a nature that is hard to please and overly particular. Along with this goes keeping one's word, being reliable in agreements; and thus, over the past twenty-five years, I have not only had a pleasant relationship with my publisher but I have learned to love and respect him too.[23]

In 1934, when Fischer died, Hesse wrote:

> In the course of thirty years I got to know S. Fischer as a publisher, and during this process my respect for him grew and with the years turned into a proven and heartfelt devotion.... Not always was I of his opinion over the years and not always pleased with him.... Gradually I too learned a thing or two from experience and gained an understanding for the publisher's function that transcended my personal wishes. And I saw that Fischer had a specific conception of his firm, of the way it was then and of how it was to develop, to which he dedicated himself with a feeling of lofty obligation but also with a keen instinct for the practical.[24]

S. Fischer did not make his job easy for himself. He was always thinking about his work; he chose staff who could grasp his conceptions and were attached to him for decades, such as his editors Moritz Heimann and Oskar Loerke. The firm was his life. His work was to realize, to transform, the work of others, i.e., his authors, into what Brecht called that "sacred commodity, the book." His imagination had to be devoted to the imagination of his authors, his idea had to be to disseminate the ideas of his authors. In his later years he attempted to collect the works of his authors in complete editions. Twenty-two complete editions were in existence by 1925; the brochure describing them had as its title *Die Bibliothek des modernen Menschen* [The library of modern man]. In this brochure we read: "Our complete editions of leading writers and thinkers of the present make up, taken together, the library of modern man. The great representatives of German—of European—intellectual life are joined here to form an extremely impressive image of contemporary humanity." Mendelssohn notes, correctly, that there was no other German publisher who could have made a comparable claim.[25]

Through his literary activity, Hesse was well acquainted with Fischer's contemporaries in the publishing field: Albert Langen, Georg Müller, Kurt Wolff, Ernst Rowohlt, Eugen Diederichs, and others. He felt a close attachment to many of them. With Albert Langen, for example, he succeeded in accomplishing what had been impossible with the more serious Fischer: "over a glass of wine talking him into making daring plans." Langen, who published Hesse's *Gertrud* and to whose periodicals *März* and *Simplicissimus* Hesse regularly contributed, presented him with a different image of the publisher. Langen, Hesse wrote, was brisk and flexible.

This man with his quick capacity for enthusiasm and eagerness to try something new was expressly created to live among a circle of gifted, creative people, to be sometimes the inspirer, sometimes the doer, sometimes the pusher and sometimes the person being pushed. He conducted his affairs with the whimsical zeal of the sportsman, stubbornly or relaxedly, intently or jovially, the way nervous people do, but in any case honorably and with personal dedication.[26]

Langen had a "passionate relationship" with literature, not, however, as a publisher but as an "admirer and gifted aesthete."[27] The contrast to S. Fischer's thoroughness, stability, and reliability is obvious.

Hesse sketched a portrait of still another publisher whom he carefully distinguished from Fischer. He used Diederichs's prospectus entitled *Wege zur deutschen Kultur* [Paths to German culture] as a point of departure for describing Eugen Diederichs. Whereas Hesse emphasized the unswerving direction of the works Fischer published (which had earned Fischer the title of "the Cotta of naturalism," a description that Thomas Mann had found very apt[28]), he found in Diederichs, whose "joyful optimism" he mentions, a multiplicity of opinions and tendencies:

And since he isn't narrow-minded . . . not subject to the one-sidedness of an original thinker or author but enterprising and full of joyful faith and admiration, he has made of his firm not so much a narrow, sectarian path and way to knowledge as a garden containing only beautiful and good things but at the same time not excluding contrast and variety. It even seems as if this idealistic publisher takes delight in creating an antipode or balance for each one of his books and each tendency represented in his firm. [Diederichs is] original, and his relationship to old cultures is a warm and positive one, not that tired rummaging about in old debris and impotent sniffing out of new thrills that we presently sense in many publishers' prospectuses.[29]

Hesse had always reacted negatively to publishers' "impotent sniffing out of new thrills." He always directed them to that path he had taken himself, which he describes in "Kurzgefaßter Lebenslauf" ["My Life: A Conjectural Autobiography"]: "Of course I noticed after a while that in intellectual matters a life lived in the pure present, concerned merely with the newest and latest, is unbearable and senseless, that it is only an enduring relationship to the past, to history, to the old and the ancient that makes an intellectual life possible."[30]

Hesse's contribution as reviewer and editor of world literature has not yet been sufficiently appreciated. His essay "Eine Bibliothek der Weltliteratur" [A library of world literature] is still valuable both as an outline of a model library and as a guide for readers. During his career, Hesse wrote some three thousand reviews. In the second volume of *Schriften zur Literatur* [Writings on literature], Volker Michels put together approximately three hundred of Hesse's reviews, making them into a "history of literature in reviews and essays." The selection begins with reviews of *Gilgamesh,* the speeches of the Buddha, and Chinese philosophy, and it proceeds, by way of reviews of works by Kafka, Proust, and Robert Walser (Hesse was one of the few to discover Walser in the twenties), to the present, with reviews of works by Walter Benjamin, Anna Seghers, Arno Schmidt, Max Frisch, J. D. Salinger, and Peter Weiss.[31]

Just as impressive as his list of reviews is the number of works of world literature that Hesse edited. Sixty-six editions are cited in Volker Michels' "Bibliographie der von Hermann Hesse herausgegebenen bzw. mit Vor- oder Nachworten versehenen Buchausgaben" [Bibliography of books edited by Hermann Hesse or in-

cluding forewords or afterwords by him], which appears
in my history of Hesse's writings.[32] The first reference is
a *Sammlung deutscher Volkslieder* [Collection of German
folksongs] from the year 1910, which Hesse edited for
S. Fischer. There follow *Die heiligen Schriften* [The holy
scriptures],*Des Knaben Wunderhorn* [The boy's magic
horn], *Morgenländische Erzählungen* [Tales from the
East], *Gesta Romanorum,* the series *Merkwürdige Geschichten und Menschen* [Remarkable stories and people],
Der Wandsbecker Bote [The Wandsbeck messenger], *Das
kleine Buch der Wunder* [The little book of miracles],
Mittelalterliche Literatur [Medieval literature], *Sagen und
Schwänke* [Sagas and humorous tales], *Das
Alemannenbuch* [The Alemannic book], and works by
Goethe, Keller, Hölderlin, Novalis, and—
repeatedly—the Romantics. Mendelssohn notes that the
manuscript of an ambitious collection, "Geist der
Romantik" [The spirit of romanticism], which Hesse
had discussed with S. Fischer, has been lost. In the
meantime, however, the complete table of contents has
been found among Hesse's posthumous papers. So we
may still be able to carry out this significant plan after
all.

The author to whom Hesse devoted himself most in-
tensively was Jean Paul. Essays, reviews, editions, introductions, and afterwords were dedicated to him. Un-
tiringly, Hesse called attention to the unknown Jean
Paul: "All the more happily can one recommend Jean
Paul. As a delight for the poetically minded, as an in-
exhaustible source of excitement for the thoughtful, as a
marvellous mustard plaster for the philistine." Jean
Paul, "our greatest dilettante and master, is the only
German poet who possesses every charm, every talent,
every fervent gesture of romanticism but at the same
time has over his head the cool, high, starry heaven of
classical German humanism."[33] Two-thirds of the

obituary notice Hesse wrote for the publisher Georg Müller is taken up with a discussion of the "old shame of modern Germany," the fact that for decades there has not been one sensible edition of Jean Paul, this "most German of all German poets." And now, as a result of Müller's death, Hesse fears that his long-standing favorite plan for a new edition with this publisher is in jeopardy.[34] In my dissertation, "Hermann Hesses Anschauungen vom Beruf des Dichters" [Hermann Hesse's views of the poet's calling], I was able to point out Hesse's relationship to Jean Paul and to demonstrate that Hesse frequently formulated his own literary theories while writing about that author.[35]

As a result of Hesse's active involvement with literature, he carried on an extensive correspondence with publishers, which fortunately has been preserved, and he wrote numerous essays on the publisher's task.[36] Hesse wrote, "As a bookseller, as a dealer in rare books, as author and critic, as the friend of many publishers and many artists I became acquainted with a fair cross section of the modern book trade."[37] From this broad acquaintance, from his activities, his literary works, and the nature and sequence of his books, we can deduce a clear publishing strategy on Hesse's part. Space, however, permits only a few brief examples.

THE PHYSICAL APPEARANCE OF HESSE'S BOOKS

For his own books, Hesse wanted a format "without any extravagance." That he had a definite taste for elegance in general is shown by the fact that he wanted the Diederichs edition of Jacobsen bound in "marguerite volumes" for Helene Voigt Diederichs. This was to be a leather binding with a fanfare pattern enclosing marguerites, as had been specially prepared for Marguerite of Valois in the seventeenth century.

The most important thing, however, was the right format, and "paper and type" had to be "good," as he wrote to the editor in charge of his first book of poetry on February 27, 1902.[38] As a rule he continued to make suggestions concerning format and appearance to his publishers, often requesting that graphic artists who were friends of his (Otto Blümel, Hans Meid, Gunter Böhmer, et al.) be assigned the design of the book jacket.

He was fond of the leather-bound volume but saw some purpose to the soft-bound one. In answer to a questionnaire, "What do you think of soft-bound books," he said: "Whenever I read a soft-bound book that I like, I think as I turn each page, 'Too bad that it isn't hard-bound!' If I read a soft-bound book that strikes me as poor, then I think, 'how fortunate that they haven't wasted a binding on it.'"[39]

THE ANNOUNCEMENT
OF HIS BOOKS

Hesse insisted that the announcements of his books be discussed with him. This procedure was followed from the very beginning, and even Peter Suhrkamp had to send the book-jacket blurbs he composed to Hesse in Montagnola. Nor was he indifferent to the language used in the advertisements for his books; he hated sensationalism, believing that one shouldn't advertise books the way hucksters advertise their wares. As a positive example he pointed to Diederichs, who spoke of his books "as a preacher does of his ideals, as the disciple does of his teachers."[40]

FINANCIAL ARRANGEMENTS

Hesse was not bashful and he expected generous royalties: he considered 20 percent or 25 percent of the soft-bound book's retail price appropriate. He was against advances, which robbed him of his independence. Exact in his figuring, he was never petty. Although he was never in dire financial need, there were recurring periods of poverty in his life. During the Nazi regime his royalties from Berlin arrived irregularly if at all. Only after he received the Nobel Prize in 1946 did the stream of royalties begin to flow more liberally. Incidentally, Hesse shared the fate of many other authors: his heirs enjoy a larger income from his books than he did when he was alive. He found the amount of his income completely in keeping with the general state of public consciousness; in response to the news that the *Kölnische Zeitung* had to lower its rate of payment, he noted, "One more sign of the esteem that intellect enjoys in Germany."[41]

WORKING WITH THE PROOFREADER

Author and proofreader, according to Hesse, are dependent on each other and must work together to vanquish the demon of misprints. But in a letter to a proofreader (October 1946) Hesse forbade the slightest correction or alteration of his text without his permission. He refused to accept changes that mechanically followed the *Duden* dictionary, "that bugbear and God of iron rules," which had become "an omnipotent lawmaker under a dreadful police state."[42]

In 1954, the Swiss periodical *Die Weltwoche* issued a questionnaire about some recommendations for orthographic reform made by the German-Swiss-Austrian Arbeitsgemeinschaft für Sprachpflege (Committee for the Cultivation of Language). Both Thomas Mann and Friedrich Dürrenmatt were against the reform. Hesse answered laconically, "I reject completely the proposed new orthography as I do every impoverishment of language and the printed word."[43] In another context, he wrote:

In the process of "unifying" and at the same time banalizing language, the writer, I believe, stands unequivocally on the side of the conservative, reactionary party and should therefore take this stand whenever possible on the formal question of orthography, etc. as well. . . . Even if the author cannot always explain why he writes something one way one time, another way another time, he is simply doing it out of an artistic need for differentiation in expression. In a Schubert quartet, when the third from last note of a movement's coda is dotted, but in another movement the otherwise identical final phrase of the coda is undotted, then every musician knows that it could have been made uniform but that this would have made it far more boring.[44]

Hesse also rejected the noncapitalization of German nouns, which is now being called for again.

THE PUBLICATION OF HIS COLLECTED WORKS

As early as 1920, Fischer had asked Hesse to think about "a popular selection" from his works. Instead of suggestions for such a selection, Fischer received a "Vorrede eines Dichters zu seinen ausgewählten Werken" [Author's preface to his selected works], which Hesse also published in the *Neue Zürcher Zeitung*. In this preface, in which he admonished himself to "pack up and go home" because his work did not bear comparison with the best literature, he explained why an edition of selections was impossible. Anyone interested in Hesse ought to read this essay.[45] The proposed edition did not materialize. Hesse decided merely on a selection of his poems, *Ausgewählte Gedichte* [Selected poems], which appeared in 1921 and one third of which was devoted to youthful verse from the period before

1902. The only complete edition of his poetry to appear was *Die Gedichte* [The poems]; in 1961, at my request, a second volume of selections was published, *Stufen: Alte und neue Gedichte in Auswahl* [Stages: a selection of old and new poems], which remained the authoritative selection.

Finally, in 1925, Hesse acceded to the urgings of Fischer, who wanted to mark his firm's fortieth anniversary by rounding off the pantheon of his Bibliothek des modernen Menschen with a complete edition of Hesse's works. On September 12, 1924, the publisher received from Hesse a detailed plan titled "Stipulations Regarding My Books to Date." The contract itself (signed on October 25) provided for royalties of 18 percent of the retail price and an annual payment of 1500 marks. The first work in this complete edition, *Kurgast* [A Visitor at the Spa], appeared in 1925; from then on, his new books were published in a uniform format handsomely designed by E. R. Weiß: light blue balloon cloth, black spine label with gold lettering, the initials H. H. on the front cover, and uniform typography (Unger Fraktur). This same format was retained for thirty-five years—a rare occurrence in publishing.

Then roman was substituted for gothic type, a change Hesse found difficult to accept. Suhrkamp and I had repeatedly urged it on him, with the result that the six volumes of his *Gesammelte Dichtungen* of 1952 and the seven-volume edition of the *Gesammelte Schriften* of 1957 finally appeared in roman type (Garamond Medieval). At that point, Hesse admitted he had become convinced that there were young people in Switzerland and Germany who were no longer able to read gothic type; nevertheless, he described for his readers his difficulties with the new appearance of his books. The new format, however, was basically a modern adaptation of E. R. Weiß's design: the blue cloth, the black spine label, and the gold lettering remained; only the jacket decorations were omitted. Thus, it can be said that the format of 1925 has remained the model up to the present.[46]

Hesse decided on the sequence of his works himself. He wrote when he had to, following his own inner timetable rather than an external one. He did not accept assignments, nor would he tolerate editorial intervention or accept ideas imposed on him by someone else. Moreover, the titles he chose were not to be tampered with. By the time the manuscript reached the publisher, it was in its final form. Peter Suhrkamp found this out during his first month at S. Fischer as editor of the *Neue Rundschau.* In an unpublished letter (January 28, 1933) to Fischer's son-in-law, Gottfried Bermann Fischer, Hesse spoke of the difficulties of the times as well as of his longing "for the naïve happiness of creativity" (he had just begun *Das Glasperlenspiel* [*The Glass Bead Game*]). He then went on to complain strongly about Suhrkamp:

> Now just a word about Suhrkamp. I am glad to hear what you have to say about him. I must have gotten the wrong impression from the letter he wrote me. In any case, it was not one of insecurity but just the opposite. He wrote me, for example, about a little essay of mine that Kayser has had since November, saying he would like to publish it, for it "fits in with his program"—which suggests to me that in the future the editor's episcopal imprimatur for my works will depend upon whether they fit in with Suhrkamp's program. In addition, he suggested a different title for my little essay; he wanted one that was peppier, promised more, and was more programmatic.... I will not have him make a mess of my titles and then have to take responsibility for them myself.[47]

At the time the author was criticizing his future publisher so roundly, Hesse was fifty-six and Suhrkamp forty-two.

THE MATTER OF LOYALTY

During this first period of his relationship with Suhrkamp, Hesse was working on *Das Glasperlenspiel.* The plan for this, his last work, had been conceived, as he often mentioned, in February 1932. On April 29, 1942, he completed the book, and in May he sent the manuscript to Suhrkamp in Berlin.

In 1932, S. Fischer named Peter Suhrkamp editor of the *Neue Rundschau,* his duties to begin on January 1, 1933. Suhrkamp published forty-six pieces in the periodical, thus becoming one of its leading contributors. He characterized the journal in these words: "It is no falsehood to point out that this journal was not founded for a movement, a school, or the like, but for the creative, or better still, artistic individuals of the present; for artists, that is (in all areas of culture), and not for a special elite and not for the general public."[48] This was Suhrkamp's intention as a book publisher as well. In the fall of 1933 he became a member of the management of S. Fischer Verlag.

It was in the Berlin of the twenties that Fischer had met him; the older publisher, who had a presentiment of approaching disaster, was bound to like this tall German with his conservative manner. On December 18, 1936, the part of the S. Fischer firm remaining in Germany was bought by a limited partnership, also calling itself S. Fischer; Suhrkamp was the personally liable partner, in other words, the sole publisher. This firm was forced to change its name to "Suhrkamp Verlag, formerly S. Fischer" on July 1, 1942. On April 11, 1944, Suhrkamp was arrested by the Gestapo on strong suspicion of high treason and taken to Ravensbrück prison and, subsequently, to the concentration camp at Sachsenhausen. There he became seriously ill and, for this reason, was released on February 8, 1945, at the height of his illness. In Berlin, on October 17, 1945, he was the first publisher to receive an English license to resume operation of his firm.

I have described the period in Hesse and Suhrkamp's relationship extending from 1933 to 1945 in an afterword to the Hesse-Suhrkamp letters.[49] Thus, I can restrict myself to a few brief aspects here.

There were three recurring themes in the correspondence and in the rather infrequent conversations between author and publisher: the completion of the manuscript of *Das Glasperlenspiel* and discussion about its publication; the situation of Hesse's books in Nazi Germany and his legal, moral, and political ties to the firm and its publisher; and the difficulty, and eventually the impossibility, of sending royalties from Berlin to Switzerland and the transfer of a part of Hesse's publications to Zurich.

The fascinating story of the origins of *Das Glasperlenspiel,* which was first entitled "Josef Knecht" and then "Der Glasperlenspielmeister" [The master of the glass bead game], can be traced by interested readers in a book containing material connected with the writing of the novel.[50] There one can see how intimately the creation of Hesse's last great work is connected with German history and with the history of his German publisher.

Hesse, never one to be taken in during his long life by any political system, also assumed the correct position vis-à-vis the Nazis from the beginning. But he knew that his works and his readers were rooted in Germany, and he wanted to retain his gradually weakening position there as long as possible. He did not let himself be swayed by attacks either by the Nazis or by those emigrants who, for example, accused him in the *Pariser Tageblatt,* the German emigrants' voice in France, of serving as a figleaf for the Third Reich and its Dr. Goebbels. Hesse fought against the regime in his own way. He published in the *Neue Rundschau* as long as he could; altogether he made forty contributions—a number second only to Suhrkamp's—among them (in February 1934), the famous poem "Besinnung" ["Reflection"]. Parts of *Das Glasperlenspiel* were published there, too. He reviewed books by Jewish authors, and when this was no longer possible in German newspapers, he began to write literary reports for Bonnier's *Litterära Magazin* in Stockholm.[51] Suhrkamp had to bear the brunt of Hesse's anti-regime activities as well as of his support of German emigrants in Switzerland and his correspondence, of which the Gestapo was well aware. All this complicated Suhrkamp's position as a publisher. Nor did it make his relationship with Hesse, who was often in a highly nervous state, any simpler.

At first, they each had personal difficulties with the other; their character and temperament were simply too different. Each, however, was an absolutist in his own way; as a result, each had to make compromises. Their first encounter (in August 1936 in Bad Eilsen) took place in the dark shadow cast by Hesse's strong words of January 1933, and Suhrkamp was uneasy at the prospect of the meeting. Looking back on it, Hesse wrote:

I saw your position at that time as threatened but still relatively brilliant; I saw you as the chivalrous, self-sacrificing, and courageous successor and deputy of dear old S. Fischer, and although we had the same thoughts about the future, we did not yet discuss the bitter struggles and sacrifices that your perhaps all-too-chivalrous loyalty would bring you. In any case, you were even then a partisan of resistance against the prevailing methods and ideologies of terror, and I must have had some presentiment, some intimation, of the trials and suffering awaiting you.[52]

The longer the two worked together to oppose the censors' machinations, to obtain rationed paper, to get around prohibitions, and to expedite royalty payments, the more intense their association and friendship became. The contract with Suhrkamp ran until 1939. "For the time being I am committed to my publisher," Hesse wrote to friends in 1936. In 1937, he wrote, "I am keeping to my contract for the time being in spite of everything but am prepared hourly for a change in the situation." "My chief concern," he confessed in July 1938, "is what will become of my books, since my contract in Berlin will expire soon and I can't renew it, and my Viennese publisher has also been ruined. I am not getting any money whatsoever from Germany in spite of the contracts."[53]

His Viennese publisher was Gottfried Bermann Fischer, who had founded the Viennese branch of S. Fischer, but soon thereafter emigrated again, this time to Stockholm. In June 1938, Bermann Fischer reported from Stockholm and requested the manuscript of *Das Glasperlenspiel*. Hesse answered:

Thank you for your letter, I am happy at its news. But there are a couple of sentences in it that I must correct. When you say, for example, "What can be holding you [in Germany]?" then I must answer, I am held by my contract with the firm I have been connected with all my life and which to the present day is making every effort it can on my behalf. I don't like the fact that you make light of this. But in addition to the contract, which runs until the end of '39, my

73

readers are also holding me there. Outside of Germany I have few readers, and a book like "Josef Knecht" will be understood almost completely by tens of thousands in Germany, especially in today's oppressed Germany, whereas in all America, for example, there aren't three people who will see anything in it. These are no light matters.[54]

Hesse didn't renew the German contract, hoping to improve Suhrkamp's position in his negotiations with the Nazi officials, who then did speak of prospects for the transfer of royalty payments. Still, Hesse did not want to break off ties with his German readers any sooner than he had to; he also hoped his books might "be instrumental in illegally strengthening German readers within the Reich" against the Nazi regime. On February 12, 1936, he wrote to the Swiss critic Eduard Korrodi:

As far as I myself am concerned as an S. Fischer author, the choice of whether to remain with the old firm in Berlin or go along with the others to Bermann's new firm is not mine at all. Likewise, Bermann himself has nothing whatever to say about what authors he wants to take with him in a new firm. The old Fischer Verlag will and must (there is no other solution) continue to exist in Berlin after Bermann has sold it. According to German law, the buyer of a publishing house also takes over its contracts with its authors. I with my author's rights, for example, would be committed to the new owner during the years my contract with Fischer runs, without being able to do anything about it.

A short time later, in a letter to a German inside the Reich, he wrote:

As far as the question of the publisher is concerned, I see it with completely different eyes than you do. I am neither [Hermann] Stehr nor [Emil] Strauß, who abandoned the "Jewish" publishing house (it hasn't been that, by the way, for a long time now) when that seemed opportune to them. For me, on the contrary, the way my good, old, tried and true publishing house has been treated, harrassed, persecuted, and humiliated by foul means in these last years was another compelling reason for me to remain loyal to it. I do not intend to resist being gradually forgotten and erased as an author in your country. And it is not my publisher's fault that I am presently not even receiving the much reduced income from my books but am being starved out; it is the fault of your government officials there.[55]

Here the reasons that moved Hesse to stay with Suhrkamp are clearly described: his ties to his readers and his intention to make *Das Glasperlenspiel* available to the German reader, if at all possible. That book is a repudiation of all ideological systems and thus a repudiation and rejection of National Socialism as well. The German officials moved cautiously, for Hesse was a Swiss citizen. Initially they didn't ban anything; they simply cut down Suhrkamp's paper rations more and more, finally cutting them off altogether. However, they permitted Suhrkamp to sign a new contract with Hesse (October 25, 1939) dealing with the publication of "Josef Knecht." In his letter to Rudolf Jakob Humm, Hesse comments on this contract, which represented a nice tie-in between "world history and my private life": "I signed it solely for the sake of my publisher; he is, I believe, a completely loyal person, and to rely on someone like him seemed to me, in spite of everything, better than anything else."[56]

It wasn't possible, after all, for Suhrkamp to fulfill the contract, because the Nazi officials rejected his request for publication. They also made it impossible for any royalty payments to be made to the author. Suhrkamp then returned all foreign rights to Hesse, since he could no longer manage them from Germany. Two excerpts from *Das Glasperlenspiel* appeared in the *Neue Rundschau* as late as July and August of 1942, but Suhrkamp personally returned the manuscript to Hesse in November for fear that it might be confiscated in Berlin. *Das Glasperlenspiel* was finally published in Zurich on November 18, 1943.

Thus ends the first period of the relationship between Hesse and Suhrkamp. The second, a long story, may be described briefly. The former owners of S. Fischer returned from America in 1947. It turned out to be difficult for Suhrkamp to work with them. At first he was willing to regard his role as that of a deputy and return the business to Fischer's heirs, but later he changed his mind. Eventually a compromise was reached out of court: it provided for the establishment of two firms, the old S. Fischer, under the direction of Fischer's heirs, and a new Suhrkamp firm under the direction of Peter Suhrkamp. This episode in German publishing history has been described in detail by Gottfried Bermann Fischer himself and by me, in a conflicting account.[57] Bermann Fischer had, as he wrote in his memoirs, no "key to Suhrkamp's behavior" at that time, but there was a key, as we can demonstrate, and it was Hermann Hesse.

Hesse urged Suhrkamp to remain his publisher, either at S. Fischer or by founding his own publishing house. When the new Suhrkamp Verlag was founded in Frankfurt (on July 1, 1950), the last portion of the relationship between the two men began. In these eight-and-a-half years, Suhrkamp, marked by sickness and "constantly at death's door," built up his firm between the poles of Brecht and R. A. Schröder, Hesse and T. S. Eliot, Shaw and Proust, and the Dioscuri Theodor W.

Adorno and Walter Benjamin. It was a firm dedicated exclusively to literature, to literature that did not satisfy needs but created them. "Peter Suhrkamp's achievement," Adorno wrote in his eulogy,

> was paradoxical: to sell the unsalable, to find success for that which doesn't seek it, to turn something strange into something familiar. This accomplishment was possible only by virtue of its concealed objective precondition: that today what seems strange to people is what leads them to expression and that they mistakenly accept alienation, dehumanization— which reduces them themselves to objects—as something familiar. . . . [Suhrkamp] proved that even today the spontaneity of one individual can make possible the socially impossible.[58]

Suhrkamp obtained the capital he needed for his firm partly from the growing sales of Hesse's works during the Hesse boom in West Germany, Switzerland, and Austria that reached its height in 1957. When Suhrkamp died in March 1959, at the age of sixty-eight, Hesse's works were once again available in an edition that fulfilled the author's wishes, an attractive complete edition consisting of the familiar blue volumes. The author, by generously accepting delayed payment of his royalties, made it possible for the publisher to build his firm. In his eulogy of Suhrkamp, Hesse wrote, "I have lost the most loyal of my friends and also the most indispensable." Hesse again referred to Suhrkamp as author: "I prefer the approximately one hundred pages of that significant work "Munderloh," which tells of Peter's life as a young village schoolteacher, to many celebrated books that Peter worked on as editor with touching devotion." Then Hesse continued, "I see it as one of the positive aspects of my life that I was able to help him, after the martyrdom of the Hitler years and his deep disappointment over the old firm, to build up the new one."

This relationship between author and publisher is, I believe, exemplary for the loyalty displayed on both sides.

In a letter sent to me in early April 1959, after Suhrkamp's death, Hesse once again described the publisher's responsibility:

> You are now taking his place. I wish you strength, patience, and good cheer; it is a fine and noble kind of work you are doing. It is also difficult and full of responsibilities. The publisher must "move with the times," as they say, yet he should not simply follow the fashions of the times but also be able to resist them when they are undesirable. The function, the very breathing in and out, of a good publisher consists of accommodation and critical resistance. This is the kind you should be. I mourn sincerely with you over the loss of our friend, and I sincerely wish us a good association.[59]

The period for which Hesse wished us a good association lasted nearly four years. His wish was completely fulfilled. To be sure, the relationship was that of a disciple to his master, of a young man just getting used to his job to an author he highly esteemed. Frequent visits in Montagnola and elsewhere (for example, Sils-Maria), an extended correspondence, and numerous telephone conversations with Hesse's wife Ninon strengthened the ties.[60]

The beginning of our association was overshadowed by Peter Suhrkamp's death and by the question of how we could carry on the work of the firm without him. But Hesse's works had already been written, and I was familiar with his ideas about the production and distribution of his books. There was no reason for basic problems to arise. When new questions did come up after all, Hesse answered them in a friendly, clear, and decisive fashion. He didn't want any film versions of his works to be made during his lifetime; after that, his heirs and his publisher could decide. When (in August 1961) a "lady in California" had the idea of creating a Siddhartha ballet, he requested that the lady be told "politely but emphatically . . . that her interest pleases me but that I consistently reject all dramatizations of my books; she must give up her plan, which I find offensive."

Nor was Hesse interested in larger printings and editions of his works in paperback format. At my initiative, and with Ninon Hesse's cooperation, the firm retrieved the translation rights, which she had managed for a very long time; we could then encourage new versions of his works in the United States and other countries.[61] The fate of his books abroad was of little concern to Hesse, least of all in the United States, but he did take pleasure in translations into Indian and other Asian languages.

He was most emphatic in his refusal to have changes made in his own compilations of his stories, fairy tales, and essays. As early as May 26, 1959, when I made my first suggestion to him after Suhrkamp's death—to include, in a new printing of *Traumfährte* [Dream trail], two significant essays, "Mein Glaube" ["My Faith"] and "Ein Stückchen Theologie" ["A Bit of Theology"], which had not yet appeared in book form—Hesse reacted with "distinct uneasiness": "You have the urge to shape and edit," he answered me, "whereas I am more for protecting and preserving what has grown naturally." The new printing appeared without the additions.

Hesse's scrupulousness had to be taken into account; thus, suggestions for changes could be presented only with great tact and adequate justification. Still, as mentioned earlier, I was able to convince him to make a selection of his poems himself, which then appeared in

1961 under the title of *Stufen: Alte und neue Gedichte in Auswahl.* It took much time and effort to win him over to a chronicle of his life in pictures, for he was of the opinion that the work, not the person of the author, is what counts, but he finally agreed. (While the book was being prepared, he emphatically rejected the cover design by Willy Fleckhaus; it was the very first cover Fleckhaus had done for Suhrkamp.) When the chronicle finally appeared, however, Hesse's reaction was positive.[62]

There was a short and lively debate in April 1962 over the question of whether *Das Glasperlenspiel* could appear in paperback, for the Deutscher Taschenbuchverlag had applied for the rights. I suggested to Hesse that we give our permission, but he saw this as a "bargain sale" and a "dumping" of the book on the market. "I suppose I can't prevent it," he wrote in his answer of April 4, "but I should at least like to delay it. . . . For this year at least I ask to be spared, and until we have talked the whole thing over again." A year earlier, Hesse had turned down a request for reprint rights from S. Fischer Verlag, although he agreed "in principal" to paperback editions. This refusal strengthened my own plan to publish something like paperbacks myself. At that time, we reacted with a series of publications that we called Suhrkamp Texte, volumes 7 and 8 of which were devoted respectively to the "Traktat vom Steppenwolf" ["Treatise on the Steppenwolf"] and to three stories; later, we added the series known as edition suhrkamp. Thus, Hesse's negative response to Fischer's request was one of the incentives that led directly to Suhrkamp's expansion into the paperback field.

During the last years of his life, we repeatedly discussed my request to print Hesse's texts in roman type instead of the Unger Fraktur. Here too he did not want

to be an "innovator," as he said to me, adding that whoever was no longer able to read gothic type should simply learn it or give up reading the works in question. I
can't remember how many times in Montagnola I sum-
moned up the courage to raise this sensitive topic; each
time he stuck to his decision. On one occasion I dared to
be decisive. I explained to him that schoolchildren in
Germany were no longer learning to read gothic type
and that he was therefore denying access to his works to
this group of readers that was so important to him. This
time he gave in. We then gradually published his books
in the new Medieval Antiqua. In July 1962, we sent him
two works set in roman type, *Gedenkblätter* [Memorial
pages] and *Kurgast—Die Nürnberger Reise* [*A Visitor at
the Spa—Journey to Nuremberg*]. His letter acknowledg-
ing receipt of these editions was the last one of any
length I received from him:

> The two new volumes in Antiqua are beautiful and
> your accompanying words are beautiful, too. I thank
> you very much and wish I could express this better,
> but I am not in very good shape, and recently when
> the weather suddenly turned hot, a fever with chills
> weakened me even more. . . . The doctor is helping
> out with injections. Please take this into account, and
> accept my heartfelt gratitude for your loyalty.[63]

Hermann Hesse died on August 9, 1962.

Bertolt Brecht
and His Publishers

Everything needs to be revised.
Bertolt Brecht to Peter Suhrkamp, October 1945

To read Brecht is a pleasure; to interpret him is comparatively difficult; to explain the theory and practice of editing his complete works is extremely difficult. The author has reported on "five difficulties in writing the truth"; the publisher and editor can report on numerous ones in editing this author's oeuvre. "I fear," we read in Brecht's play *Leben des Galilei* [*Galileo*], "all that is not so very simple."

Indeed, the history of editing and publishing Brecht's works is not very simple. How uncomplicated this history was in the case of Hesse, of Rilke, of Thomas Mann, progressing logically from point to point! With Bertolt Brecht, on the other hand, everything is always entirely different. One of his publishers, Wieland Herzfelde, commented, "His publishers didn't have an easy time with him."[1]

THE FIRST EDITIONS

Five versions of Brecht's first play, *Baal,* have been preserved. They exist in two typescripts—carbon copies of the missing original—and in five different final drafts for the printer. The first version dates from the year 1918, the fifth and last from the year 1955.[2]

Brecht sent the second version, a more unmannerly
and uninhibited variant of the previous year's version, to
Musarion-Verlag in June 1919, but the manuscript was
returned immediately "with a very impertinent accompanying letter."[3] After that, Lion Feuchtwanger tried to
put in a good word for Brecht at Drei Masken Verlag;
but here again, just a few days after the manuscript arrived at the publishers, Brecht received a rejection
notice. Then he approached the publisher Georg Müller, this time with a new, third version that was considerably shorter and poetically inferior; nevertheless, the
publisher reacted positively and had the type set. When
Müller became involved in legal proceedings because of
another book, however, he regretted his boldness and
backed out of the contract, offering the plates to the
author free of charge. Feuchtwanger recalls that twenty
to thirty sets of galley proofs were printed from these
plates; each and every one has disappeared. All the attempts made by Brecht's friend Hans Otto Münsterer to
interest the publisher Franz Bachmeier in the play were
unsuccessful. The paper for printing the book was to be
donated by Brecht's father's paper factory, but not even
this substantial assistance—the use of free plates and
paper—helped find a publisher willing to produce the
book.

The second work Brecht tried to publish, in the
summer of 1919, was "Meine Achillesverse" [My
Achilles verses—the title contains a pun: when spoken
it is also "my Achilles heel"]. It was intended to be
printed privately by Lampart & Co.'s Augsburg Press, as
their second publication. The "Achillesverse" were
erotic, pornographic poems, with echoes of Aretino,
that later became known as the *Augsburger Sonette* (Augsburg sonnets). After the plates had been set up for the
first proofs, work was stopped and the plates destroyed.
The original manuscript has disappeared but the galley

sheets are today counted among the treasures of the Brecht Archive.

A third attempt in early April 1921—an edition of Brecht's ballad entitled "Apfelböck" and described as a "musical work"—was confiscated before it was distributed and subsequently turned into pulp. The history of his publications finally took on more real and tangible form when a twenty-five-year-old editor at Gustav Kiepenheuer Verlag in Potsdam had the following experience: "In 1921 in my capacity as editor I received from a completely unknown author the proofs of a play originally supposed to be published by Georg Müller and a manuscript containing ballads and poems that I found so fascinating I took them straight to Loerke. He, too, was surprised by the unusual nature of these poems. They turned out to be a first draft of the *Hauspostille* [*Domestic Breviary*] by Bert Brecht."[4]

The editor in question was Hermann Kasack, who later became a writer and a friend and associate of Peter Suhrkamp. Kasack was the first editor to work with Brecht, and he later wrote: "Then one day [Brecht] was standing there, of medium height, in his early twenties, with a thin, masculine face.... We frequently talked and worked together in those days, and it was remarkable with what integrity of feeling he presented his ideas and with what unyielding assurance and dialectical finesse he unfailingly managed to get what he wanted."[5] It was Kasack who prevailed upon Gustav Kiepenheuer to publish *Baal.* In 1922, both of the famous first editions appeared in quick succession, the first in a limited printing of eight hundred copies, the second as a regular edition with an unsigned drawing by Caspar Neher on the cover. As his collaborator Elisabeth Hauptmann reported, Brecht signed a contract with Kiepenheuer extending for several years "based on a monthly income that was then charged to his account at the end of the year. That made his work go much easier." In both first editions, *Die Hauspostille,* a volume "by the same author," was announced. Brecht had already finished the manuscript, but he envisioned a book that looked completely different from the one Kiepenheuer had originally agreed to produce. He wanted to see the poems and songs printed "on India paper in the format of a little New Testament or hymnal," and his wishes "were then all followed exactly." The text was printed by Poeschel & Trepte and the accompanying music by C. G. Roeder in Leipzig. The title, however, was no longer *Die Hauspostille* but *Bertolt Brechts Taschenpostille* [Bertolt Brecht's pocket breviary]—"With Instructions, Music to the Songs, and an Appendix: 1925: Gustav Kiepenheuer Verlag, Potsdam." The edition, we read on the verso of the title page, was produced by order of the author in a limited private printing of twenty-five copies, not for sale. The pages were set in two columns of black print with the headings in red; the book was bound in soft leather. One year later *Die Hauspostille* appeared, after all, but with the Propyläen-Verlag in Berlin, not with Kiepenheuer. "Kiepenheuer Verlag came into some new money," Elisabeth Hauptmann reminisced. It turned out that this was reactionary money, and protests were lodged against the "Legende vom toten Soldaten" ("Legend of the Dead Soldier"), one of the ballads in the collection. Arguments ensued, but Brecht was unyielding. The contract with Kiepenheuer was dissolved, and the rights to the three publications reverted to Brecht, who then included them in his new contract with Ullstein's Propyläen-Verlag.[6] The new publisher found "pocket breviary" too inappropriate a title, and Brecht agreed to *Die Hauspostille* without hesitation.[7]

Indeed, his publishers did not have an easy time with him. In spite of the "reactionary" money, Brecht's fa-

mous series, Versuche (Attempts or Experiments) re-
mained with Kiepenheuer; in 1932 volume 6 appeared
with twenty-five drawings by George Grosz and, in
1933, volume 7, which included *Die Mutter* [*The
Mother*]. Volume 8 did not get beyond galley proofs.
Propyläen-Verlag brought out the plays *Trommeln in der
Nacht* [*Drums in the Night*], *Im Dickicht der Städte* [*In the
Jungle of Cities*], and finally *Mann ist Mann* [*A Man's a
Man*].The places where Brecht's books were published
thereafter reflect the stages of his exile: Paris, London,
Moscow, New York.

WIELAND HERZFELDE: THE FIRST COMPLETE EDITION

Wieland Herzfelde, the head of Malik-Verlag (founded
in 1917), emigrated in 1933 and founded the Publishing
Company Malik Verlag in London with a branch in
Prague. In 1938 he undertook the difficult task of mak-
ing a new collection of Brecht's works and bringing
them out in a complete edition of four volumes. That
same year the first two volumes appeared (Volume 1:
Die Dreigroschenoper [*The Three-Penny Opera*],
*Mahagonny, Mann ist Mann, Die heilige Johanna der
Schlachthöfe* [*St. Joan of the Stockyards*]; Volume 2:
Rundköpfe und Spitzköpfe [*Roundheads and Peakheads*],
Die Mutter, Der Jasager und der Neinsager [*He Who Says
Yes and He Who Says No*], *Die Ausnahme und die Regel*
[*The Exception and the Rule*], *Die Horatier und die
Kuriatier* [*The Horatians and the Curiatians*], *Die
Maßnahme* [*The Measures Taken*], and *Die Gewehre der
Frau Carrar* [*Senora Carrar's Rifles*]). The copyright
read, "Copyright 1938 by Malik-Verlag, Publishing
Company, London C.C. 1 Wieland Herzfelde (Ger-
man): Druck von Heinr. Mercy Sohn in Prag."
The circumstances surrounding the proofreading

were complicated because Brecht, who was in exile in
Denmark, felt an urgent need to make changes in the
text, which was being printed in Prague. In a letter from
Svendborg to Herzfelde in Prague, Brecht expressed his
gratitude for a check, which "in these difficult
times . . . represents a gesture of historical magnitude
that I really appreciate." To be sure, Brecht wanted to
wait for Herzfelde to publish him, but the special edition of *Svendborger Gedichte* (Svendborg poems) was a
matter of great urgency for him. "We must stick together," Brecht wrote in this letter, but in the very next
sentence he added, "when you print the other things,
don't forget that the Prague printer has not acknowledged my corrections; that means the plates as they now
stand have not been completely corrected."[8] One can
imagine how Herzfelde, in Prague, felt about these requests for changes that came from Denmark.

Volume 2 carried an announcement of the third volume, which was supposed to contain the following
works: *Deutschland, ein Gräuelmärchen* [*Germany, a
horror story*], *Baal, Leben König Eduard des Zweiten von
England* [*Life of Edward II of England*], *Im Dickicht der
Städte,* and *Trommeln in der Nacht.* Intended for volume
4 were: *Die Hauspostille,* "Die drei Soldaten" [The three
soldiers], excerpts from *Lesebuch für Städtebewohner*
[Primer for city-dwellers], *Lieder, Gedichte, Chöre 1933*
[Songs, poems, choruses], and *Gedichte im Exil* [Poems
in exile].

Herzfelde reported that parts of volumes 3 and 4 had
already been printed and the sheets already at the bind-
ery when they fell into the hands of Hitler's troops, who
were marching into the Sudetenland. Franz Fühmann
claims to have seen the four volumes in Reichenberg's
Bookstore for Workers, but neither Herzfelde nor
Brecht ever received them. Brecht, however, did mar

age to hold on to the galley proofs of volumes 3 and 4 throughout his exile: today they make up another part of the treasures in the Brecht Archive.

Herzfelde succeeded in convincing Brecht of two points as the edition was going to press. Brecht wanted to use the term "Versuche" (attempts or experiments) for the complete edition since the word "Werke" (works) was too final for him. "I was of the opinion," Herzfelde recalls, "that it was time to give up this designation because I feared, on the basis of my publishing experience, that people would take it to mean something of a merely technical nature. I succeeded in convincing him." His attempts at persuasion met with more difficulty on the second point: Brecht did not want to have his nouns capitalized. Here, too, victory went to the publisher, who saw non-capitalization as "one more obstacle between literary production and the reader."[9] Herzfelde's arguments had such a lasting effect that Brecht, who did not capitalize nouns in his letters, never brought up the subject again in connection with the printing of his works.

The first two volumes of the collected works appeared in 1938 in a printing of two thousand copies each. Herzfelde sold the remaining stock along with his other books in order to pay for the crossing to New York for himself and his family in May 1939. There he founded the Aurora Verlag New York, an authors' press, one of whose owners and founders—along with Ernst Bloch, Alfred Döblin, Lion Feuchtwanger, and Heinrich Mann—was Bertolt Brecht. The firm, founded in December 1943, published twelve titles between 1945 and 1947, among them a book by Brecht, *Furcht und Elend des Dritten Reiches* [*Fear and Misery of the Third Reich*]. In 1948, Herzfelde had to liquidate the firm to get the money to return to Europe.[10]

BRECHT—SUHRKAMP

In his *Arbeitsjournal* [Working journal] Brecht commented (on May 8, 1945) on the momentous event of Germany's capitulation: "Nazi Germany surrenders unconditionally. At six o'clock this morning the President speaks on the radio. Listening, I look out at the California garden in full bloom."[11] In October, he made contact with Peter Suhrkamp for the first time after the war, writing a letter whose political, biographical, moral, and linguistic aspects merit a separate essay. Suhrkamp had written to Brecht, and the latter replied:

> Your letter is the first one to reach me from Germany, and you were one of the last people I saw in Germany—for it was from your place that I went to the train the day after the burning of the Reichstag: I have never forgotten how you helped me to escape.
>
> We spent five years in Denmark, one in Sweden, one in Finland, waiting for visas, and now we have been in the United States, in California, for almost four years. Of course I've done a lot of writing, and I hope we can go through some of it together (by the way, please state, whenever you have the chance, that I urgently request that no major work of mine, old or new, be performed without my having a say about it. Everything needs to be revised).[12]

Suhrkamp's reply bears no date: "I was exceedingly pleased to receive word from you, even though basically I have always known that we would get together again some day; yet there were times when I really was afraid I wouldn't live to see the day. Now I hope very much it is not too far off.

"Meanwhile, I have been able to resume publishing here; you can have hardly any idea over there of the practical and especially the technical difficulties involved." In the meantime, *Die Dreigroschenoper* had been performed in Berlin, a fact Brecht had noted in his *Arbeitsjournal.* Suhrkamp then asked for written authorization to do what Brecht had asked of him in his first letter.

In his next letter, also undated, Brecht sent Suhrkamp the power of attorney requested: "I limited it so that it will be easier for you to say no, for I can imagine only too well how necessary that will now be in many cases. The reconstruction of the German theater cannot be improvised." He went on to suggest that *Mutter Courage* [*Mother Courage*], a play of proven success, be performed; of course his wife Helene Weigel must be invited to play the leading role.[13]

By the time Suhrkamp answered (April 3, 1946), difficulties had already begun to arise. An old contract for *Die Dreigroschenoper,* with Felix Bloch Erben, reserved all rights to that firm. Suhrkamp asked Brecht to grant him intellectual supervision of the performances, so to speak, and wrote that he was perfectly willing to grant the "settlement," i.e., the royalties, to Felix Bloch Erben. A short time later, on April 15, Suhrkamp reported a further difficulty. He was involved with *Mutter Courage,* but it turned out that the rights were with Reiss Verlag in Basel, which had transferred them to its German affiliate, Kurt Desch's Zinnen Verlag in Munich. It was not only a question of *Mutter Courage* but also of *Galilei* and *Der gute Mensch von Sezuan* [*The Good Woman of Setzuan*]. Suhrkamp made an urgent request for clarification, for "there is an extremely strong demand for your plays."

Brecht made an attempt at clarification himself. He wrote to a German lawyer, presenting information to prove that Bloch Erben no longer had the rights to *Die Dreigroschenoper.*[14]

The year 1947 did not bring any substantial changes.

Helene Brecht-Weigel sent Care packages to Suhr-kamp, and there was a significant exchange of letters between the two. Suhrkamp wrote to her on May 7, 1947, "There is no one I am looking forward to seeing as much as Brecht." This correspondence also contains "an application for duty exemption" for the luggage the Brecht family intended to take along from the United States to Switzerland and from there to Germany. There were thirteen pieces, among them two boxes of books and two trunks filled with books.[15]

On March 17, 1948, Suhrkamp sent his first letter to Brecht in Zurich. He again asked for an answer about contract questions, then referred to a new difficulty:

> To begin with, I have received the news from Aufbau Verlag in East Berlin that they have taken over the former Malik Verlag, now the Aurora Verlag of New York, as a division of their company, and that means they have taken over the rights to your works in Germany as well. What makes this run counter to our conversations is the fact that you told me in Zurich that you felt unconditionally obligated to Wieland Herzfelde but would be against this sort of takeover en bloc by the Aufbau Verlag.

Suhrkamp did not want to put pressure on Brecht nor make him "feel beholden in any way to my firm," but how was Suhrkamp to exercise supervision over the performances if he did not have any rights to the works in question? On July 24, 1948, Suhrkamp wrote Brecht again: "I still haven't received an answer from you to my last letter. This wouldn't make me impatient if the question of your representation in Germany were not becoming more complicated all the time. It can't go on like this; you must produce final clarification your-self.... So please let me know quickly how we are to act." Brecht wrote immediately, but he didn't answer

Suhrkamp's urgent question; on the contrary, he indicated that he was negotiating with the Swiss publishers Oprecht and Reiss. He wrote: "I hear that you will be seeing Reiss in Basel soon. Perhaps you can come to a final agreement with him over the distribution of my books? Reiss could pay me a salary here. That would be tremendously important, as you well know." A salary, and it would be "tremendously important."

In September, Brecht wrote another letter to Suhrkamp, letting him know he wanted to continue the series, Versuche, for it provided him with a "certain freedom in publishing, especially of works in an unfinished state. In addition, that way I can keep my word to Wieland Herzfelde, i.e., he gets the collected works, which he had already started to publish in exile at great sacrifice." Brecht wanted to do the Versuche, his "major works," with Suhrkamp. Further questions were cleared up in conversation. In a letter of February 7, 1949, Suhrkamp mentioned a "memorandum concerning an agreement with Bertolt Brecht," according to which the Versuche are to be done exclusively with Suhrkamp. The *Gesammelte Werke* [Collected Works], still to be edited, were also to be handled by Suhrkamp; Aufbau Verlag, however, was to receive rights from Suhrkamp for publication in the German Democratic Republic. For the time being, stage rights were still to be handled in Switzerland.

Suhrkamp began work on the Versuche in 1949. The first Brecht publication was Versuche, volume 9, *Mutter Courage und ihre Kinder,* with the copyright "Suhrkamp Verlag formerly S. Fischer." Versuche, volume 10, *Herr Puntila und sein Knecht Matti* [*Mr. Puntilla and His Hired Man, Matti*] appeared under the same imprint. Volume 11, *Der Hofmeister* [*The Private Tutor*], appeared with the new Suhrkamp Verlag, for in the meantime Suhrkamp's association with Bermann Fischer had been terminated and, on July 1, 1950, the new Suhrkamp Verlag had been established.

BERTOLT BRECHT

Lieber Suhrkamp,

natürlich möchte ich unter allen Umständen

in dem Verlag sein, den Sie leiten.

Herzlichst Ihr

brtholt bmft

Berlin, 21.5.50

One of the major events in the firm's history occurred quite casually. On May 17, 1950, Suhrkamp sent Brecht a letter, two-thirds of which was devoted to winning Brecht's approval for a performance of Ernst Barlach's play *Der Graf von Ratzeburg* [The Count of Ratzeburg] by the Berliner Ensemble. Then, at the end of the letter he wrote: "Now something entirely different. You have said that, now that I am no longer associated with S. Fischer Verlag, you want your works to be published by my firm. But I do not yet have your official written confirmation. Would you please send it to me as soon as possible?" Brecht complied with a laconic letter from Berlin on May 21: "Dear Suhrkamp, of course I would definitely like to be part of the firm you are the head of. most cordially, your Bertolt Brecht." Such a letter is the dream of every publisher! The rest of the correspondence of 1950 was devoted to completing work on the Versuche; in 1951, Suhrkamp requested the publication and performance rights for Austria as well. On February 21, Elisabeth Hauptmann answered on Brecht's behalf:

> Brecht certainly agrees to your taking over the distribution of his books in Austria . . . the provision is . . . that Brecht be notified before every contract is signed and that his okay be required. . . . Besides what has just been said, the principle also applies to Austria that the plays Brecht himself has not yet produced in Europe or whose performance he has not yet approved are not yet to be released—among these are *Galilei, Der kaukasische Kreidekreis* [*The Caucasian Chalk Circle*], *Der gute Mensch von Sezuan, Die heilige Johanna, Schweyk. Mutter Courage,* on the other hand, can be performed anywhere.

The correspondence of 1951 did not contain anything essentially new. It did, however, establish that *Mutter Courage* could not be performed so readily, after all, because the publisher Desch was able to produce an earlier contract. For the rest, it was primarily concerned with requests for money and the sending of money. Then there was the question of publishing the missing Versuche numbers 1–8 in two volumes, thus completing in reverse order Brecht's "major works," for only numbers 9, 10, and 11 were available at that time. Suhrkamp decided to do this, and while the two volumes were in preparation (they did not appear until 1959) a proposal was made (in a letter of November 11, 1951, from Elisabeth Hauptmann). The director of the Städtische Bühnen in Essen had asked to produce Brecht's *Leben Eduards des Zweiten.* "This request gave us the idea of publishing a volume of Brecht's early dramas: *Baal, Trommeln in der Nacht, Eduard der Zweite, Im Dickicht der Städte, Mann ist Mann.* Brecht thinks that these five plays, for example, could appear as the first volume of his *Gesammelte Dramen* [Collected dramas]. And he says that now is just the right time for the *Hauspostille.*" In his response of November 29, Suhrkamp seemed somewhat unhappy with the idea of publishing a volume of early dramas. Furthermore, he regarded the two-volume edition of Versuche as part of the complete works.

In another letter (December 4, 1951), Elisabeth Hauptmann wrote that Brecht would like to see both—the two volumes of Versuche and "apart from that, he would like the collected dramas [to be published], that is, just the plays. And he thought that the five early dramas should make up the first volume—and possibly should be published in an entirely different format from the Versuche, somewhat in the manner of Collected Dramas by Classic Authors (and Those Who Will Become Such)." The texts for this volume were in final form, she wrote, "and Brecht has nothing more to do with them." She was wrong about that.

Once again, Suhrkamp demurred (in a letter of December 14): "The Versuche are only a form of popular edition, even though the contents are arranged in an unusual way. Brecht would surely never think of taking the plays from the Versuche and publishing them separately in an edition of collected dramas. In any case, I would regret it." A solution was proposed in Hauptmann's letter to Suhrkamp of January 9, 1952:

Brecht now sees two editions: a kind of popular edition (the Versuche) and then the *Gesammelte Werke des Klassikers* [The collected works of the classic author], which would have to begin with the collected dramas. For this reason the two volumes of the Versuche should have the format of the other Versuche; the classic edition, on the other hand, ought to have a classic format.... The format, the whole appearance of this edition, lie very close to

Brecht's heart. It would be splendid if you came to
Berlin again soon to talk about it . . . How fine it
would be if the *Gesammelte Gedichte* [Collected
poems] could be done—and much more comprehen-
sively than the Aufbau edition—including the earlier
poems too.

Suhrkamp gave in and granted Brecht his wish. But
the whole thing didn't move that quickly; questions of
format and typography were discussed very carefully
with Brecht. Sample volumes were sent to the author
and he countered with photocopies of old editions of
the classics as examples of the typography that should be
used. The final format, which was decided upon in close
collaboration with Brecht, had a large typeface, for it
was the author's wish that his complete works make up
at least five volumes. On August 19, 1953, Brecht wired
Suhrkamp: "'First Plays' much better [title] than 'Early
Plays.' Revision pays." In the end, then, it was not a
single volume of four hundred pages with the title
"Frühe Dramen" [Early dramas] that appeared, but two
volumes of approximately three hundred pages each,
entitled *Erste Stücke* [First plays].

It seems that these volumes encouraged Brecht to
continue the series: "I myself have fallen for the edition
of the *Erste Stücke;* thank you very much," he wrote.
And in another letter, written in November: "The *Erste
Stücke* have turned out beautifully, so beautifully that I
really wish we could continue the series quickly—and
not only because in this country the significance of a
writer is measured by how much room his books take up
on the shelf. Instead of Versuche volumes 1–8, why not
simply reprint the dramas from those volumes? with a
volume of theoretical writings in addition? and the
poems in addition?" It was as easy as that for Brecht, in
his enthusiasm, to conceive a plan for a complete edition

of his works, a plan, however, which certainly turned out to be philologically unsound.

At first, the publication of such an edition was unthinkable, although there was a definite desire to continue with the publication of the plays. When Brecht died on August 14, 1956, only two more volumes of plays had appeared. In an obituary notice, Suhrkamp wrote:

It will be the special concern of this publishing house to preserve and promote Brecht's work. His death removes him from the conflicts of the day. Many people will only now recognize the greatness of this poet. He has already won himself an outstanding reputation abroad. International critics see him, quite simply, as the most significant contemporary dramatist. Publication of the complete edition of the plays and of the Versuche will be continued at a rapid pace.[16]

THE COMPLETE EDITION

Suhrkamp's words were the first public mention of a complete edition, even though only of a complete edition of plays. But after Brecht's death, his publisher's task was clear: a significant oeuvre had been brought to the conclusion and a complete edition had to be collected and edited. This was done by Elisabeth Hauptmann, Brecht's "best collaborator" since around 1922, whom he called "one of the most reliable and efficient people I know."[17]

The first volume to appear with the notice "under the editorship of Elisabeth Hauptmann" was the reprinting (four to six thousand copies) of the *Erste Stücke* in 1957. Selection of works and correction of errors were less important in this new complete edition than a text that was as complete as possible and that would serve as a pattern for the whole undertaking. Out of the plan to bring out at least five volumes, there grew an edition that was still not completed in the thirty-nine volumes that were published before Elisabeth Hauptmann's death. The edition was divided into categories: Poems (ten volumes), Prose (five volumes), Writings on Literature and Art (three volumes), Writings on Politics and Society (one volume), Writings on the Theater (seven volumes), and Plays (fourteen volumes). Since the edition was intended to be as complete as possible within each category, overlapping and duplication could not be avoided; thus, in the course of the next ten years, the edition became too confusing and cumbersome for use.

In 1955, two years after our edition, the *Erste Stücke* was also published by Aufbau, in East Berlin. From that moment, editorial problems that had been known to a mere handful of experts became common knowledge and moved into the glare of the political controversy between East and West. The growing Suhrkamp edition was always at a disadvantage, compared to its Aufbau counterpart. This was not because of Aufbau's popular cloth binding, which many buyers seemed to prefer—we could claim, to our credit, that expressly at Brecht's request (and with great pains on Peter Suhrkamp's part), we had specially tinted the extra-heavy paper covering our board volumes in the greenish color that unintentionally turned out to be a different shade for each category. Nor was it due to the fact that anyone could buy Aufbau's cloth volumes at a non-competitive low price in the bookshops of East Berlin.

No, what really distinguished the Aufbau edition from ours were the textual changes; actually, these were not only changes but corrections and additions. In other words, these volumes, despite their lower price, contained improvements. This was in violation of our contract, which stipulated that Aufbau-Verlag was to issue editions with texts identical to ours, for up till now, and for the foreseeable future, the East Berlin volumes are published with the express permission of Suhrkamp Verlag in Frankfurt. But the lapse of time between the appearance of our edition and theirs enabled them to make revisions that Brecht had wanted and to correct errors in our edition. These first Aufbau volumes of the *Erste Stücke* contained such striking differences as the addition of Brecht's famous preface (dated March 1954) "Bei Durchsicht meiner ersten Stücke" ["On Looking through My First Plays"], that had been inspired by the appearance of the Suhrkamp *Erste Stücke*. Brecht reread these plays in the Suhrkamp version and revised them for the Aufbau edition. The "Choral vom Großen Baal" ("Chorale of Great Baal") preceding the play *Baal* had eighteen stanzas, compared to fourteen in our edition and to nine we had published in *Die Hauspostille*. The text of *Baal* was not identical: Brecht called our version a "first draft" and revised the first and last scenes. "Otherwise," he wrote in his preface, "I am leaving the play as it is, since I don't have the energy to revise it. I admit (and warn): the play lacks wisdom."[18]

When the two editions were compared, the reaction was immediate. There was a storm of protest. Our tribulations with our critics had begun: we were charged with being politically motivated, with censorship, with making unwarranted omissions, and with shortchanging and generally taking advantage of the buyers of our edition.

THE WAY BRECHT WORKED

The criticism dating from the appearance of the Aufbau edition of the *Erste Stücke* in 1955, which grew louder and louder, had the effect of calling the attention of the public—at least of that growing segment of it consisting of careful readers of Brecht—to this author's peculiar way of working.

"Everything needs to be revised" was his creative

motto. His goal was change, not a static achievement but a continuous process: "Real progress is not having progressed but progressing."[19] Since the mid-twenties he had called his literary productions Versuche. "It was not false modesty that led him to call his dramas Versuche," wrote Lion Feuchtwanger; "these plays were indeed 'attempts' to make his inner world visible to the spectator in continually new and different ways. The poet, he found, has to experiment, the way an Archimedes, a Bacon, a Galileo did."[20]

Two of Brecht's statements are typical of many. In the preface to the first volume of the Versuche (1930), Brecht defined the concept: "The publication of the Versuche takes place at a time when certain works should no longer be so much individual experiences (having the character of an individual work) as be directed to the use (transformation) of specific enterprises and institutions (having experimental character) for the purpose of continuously explaining the various and very complicated projects in their context."[21] "Attempt" and "experiment" thus became central categories in Brecht's work. Again, in notes made in January 1956, half a year before his death, for his address to a Writers' Congress, we find the words:

> If we want to make the new world our own in our artistic practice, we must create new artistic methods and modify the old ones. The artistic methods of Kleist, Goethe, and Schiller ought to be studied today, but they are no longer adequate if we want to depict what is new. The unceasing experiments of the revolutionary party that are transforming and reforming our country [the German Democratic Republic] must be matched by experiments in art, equally bold and equally necessary. To reject experiment means to content oneself with what has been attained, that is, to lag behind.[22]

This view leads to a special attitude toward work, a special way of working. Let me attempt to characterize it here. Its most striking feature is that friends, visitors, and specialists unexpectedly became Brecht's collaborators. "He made friends out of people by turning them into collaborators," Wieland Herzfelde reported.[23] It would be easy to name approximately fifty people whom Brecht called "collaborators."[24] Whoever didn't qualify as such was soon dropped from his circle of acquaintances. Brecht behaved in a very interesting way during his American exile, about which we learned more after the publication of his *Arbeitsjournal*. For example, he complained there about the paucity of his contacts with such people as Herbert Marcuse and Leonhard Frank. His dislike for Thomas Mann was well known: face to face with Mann, Brecht felt as if "three thousand years were staring down at [Mann]." Yet Brecht was often struck by the "decided wretchedness of these 'upholders of civilization.'" Brecht found "bestial" Mann's statement, "Yes, half a million will have to be killed in Germany"; from the moment of that utterance there was no further contact between the two.[25] With very few exceptions, Brecht did not come into contact with the ranking American authors of the day; he never discovered Hemingway, Dreiser, Steinbeck, Faulkner, or Thomas Wolfe. Dos Passos is mentioned only occasionally. His mind, otherwise so eager to assimilate, shut out impulses that he could not use in his work. Obviously, language was a barrier; in the six years of his stay in America, Brecht showed no interest in learning English. His accent, when he was called upon to testify before the House Unamerican Activities Committee on September 19, 1947, must have come straight from the Gymnasium in Augsburg! Brecht assimilated what was useful, taking note of what was foreign to him if he had to. Faced with the radicalism and significance of James Joyce's epoch-making literary innovations,

Brecht merely repeated statements made by Döblin; he mentions Joyce, for example, in the stereotypical formula "Gide, Joyce, Döblin" in his debate over expressionism and realism with the Hungarian Marxist critic Georg Lukács.[26]

By 1928 Franz Kafka was already a "truly serious phenomenon" to Brecht; but in a brief homage containing more criticism than praise, Brecht declared himself *"very far* from suggesting a model here."[27] Thus, he remained untouched by these writers, who were perhaps the greatest literary figures of the century. His collaboration with such composers as Kurt Weill, Paul Hindemith, Hanns Eisler, Paul Dessau, and Rudolf Wagner-Régeny was similar. Collaboration came to an abrupt end if the composers were no longer willing to follow Brecht or attune their compositions to the text of the play, or if Brecht's musical ideas were not in accord with the musical tendencies of the composers. Brecht called his own ideas about music *misuk,* a musical art form that was supposed to be popular but was not to stir up the emotions.[28]

In this connection, mention must be made of Brecht's habit of adapting the works of other writers. We know his famous remark about "laxness as a matter of principle in questions of intellectual property." This had nothing to do with plagiarism, but much to do with inspiration for his work. In a letter to Döblin, Brecht wrote:

I should therefore like to call the attention of many people to the extraordinary industry with which I have studied your literary works and adopted the manifold innovations you have introduced in our way of seeing and describing our world and our social relations.... I see your works as an abundant source of pleasure and instruction and hope that my own writings contain borrowings from them. I believe there is no more worthy form in which I can present myself to you than as an exploiter.[29]

Brecht drew inspiration from the reality around him as well as from reality as transmitted by literature. The most outstanding example is afforded by the history of *Leben des Galilei,* a play he wrote in 1938 and 1939, during the first years of his Danish exile. While he was producing an American version with Charles Laughton, the atom bomb fell on Hiroshima: "The 'atomic age' made its debut in the middle of our work," Brecht wrote, and thus "from one day to the next the biography of the founder of modern physics had to be read differently." "Everything needs to be revised": in this instance, the motto led to his second, or "American," version of the play, which is a considerably less flattering portrait of the scientist. Still, Galileo's obsessive demand, "I must know," is characteristic of Brecht's own attitude,[30] an attitude of curiosity that was responsible for the wide range of materials he chose to treat in his works.[31]

It was also characteristic of Brecht to return to a plot, an idea for a play, a sketch, a line of verse again and again over the years. No published version was final, and he himself scarcely knew in the end what had been revised. Lion Feuchtwanger wrote about this:

Brecht himself seized upon all the themes and forms that attracted him, played with them, remodeled them, appropriated them, transformed them to such an extent that they belonged to him completely. The masks of the Chinese theater, the path of flowers of the Indian drama, the chorus of Greek tragedy—he made everything serve the shaping of his own vision. . . . Brecht himself considered everything he had created as preliminary, as a work in progress. Books he had published long ago, plays he had produced countless times were by no means finished in his eyes, and he regarded his favorite works, *Die heilige Johanna der Schlachthöfe, Der gute Mensch von Sezuan, Der kaukasische Kreidekreis,* as fragments. For him, as for so many great Germans, the completion of a work meant less than the process of creation.[32]

We do not have to agree with Feuchtwanger's evaluation, and yet we must acknowledge that there was a basic lack of finality in Brecht's creative process. In one of the first typescripts for *Trommeln in der Nacht* we find his handwritten note: "For the typist: lots of room for corrections and crossing out. A blank page between the individual acts."[33] Brecht was always ready to make corrections and to have doubts about what he had written. The image of the man with doubts is a pervasive one in Brecht's works: Galileo's words, "We shall have to question everything again," apply to Brecht as well.

"Everything needs to be revised." Brecht was not one of those authors—like Thomas Mann, for example—whose first drafts could be sent directly to the printer or who—like Hesse, like Martin Walser—were unable to reformulate what had once been formulated but were merely able to delete if they had to. For him the process of creation did not end with the writing: each new version was a new attempt or experiment. There are numerous handwritten sketches and originals, numerous manuscripts and typescripts of almost all the plays and poems; to an unusual degree, there are different levels and stages in the creation of a single work. Understandably, the longer the process of creation lasted, the more variants there were. Brecht worked on *Das Verhör des Lukullus* [*The Trial of Lucullus*] for two weeks in 1939, on the original version of *Baal* for two months in 1918, and on *Der gute Mensch von Sezuan* for twelve years. First drafts were usually written quickly, later drafts much more slowly. By far the greatest difficulty in verifying texts results from the fact that, when he set out to revise, Brecht did not always proceed from the last version he had written; he often continued working on whatever text he happened to have at hand or that seemed, at the moment, to need improvement. "Characteristic products of Brecht's way of working," observed Hans J. Bunge, "especially in writing plays, are manuscripts he cut up and then reassembled, neatly pasting them together. Brecht described himself as a 'master of pasteology.'"[34] To the despair of future philologists in particular, this master of pasteology saved the deleted portions of the manuscripts he had cut up; they, too, were kept over the decades.

Thus, there are numerous versions of all Brecht's works. When he decided to publish a given version, it was still far from clear that this was the definitive and final one. In each case, the publication process—the progress from manuscript to galley to page proofs to author's imprimatur—was repeatedly used for revisions; he seems to have been especially inspired to make changes when he read newly issued reprints of his works. For the plays, there was the additional requirement that the texts had to prove themselves on the stage. Brecht worked on the language of his productions, cutting scenes, adding new ones, changing their order, rejecting old endings and writing new ones— regardless of whether Suhrkamp Verlag had just sent the printer a "definitive" version that was often to be superceded by the time it appeared.

Brecht applied to his own works his famous motto: the poet's word is sacred only insofar as it is true. That is why we find so many versions, preliminary versions, variants, and fragments of all his works. Above all, we find the variants corrected again and again. There are suggestions about wording neatly typed or written above one another. Who was supposed to make the selection among these suggestions? Often the date of a work could be determined only because Brecht had saved the manuscript pages from which he had cut out portions of the text. We know that he was unable to throw anything away. Through the stages of his exile, he (or his friends) lugged around boxes full of manuscripts as well as reviews and newspaper clippings he had collected. In May 1941, he had to leave a considerable part of this material behind in Helsinki; friends kept it for him, and it formed the basis of the Brecht archive in East Berlin. When he gained a more permanent residence in America, he began to collect manuscripts, proofs, and newspaper clippings anew. Brecht's *Arbeitsjournal* shows how important these clippings were to him: of the thirteen pieces of luggage he took back to Europe with him, six pieces consisted of trunks and boxes containing this material as well as "book-binding material."[35] This explains the tremendous scope of the Brecht Archive, arranged by Helene Weigel. In addition, the collection was augmented in the years following Brecht's death by gifts and purchases; according to its director, Herta Ramthun, it contains 2,210 folders, each of over 175 pages. The portion consisting of the manuscripts alone is estimated at 75,000 pages; the *Bestandsverzeichnis des literarischen Nachlasses* [The index of (Brecht's) posthumous literary papers], three volumes, cites 18, 242 different items.[36]

The Brecht Archive probably contains the most significant and extensive collection of a contemporary writer's texts we have. Brecht, who had a low opinion of philologists, left a great deal of work for them nevertheless: in 1924 he wrote, "if drama is to make any forward strides at all, then it must in every case stride with equanimity over the corpses of the philologists."[37] To give just a few examples, there are *ten* versions of the "Horst-Wessel Legende" [Horst Wessel legend]; the first draft, typed by Brecht, has not been preserved in its entirety, but it shows indications of four separate stages of work. The ninth version reveals at least three stages of corrections, one written above the other. The 1976 edition of the *Gesammelte Werke* presents, as the final version, a reading of the ninth one. Then there is Brecht's versification of *Das kommunistische Manifest* [*The Communist Manifesto*], his "Lehrgedicht von der Natur des Menschen" [Didactic poem on the nature of man]. The model for this poem, which he gave the alternate title "Über die Unnatur der bürgerlichen Verhältnisse" [On the unnatural nature of bourgeois conditions] was Lucretius' great didactic poem "De Rerum Natura," whose form and "respectable meter," the hexameter, he borrowed. An early overall plan envisages four cantos as its main divisions: in the first one, Brecht wanted to show how difficult it is to find one's way in human society, and he wanted to add to it a section of the third chapter of *Das kommunistische Manifest*. The verse version of that work's first chapter was to be reserved for the second canto. The third canto was supposed to be devoted primarily to the second chapter of Marx's work, and the fourth to "the tremendous growth of the barbarization of society." There are more or less complete versions of the second canto, but only fragments of varying length of the remaining cantos are extant. Some pages of this poem bear the title of the section, but the beginning of the section is often missing. Some pages are identifiable by the phrases, "from the first canto," "from the second canto," and so forth. In the *Gesammelte Werke* of 1967, Brecht's second version, which contains many handwritten suggestions for changes as well as alternative formulations, was used.

Dating the texts is just as difficult as verifying the various stages they have gone through. It is relatively easy to date the first draft. The big problems arise simply because there are so many variants and corrections. For the time being, the examples we have adduced will suffice to convey a general idea of the difficulties of publishing a new edition of Brecht as well as the even greater difficulties of a future historical-critical edition that must include not only the works but also show the gradual process of their growth by means of editorial methods not yet developed. One thing is certain: no matter how attractive such an edition may be to the scholar by virtue of its philological refinements, there will be no revelations such as there were in the case of Nietzsche, whose pristine texts were not established until the second half of the twentieth century, thanks to the efforts of such editors as Karl Schlechta. Nor will there be any "earthquake" such as was experienced by Goethe scholars in 1950, two hundred years after his birth, when Ernst Grumach presented his *Prolegomena zu einer Goethe-Ausgabe* [Prolegomena to a Goethe edition], a criticism of the texts of all previous editions of Goethe.[38]

Of course, there will have to be a historical-critical edition, and Suhrkamp Verlag, which possesses publication rights to Brecht until the expiration of the copyright in the year 2026, will do everything in its power to support and encourage this undertaking. But it is premature to call for such an edition now. A meeting of leading Germanists, among them Friedrich Beißner, the outstanding Hölderlin editor, came to this very conclusion, for, in order to do justice to the scholarly requirements of this project, certain editorial prerequisites must be satisfied. It is impossible to satisfy them all in this decade: the collecting, sorting, and eventually the publication of the letters; the examination and publication of the diaries, notebooks, and workbooks; the evaluation of all the tapes made during Brecht productions at the Berliner Ensemble. And it is not only these writings by Brecht himself that must be gone over and published in a scholarly way. Just as crucial for the dating, verification, and rectification of the texts and their variants are the writings of his friends, classmates, and collaborators; contemporary reactions to Brecht's statements and documents; the publication of letters and remarks of people who corresponded and worked with him. Only after all this material has been gone over can we begin to think of a historical-critical edition, which will be of huge proportions indeed: a preliminary plan called for over a hundred volumes. For such an undertaking, we shall have to invent a new system of editorial techniques as well as a whole new method of reproduction.

A glance at history is instructive in this regard: Schiller had to wait 138 years for a historical-critical edition, Hölderlin 100 years. The first volume of Büchner (by no means philologically undisputed) has only recently appeared; Klopstock, Brentano, and Arnim—to mention only a few—have not yet been edited in this way even today, to say nothing of modern authors: of Kafka (who died in 1924) or Musil (who died in 1942). One scholar at the Joyce Symposium in Dublin (June 1969) described the English text of *Ulysses* as "corrupt" and of *Finnegan's Wake* as "absolutely corrupt." Goethe was dead fifty-five years before the Weimar edition was begun, and there are people who claim, in all seriousness, that there is still no reliable Goethe edition. After preparations extending over decades, a historical-critical edition has been initiated for Hegel, whom Brecht called the "greatest humorist among the philosophers"; the last volume will not appear in this century. The people working on this edition are well aware that there can never be a reliable edition of Hegel. We must realize that neither Marx, Heidegger, Ernst Bloch, Lukács, nor Jürgen Habermas read texts by Hegel himself— only the notes taken by his students. From this we may draw the conclusion that an author's impact never stems from a historical-critical edition.

THE DOUBLE EDITION OF THE
Gesammelte Werke

In 1967, in commemoration of the seventieth anniversary of the author's birth (February 10, 1968), Suhrkamp Verlag published a double edition of Brecht's collected works, consisting of a cloth and leather-bound edition on India paper in eight volumes as well as a paperback one in twenty volumes.

Why this double edition? In addition to the pragmatic reason that we wanted to produce an inexpensive edition as well as a finely bound one, there is a historical precedent that sheds light on our enterprise. I had always wondered why Schiller left his publisher Georg Joachim Göschen and transferred to Cotta, when the writer had repeatedly expressed friendship and liking for Göschen and a sense of obligation to his "generous paymaster." The publisher constantly came to Schiller's aid in times of need and sickness, often surprising him with spontaneous demonstrations of magnanimity. Again and again, Schiller stated that his publisher's interests were the same as his and that he looked forward with pleasure to their life-long cooperation. Göschen even paid for his country house, and Schiller assured him of his eternal gratitude. As late as October 27, 1790, Schiller thanked Göschen effusively: "You have rewarded me, not paid me, and have surpassed the wishes of even the most hard-to-please author.... Eternally yours." Three years later, Schiller was negotiating with Cotta, and soon the die was cast. What had happened? Göschen had made a mistake, the most unforgivable one a publisher can make: in answer to the question of who the most important writer of the time was (a publisher must never answer this question with a specific name), Göschen named Christoph Martin Wieland instead of Schiller. Schiller then saw that his publisher was completely taken up, indeed brought almost to the brink of ruin, by the simultaneous publication of *four* separate editions of Wieland's works, each one consisting of *thirty* volumes! When this most ambitious of publishing feats was finally concluded in 1795, Wieland wrote to Göschen: "To none of my friends do I owe so much as to you."[39] When, in the last days of 1965, I read the story of Göschen's "great undertaking" in the biography written by his grandson, the historical precedent inspired me to go ahead with a long-standing if less grandiose plan and pay similar homage to Brecht on the seventieth anniversary of his birth.

The existing complete edition, thirty-nine volumes, was clearly too cumbersome for the everyday use that an author like Brecht certainly invites. In February 1966, conversations were begun with Helene Weigel and Elisabeth Hauptmann and, shortly thereafter, preliminary work began on the new edition, which appeared on September 30, 1967. For this double edition, identical in text and pagination, all the texts were rechecked and again compared with the handwritten or typed originals in the Brecht Archive in Berlin. Brecht's last revisions were adopted and, quite naturally, textual criticism up to that time was taken into account. The most important editorial decision was to avoid the overlapping and duplication that had made the old edition so voluminous. Variants and different versions could not be included; but how were we to decide between the text of a poem in a play and the poem as Brecht wished it to appear in a volume of his verse? In this new edition, the poems and songs in the plays are printed only in their dramatic context, not in the volumes entitled *Gedichte* [Poems]; the index to the volumes of poems, however, also lists the poems in the plays. A portion of the fragments was published for the first time. Shortly before the editorial work was concluded, the mimeographed manuscript of fifteen-year-old Berthold Eugen Brecht's first play, bearing the significant title "Die Bibel" [The Bible] was discovered in his Augsburg school newspaper *Die Ernte* [The harvest][40]—in time for its inclusion.

In the course of all this work, as it turned out, the texts themselves underwent relatively few revisions for the double edition; the substantially new material from the posthumous papers was printed separately. In other words, the owners of the earlier thirty-nine-volume edition could rest assured that they possessed essentially the same Brecht. Footnotes were included in the double edition, giving details about reactions to Brecht and—insofar as they could be reconstructed—the dates when the individual works were written.[41]

A future age will be able to assess the significance of this double edition in the history of the reception of Brecht's work. One fact can already be mentioned: there is no other complete edition of an author who wrote in German that has been distributed so widely so soon after his death. And Brecht—like Kafka and Rilke—belongs among those authors whose great impact was produced by their total oeuvre, not by individual titles or individual genres. For this very reason, complete editions, especially if they are reasonably priced for students, are indispensable to winning a wider readership for these authors.

OBSERVATIONS ON BRECHT'S POPULARITY

In any future history of Brecht's popularity, the following points ought to be considered.

First, in the first three years following their appearance, the *Gesammelte Werke* of 1967 in the double edition (especially because of the popular one in twenty volumes) reached a total printing of 100,000 copies. By

1977 the number had climbed to 132,000. Of the individual works, *Mutter Courage*—in the edition suhrkamp—was the first to reach the 1,000,000 mark: a total of 1,370,000 copies of *Mutter Courage* has been distributed to date (1977). In addition, 130,000 copies of the volume of documents relating to the play have been printed.

Second, the *Bibliographie der deutschen Sprach- und Literaturwissenschaft* (Bibliography of studies of German language and literature) indicates that scholarly interest in Brecht has grown since the appearance of the 1967 edition. For the years 1967 and 1968, the bibliography lists 143 items, a yearly average of 71 scholarly publications about Brecht. In 1969, there were 74 publications; in 1970, 64; in 1971, 88; in 1972, 84. In 1973, the number of entries jumped to 173; in 1974, it fell back to 70; in 1975, there were 101. The bibliography lists a total of 1373 publications about Brecht since 1945, not including shorter articles and reviews, of which there are simply too many to keep track.

The first volume of a Brecht bibliography by Gerhard Seidel was published by Aufbau Verlag in 1975. In his preface, Seidel wrote:

> Today, less than twenty years after the poet's death, the international literature on Brecht can no longer be encompassed, even by specialists. In spite of all the bibliographical efforts, what has already been established is forgotten again. Duplication in research is the inevitable result. There are not even any comprehensive or reliable maps for the path into the labyrinth of the available sources. The fact that there are so many and frequently contradictory Brecht editions is impressive proof of the worldwide popularity of his work; however, until some standardization and order have been introduced, the existence of these various editions impedes progress in research and, since there is not yet a historical-critical validation of

Brecht's texts, accelerates the process of their falling into neglect.[42]

Third, a year after the appearance of the popular edition of Brecht, Suhrkamp Verlag conducted a survey of readers; it turned out that 80 percent of the purchasers of Brecht editions were pupils and students. The large sale of *Mutter Courage* is accounted for by the use of this work and this edition in the schools. Naturally, Brecht's works are among those read in all German schools; he is the author most frequently included in the teachers' guides and anthologies that publishers of schoolbooks produce. The Brecht of school textbooks is not only an assigned author, however; in a questionnaire distributed in the senior class of a Darmstadt Gymnasium, two-thirds of the students named Brecht as their favorite writer (their favorite poem was "Die Liebenden" [The Lovers]).

Fourth, Brecht is cited in editorials and quoted in political speeches. People are no longer even aware that many popular quotations come from Brecht. His words have become household words.

Fifth, statistics compiled from German-speaking theaters (in the Federal Republic of Germany, Austria, and Switzerland) for 1971–72 show that Brecht, with 1,458 performances, was the most frequently produced dramatist, ahead of Shakespeare (1,311), Molière (1,000), and Nestroy (808). Every second theater in the Federal Republic has a Brecht play in its repertory. The February 17, 1973, issue of the periodical *Die Furche* commented that he is "far and away the most successful dramatist of the twentieth century."

Sixth, Brecht's theory of the epic theater, which he began to develop in the late twenties, his attempt to replace the theater of illusion, which has a purely emotional influence on the audience, with a theater of demonstration and situations that uses the epic statement, "That's how it was," to provoke the audience to critical thought and to drawing its own conclusions, has become theatrical history. It has won adherents like no other dramatic theory; it has been made use of and carried to extremes. Many producers, to be sure, feel it is already past history.

Seventh, these tendencies and developments find their expression in essays about Brecht. Substantive themes are sounded in the three essays in Hans Mayer's important book: Brecht and tradition, Brecht and humanity, and Brecht in history (that is, Brecht's Marxist position).[43] Some topics that have been treated in recent studies: Brecht in the seventies (by G. E. Bahr), Brecht's significance for current developments in West German literature (by K. Pezold), and Brecht and his social significance in the seventies (by Erich Schumacher).

It is interesting to note that, in the *Bibliographie der deutschen Literaturwissenschaft* (Bibliography of studies of German literature), new points of comparison continue to appear under the heading of "Relationships, Comparisons": in 1973, Brecht and naturalism (Hans-Joachim Schrimpf), Brecht and Rudyard Kipling (James K. Lyon), and Brecht and Bernard Shaw (Karlheinz Schoeps); in 1974, Aristotle and Brecht (Hellmut Flashar), Brecht, Freud, and Nietzsche (Reinhold Grimm), and Brecht and Karl Valentin (Denis Calandra); in 1975, Brecht and Beckett (Hans Mayer), Brecht and Diderot (Theo Buck), Brecht and Heinrich Mann (Klaus Schröter), and Brecht and Shakespeare (R. T. K. Symington).

The Brecht yearbook for 1976 (edited by John Fuegi, Reinhold Grimm, and Jost Hermand, edition suhrkamp, vol. 853) includes a description of the development of Brecht's theory of radio, a comparison with Marieluise Fleißer, and a review by Martin Esslin of the report on Brecht research by Jan Knopf entitled "Bertolt Brecht: Ein kritischer Forschungsbericht" [. . . A critical report on the research]. Esslin remarks, "It probably would have amused Brecht to see how his works—or rather, commentaries on commentaries of his works—are being busily scrutinized by an army of Läuffers" (Läuffer is the pedantic schoolmaster in Brecht's adaptation of Lenz's play *Der Hofmeister*). The 1977 yearbook contains "Geziemendes über Brecht und Kafka" [Fitting remarks about Brecht and Kafka] by Uta Olivieri-Treder and "Brecht und Wagner" by Marianne Kesting. Studies of Brecht and Büchner or Brecht and Schiller are still to be written.

Eighth, for a long time now, Brecht's impact has not been limited to the German-speaking world: a striking example is *Die Dreigroschenoper,* which has conquered the globe, even being performed in Calcutta in a Bengali version in 1971. Brecht's works have been translated into many languages, even though individual titles are not available in all of them, and complete editions are now in preparation in the major languages of the world. Literary criticism and scholarship follow in the wake of popular reception. There are countless essays on such topics as Brecht in England (by John Willett), Brecht in France (by Bernard Dort), Brecht in Poland (by Andrzej Wirth), Brecht in the USSR (by Käthe Rülicke), Brecht in Yugoslavia (by D. Rnjak), and Brecht in Mexico (by D. Rall). The New York literary scholar Lee Baxandall wrote on Brecht's Americanization in 1971, stating that Brecht's influence on the contemporary American consciousness had developed to a degree scarcely considered possible only a few years earlier.[44]

A fortunate event should be noted here: the book *Bertolt Brecht: Poems, 1913–1956* has been published by Methuen in London, edited by John Willett and Ralph Manheim, who devoted over a decade to its preparation. This is an exemplary edition that should be influential in the English-speaking world. Brecht the dramatist is already familiar to that world, which recognizes him as the outstanding German dramatic writer of the twentieth century. The contemporary English theater, under the guidance of Shakespearean directors like Peter Brook, is unthinkable without Brecht's revolutionary influence. The public, in other words, has gotten to know Brecht primarily or even exclusively as a dramatist. But the editors of the English edition of his poems maintain that Brecht is greatest as a lyric poet, a thesis they substantiate by showing his development from the cynically romantic street singer and anarchist of the big cities to the political rhapsodist of exile and the laconic, epigrammatic, wise poet of the final years. The editors' remarks make clear the connection between these poems and the unusual history of this century, for this collection emphasizes not only Brecht's poetic qualities but, at the same time, the way the history of Europe—the phenomenon of fascism and its impact on the suffering individual—has been authentically caught in his poetry. John Willett describes these poems as a secret diary recounting the "tragedy of our times." When the critic Karlheinz Bohrer reviewed the book in the *Frankfurter Allgemeine* (October 28, 1976), he wrote of an "epoch-making discovery": "Suddenly there appears behind the Anglicized Brecht the long tradition of German singers: Hölderlin, Stefan George, and Walther von der Vogelweide."

Ninth, future chroniclers will provide evidence and documentation to show that, in the twenty years following Brecht's death, his popularity was more pervasive in the nonsocialist countries than in the socialist ones. At present, interest in this writer seems to grow and decline at ever-shorter intervals. In the 1976–77 season, the number of performances rose in the non-German-speaking Western world and declined in the

German-speaking countries. We shall probably see another increase in performances in the latter countries during the 1977–78 season.

The number of performances rises and falls, as does the number of publications on the subject of Brecht, but the number of copies of his works sold remains fairly steady. In 1977, the critics are displaying a certain disenchantment with Brecht. In its issue of September 27, 1977, the *Frankfurter Allgemeine* printed two symptomatic reviews. For the first time, Giorgio Strehler produced a Brecht play *(Der gute Mensch von Sezuan)* in a German theater, and Peter Palitzsch, one of the few true disciples of Brecht, ended his long abstinence from Brecht by producing *Die Tage der Commune* [*The Days of the Commune*]. Critics of both productions considered them flops, Strehler's on a high level, Palitzsch's on a low one. Hellmuth Karasek wrote, in *Der Spiegel* (October 3, 1977), "Time for a Closed Season on Brecht."[45]

Brecht's popularity will scarcely take its cue from the theater critics, for reviews are merely periodic surface reactions. The reception of every literary work moves between the poles of high and low, even though the oscillations may be more rapid in our day. Behind the fluctuations of interest in Brecht, however, lies the unchanging and unchallenged fact of his significance for our times.

In his "descent into fame" (to use the phrase he himself applied to Helene Weigel), Brecht has become a classic. When Max Frisch wrote about "Brecht as a classic" in 1955, he meant the phrase ironically, but his statement about the "thoroughgoing ineffectiveness of a classic author" was not borne out by Brecht. Despite the fact that Brecht is a classic author, he can still have an "irritating" effect, as Marianne Kesting wrote in 1959:

"Even after his death Brecht remained a scandal, one of those fruitful, irritating figures destined to kindle controversy again and again. His work, which is a lasting one, is lodged like a thorn in the flesh of our times."[46]

Peter Suhrkamp pointed out why this work will remain a lasting one and why it has the effect of "a thorn in the flesh of our times." In the foreword to his selection of Brecht's poems and songs he wrote, "It has been all too little recognized that Brecht as poet, both in his poetry and drama, has been writing the history of our nation since 1918; this becomes unmistakably clear, however, to someone who has experienced these times deeply when he or she reads Brecht's poems as well as his dramas in their historical sequence."[47] The presentation of the history of the times in language and on the stage is a sign of classic literature. This has nothing to do with that "pious path to the classic author" with which Manfred Wekwerth reproaches those who emphasize the classic element in Brecht.[48]

BRECHT AS A CLASSIC AUTHOR

Brecht's relationship to classic works and authors dates back to the time when he began to think and to write, as Hans Mayer pointed out in an early essay. Just a few brief examples here: there is the large role played by Latinisms in Brecht's style, to be seen in his use of the present participle (uncommon in German): one of the last poems he wrote before his death begins, "standing at my desk," and in the very first play by the fifteen-year-old Berthold Eugen (mentioned earlier), the first stage direction reads, "The grandfather reading at the table." (Queried about his use of the participial form, Brecht responded, "You should do that only if you got a grade of 'very good' in Latin, as I did.")[49] Then we see Brecht's affinity for Roman subject matter: *Die Horatier und die Kuriatier,* based on Livy; *Das Verhör des Lukul-*

lus, based on Plutarch; *Die Geschäfte des Herrn Julius Caesar* [The business deals of Mr. Julius Caesar], based on Sallust and Suetonius; *Coriolan* [*Coriolanus*], based on Shakespeare and Plutarch. The novel fragment, *Die Geschäfte des Herrn Julius Caesar,* the radio play about the Roman general Lucullus, and the late adaptation of *Coriolan* are three works in which Brecht takes the side of the Roman plebians; in them, the ruler and oppressor is seen from the standpoint of those who are ruled and oppressed. We find another expression of the plebian point of view in Brecht's famous poem, "Fragen eines lesenden Arbeiters" ("A Worker Reads History"), which ends: "Every page a victory. Who cooked the victory feast? / Every ten years a great man. Who paid the costs? / So many reports. / So many questions."[50]

Brecht's late paraphrase of the Horatian "Exegi monumentum aere perennius," the poem "Beim Lesen des Horaz" [On reading Horace] should also be mentioned. And, finally, the famous invocation of "great Carthage" as a symbol of our own situation, written on September 26, 1951: "Great Carthage waged three wars. It was still powerful after the first, still habitable after the second. It could no longer be found after the third."[51]

In the indexes to Brecht's theoretical writings, the most frequent references are to Shakespeare, Schiller, and Goethe. Later, Karl Marx and Friedrich Engels joined his roster of classic authors, of whom his sage Me-ti reports: "The classic authors lived in the darkest and bloodiest of times. They were the most serene and optimistic of people."[52] In the *Arbeitsjournal* for the years 1938 to 1955, Goethe is assigned twenty-two lines in the index of names and Shakespeare twenty-three; the greatest number of entries, however, follows the name of Adolf Hitler.

"I observe," he wrote mockingly in the twenties, "that

I am beginning to become a classic author"; he resisted the way these worthies had of "tossing off certain banal statements at every opportunity,"[53] for his attitude toward everything classic was one of provocation and criticism—he refused to be intimidated. He was interested only in the practical use the classics could be put to. His criticism of Goethe and Schiller was severe: an example is his ironic treatment, in the sonnet "Über Schillers Bürgschaft" ["On Schiller's 'Pledge'"], of a Schillerian ballad in which a tyrant is converted from his nefarious ways by the example of one friend's self-sacrifice for another. Other examples are the parodistic insertions in *Der aufhaltsame Aufstieg des Arturo Ui* [*The Resistible Rise of Arturo Ui*]—such as verses by Schiller, the garden scene from *Faust,* and scenes from Shakespeare's *Richard III*—and the parody of classic authors in *Die heilige Johanna der Schlachthöfe* as well as of classic composers in the music accompanying the plays.

After his study of Marx, Brecht's relationship to the classics and to tradition underwent a change; he now made an effort to emphasize the progressive and militant spirit of classic authors and to teach his readers to apply it to contemporary life. The didactic element was, of course, very strong in Brecht right along, in his plays as well as in the didactic poems of his later years, "Von der Entstehung des Buches 'Taoteking'" ["On the Origin of the Book Tao Te Ching"], "Die Erziehung der Hirse" ["The Nurture of Millet"], and "Das Manifest" ["The Manifesto"]. Late in his life Brecht once said to Käthe Rülicke, "Simply describe me as what I am, as a teacher."[54] Brecht's companion of many years, Wieland Herzfelde, wrote (in 1956), "Brecht the imaginative poet and good fighter was a teacher and educator."[55]

There is much in Brecht's writings and in his method of working to lend support to the claim that he is a classic author. Just a few examples: his archivistic tendency to save every little snippet of a work in progress and the form and typography of the complete edition of his works (we have already mentioned that Brecht wanted "a classic format"). His close relationship to the sister art of music also belongs in this context, as does the fact that he was at one and the same time playwright, producer, and practical man of the theater. The unified structure of his theory of the contemporary theater and his way of associating with his disciples fits in here, too. Also typical of classic authors is the inescapable influence Brecht exerted on his successors: in the drama we think of Frisch, Dürrenmatt, Peter Weiss, Heiner Müller, Martin Walser, Franz Xaver Kroetz, Volker Braun, and Thomas Brasch; in lyric poetry, names such as Enzensberger, Volker Braun, and Wolf Biermann come to mind. Classic, too, is his reaction to the question of the permanence of his works in his poem "Beim Lesen des Horaz." Finally, there is the wisdom expressed through his figures Ziffel and Kalle in *Flüchtlingsgespräche* [Dialogues between exiles], Herr K. in *Geschichten vom Herrn Keuner* [Stories about Herr Keuner], and the Chinese sage Me-ti in *Buch der Wendungen* [Book of changes].

In Leipzig, in 1951, when Brecht made one of his few public addresses, he said, "The watchword of German classicism is just as valid as ever: we will have a national theater or none at all."[56] Hans Mayer commented on this speech at the time: "When Brecht speaks here about classicism and classicality, he is thinking like a German classicist himself. With full awareness." Mayer points to a parallel: "Brecht in Leipzig in 1951 echoes the question raised by Goethe in his essay of 1795, 'Literarischer Sansculottismus' [Literary sansculottism], written in the wake of the events of the French Revolution: 'Where and when will a classic national author arise?'"[57] Later, in 1954, Brecht returned to this idea:

"We must bring to the fore the original ideas contained in a [classic] work and grasp its national and thereby its international significance."[58]

The Age of Goethe saw the classic element of a "classic national author" in his ability to create "something noteworthy" in all genres. This ideal held sway until the end of the nineteenth century. It is typical of twentieth-century writers, on the other hand, that they often limit themselves to one genre: Kafka, Thomas Mann, Hermann Hesse, Hermann Broch, and Robert Musil to fiction; Rilke and Benn to poetry. Hugo von Hofmannsthal did produce works of distinction in a wide variety of genres (although he left behind only a few isolated examples in some of them), but it was Brecht alone who displayed this characteristic to any great extent among modern authors writing in German, creating works in the categories of fiction, poetry, and drama that are more than merely "noteworthy." Consider his prose forms alone: novel, novella, tale, fairy tale, legend, saga, idyll, epic, fable, parable, story, short story, short short story, anecdote, and aphorism. His poetry likewise encompasses a variety of forms: ballad, chorale, elegy, epigram, gloss, heroic song, song of songs, hymn, canzone, lied (children's song, folk song, popular hit, song), ode, psalm, romance, sonnet, and terza-rima. (The poem, "Die Liebenden," for instance, is written in terza-rima. According to Ernst Bloch it was composed in *one* night, after reading Shakespeare, in order to create "high art" and to save the production of *Mahagonny* from being closed down by the censors.)

In his poetic technique Brecht is a master of trimeter, blank verse, pentameter, and hexameter, a master of meter, of rhyme and assonance, of formal as well as free rhythms. Forms are observed, forms are shattered. The more important the subject matter, the more classical the form of the verse. The didactic Communist poem "Das Manifest" is written in that "respectable verse form," the hexameter. Brecht expressed his doubts and his skepticism about the permanence of his works in the form of a shortened and therefore "imperfect" hexameter in his poem "Beim Lesen des Horaz."[59] The best commentary on his own practice and—beyond that—on his significance as an artist was written by Brecht himself: "But he who wants to make the great leap must first go back a few steps. Today, nourished by yesterday, proceeds into tomorrow. Perhaps history does make a clean sweep, but it abhors a vacuum."[60]

Rainer Maria Rilke
and His Publishers

. . .it is very important to me to have my future things
in the hands of a single publisher.
Rainer Maria Rilke to Carl Ernst Poeschel, November 8, 1905

My topic, "Rainer Maria Rilke and His Publishers,"
treats the unique relationship between *one* author and
one publisher; this is the kind of association I find
highly desirable although virtually unattainable. To introduce my topic, I am happy to be able to quote
from an unpublished letter in the Insel Archives in
Frankfurt that Rilke wrote to Carl Ernst Poeschel,
who, at that time, headed the Insel Verlag in Leipzig
together with Anton Kippenberg. The letter, dated
November 8, 1905, was sent from Paris, that "infinitely variegated scene" (where he had just moved
into Rodin's home to study the master's art and, later,
Cezanne's so that he could learn to understand his
own art better), and contains three themes characteristic of the relationship between author and publisher.

"My dear Herr Poeschel: . . . You know that it is very
important to me to have my future things in the hands of
a single publisher." Actually, both publisher and author always hope for this, and yet, in the past as in the
present, some notable associations between the two
have foundered because of this wish.

The second theme follows directly on the heels of the first: "But that [publisher] would have to be someone who, aside from idealistic considerations, would be willing to render adequate monetary compensation (not exceeding the normal), which my circumstances unfortunately do not permit me to disregard."

"Adequate monetary compensation" that Rilke cannot disregard—how reasonable this sounds. Indeed, Rilke was dependent all his life on such compensation. It should give us pause to realize that two great German literary figures of this century, Rilke and Kafka, were not able to live on the proceeds from their work. Rilke was the most modest of men, and in financial matters the most helpless. He thought highly of his literary gifts, but his expectations of the fees and income they might bring him were low. The most modest payments made by Insel Verlag and Kippenberg's rather meager additional assistance evoked effusive expressions of gratitude from Rilke. One of the last letters from the poet, who was aware that his death was approaching, is addressed to Kippenberg; it is extremely moving:

> Chateau de Muzot, June 10, 1926
> My dear friend, just this hasty addition to yesterday's letter: there is such an uncanny and wonderful rapport between us that every time I complain to you that I haven't received my remuneration, the next mail comes to cancel out my complaint (so that I am ashamed of having put it prematurely into words at all!). Just now, for example, the bank in Val-Mont informs me that my account has been credited with ...francs as of the 8th, which to my relief and satisfaction leaves everything in good order![1]

All reference to specific amounts of money was deleted when Rilke's letters to his publisher were printed. In this case, the sum was 850 Swiss francs.

Let us return to that first letter, written in 1905, to the third passage, which follows those expressing his desire to have a single publisher and to receive monetary compensation. These words occur at the conclusion of the letter: "the fate of the book and its early appearance are naturally far more important than anything else." This too is characteristic. The poet ranks the publication of the book—he is talking about *Das Stunden-Buch* [*The Book of Hours*] here—above the publisher's imprint and certainly above any financial considerations. This letter seems to me to be typical of Rilke's view of his relationship to his publisher. Certainly, the three themes in the letter also characterize every relationship between an author and a publisher.

THE FIRST PUBLICATIONS

Before we mention the publication of Rilke's first book, let us go back to the beginning of his career as a writer. He himself gives us the biographical details in a letter to Hermann Pongs (August 17, 1924):

> When I was about seventeen years old, I was as unprepared as anyone can possibly imagine for the life and work that I was to realize for myself. My training in a military school for five years had finally become so patently absurd on account of my state of health and mind that it had to end with a complete break. An additional year was spent in poor health and with a lack of direction. The military lower school and later the upper school in Mährisch-Weisskirchen gave me nothing that might have served my inclinations and talents.... Moreover, the isolation of the boys in those rigid educational institutions was so complete that I didn't have access to the books that would have been nourishing and appropriate for my age or to the slightest bit of ordinary reality that might affect my life.[2]

Rilke then reports that he was prepared for the Abitur by "beneficial private tutoring." It was just during these most difficult times that his productivity was at its liveliest. He was writing

> all those attempts and improvisations that I could only wish a little later on I had had the good judgment to leave in the drawer of my school desk. The reason they found their way out after all, were even forced out by every means at my disposal, is the same reason they appear to me today so ill-suited to represent the beginnings of what I was then gradually able to do successfully. If I was foolish enough to want to lead off with those worthless pieces, it was because I was driven by the impatient desire to prove to a reluctant world my right to such an activity—a right that, once these attempts were made public, others who had already made a name for themselves might show themselves inclined to support. Yes, more than anything else, this is what I was probably hoping for by making myself known: to find people who could help me make contact with those intellectual movements from which I believed myself quite cut off in Prague, and I would have felt the same even if my circumstances had been better than they actually were. It is the only time in my life when I was not struggling with writing itself but was making use of its meager beginnings to try to win recognition.

Rilke then speaks of the assistance given him by Prague writers—by Alfred Klaar, Friedrich Adler, Hugo Salus—by Orlik the painter, and also by August Sauer:

> I will never forget that Detlev von Liliencron was one of the first to encourage me in this most immeasurable of projects—and when he occasionally began his cordial letters with the generous salutation that I

loved to say aloud, "My splendid René Maria," it seemed to me (and I made an effort to convey this conviction to my family) as though I possessed in these words the most reliable indication of the boldest of futures!

It was during this period that Rilke's first poem was published. It appeared in the journal *Das Interessante Blatt* in Vienna on September 10, 1891, with the opening line, "The train [of a gown] is now the fashion." It has always surprised me that Rilke took part in this contest (his poem was chosen by the judges and printed along with twenty-seven other entries). When I attended the Rilke Symposium in Vienna in 1975, I looked up the announcement of this competition, "Train or No Train," in the library. It is published in the August 6, 1891, issue of the journal. There we read that the train is again the order of the day; it is a matter of concern not only for the seamstress but "also for the authorities": "The head of the Board of Health scathingly condemned the wearing of trains on the street; he was of the opinion that the police should consider the possibility of taking official measures against the train." The editors of the journal followed the issue with interest and expressed the view "that neither the public health officer nor the police were the proper authorities" to make a decision in this matter. Rilke's poem, which he never allowed to be reprinted, must be read with this background in mind:

Die Schleppe ist nun Mode—
verwünscht zwar tausendmal,
schleicht keck sie sich nun wieder
ins neueste Journal!
Und so dann diese Mode
nicht mehr zu tilgen geht,
da wird sich auch empören

die "strenge" Sanität;
ist die dann auch im Spiele
und gegen diese Qual,
daß man geduldig schlucken
soll Staub nun sonder Zahl—
schnell, eh man es noch ahndet,
die Schlepp' vergessen sei,
eh sich hinein noch menget
gar ernst die Polizei.
Die müßte an den Ecken
mit großen Scheeren stehn,
um eilends abzutrennen,
wo Schleppen noch zu sehn.

                    René Rilke in Prag, Smichov

The train is now the fashion—
Though cursed a thousand times
Pertly it slips back into
The latest magazine!
And since this newest fashion
Can no longer be denied,
Outrage is the answer of
The "rigid" Board of Health;
Once it gets in the act
In protest of our plight
That we patiently must swallow
Dust in large amounts—
Quick, ere punishment is meted,
May the train be soon forgotten,
Ere there is mixed in with this
The earnest force of the police.
On every corner they would have
To stand with great long shears
And hastily cut off the trains
Where they continued to appear.

We see that the question, train or no train? hardly concerns the young Rilke, but he does criticize "the 'rigid' Board of Health," and he treats the police ironically. Can it be said that Rilke's first published poem already evinced an emancipatory character?

The publication of this poem gave him encouragement; the fifteen-year-old boy wrote his mother that he was now "a man of letters through and through."[3] The first poems were written at that time, then the first stories, fourteen of which, from the years 1891 and 1892, have been preserved but not published. He also wrote, during that period, the series of dramatic scenes entitled *Der Thurm* [The tower].

On November 29, 1892, Rilke wrote to the Austrian writer Franz Keim, then a professor at the Landes-Oberrealschule in St. Pölten, asking for an evaluation of his poems. On December 17, he thanked Keim for an apparently encouraging appraisal, and the boy, now turned sixteen, answered the professor with these lines of verse:

Nein!—Schafft die Zeit
sich keine großen Männer,
so schafft der Mann sich eine große Zeit!

No!—If the times
Do not create great men,
Then the man will create great times!

On December 30, he wrote to Sedlakowitz, his German teacher at St. Pölten: "Meanwhile Mistress Poesy is not completely idle—the strings of my lyre are not rusting, a busy hand awakens in them the soothing harmony of sweet tones, and its sounds are purer than ever."[4]

On January 3, 1893, Rilke offered the publishing

house of J. G. Cotta in Stuttgart a book of poems entitled *Leben und Lieder* [Life and songs], pointing out in his
accompanying letter that "these have received a lauda-
tory reception by Franz Keim, Alfred Klaar, and others,
and up to now have only appeared individually in journals." Cotta turned the book down. A historic case of
misjudgment?

In this same month, something happened that was to
remain characteristic of Rilke's life and was to influence
him, although the poet never mentions this influence in
retrospect. He began a friendship with the artistically
gifted Valerie von David-Rhonfeld, whose mother was
the sister of the Czech writer Julius Zeyer. To Valerie,
who was a year older than he, Rilke dedicated his first
volume of verse, *Leben und Lieder*. The 130 letters in
prose and verse chronicling this relationship have been
lost. Valerie was the first of a series of, usually, older
women to whom he became attached because he, the
restless and homeless poet, recognized the inspiring
force of such relationships. Her mother's connections
brought Rilke into contact with new periodicals, *Das
deutsche Dichterheim Wien* and, in 1894, *Jung-
Deutschlands Musen-Almanach,* in whose first volume
the series of six poems, "Lautenlieder" [Lute songs],
appeared. This almanac was under the same editorship
as the bimonthly journal for poetry, criticism, and modern living, *Jung-Deutschland und Jung-Elsaß,* published
by G. L. Kattentidt in Straßburg.[5]

RILKE'S PUBLISHERS PRIOR TO INSEL

Rilke himself jokingly named the epochs of his life after
his publishers: he called his early period the "Katzen-
zeit" (the cat period), after the Straßburg publisher
Kattentidt; the years from 1899 to 1904, the Juncker
period, after Axel Juncker, the publisher of *Die Weise
von Liebe und Tod des Cornets Christoph Rilke* [*The Lay of*

Love and Death of Cornet Christoph Rilke]. He called his late period the "Insel-Zeit" [the "island" period].

The Rilke bibliographies list nineteen titles that had not appeared with Insel before 1905, the year Kippenberg joined Isel Verlag, and a twentieth, *Cornet,* that was brought out by the firm of Axel Juncker after Kippenberg had joined Insel.

In September 1894, Rilke's first book appeared: "*Leben und Lieder: Bilder und Tagebuchblätter* [... Pictures and diary pages] von René Maria Rilke: Straßburg im Elsaß und Leipzig: G. L. Kattentidt: Jung-Deutschland Verlag." The appearance of this book was preceded by correspondence with Kattentidt, for Rilke probably contributed to the printing cost. The slim volume of verse bears the dedication, "for Vally von R . . ." The poems in this volume were written, beginning in September 1891, in Linz; during the summer of 1892, in Schönfeld; and, after that, in Prague until the end of 1893. Rilke never permitted his first publication to be reprinted, not even in his later *Gesammelte Werke in 6 Bänden* [Collected works in six volumes], and most of the copies were probably turned into pulp. We know of only seven extant today.

His second book appeared at Christmastime 1895. Rilke, now twenty and a student of the history of art and literature in Prague, published his second volume of verse, *Larenopfer* [Offering to the lares] with the firm of H. Dominicus in that city. In a notice he himself wrote, he says, "This work, which is 'strongly rooted' in Bohemia, nevertheless reaches far into the realm of universal interest and because of its elegant layout is ideally suited for gift purposes." There is an advertisement for his first collection of poems, *Leben und Lieder,* in the back of the book, along with an announcement of his coming third publication entitled *Wegwarten* [Wild chicory].

We read, on the title page of *Wegwarten:* "Songs presented to the people by René Maria Rilke: Free: Appears once or twice annually: Privately printed by the author: Prague." The first issue appeared in January 1896, the second in April, the third in October; Rilke donated copies to hospitals and community and workers' organizations. In a preface, he explains the title: "Paracelsus relates that once every century wild chicory turns into a living being; and the legend comes true readily in these songs; perhaps they will grow into a higher form of life in the soul of the people. I myself am poor, but this hope makes me rich."

In January 1896, Rilke took over the editorship of *Jung-Deutschland und Jung-Österreich.* Owing to a lack of subscribers, however, the publication soon ceased to appear. In 1897, Friesenhahn in Leipzig published the books *Traumgekrönt* [Dream-crowned] and *Advent.* In 1898, a volume of novellas and sketches entitled *Am Leben hin* [On life's rim] was published by Adolf Bonz in Stuttgart. Later, on April 22, 1900, Rilke promised Bonz the first option on "every novel, every story, and every novella containing more than five printed sheets," a pledge that turned into an onerous obligation.

The book of poems, *Mir zur Feier* [In celebration of myself], published by Georg Heinrich Meyer in Berlin, appeared in late 1899, with decorations by Heinrich Vogeler. In 1902, a drama in two acts, *Das tägliche Leben* [Daily life] was published by Albert Langen in Munich.

With *Die Letzten* [The last ones] and *Das Buch der Bilder* [*The Book of Pictures*], Rilke began his association with Axel Juncker in Berlin. In 1906, this publisher brought out *Die Weise von Liebe und Tod des Cornets Christoph Rilke,* written in 1899 and first printed in 1904 in the periodical *Deutsche Arbeit, Prag.* Looking back in later years, Rilke wrote "*Cornet* was the unexpected gift of a single night, an autumn night, written down in a single stroke by the light of two candles flickering in the night wind; clouds passing over the moon gave rise to it several weeks after I had been inspired by the material as a result of my discovery of certain inherited family papers."[6]

At the end of March 1903, Julius Bard of Berlin published Rilke's *Auguste Rodin* in the series Die Kunst: Sammlung illustrierter Monographien [Art: A collection of illustrated monographs]; the edition, "with two photogravures and six full-page colored etchings," bore the dedication, "To a young sculptress" (Clara Westhoff, Rilke's wife). A year later he almost came to regret the appearance of this edition, "for the little book on Rodin's works excluded, precluded (it is becoming increasingly clear to me) a larger and more ambitious Rodin book, which should have been composed and formed completely in my own way. I can never write two things [on the same subject], and if I have to write one, then that destroys the other one that I want to write—"Rilke to Arthur Holitscher, March 16, 1904.

The same year, 1904, he received two requests, one from the publisher Bard and the other from the editor of the series *Die Dichtung*[Poetry], published by Schuster & Loeffler, to translate Jens Peter Jacobsen. He turned down both offers; he was already planning to translate Jacobsen, but only after he had become more proficient in reading that writer's works and letters in Danish.

We can see from all this that Rilke's associations with publishers were extremely varied and lively, like his literary activities in general. He wrote to colleagues with whom he was on friendly terms, asking for their opinions and recommendations. He was untiring in seeking out the right publisher for books or authors he considered important: he urged Kippenberg to consider a German edition of Marcel Proust, and we now know that he sought a publisher for the manuscript of *Trac-tatus Logico-Philosophicus* by Ludwig Wittgenstein, whom he did not know personally. Altogether, he corre-sponded with many publishers, including almost all the prominent ones of the day: Adolf Bonz, Eugen Die-derichs, Kurt Wolff, Samuel Fischer (to whom he sub-mitted his first drama, which was rejected), Bruno Cas-sirer and Korfiz Holm, Julius Bard, and E. J. Mayer. Just because Rilke's publishing connections were so widespread, it is all the more important for us to con-centrate on the main associations.

RILKE AND INSEL
PRIOR TO THE KIPPENBERG PERIOD

In March 1900—we are jumping back a few years here—the monthly journal *Die Insel* brought out Rilke's poem "Die Heiligen Drei Könige" ["The Three Wise Men"], with marginal drawings and a full-page illustra-tion by Heinrich Vogeler of Worpswede. At Christmas-time of the same year, two books by Rilke were pub-lished by Insel Verlag, the publisher of the monthly: *Vom lieben Gott und Anderes: An Große, für Kinder erzählt* [About the dear Lord and other writings: Meant for adults, told for children], with decorations by E. R. Weiß, and *Mir zur Feier,* which Insel took over from the Berlin publisher Georg Heinrich Meyer.

How did this association between Rilke and Insel Verlag come about and why didn't it last? The fact that Anton Kippenberg took notice of Rilke only after 1906, after he himself had established connections with the poet, does not diminish that publisher's accomplish-ments. It is amusing to learn, by the way, that Kippen-berg, who deserves great credit for his efforts on behalf of Rilke's work, actually tried to draw a cloak of silence over the connections between Rilke and Insel Verlag that existed before he himself joined the firm.

Two men, an artist and an author, originally led Rilke to Insel: Heinrich Vogeler and Rudolf Alexander Schröder. In Florence, in April 1898 (where he happened to meet the German poet Stefan George, who reproached him for his premature and immature publications), Rilke attended an evening gathering at the Pension Benoit, where he was staying, and became acquainted with Heinrich Vogeler, who then became his "dear, dreamy-eyed companion." Later, when they got together in Berlin, Vogeler invited the poet to visit him in Bremen; it was there, at Christmastime 1898, that Rilke met Rudolf Alexander Schröder.

Schröder wrote, in his 1935 report *Aus den Münchner Anfängen des Insel Verlages* [Insel Verlag's Munich beginnings] that, ever since 1897, he and Heymel had been discussing a plan: "we wanted (once we had come of age) to edit a periodical of a literary-artistic nature that would create a sensation in Germany."[7] In March 1899, Heymel went to Schröder and suggested enlisting the support of Otto Julius Bierbaum, who was approximately fifteen years older and already famous. From the very beginning, the journal was supposed to be connected with "a publishing house or at least some kind of publishing venture." The name "Insel" [island], which Schröder proposed for the undertaking, met with approval.

In the first issue, the editors explained why they chose this name:

> It was far from our intent to emphasize, by this name, a tendency toward an unjustified exclusivity or an excessive display of elegance; rather, we want to attempt to do justice to all *artistic* efforts, if not to *all* artistic efforts, that are relevant to an undertaking like ours. By giving our publication the name "Die Insel," we merely wanted to make clear how little we

are inclined to join in the cries of triumph, now so prevalent, over the glorious results of any and all modern artistic efforts and how very conscious we are of the immense internal and external difficulties standing in the way of a desirable development of our artistic life.

Emil Rudolf Weiß designed a poster showing an island studded with fortresses from which the mainland could be reached only by boat; hence, a sailboat was chosen as the colophon of the house.

Ingeborg Schnack gives the following description in her history of the firm:

> Thus, three writer-publishers stand around Insel's cradle. In this trio, Heymel represented wealth, Schröder talent, Bierbaum experience. For the new firm this meant: Heymel provided the stimulus, Bierbaum was in charge, Schröder came to the rescue—whenever artistic standards seemed to be threatened by Bierbaum's willingness to compromise. In addition, Heymel displayed great human sympathy as well as a deep respect for artistic creativity and Bierbaum possessed knowledge of human nature and was familiar with the currents in the literary world that the novices Heymel and Schröder were eager to enter.

"The turn of the century," Schröder reminisces, "was an extraordinarily rich and happy time; a large part of an old, great heritage was still alive and just at that moment seemed to be emerging with its full impact for the first time. Countless new forces were at work, myriad developments were appearing or seemed to be appearing."[8]

What seemed to be emerging? Two things: a feeling of the decline of an age and a society and, simultaneously, the burgeoning of new literary forces.

Schröder's reminiscences are again instructive about the former point. He reports on a conversation he had with Hofmannsthal in Vienna shortly after the turn of the century; the two had walked from the Opera Ring across Karlsplatz, and Hofmannsthal spoke about the last song sung by Girardi, a popular Viennese actor of the day:

> Es wird a Wein sein,
> Und wir wer'n nimmer sein;
> Es wird an Sommer geben,
> Und wir wer'n nimmer leben.
>
> There will be wine,
> And we won't be here,
> There will be summer,
> And we won't be alive.

In spite of such melancholy assessments, the literary life was flourishing.

When Schröder tells about the early days of Insel Verlag, he doesn't mention that these beginnings were mainly characterized by the fact that the publishers Bierbaum, Heymel, and Schröder were primarily interested in the authors Bierbaum, Heymel, and Schröder. Still, the list of authors who appeared in their journal is an unusual one and attests to the publishers' literary flair. The first issue, containing illustrations by Thomas Theodor Heine and Vogeler, began with a poem by Rudolf Alexander Schröder entitled "Goethe." There followed pieces by Franz Blei, Hugo von Hofmannsthal, Detlev von Liliencron, and four poems by Robert Walser. In the second issue there were contributions by Richard Dehmel and Julius Meier-Gräfe; in the third issue, by Paul Verlaine; in the fourth, by Hugo von Hofmannsthal and, again, Robert Walser; in the fifth, by Arno Holz and Paul Scheerbart. The sixth issue contained, along with works by Maurice Maeterlinck and

Richard Schaukal, Rilke's poem "Die Heiligen Drei Könige." These authors, who were later to be joined by Paul Heyse, Hermann Bahr, Paul Ernst, Frank Wedekind, and Max Dauthendey, formed the core of Insel Verlag.

The firm could have become the most flourishing publisher of contemporary German literature. Compared with other publishers at the turn of the century, it had the greatest wealth of authors, and Heymel's fortune would have provided a sound economic basis. But things turned out differently, for the three publishers were really authors and, in the last analysis, not publishers. They recognized the stature of individual authors, but they did not cultivate relations with these authors and thereby ensure continuity. Just one example: in 1904 Insel published a book by Robert Walser, *Fritz Kochers Aufsätze* [Fritz Kocher's essays], with a double title page and eleven drawings by Karl Walser, the author's brother. Schröder wanted to bring out Robert Walser's poems as well, for in his opinion they contained "such density and daemonic quality and, at the same time, such delicacy and purity of expression that I don't know of anything in our language that measures up to them." But the firm's later directors did not maintain the connection with Walser.

Schröder's remarks about Rilke are also interesting: "Rilke, too, who was almost the same age as we, could already be counted as one of ours in many respects, especially in view of his unswerving admiration for Hofmannsthal; I am glad today that when we published his first book of prose, *Die Geschichten vom lieben Gott* [Tales about the dear Lord], we were laying the foundation for his later connection with the firm."[9] But this foundation soon became unsteady. On October 12, 1901, Rilke offered Insel a book of poems, writing Bierbaum that this new book had "from the outset close associations with Insel, for you accepted several of its best poems . . . for the journal." Rilke explained that he was turning to Insel because it was the only publishing house that

> possessed enough artistic distinction to promote lonely books (of which the book about the dear Lord is one). In addition, it is my misfortune that all my previous books of verse are in the worst possible hands, with the result that my lyrical works cannot really become known yet. . . . I visualize the format completely without decoration, grand, serious, simple—something like the books of the young Dutch poets. The contract could be worded like the one for the book *Vom lieben Gott,* since this new book, too, is not for "the many" but could well be valuable to those few people whom Insel has undertaken to search out and bring together.

Rilke offered to meet Bierbaum in Berlin, but nothing came of it, and the book was subsequently published (in 1902), not by Insel but by Axel Juncker. This is extremely hard to understand, for Bierbaum had warmly greeted "Die Heiligen Drei Könige": "you have brought us great joy. It is a delightful poem, the kind of success one seldom finds"—Bierbaum to Rilke, December 10, 1899, Insel Archives.

Insel's economic situation became increasingly difficult. The periodical got off to a daring start with a printing of 10,000 copies, but later this number fell to 3,000; steady subscriptions, which reached a peak of 400, finally dropped to 80. The firm's vitality was exhausted in the search for literary talent and in the artistic production of their books. Heymel paid his authors well, but there was not sufficient commercial activity in the form of sales, distribution, and promotion. The authors therefore became dissatisfied and gradually dispersed: Hofmannsthal went to Fischer, Rilke's book was published by Juncker. In 1904, Heymel transferred to Rudolf von Pöllnitz the management of a new firm, Insel-Verlag GmbH in Leipzig. It is to Pöllnitz's credit that he soon suggested a second printing of *Die Geschichten vom lieben Gott,* a book to which Rilke hoped to add a second part but never did. On January 16, 1904, he wrote to this publisher, "There is (as may also be mentioned in passing today) still another manuscript in which I someday hope to interest Insel Verlag, but it will be another year or two before it can be discussed"; the manuscript in question was *Das Stunden-Buch.* Rilke also asked about possible remuneration: for *Die Geschichten vom lieben Gott* he received only one payment of 50 marks. If Insel couldn't offer him "good prospects," he wrote, he would have to accept Axel Juncker's publishing proposals.

A year later (April 13, 1905), Rilke turned to Insel again. Referring to his correspondence with Pöllnitz, who had died the previous year, he mentioned he had completed *Das Stunden-Buch:*

> It is a long, highly cohesive poem cycle into which have gone almost all the progress I have made and the best of all the work I have accomplished since my last book of poems, published more than two years ago. In it, a series of hymns of praise and of prayers is meant to be ... united into a visible whole and, in remembrance of the *livres d'heures,* the volume is to be given the name *Stunden-Buch,* with the subtitle *Erstes, zweites und drittes Buch der Gebete* [*First, Second, and Third Book of Prayers*].

Insel's Carl Ernst Poeschel responded positively to this letter, and so, on May 16, Rilke sent the publisher the "completed manuscript, ready for the printer," requesting that a typewritten copy be made of his holograph. He had suggestions about the book's appearance: "I visualize *Das Stunden-Buch* as making a simple and strong impression and as resembling that type of tasteful, serviceable book exemplified by the prayer books of the sixteenth century . . . intentional archaisms should naturally be avoided." He also made recommendations about the format, title page, size of type, and quality of paper. Poeschel took charge of *Das Stunden-Buch*'s production and discussed these matters with Rilke.

At this point (July 1, 1905) Anton Kippenberg entered the firm, assuming the management of Insel together with Poeschel. In a speech on Poeschel's birthday in 1934, Kippenberg looked back on those days:

> The head of Insel Verlag [Pöllnitz] died in late 1904 after a brief illness. During his last days, you took over for him and stayed on for a while after his death as the interim head. The future of the firm was uncertain. It is true that most of the books that came out of your house, designed by Walter Tiemann and Marcus Behmer, were unusual in appearance; individual works by Rilke, Ricarda Huch, Hofmannsthal were among those that appeared there . . . but the main body of books was put together more at random and all too arbitrarily. The young firm had a good name among circles of confirmed book lovers, but wider circles detected a hint of snobbery and decadence. There was, however, sufficient foundation for the house to be built upon. Of course, its financial situation was wretched.[10]

It is not to denigrate Kippenberg's achievements and his history-making efforts on Rilke's behalf that we point out that, in 1905, when Insel published *Das Stunden-Buch,* he was probably not yet convinced of the poet's significance. In the above-mentioned speech for

Poeschel he spoke of four important events in the firm's early history: "the connections established with the Nietzsche Archive and with the Goethe Society, the appearance of Rainer Maria Rilke's *Stunden-Buch,* and the birth of the Insel Almanac." Kippenberg went on to give an enthusiastic account of his idea to have the Almanac present a cross-section of selections from Insel books and introduce its most important authors. Just six weeks after he took over the firm, the first Insel Almanac (1906) appeared, with the motto:

Ältestes bewahrt mit Treue
Freundlich aufgefaßtes Neue

The ancient faithfully preserved
The modern favorably observed

This Insel Almanac did not contain a contribution from Rilke.

A year later (December 1, 1906), Kippenberg wrote to Hugo von Hofmannsthal:

I believe that I am now relatively certain about the path I have to follow in the future. If I judge correctly, the direction Insel Verlag has taken until now points primarily to the following goals, which are to some extent related: to serve world literature in the Goethean sense, to adapt the form of a book to its content, to cultivate increasingly an appreciation of the art of the book and its refinements, and to publish only a small part of contemporary literature but, if possible, the part that promises to endure. . . . Insel Verlag certainly has a cultural mission to fulfill in its own modest way, but in the last analysis it is a business, and just as Goethe, in his role of theater director, mounted many productions displeasing to the poet and connoisseur solely in order to make money, so too the publisher will print books that will not long survive the time that gave them birth.

When Kippenberg mentioned to Hofmannsthal books that were meant to indicate the direction he intended Insel to take in the future, there was not one Rilke title among them. Nor did he express the wish to make any further efforts on Rilke's behalf.

We can only speculate about the reasons for Kippenberg's aloofness in this early period. *Die Geschichten vom lieben Gott* were anything but a best-seller, nor did *Das Stunden-Buch* promise great sales in the beginning, and Kippenberg must have had in mind Insel's "wretched" economic condition. Another important factor in his attitude was probably his impression that Rilke was the property of his colleague Poeschel, with whom he was increasingly at odds (in fact, relations between these copublishers were finally severed in anger and discord). It can be surmised that Kippenberg took the words Rilke had addressed to Insel Verlag in his letter of November 8, 1905, expressing his hopes for an enduring association with one publisher, as a message to Poeschel. And presumably the decisive factor: Kippenberg had intended to dedicate his main efforts to the publication and promulgation of Goethe's works. Very symptomatic was his assertion: "We had already taken on board our ship the best pilot of all: Goethe. He advised us, above all, what ballast should be thrown overboard."

RILKE, INSEL, AND ANTON KIPPENBERG

If the Insel records are correct, Kippenberg's first act in connection with Rilke was to draw up the contract for *Das Stunden-Buch*. The agreement, signed by Kippenberg on December 7, 1905, and by Rilke on December 11, contained a paragraph that strikes us today as unusual: in place of the standard method of payment there is reference to "sharing": "The partners to the contract will divide equally any net profit that may occur." Kippenberg's first letter to Rilke (April 7, 1906) continued the businesslike association almost on a bookkeeping basis: "I scarcely need to say that we are happy to comply with your wish that the copies of *Das Stunden-Buch* you have received be deducted at a later date from your share of the profits." On August 21, 1906, Kippenberg reported to Rilke that, altogether, 280 copies of *Das Stunden-Buch,* including the free copies that had been sent out, had been distributed. In this letter, he also announced that he had broken with Poeschel. A year later (December 31, 1907), Rilke learned that a second printing of *Das Stunden-Buch* had brought him a total of 473.25 marks. The correspondence during 1906 had been quite aloof, with no particular rapport developing between publisher and author. In fact, a conflict threatened: in a brusque letter (November 7), Kippenberg wrote: "Very honored Herr! To my great regret and— frankly—amazement, I have learned from the booksellers' trade journal that you have given your new books to another publishing house. . . . If the reason should be that the other firm has offered you more favorable terms, then I very much regret that in this case you did not inform me of the fact."

Rilke's reply must have astonished Kippenberg. It is the first letter in Rilke's collection, *Briefe an seinen Verleger* [Letters to his publisher], and perhaps it was Rilke's response that finally won Kippenberg over. Rilke wrote that he had no "intention of overlooking or underestimating the friendly and valuable interest of Insel Verlag; I am, quite on the contrary, certain that it will be of truly substantial significance for my work if the association with your firm, begun under such cordial auspices, be allowed to continue and endure." Kippenberg must not have been prepared for this or for the way the letter continued: "My sincere need, finally to bring my future books under one roof, would be fulfilled in a welcome way surpassing all my expectations if I could put them in the hands of those in whom I take pleasure and have confidence."[11] And then Rilke cleared up Kippenberg's error: it was not a question of giving his new books to another publisher, but of a somewhat expanded second edition of *Das Buch der Bilder,* which Insel Verlag had turned down. Rilke assured Kippenberg that "ever since *Das Stunden-Buch,* it has been my firm policy to inform you of each new work of mine as it nears completion. At the moment there are all kinds of things growing and developing, but a completed work will not be ready for the printer until the beginning of next year, at the earliest."[12]

Kippenberg's reaction was expressed in a letter (November 12) that began with "Highly honored Herr Rilke" instead of the earlier "Very honored Herr": "It was with very special pleasure that I received yesterday, Sunday—along with several unpleasant things that are the lot of every publisher—your very cordial letter of the tenth of this month. I was comforted to know that there is nothing that could give you occasion to have any second thoughts about a continuing association with us but that you have the intention of entrusting your works to us in the future." Rilke saw in this letter Kippenberg's "probable confidence in my future books."[13] It appears that this "misunderstanding" (stemming from an out-and-out error by Kippenberg, who—as we know—was aware of the contents of Rilke's letter of November 8, 1905, to Poeschel), which could easily have resulted in a clear-cut rupture, led instead to a lasting association. In any case, from then on, their correspondence reflected a working relationship that improved from year to year and encouraged Rilke in his productivity. The correspondents' attitude toward each other also became more open and friendly, despite the formal tone that was retained.

Rilke and Kippenberg were both about thirty when they began to correspond. Rilke was working on *Die Aufzeichnungen des Malte Laurids Brigge* [*The Notebooks of Malte Laurids Brigge*] and had the feeling that he was writing his magnum opus. Kippenberg noted, in one of his few autobiographical records, *Aus den Lehr- und Wanderjahren eines Verlegers* [From the apprentice and travel years of a publisher], written in 1944–45, that the beginning of his career at Insel had been easy but that "progress along the path predetermined by fate, 'managing to continue in spite of all adverse forces', was infinitely more difficult." The decade devoted to building up the firm, from 1906 until the First World War, was one he said he would not want to live through again, happy as he had been in his work.[14] The difficulty in his association with Rilke was that Kippenberg (like so many other publishers) had to learn from experience that a major author could not be influenced by outside pressures, even of the most well-meaning variety. For example, Rilke continued to work imperturbably on *Malte,* finally sending it to the printer in the form in which he had originally conceived it, in spite of the fact that Kippenberg and his wife were quite disturbed by the criticism of Goethe contained in that work and had tried to convince its author to modify it.[15]

Given the fondness of Rilke and of both Anton and Katharina Kippenberg for writing letters, it is not surprising that there was an enormous correspondence among the three. The Deutsche Literaturarchiv has preserved more than five hundred letters from Rilke to the Kippenbergs, the majority of which have been published. One volume contains only Rilke's letters to Anton; the other contains his letters to Katharina together with her replies. Unfortunately, neither of these editions is completely reliable, owing to a lack of critical editing.

The history of the relationship between Rilke and Kippenberg can be deduced directly from the salutations, the complimentary closes, and the forms that greetings take in their letters. Kippenberg's "very honored Herr" (in his 1906 letter) was changed to "Very esteemed Herr Rilke," "Highly honored Herr Rilke," "My very esteemed Herr Rilke," "My dear and esteemed Herr Rilke," and, finally (November 29, 1911, and thereafter), "Dear friend." The complimentary closes were: "Yours sincerely," "With respectful devotion," "With sincere devotion," "With cordial esteem for you as ever," "Yours," "Yours as ever." Rilke's salutations and complimentary closes were far more ornate. In 1907, they were usually "Esteemed Herr Doktor" and "Greeting you with sincere wishes," "My dear and esteemed Herr Doktor . . . Your cordially devoted . . ." After their first meeting in 1910, the salutation was "My dear Doktor Kippenberg"; a month later, "Dear and very valued friend . . . Yours in friendship." Then the form of address remained "My dear friend," whom Rilke always wished all the best from the depths of his heart. The last letters have the heading, "My good friend." And a letter of 1926 closes very characteristically: "Farewell, my good old friend and for your Lady the most cordial and fair wishes." Kippenberg probably took special pleasure in Rilke's letter on the publisher's fiftieth birthday; it begins, "Muzot, prior to May 22, 1924: My dear, constant friend." The poet speaks of the

moments of the greatest mutual trust and the most

joyful understanding over so many years. . . . May everything you have lovingly accomplished in your home and profession and in the pure circle of your interests and obligations come to the surface of your consciousness for a moment so that you may involuntarily repose and refresh yourself therein. . . . So much for what can be said; let the rest remain between us in deed and in thought. In deed and in thought let there also be present that which binds me indescribably to you, my gratitude.

And then Rilke writes the verses, "Anton Kippenberg in Freundschaft zugewendet zum 22. Mai 1924" [Presented to Anton Kippenberg in friendship on May 22, 1924]. I myself would place an even higher value on the letter Rilke wrote his publisher after completing *Duineser Elegien* [*Duino Elegies*]. We shall return to this later.

During the years prior to the publication of *Malte* in 1910, Kippenberg tried to obtain the rights to those of Rilke's works that had appeared earlier with other publishers. This turned out to be a tedious process. In the course of time, Insel published *Neue Gedichte* [*New Poems*] (1907), and *Der Neuen Gedichte anderer Teil* [*New Poems: Part Two*] (1908). Both volumes contain those great poems signaling Rilke's mastery of his craft: "Archaischer Torso Apollos" ("Archaic Torso of Apollo," written in Paris, early summer of 1908); "Lied vom Meer" ("Song of the Sea," written in Capri, January 1907); "Venezianischer Morgen" ("Venetian Morning," Paris, 1908); "Die Liebende" ("Girl in Love," Paris, August 1907); "Der Fremde" ("The Stranger," Paris, 1908); and "Die Flamingos," Capri, 1908. Despite frequent urgings, Kippenberg never received a third book of these poems from Rilke. Also published before 1910 were *Die frühen Gedichte* [The early poems], "Requiem für eine Freundin" [Requiem for a friend, Paula Modersohn-Becker], "Für Wolf Graf von Kalckreuth" [For Count Wolf von Kalckreuth] and, finally, the translation of Elizabeth Barrett-Browning's *Sonnets from the Portuguese.*

A slightly complaining and sometimes critical undertone can be detected in Rilke's statements about his financial situation. In the letters to Kippenberg appearing in *Briefe an den Verleger,* these passages usually contain ellipsis points to indicate omission. It is evident that Rilke was in financial difficulties during his entire career; quite naturally, the income from the sale of his books did not begin to cover his living expenses. On June 21, 1907, he wrote his wife, "I have given up everything, first the taxis, second drinking tea, third buying books. And still... I have done a lot of figuring again in these last days and haven't managed to discover how I am going to get along."[16]

Rilke began to give readings for the sake of the fees. From November 8 to 18, 1907, he was in Vienna to give his Rodin lecture at the invitation of the bookseller Hugo Heller. Right after the lecture began, Rilke suffered a severe nosebleed: "During this unfortunate incident, Hofmannsthal came backstage, spoke some comforting words, was charming; 'If necessary, I will read your talk,' he said" (to Clara Rilke, November 9, 1907).

Rilke's first meeting with the Kippenbergs was planned for Februrary 13, 1908, in Leipzig, but Rilke, who was in Bremen at the time, changed his mind and didn't make the journey. Was he perhaps disappointed that Kippenberg had offered him only 300 marks for the translation of the Elizabeth Barret-Browning sonnets? He wrote Kippenberg that he was too exhausted from an illness; nevertheless, he proceeded to visit Berlin (from February 19 to 23) at the invitation of Samuel Fischer.

This may be the place to devote a few words in our account of Rilke and his publishers to the subject of his association with Samuel Fischer and his wife Hedwig. The letters the Fischers wrote to Rilke have been preserved, although they have not yet been sorted through. Some of them are in the Rilke Archive, but the larger portion was presented to the Landesbibliothek in Bern by Nanny Wunderly-Volkart. Rilke's letters to Samuel and Hedwig Fischer, on the other hand, are available in a selection published by Hedwig Fischer in 1952. From these letters, and also from Peter de Mendelssohn's comprehensive study of the S. Fischer firm, we can gain a clear picture of this relationship. It was marked, for one thing, by a lack of any great enthusiasm on the publisher's side for Rilke *qua* poet. Peter Suhrkamp once told me that Fischer had no feeling for lyric poetry; for example, he made no effort to obtain the rights to those volumes of Hesse's verse that had been published before Fischer added Hesse to his list. Samuel Saenger observed that lyric poetry as "the ancient preserve of the soul" within literature was basically alien to Fischer: "His aspirations as publisher never extended as far as Rilke or Stefan George."[17]

Rilke had met Fischer as early as 1897: in December of that year, he and Lou Andreas-Salomé attended a literary gathering at the Fischer home in Berlin. This occasion marked the beginning of a friendly relationship between Rilke and Hedwig Fischer that lasted until the poet's death. "Rilke's poems," Frau Fischer wrote, "which I came to know little by little, were at first a strange world to which I only gradually gained access, and for a long time I felt closer to Rilke the man than I did to his work." Later, Rilke was invited to read from his poetry in the Fischer home; he also saw the couple in Italy and once in Paris, and he remained an occasional correspondent. Over the years, Fischer had been pressing Rilke for contributions to *Die Neue Rundschau* (Hofmannsthal, for example, had hoped to have some of his prose works reviewed there by Rilke).

Thus, during those February days of 1908 when Rilke did not go to see Kippenberg in Leipzig but visited Fischer in Berlin instead, poet and publisher were far from strangers. In the course of their conversations, Fischer offered Rilke financial support on condition that he submit a prose work to the *Rundschau* or even to the Verlag for publication as a book. In a five-page letter from Capri (March 19, 1908), Rilke replied that this suggestion opened up to him "a most favorable possibility that just a moment ago was still impossible: I would go to Paris, shut myself in, be able to work, throwing myself into it headlong as I hardly ever have before." Then he added:

> My relationships with publishers are not quite clear even to myself; for a long time there were, so to speak, none. But now in recent years an association with Insel Verlag has developed in a very natural way. I think I would not be playing fair if I concealed from you the fact that this relationship is a friendly one and that I consider myself, as far as my feelings are concerned, obligated to Insel Verlag to a certain degree. . . . In the meantime, however, I have . . . called attention to my situation and, because of the pressure it puts me under, have urged Insel Verlag to clarify more precisely the nature of our association and of their claims on me. . . . I cannot, it seems to me, assess my . . . obligations until I know what their intentions

and suggestions are. Now, in any case, I am determined to offer you...authentic poetic recompense over the next few years.

Rilke had always meant to ask Kippenberg for payment on a regular basis, and now, backed by Fischer's offer, he requested a salary ("a very little one," in Hofmannsthal's words). This letter to Kippenberg,[18] written from Capri on March 11, 1908, should actually be reproduced here in its entirety, but we shall limit ourselves to the most important passages.

Rilke expresses his regret that the visit to Leipzig did not materialize; he would now like to attempt to make his association with the firm "even more definite and beneficial"; as it is, this association has been "happily strengthened by four books." Rilke is concerned because he has not been able to devote himself undisturbed to his work. To be sure, whenever he made a monetary request, he also kept the publisher's interests in mind: "In taking it upon myself to ask you to consider my situation, I am aware that you are not free to respond to this confidence in a personal way but that your attitude must be determined and modified entirely on the basis of financial considerations." There follows the modest inquiry "whether the firm might see any possibility of working out arrangements between us in a way that might be beneficial to me in the sense I have indicated." Then the letter takes on an impressive tone as Rilke turns to the future:

> I realize that a lyric work, commercially speaking, must be regarded as a precarious security, so that any advance agreement based on it may be considered somewhat rash. As far as one can foresee, however, my lyric work (no matter how unconditionally it may and will continue to present itself in individual re-

alizations) is an act of taking personal possession, a conquest of the external world, behind which other tasks, crystallizations, solutions are in preparation; for if I now wish with all due care to secure for myself a period for intensive work, I am not thinking only of the completion of the next book of poems but, with just as great dedication, of the expansion of my prose and, beyond that, of a certain dramatic inevitability that may some day arise from an artistic versatility expanded to its utmost.

When Kippenberg received this letter, he had no way of knowing that a competitor was lurking behind this impressive plan to ensure an artist's subsistence. Entirely of his own accord, he proposed paying quarterly installments of 500 marks to Rilke's account for a period of one year beginning in April 1908 (the letter is in the Insel Archives). Rilke expressed his gratitude "for this new convincing proof of your kind understanding" and for the fact "that in making arrangements for the immediate future you still knew how to preserve that spontaneous vitality that has accompanied our association from the beginning." Accordingly, he sent the next things he wrote to Insel, including *Die Aufzeichnungen des Malte Laurids Brigge.*

On March 20, Rilke wrote Fischer that he had to accept the "reasonable offers from Insel Verlag." "Consider, dear friend, whether the assistance you offered me might be reduced so that I could be reasonably certain of offering you contributions for the *Rundschau* in the next years as a really suitable recompense."[19] On April 3, Fischer informed the author that he would stick by his original offer. Rilke received the subsidy, but the only "really suitable recompense" Fischer ever got in return was the opportunity to publish a chapter from

Malte in the February 1909 issue of *Die Neue Rundschau* before Insel brought the book out.

There was no further correspondence between poet and publisher, but letters continued to flow between Rilke and his friend Hedwig Fischer. Years later, in April of 1922, she inquired more or less privately whether he didn't have something from *Duineser Elegien* for *Die Neue Rundschau,* and Rilke answered in the negative. Not until after Rilke's death was *Die Neue Rundschau* able to publish (July 1927) his "Briefe an eine Freundin" [Letters to a female friend], the last work by him to appear in that journal.

But back to 1908: on New Year's Eve, Rilke again informs Kippenberg of his "worries about external life" and Kippenberg sends a check for 1,000 francs, "which you need to cover last year's deficit," notifying him that the agreement according to which the firm pays him 500 marks quarterly has been extended for another year (from a letter dated January 2, 1909, in the Insel Archives). In the meantime, Juncker had published *Cornet.* Kippenberg discovers, however, that according to the contract between Rilke and Juncker

Herr Juncker has the rights for only a single printing of 300 copies, and since these have all been sold, his rights are no longer valid. Herr Juncker cannot very well publish the book again, since he expressly announced a single printing. I should like to suggest that you now write Herr Juncker that, under the circumstances, it is impossible to have the book published again by itself and that, when you get a chance, you intend to give it to another firm along with other works. Perhaps it could then be combined with "Requiem" and some work or other that is already on hand or might present itself at the opportune moment. In my opinion it would not do any harm, especially since a limited edition was specified, for the book to be out of print for a year.

Rilke follows this advice and attempts to get Juncker to relinquish the rights to *Cornet*. But that proves difficult: Juncker replies that he has just bought up the rights to *Advent* and *Traumgekrönt* and would like to bring them out again.

Rilke works on completion of *Malte* in Paris in 1909. Once again, on September 10, he has to ask Kippenberg for additional funds: his treatment at the spa of Bad Rippoldsau turned out to be more expensive than he expected. On September 12, he reports to Kippenberg that *Malte* is progressing well: "When I next come to Germany, my trip will definitely take me to Leipzig. I wish to heaven I might have [Malte] *Laurids Brigge* with me. Shouldn't its completion be a condition of our meeting? If life is only relatively well-disposed toward me again, then I intend to hasten rather than delay my departure."[20]

On October 20, 1909, Rilke tells Kippenberg that a good half of his prose work is finished, but he has a problem—does Kippenberg know someone reliable who could type his handwritten manuscript or type from Rilke's dictation from his notebooks? On October 23, Kippenberg replies:

The calamity brought upon you by the necessity of having to have Laurids Brigge transcribed by way of dictation, is, frankly speaking, very welcome to me. . . . it seems to me to be the most practical thing, by far, for you to come to Leipzig for a week or longer and do the dictating here. Of course you must stay with us, and in addition to your sleeping quarters there is a tower room completely at your disposal, which is very sunny and bright and always struck us as a suitable haven for a poet.

Rilke accepted and left for Leipzig on January 11, 1910. He stayed with the Kippenbergs from the 13th to the 31st, and there produced the definitive typescript of *Malte*.

Here I should like to return for a moment to the topic of Rilke and Goethe. How did it come about that Rilke, who at one time had had a deep admiration for Goethe, then began to reject him more and more and finally launched his sharpest poetic attack against that classic poet in *Malte*—in, of all places, the home of Kippenberg, the great Goethe specialist? The answer has to do with the deep-seated conflict in Rilke between life and work, which he believed Goethe had solved for himself in an exemplary way, whereas he, Rilke, was in constant danger of being destroyed by it. In any case, the Kippenbergs did not seem to hold their friend's attacks on Goethe against him, and the success of *Malte* was reassuring in this connection. On occasional visits with Rilke in Weimar, Katharina Kippenberg tried in vain to win him over to her and her husband's enthusiasm for Goethe. But Anton Kippenberg met with success in 1913 when he read aloud Goethe's erotic poem "Das Tagebuch" ["The Diary"], which inspired Rilke to write a series of seven erotic poems of his own. In Kippenberg's only essay on Rilke (1947), portraying Rilke as a German poet who had been "born for the world," Kippenberg quotes verses by Goethe in Rilke's honor! Rilke's failure to appreciate Goethe was not an isolated occurrence; Thomas Mann's appraisal of Rilke affords another example of how unjust one major author can be to another. Juxtaposing Rilke and Goethe, he found that

> the confrontation between a life exhibiting the highest abilities and fulfillment and one of passive weak-

ness that is in love with nothingness is naturally not very flattering for the modern age. A grandson of Goethe's, Walter, used to say: "What do you expect? [Goethe] was a giant and I am a chicken."[21] Rilke could have said the same thing. But it cannot be denied that this chicken laid some golden eggs.—Mann to Harry Slochower, September 8, 1942.

Perhaps one should take a statement such as this with a certain degree of humor, and yet it was one of the reasons why I dealt with the topic of Rilke's relationship to Goethe at some length in my book, *Das Tagebuch Goethes und Rilkes Sieben Gedichte.*

Die Aufzeichnungen des Malte Laurids Brigge, which appeared on June 1, 1910, is one of those works of modern world literature that will endure; its epoch-making significance lies in its being one of the earliest successful and convincing descriptions of our modern existential predicament. The themes of man's loneliness, anxiety, and forlornness in huge cities is presented in visions that possess a concrete and exact character. "He was a poet and hated imprecision," Rilke said in describing a dying poet in *Malte* with words that might be applied to himself. The Rilke critic Peter Demetz wrote, in 1965, "There is nothing more replete with the future than *Die Aufzeichnungen des Malte Laurids Brigge,* in which Rilke the lyric poet initiates a new epoch of precise German prose and, in his radical questioning of the nature of reality, is far ahead of his contemporaries on the path leading to a Robbe-Grillet."

One wonders what writer today possesses the exactitude of Rilke's double, the young Malte in the Rue Toullier: "Is it possible that in spite of all the inventions and progress, in spite of art, religion, and philosophy, we have remained on the surface of life? Is it possible that we have covered over even this surface, which might after all have been something, with an incredibly uninteresting material so that it looks like the drawing-room furniture during summer vacation?"

On October 2, 1911, Anton Kippenberg informs Rilke that from then on he can count on receiving 500 marks a month. The correspondence between Rilke and Kippenberg for the years 1911 and 1912 constantly returns to the question of how they can get *Das Buch der Bilder* and *Cornet* away from Juncker. Kippenberg writes, on September 18, 1911:

> I must say frankly that I had not expected Juncker's answer to be any different. He is clinging with Nordic tenacity to this book, which he probably considers the best by far on his list, and I must confess, I would do the same myself. You approached the matter quite properly and the fact that Juncker is unwilling is anything but your fault. My advice is that we do nothing further in this matter. Don't answer his last letter, and we will leave everything up in the air. I shall keep *Das Buch der Bilder* in mind and, when the right moment has come, I'll surprise him with a check. The whole question of *Cornet* is dubious. In the near future I intend to talk to a lawyer who is experienced in the area of copyright and discuss with him what can be done.

Later (November 29, 1911), Kippenberg seems to have decided to take advantage of the legal uncertainty of the situation and bring out a new edition of *Cornet*. He wants to sign a contract with Rilke: "I will then inform Juncker of this fait accompli. If he should raise any objections, then they will have to be dealt with. The contract signed with him, which I have here, does not give him any rights to a new edition." In January 1912 Kippenberg suggests publishing two prose stories or a selection of poems making up about forty pages for his Dreißig-Pfennig-Bücher [thirty-cent books]—which, in

the following weeks, became fifty-cent books and were
to become the famous Insel-Bücherei—and Rilke is
to receive 150 marks for every 10,000 copies sold. On
January 22, Kippenberg tells Rilke that Axel Juncker is
now ready to give up *Cornet* for 400 marks, after all.
Kippenberg wishes to include that work in his fifty-cent
series and increases the royalties from 150 to 400
marks. In late June of 1912, the first twelve volumes of
the Insel-Bücherei appear, set by hand in the best type
available, printed on rag paper, and—something new for
a series in this price range—solidly bound in cardboard.
The first book in the series was *Cornet,* which sold
22,000 copies the year it was published. By the end of
1916, 88,000 copies had been printed; by 1922,
251,000; by 1934, 500,000. In 1962, the number of
copies printed passed the one-million mark.

Rilke was correct in his assessment of the situation
when he wrote to Kippenberg from Venice, after Kippenberg reported that the appearance of *Cornet* had
triggered a veritable Rilke boom: "For four or five days
now I have been meaning to thank you for this supply of
good news. . . . Juncker is really beside himself—
although my *Cornet* didn't get very far at all on the nag
he provided him with. Dear friend, what a fine steed you
have given our good Christoph Rilke. Who would have
thought it!"[22] A short time later (August 9, 1912), Rilke
again wrote from Venice: "You work on a Herculean
scale, dear friend. What can I say? I am almost alarmed
by the boldness with which you have now liberated *Das
Buch der Bilder,* too, burying the dragon in a mountain of
gold."[23]

A new phase in Rilke's development as well as in his
relationship with Kippenberg followed. In 1912–13, he
managed to write the first two *Duineser Elegien* and *Das
Marien-Leben* [*The Life of the Virgin Mary*], but then
came those ten years that were "name-less," years of

silence, of faltering, ten years in which—in his own words—he inhabited the land of psychic suffering. But they were by no means totally sterile, for some of his most beautiful poems were written during this period: "Hebend die Blicke vom Buch, von den nahen zählbaren Zeilen" ["Raising One's Eyes from the Book, from the Close, Countable Lines"]; "Es winkt zu Fühlung fast aus allen Dingen" ["Nearly All Things Signal to Us to Perceive Them,"] (Munich, September 1914); and "Ausgesetzt auf den Bergen des Herzens" ["Exposed on the Mountains of the Heart,"] (Irschenhausen, September 1914). In this last-mentioned, especially significant fragmentary poem, we find the emphatic statement that words cannot reach and, in the last analysis, cannot express, feelings:

> Ausgesetzt auf den Bergen des Herzens. Siehe, wie klein dort,
> siehe: die letzte Ortschaft der Worte, und höher,
> aber wie klein auch, noch ein letztes
> Gehöft von Gefühl. Erkennst du's?

> Exposed on the mountains of the heart. Look, how small there,
> Look: the last habitation of words, and higher,
> But how small too, still one last
> Farmstead of feeling. Do you see it?

As I said, this was not an unfruitful time. Yet Rilke had the feeling that the *Elegien,* which he had begun with such intensity, to which everything was impelling him, and in which he saw the fulfillment and ultimate achievement of his poetic work, would never be completed.

Another sidelight on Rilke's encounters with publishers: Rilke thought highly of Kurt Wolff and his "fine publishing house," as he stated in his first letter (December 6, 1913) to Wolff. He took note of the firm's books, was a subscriber to its famous series Der Jüngste Tag (Judgment Day), and recommended titles for the firm's list. On January 7, 1914, however, Rilke turned down an offer from this publisher to translate the Indian writer Tagore.

No book of his ever appeared under Kurt Wolff's imprint, although once his name did appear in the firm's catalog: on February 10, 1914, Rilke offered Wolff a "short manuscript" for his periodical *Die Weißen Blätter;* the essay, which dealt with Lotte Pritzel's wax dolls, appeared in volume 1 (pp. 634–42) and elicited an immediate letter of alarm from Kippenberg:

> to tell you frankly . . . it is with a feeling of real uneasiness that I saw you among the contributors to *Die Weißen Blätter*. You have been unique for many years in holding aloof by not contributing to periodicals, and that has been one of the factors responsible for your outstanding special position—even in the eyes of the broad public—in the midst of the confusion of our times. I am not the only one to regret that you have not remained faithful to this principle, which I have always admired and supported—there are quite a few who have expressed the same sentiment to me. People are already saying that you are now going to emerge from your self-imposed isolation and make a general practice of publishing your works in advance in periodicals . . . I regret, above all, the place where you published your essay on the dolls. I can't help telling you that I do not find this publication of Franz Blei's, where so much helpless dilettantism and sterile arrogance parades itself along with precious little of quality, at all worthy of you. And you mustn't overlook the obvious danger that you will be made use of to give periodicals like this a boost—March 28, 1914.

Kippenberg made himself more than clear. It is understandable that he was anxious to continue to be the publisher of original material and not of reprints; on the other hand, he should have considered the particularly severe difficulties Rilke was having with writing at this time and respected the wishes of his faithful author. Rilke remained firm in the matter:

Nevertheless, publication in *Die Weißen Blätter* gives me pleasure, even now that it has appeared. The motivation for this overstepping of my usual bounds stems from the pleasure I take in [Franz] Werfel, from my surprise, which has undergone many changes since last summer, at feeling such involvement with and delight in the younger generation, as has been the case for me, quite unconditionally and unexpectedly, with his poetry and since then in other places as well. I had to find expression for this somehow, and it would be unfortunate for one's attitude and self-imposed course to find oneself locked in them because of a certain force of habit. My "reserve" will certainly not be given up as a result of this, for it is within me, not something outside of me, and thus I only appear to abandon it when I act contrary to it out of impulse on one occasion—April 1, 1914.

The next sentence is not intended for publishers alone: "To keep everything alive and flexible within oneself, even such long and firmly held views, seems to me vastly more important than always being concerned about looking exactly the way one is at one's most secure."

In 1918, Rilke delivered the manuscript of the portions and fragments of the *Elegien* he had written thus far to Kippenberg for safekeeping, thinking he was never going to complete them. Two years later, at Schloß Berg, when Kippenberg suggested the idea of a complete edition and inquired about the *Elegien,* Rilke again expressed the same negative attitude.

We know that the hour for the *Elegien* finally came. In July 1921, Werner Reinhart rented the little castle of Muzot in Switzerland for Rilke (which Reinhart was later to buy), thus providing a haven for the traveler who, for the past ten years, had been wandering restlessly between Paris, North Africa, Naples, Venice, Duino, Spain, Paris again, Duino again, Munich, Vienna, Locarno, Basel. How nervous and irritable Rilke was at the time, even with the Kippenbergs, is expressed in a letter he wrote in French from his Muzot retreat to his friend Merline: "The time before November 22nd can be regarded merely as a waiting period. . . . And the time since my return from Geneva until the Kippenbergs' arrival is likewise a kind of waiting again—and once they are here, on January 2nd, 3rd, and 4th, they'll bring a kind of distraction with all their news so that until mid-January everything will again be aftermath and interruption."[24]

Rilke became more and more restless. On the last day of January 1922, he decided that he would not write a single letter in February. On February 1, he wrote a poem in which the form of the sonnet is foreshadowed; the first part of *Die Sonette an Orpheus* [*Sonnets to Orpheus*] followed between the second and fifth of February. Now, in days of "immense spiritual obedience," the storm of the *Elegien* broke, and on the evening of February 9, Rilke wrote Kippenberg a letter that I would describe as the most significant testimony we have to an exemplary relationship between an author and his publisher:

My dear friend, late and although I can hardly hold the pen any longer, after several days of immense spiritual obedience—you must . . . you must be told today, now before I try to go to sleep: I am over the mountain! Finally! The *Elegien* are here. And can be published this year (or whenever else it may suit you).

Nine long ones, of the approximate length of those you already know; and then a second part, belonging to their sphere, which I intend to call "Fragmentarisches" [fragments], individual poems related to the longer ones in time and tone . . . the whole thing is to be called *Die Duineser Elegien.* People will get used to the name, I think. And: my dear friend, this: that you have granted it to me, have shown me the necessary patience: for ten years! Thank you! And again and again believe me: thank you!

The next day, February 10, he reported the completion of the *Elegien* to Nanny Wunderly-Volkart; on the eleventh to the Princess Thurn and Taxis—to all his correspondents the message was the same: the *Elegien* are here. And not only the *Elegien,* but also the major cycle *Die Sonette an Orpheus* as well as *Der Brief des jungen Arbeiters* [*The young worker's letter*], written from the twelfth to the fifteenth of February between the Tenth and the Fifth Elegy, a marvellous work that in my opinion is in a class with *Malte.*

On the same pad on which sketches for the Tenth Elegy and a conclusion for the Fifth had been jotted, there are some passionately scrawled notes for "Erinnerung an Verhaeren" [In remembrance of Verhaeren], which gave direct rise to the imaginary letter from a worker to the Flemish poet of that name who had died in 1916. The subject matter of the work involves problems still relevant to our time—for example, the question of power and domination: "As far as the 'patron,' the powers that be, are concerned, there is only *one* measure against them: to go farther than they go themselves. I mean that in this sense: one should make an effort to see, in every form of power that claims a right over us, all power, power in its entirety, power per se, the power of God." Rilke's fictitious worker goes on to discuss "the twilight of the Christian spirit," questions of guilt and sin: "Why have they made sex a homeless thing for us instead of locating in it the celebration of our special strength? . . . The terrible inauthenticity and uncertainty of our times has its roots in our failure to acknowledge the joy of sex, in this remarkably deep offense, which is constantly growing and which separates us from all the rest of nature." Then he speaks of the debris of Christian prejudices, adding the demand, "I want to be used by God just as I am."

The worker had heard the Flemish poet read his poems, and he concludes: "The poems, however, have evoked this emotion in me. My old friend once said: Give us teachers who praise the here and now. You are such a one" (words that could just as well be addressed to the poet of the *Elegien* and *Sonette*).

From the twenty-first to the twenty-fifth of July 1922, the Kippenbergs visited Rilke in Sierre, the location of Chateau Muzot, and on this occasion Kippenberg had the impression that once again a decisive turning point had occurred in the author's life and work: "After he had penetrated to the limits of the expressible, which way would his genius lead the poet?" the publisher wondered.[25] When Kippenberg next visited Muzot (in 1923), the subject of the final form of the complete edition was again discussed, with Rilke reasserting that his literary production was at an end. Yet, in spite of his worsening illness, he did superb translations of Paul Valéry and wrote the important French poems comprising *Vergers,* "suivi des quatraines valaisans avec un portrait de l'auteur par Baladine"; this book, appearing in 1926, was the last one he saw published. But before then, in June 1923, a special edition of the *Duineser Elegien* had appeared, bound in dark green morocco, followed by the trade edition of the same work in October. The *Sonette an Orpheus,* "written as a monument for the grave of Vera Ouckama Knoop," were also published in 1923.

Rilke and the Kippenbergs saw each other one more time, in April of 1924, in Sierre. By then the poet's illness was severe enough to overshadow temporarily the sentiment he expressed on his deathbed: "Life is magnificent."

In sum, Anton Kippenberg was all these things for Rilke: partner, advisor, patient companion to the creative poet, in all ways a friend. To be sure, he was not able to eliminate Rilke's worries about practical matters or assure him of an untroubled financial basis for his work, but who knows whether Rilke would have achieved the breakthrough of the *Elegien* under different economic conditions? The most important thing Kippenberg could do for Rilke was to give him constant encouragement, be patient, and express the hope that the *Elegien* would one day be completed.

In the preceding pages we have paid little attention to Rilke's relationship with Katharina Kippenberg, the "Mistress of Insel." She played a special role, serving as a kind of sounding board when he wished to discuss literary contemporaries, fashions, trends, and the books of his colleagues. He was more open with her than with her husband: for example, in a very discreet way, he gently criticized Insel for not having published important authors he had recommended, such as Francis Jammes, Giraudoux, and Proust, whom Rilke was one of the first to discover. It was also Katharina Kippenberg who had been instrumental in securing Rilke's discharge from military service. In January 1916, he had been transferred from his company to the War Archives, where his literary colleagues Stefan Zweig, Alfred Polgar, and Franz Theodor Csokor were already working. (A witness of those days, Zega Silberer, reported later that the people in this office had to write heroic stories based on the daily news from the front, thus performing what was called a "poetic service" or also a "cosmetic treatment of heroes.") On February 15, Rilke asked

Katharina to petition for his discharge, writing that "Insel Verlag is far and away the best place to initiate and carry out this new step." She complied with his request: Insel Verlag, whose editor-in-chief had gone off to war, stated that Rilke was indispensable to the firm. Later, Katharina wanted to make Rilke a salaried advisor to Insel, but he refused to take on assignments imposed on him from outside: he preferred to make spontaneous recommendations. For example, during the war he made the unpopular recommendation that Insel-Bücherei, as well as the Insel Almanach, publish French and English literature—in other words, the literature of the enemy—something they proceeded to do.

It was during this period in particular that Rilke turned increasingly to Katharina Kippenberg. His relations with her husband remained friendly but cool over the years that followed. It was strange that Kippenberg, who had tried for twenty years to bring all of Rilke's works together in his catalog, was not interested in his last book of French poems, *Vergers*. Was Kippenberg offended because Rilke had accepted an "unexpected offer from Gallimard" for this volume? Did it disturb him that Rilke, whom he considered the great *German* poet of the times, spoke and wrote French more and more exclusively during the last years of his life, even to his friends; that the last comments on his work to reach Rilke came from France, from Paul Valéry and André Gide, who praised his command of their language in the poems in *Vergers?* In any case Rilke must have felt that Kippenberg was slightly annoyed, for on June 9, 1926, he wrote to Katharina: "My French book, *Vergers,* this lighter lyre for my left hand, this late quasi-youth on borrowed ground, was submitted to the public on June 7. As soon as my copies arrive, the first one will go to you."[26] She thanked him for the "sun-warmed lyre with its foreign and delightful sound. Hearing it, I feel the same as when we hear in a fairy tale that the fairy has turned into a rose bush.... And I imagine that such metamorphoses must be very refreshing, that this bathing in another language must be very invigorating."

Such was the sounding board provided by their correspondence: within the conventions of polite letter writing they could say on occasion those critical or not very pleasant things that had to be said. The "Mistress of Insel" had an ear and a heart totally open to such nuances.

AFTER RILKE'S DEATH

It should be mentioned that, after Rilke's death in 1926, Anton Kippenberg no longer edited Rilke's works personally. The editions composed of selections that began to appear were edited by Katharina Kippenberg or by Insel staff or, later, by the poet's heirs. Ingeborg Schnack has pointed out that "in spite of the wide range" of Kippenberg's "associations with contemporary writers he focused his attention on Goethe. His publishing activity revolved around this central literary sun more and more intensely with his advancing years."

To an increasing degree, his guiding motto was, "Pay homage to one alone." Commenting on the firm's continuing publication of editions of Goethe's works, Katharina Kippenberg said, "Looking at the Goethe collection, it can be clearly perceived how much it and the firm complement each other, how richly the one nourishes the other." Especially after Rilke's death, the harmony between collector and publisher exhibited by Kippenberg became increasingly apparent; for instance, in the mid-twenties, Insel brought out a reproduction of the *Codex Manesse,* the famous manuscript of the songs of the Minnesingers. Based on the pattern of their facsimile editions of Bach's *St. Matthew Passion* and *B Minor Mass* and reproduced by the collotype process, this volume was the most beautiful of those books and Insel's highest achievement.

The responsibility for Rilke's works rested in the hands of Katharina Kippenberg and Adolf Hünich, a staff member who, in 1921, had edited the volume *Aus der Frühzeit Rainer Maria Rilke: Vers, Prosa, Drama, 1894–1899* [From Rainer Maria Rilke's early period: poetry, prose, drama . . .]. Rilke had dedicated an ironic poem to him, calling him his "Eckermann."

> Ach in den Tagen, da ich noch ein Tännlein,
> ein zartes, war in einer Gartenecke,
> was sprach mir niemand von dem Eckermännlein,
> das später aufkommt, daß es sich entdecke
> Struktur und Stärke meiner frühsten Sprossen—?
> Wie hätte mich so mancher Vers verdrossen
> von jenen leicht und zeitig hingestreuten:
> hätt' ich geahnt: er soll mich einst bedeuten!
> Viel rücksichtsvoller hätt' ich mich erschlossen,
> Mich gründlich jeden Morgen prüfend: grün ich
> Auch schön genug für meinen künftigen Hünich?
>
> > Muzot, Ende Januar 1922

> Ah, in the days when I was still a young fir tree
> and tender, growing in a corner of the yard,
> why did no one speak to me of the little Eckermann
> who would later appear and discover
> the structure and strength of my earliest shoots—?
> How vexed I would have been by many a verse
> among those I had scattered about with early ease:
> had I only known: it was one day to denote me!
> Then I would have developed much more cautiously,
> examining myself thoroughly each morning: am I
>   growing
> beautifully enough for my future Hünich?

Now came the time of the great Rilke collections. In

the fall of 1927, the six-volume edition of the complete works, which Kippenberg and Rilke had long discussed, reached the bookstores; its appearance had originally been planned to coincide with Rilke's fiftieth birthday in 1925, but Rilke had urged his publisher to do a careful job—in his view there was no hurry. Volume 1 contains the poems, part 1; volume 2, the poems, part 2 (*Das Buch der Bilder, Das Stunden-Buch,* and *Das Marien-Leben);* volume 3 contains *Neue Gedichte, Duineser Elegien, Die Sonette an Orpheus,* and last poems and fragments; volume 4, prose works 1 (everything except *Malte*); volume 5, prose works 2 *(Malte);* and volume 6, the translations, which make up a considerable oeuvre in themselves—Barrett-Browning, Guérin, *Die Liebe der Magdalena* [The love of Magdalena], *Portugiesische Briefe* (Portuguese letters), André Gide, Louise Labé, Michelangelo, Paul Valéry, Verlaine, Comtesse de Noailles, Mallarmé, Baudelaire, Petrarch, and Moréas. In his review of this edition, Hermann Hesse wrote:

Often Rilke seemed to transform himself in the eyes of those who had been his readers for a long time, often he seemed to shed his skin, from time to time to wear a mask. Now the complete edition reveals a surprisingly uniform picture; the poet's faithfulness to his own nature is far greater, the strength of this nature much stronger than what we once called his capacity for transformation or even inconstancy.... Remarkable the path leading from the early poems with their reminiscences of Bohemian folk songs to the end, to *Orpheus;* remarkable this poet's consistency, the way he begins with the extremely simple and then—with the development of his language, with his developing mastery of form—descends deeper and deeper into essential problems, and on every step of the way he always accomplishes the

miracle: his delicate, doubting self, so in need of support, recedes and he is filled with the music of the
world, becoming like the basin of a fountain, simultaneously instrument and ear.[27]

Hesse was also describing the essential literary function of a complete edition, which is to show the development of a writer and, at the same time, the coherence
and unity of his work. In 1927, Katharina Kippenberg
also published *Ausgewählte Gedichte* [Selected poems],
followed by *Erzählungen und Skizzen aus der Frühzeit*
[Tales and sketches from the early years] in 1928. Ruth
Sieber-Rilke, the poet's daughter, and her husband Carl
Sieber edited *Briefe aus den Jahren 1902–1906* [Letters
from the years 1902–1906] in 1929, and *Die Briefe und
Tagebücher aus der Frühzeit 1899–1902* [Letters and diaries from the early years . . .]; a new, expanded edition
of the latter volume appeared in 1942. Between 1933
and 1939, *Briefe aus den Jahren 1907–1914* [Letters
from the years 1907–1914] were published; in 1934,
Briefe an seinen Verleger [Letters to his publisher]; in
1935, *Briefe aus Muzot 1921–1926* [Letters from
Muzot . . .]; and, finally, in 1937, *Briefe aus den Jahren
1914–1921* [Letters from the years 1914–1921]. In
1939, *Gesammelte Briefe in sechs Bänden* [Collected letters in six volumes] appeared.

In December 1943, the building in which Insel was
housed on Kurze Straße in Leipzig was destroyed in an
air raid and along with it all the presses and book de-
positories. When the Americans occupied Leipzig in
April 1945 and gave a few publishing houses the opportunity to continue operations in the West, Kippenberg founded a branch of Insel Verlag in Wiesbaden.
His inventory, including his valuable Goethe collection,
was brought to Marburg from the places where it had
been stored for safekeeping during the war, and there,

on September 7, 1947, three years before his death, Kippenberg opened a Rainer Maria Rilke Exhibition. For this occasion he attempted to sum up Rilke's significance:

> The young Rilke called his first slim volume, *Wegwarten,* a "gift to the people"; his work has become a gift to the world. When this poet died, there were hardly twenty foreign-language editions in existence, among them only three in English. A remarkable number, at that, when one considers the knowledge and ability that is required to translate Rilke's works. Since then, they have been translated into nearly twenty-five languages.... But Rilke is being read more and more in his own German language; in other countries the number of bilingual editions is growing—a teacher at a British university wrote recently that many of his students are learning the German language or attempting to master it more thoroughly in order to gain access to Rilke's works in the original.[28]

The publications of Rilke's works during the years from 1945 to 1949 were mostly pirated editions. When Kippenberg caught these "publishers" at it, he tried to make them send him a Care package as "punishment"! Anton Kippenberg died in Lucerne on September 21, 1950, having outlived his wife by three years. Friedrich Michael, associated with Kippenberg for many years, became the head of Insel Verlag; he was followed by six others.

As far as Rilke publications are concerned, the time around 1950 and thereafter was, with one exception, the period when secondary literature appeared in addition to his correspondence. In 1947, a book-length critical study was published; in 1948, three works; in 1950, seven; in 1951, fifteen; in 1952, twenty-four; in

1953, around thirty; from 1954 until 1963 the number remained constant, between twenty-five and thirty. Then the amount of literature devoted to Rilke began to decline.

The sheer volume of letters published after 1945 nearly matched the volume of the secondary literature. The books were not all brought out by Insel, for the firm would not have been able to handle such a deluge at the time. These editions of letters began with *Briefe an Baronesse von Oe* [Letters to the Baronness of Oe, New York, 1945]; *Freundschaft mit Rainer Maria Rilke, mitgeteilt durch Elya Maria Nevar* [My friendship with Rainer Maria Rilke, as told by Elya Maria Nevar, Bern]; *La dernière amitié de Rainer Maria Rilke* (Paris, 1949); *Lettres françaises à Merline* (Paris, 1950). Insel published *Die Briefe an die Gräfin Sizzo* [Letters to Countess Sizzo, 1950], and *Rilke und Marie von Thurn und Taxis: Briefwechsel* [Rilke and Marie von Thurn and Taxis: a correspondence, Zurich and Wiesbaden, 1951]. In 1952, the Rilke–André Gide correspondence came out in Paris and the Rilke-Lou Andreas-Salomé correspondence in Zurich and Wiesbaden; they were followed in 1953 by *Die Briefe an Frau Gudi Nölke* [Letters to Frau Gudi Nölke] (Wiesbaden) and *Rilke-Inga Junghanns: Briefwechsel* [Rilke-Inga Junghanns—a correspondence] (Wiesbaden). Then these publications came to a halt; Rilke's popularity declined.

I have already referred to an important publishing event after 1953 that was an exception and a major service on the part of Insel. In 1955, the first volume of the complete works appeared, edited by the Rilke Archive in cooperation with Ruth Sieber-Rilke and under the supervision of Ernst Zinn. Five more volumes printed on India paper followed, totaling nearly 5,000 pages. "Many years of extensive preliminary work were required," Insel wrote upon the publication of the first volume, "to do the necessary groundwork for this edition. It will contain everything already printed from the early years until the end of 1899, along with a selection of unpublished early works; the edition will present the complete poetic works from 1899 on together with [Rilke's] extensive posthumous writings."

In these volumes, Ernst Zinn produced a useful critical edition, one with reliable texts and reliable information about the origins of the individual works. Such an exemplary edition of a German writer of this century is unusual; indeed, few great contemporary writers of any nation have been so well served. Insel Verlag, in cooperation with Ruth Sieber-Rilke, took a vital step toward handing down Rilke's works to posterity in an authoritative form and can, as a result, absolve itself, with a clear conscience, of responsibility for the ever-growing decline of his popularity.

RILKE AND THE PRESENT-DAY INSEL VERLAG

On February 19, 1963, Anton Kippenberg's two daughters and numerous other shareholders transferred their shares in Insel Verlag to the owners of Suhrkamp Verlag, and since January 1, 1965, the merged firms of Suhrkamp and Insel have been under my personal direction. For me, Insel was the publisher of Rilke. I must have been around twelve or thirteen when, thanks to Hans Scholl, I discovered *Cornet;* I learned it by heart, and even today, in spite of the prevailing negative assessment of this work, I am able to accept the plot—including the Cornet's ride through the Hungarian steppe, the noctural love scene in the castle, and his death battling the Turks—because of the basically ballad-like nature of the twenty-nine prose sections. Even the linguistic mannerisms such as, "Was a window open? Is the storm in the house?" do not disturb me, given the epic-lyrical form of this ballad. Naturally, the ideology of *Cornet* derives from the vitalism of the turn of the century. In the war, when I had reason to recite to myself the lines of *Cornet,* his death struck me as all too effortlessly caught up in the cyclic festival of life.

But there were other poems, too, e.g., "Archaischer Torso Apollos," that had accompanied me from early youth. In Tübingen I "experienced" the *Duineser Elegien* through Romano Guardini's unforgettable interpretation and, later, through an equally exciting series of de-mythologizing lectures entitled "Rilke in Muzot" given by Friedrich Beißner, whose sober approach to the poet provided a beneficial modification of my own views. The *Elegien* took on a literary reality of the first magnitude for me, becoming an inescapable feature of the literary landscape of this century along with the creations of such other towering figures as Kafka and Brecht, Joyce and Proust.

Our work on Rilke at Insel met with two obstacles, one of a specific, quasi-legal, the other of a more general nature. Rilke's heirs created the first obstacle; they not only possessed the rights to the still unpublished posthumous writings in the archive—the manuscripts, versions, and variants there—they also had to give their approval for every new, special, or licensed edition. The existing contract permitted Insel to reprint the books by Rilke that had already been published, but only in the form in which they had already appeared. What was clearly needed, in 1965 and the years that followed, were volumes of selections, special editions with specific themes and, above all, inexpensive editions that would make Rilke accessible to a new generation of readers. An attempt should have been made to alter the objective situation characterized by an acute low point in Rilke's popularity and a complete absence of critical treatment of his works.

In 1945, Carl Sieber, the first husband of Rilke's daughter Ruth, died. In 1948 she remarried, and the firm's relations with her and her new husband, Willy Fritzsche, were strained from the very beginning. I paid two visits to the couple in Fischerhude, the first in 1963, after becoming head of Insel, when I spoke to both of them, and the second in July 1966, when I was not able to speak with Ruth Fritzsche-Rilke. Herr Fritzsche received me alone and our conversation was primarily a monolog in which I answered questions his wife had written in advance. To be discussed there were the plans we had made to mark the fortieth anniversary of Rilke's death, but his heirs would not give their consent for our projected publication of licensed editions, i.e., paperback editions by other publishers or even by Suhrkamp. After much preliminary deliberation, an edition of selected works in three volumes was under discussion, with a foreword by Beda Allemann, 2,100 pages, clothbound, for 36 marks. The idea behind this selection was to present the works on which Rilke's reputation rests and which are of immeasurable importance for the contemporary reader. Other topics discussed on this second visit to Fischerhude were Beda Allemann's foreword, which the heirs found unacceptable, and the composition of volume 3, which was to include important works hitherto unpublished. I also brought up our plans for an Insel Almanac for 1967, to be devoted to the influence of Rilke's works.

No final decisions were reached at this meeting, but in the following months I did obtain permission to go ahead with the three-volume edition. It appeared in November 1966 as a special edition in the series "Bücher der 19." We were permitted to print a limited edition of 30,000 copies, which seemed a large number to us at the time, but within three years all of them had been sold and the heirs refused to give us permission for

a second printing. In the almanac, intended to demonstrate Rilke's influence, we had planned to include a
collection of various "Views of Rilke," put together by
the acknowledged Rilke scholar Jacob Steiner, who introduced his selection with an entry from Robert
Musil's diary: "How often I have changed my opinion of
Rilke, of Hofmannsthal. A possible conclusion from
this: that there is no objective opinion, only a 'living'
one." With his compilation of comments about the poet,
Jacob Steiner wanted to present some of the *living*
opinions his contemporaries had arrived at, and obviously these views were not to be exclusively positive
ones, for then the depiction of responses to Rilke would
be a one-sided misrepresentation of facts. Clearly, other
views had to be presented as well, but on October 6,
1966, I received the following telegram: "Concerning
almanac plans we emphatically remind you that rilke
publisher is obliged to be extremely loyal to rilke's
memory and work especially in view of such long association between rilke and his heirs and insel stop we call
on you to make omissions rather than do something that
only other publishers could do with impunity." This
touched directly upon a matter of principle. I expressed
myself on this subject in a letter of October 18, 1966:

The case is simply that loyalty toward Rilke's work
can not mean publishing praise and suppressing criticism. His work is so significant—and will remain so
for decades—that it is quite naturally bound to attract
critics. Please remember how much criticism was
leveled at Schiller and Goethe even while they were
still alive. That is a quite natural phenomenon. Every
generation has its own set of responses to a poet's
work and often—indeed, as a rule—takes a polemical
position toward preceding generations. . . . Hermann
Hesse once told me that he preferred to have

181

Suhrkamp publish critical writings about him, for then a certain level of criticism would be assured and in the eyes of the outside world the criticism would be subsumed under the publisher's over-all advocacy of the work. I do not believe your view that other publishers could print criticism of Rilke with more impunity than I is incorrect, but now that this criticism is reaching a certain level (in the case of Peter Demetz's book, for example), it is far better for Rilke's cause if this kind of writing appears in our own house.

I never received a response to this letter.

In 1968, a last interview with Herr Fritzsche took place in Munich, in the presence of his two lawyers and our lawyer. There was a lengthy discussion of the legal, economic, and literary problems "arising from the contractual agreement between Rilke's heirs and Insel Verlag," as the notice of the meeting put it. The meeting had become necessary because the old contract did not cover contingencies for distribution in new media. It was our last contact with the heirs. Four years passed, during which there was no communication between us, and then we learned that Ruth Fritzsche-Rilke and her husband had both taken their own lives on November 27, 1972.

Today, with the passage of time and after learning more about Ruth Fritzsche-Rilke, I have a different impression of her. She was already ill when I met her, and our world was no longer her world. She and her husband, in choosing to die by their own hand rather than suffer through a protracted terminal illness, had been granted the fulfillment of Rilke's fervent plea in *Malte* that each person be granted his own death. Ever since 1927, Ruth Rilke had assisted Katharina Kippenberg in the editing of her father's works. Both lived through the time when Rilke was called "a friend of the Jews," "an offspring of Jews," and "effeminate," the latter a category completely opposite to the contemporary ideal, which was to be "hard as Krupp steel." His work, sometimes just individual poems, remained alive for a few, but he was forgotten by the public in general. It is a subject for a future study—and such a study should be encouraged—to examine how these decades of neglect nevertheless paved the way for a revival of interest and a new, mature understanding of his work. But could this new interest have come about without the publication of his complete works?

It was Ruth Rilke who made this undertaking possible. She left Weimar in East Germany in the winter of 1948–49, abandoning all her personal belongings, a splendid house with its grounds, and irreplaceable material possessions, for only one reason: to rescue the Rilke Archive, which she had brought into being through decades of labor. It had become her life's work to collect and preserve manuscripts, versions, and variants and to purchase manuscripts and ever-increasing numbers of letters. Without this archive and the opportunity of using it, Zinn's work on the *Sämtliche Werke* would not have been possible; without it, the re-establishment of Insel Verlag following Kippenberg's flight from Leipzig to Wiesbaden would have been robbed of one of its major motives.

One wonders parenthetically what use the German Democratic Republic would have made of the Rilke Archive, since the official cultural policy in that country was to appreciate Rilke's works as little as do the present-day preachers of the death of literature in West Germany. Rilke's writings did not find official acceptance in East Germany until after the Soviet Union had recognized him as a (progressive) author; clearly, before that time, a comprehensive edition of his works there would not have been possible, and thus the necessary basis for a revival of interest would have been missing, for how can an author be popular if his works are not available?

It was these facts and considerations about Ruth Rilke that changed my attitude toward her, and I know today that in spite of all the difficulties she caused, her efforts were essential in bringing Rilke back to the attention of the reading public. Three days before her death, I sent her a letter that she probably never read. As an indication of the neglect into which Rilke had fallen, I sent her a clipping from the *Frankfurter Allgemeine Zeitung* of November 24, 1972, with the heading, "Repression":

> There was a time not so long ago when it was impossible to carry on a conversation about literature without mentioning him: Rainer Maria Rilke. Today the situation is exactly the opposite: in discussions about literature, Rilke is one of those names you studiously seek to avoid in order not to be accused of being old-fashioned and conformist. Now, reasons can certainly be given for this change. For example, it is no doubt understandable that Rilke, as the idol of an epoch, has disappeared beyond the horizon along with its philosophy. But this does not completely explain the phenomenon. For every epoch seems to be characterized not only by its ideals but also by its repressions, and here Rilke's name stands for many others.

Had Rilke, the idol of an epoch, disappeared beyond the horizon? And is our epoch—or to be more modest, our decade—characterized by the repression of Rilke? I have already mentioned the specific obstacles we encountered when dealing with his heirs: for example, scholars such as Jacob Steiner, Klaus Jonas, and especially Bernhard Blume, the editor of the volume, *Briefe an Sidonie von Nádherný,* had been unable to pursue their research because they had no opportunity to examine and quote from unpublished material in the Rilke Archive. Two editors even planned legal action against Insel Verlag. This was the basic difficulty standing in the way of a revival of interest in the poet, but there was another, more general one, stemming from the plight of literature and the way it was viewed in the second half of the sixties.

In the great and extremely necessary debate about the social relevance of literature, Rilke—as a representative of a "bourgeois literature"—was completely written off by a whole group of Germanists and students, and, as if this were not enough, by a group of literary critics and intellectuals writing for journals. Literature, especially poetry of Rilke's kind, was no longer in demand by the cognoscenti of our day. It didn't seem to make any difference to them that the person in whose name they often waged their ideological battles, Walter Benjamin, had praised Rilke: "I believe," Benjamin wrote to Herbert Belmore on August 4, 1913, "that only in a community, and especially in the most fervent community of the faithful, can a person be really lonely: in a loneliness in which his individuality protests against the [generally accepted] Idea in order to attain selfhood. Do you know Rilke's 'Jeremia'? It is wonderfully expressed there."[29]

During this period of change in literary tastes, Rilke's grandson Christoph Sieber-Rilke (the son of Ruth Rilke and Carl Sieber) and his wife Hella, née Hartwig, inherited the rights to Rilke's works. They both have a deep appreciation of Rilke and his work, an appreciation of his relationship to our times and to Insel Verlag. Overnight, new opportunities became available to Insel, and the firm took advantage of them in order to make preparations for the observance, in 1975, of the hundredth anniversary of Rilke's birth.

Plans could again be made: first came the reprinting of the three-volume edition, followed by single editions of his writings, paperback editions, and volumes of documents relating to Rilke designed to revive interest in the author. Also planned, along with important new editions—such as *Das Testament* [The will], in which Rilke summed up in remarkable fashion the problems of his life and work—was a facsimile edition of the handwritten *Ausgewählte Gedichte* [Selected poems]. Principal interest, however, was focused on the issue of a popular edition in twelve volumes, a photographic copy of the six-volume Zinn edition; each section, however, is to be provided with a new index so that a person can use this edition without having to refer to the indexes of the original one.

What accounts for the new vitality of Rilke's work today, in 1977? For me there are three contributing factors:

First, Rilke once wrote that the trauma resulting from his difficult years in the military academy had led to his having an "over-life-sized experience of loneliness" for his young years. And Paris, he wrote Lou Andreas-Salomé in 1903, was "for me an experience similar to that of the military academy." Rilke gave unsurpassed expression to this modern forlornness and loneliness of people in our cities and also gave his readers hope that both feelings can be borne, perhaps even overcome.

Second, we need imagination and sensitivity, we need a new sensibility at a time when we are controlled by anonymous forces, directed by anonymous computers, and see ourselves coming more and more under the sway of impenetrable decision-making powers. The powers that be are more concerned with the demands of the present than with those of the future. But we must "go farther than they go themselves," as we read in the *Brief des jungen Arbeiters.* I think Peter Demetz is right when he says, "in his country, hungering for ideas, Rilke, as a magus of sensibility, seems to me to have more of a future than a past."

The third point is closely connected with the second. My favorite Rilke poem is "Archaischer Torso Apollos," which closes: " . . . denn da ist keine Stelle, / die dich nicht sieht. Du mußt dein Leben ändern" [" . . . for there is not a place that does not see you. You must change your life"]. This admonition to change is by no means rare in Rilke. We need only think of the sonnet to Orpheus that begins, "Wolle die Wandlung" ["Will transformation"] and of two other pertinent passages, the first from a letter written on June 28, 1915, in which Rilke commented upon the changes—at least some of them for the better—that the war made in people. He had hoped, he wrote, that art might also have this power: "What else is our metier for, if not to provide the motivation for change in a pure and grand and free manner,—have we done this with such poor, such half-hearted, such little conviction and convincingness? That has been the question, that has been painful—for almost a year now—and our task is to do it more powerfully, more relentlessly. How?!"[30] The second passage occurs in the ninth Duino Elegy of 1922, whose tone is indeed "more powerful and more relentless":

Erde, ist es nicht dies, was Du willst: *unsichtbar*
in uns erstehen?—Ist es Dein Traum nicht,
einmal unsichtbar zu sein?—Erde! Unsichtbar!
Was, *wenn Verwandlung nicht,* ist Dein drängender Auf-
    trag?

Earth, is it not this that you want: *invisibly*
to arise in us?—Is it not your dream
one day to be invisible?—Earth! Invisible!
What, *if not transformation,* is your urgent task?

187

This task of transformation, of alteration, expressed both directly and indirectly, permeates Rilke's work. Another example is one of his last poems, "Spaziergang" ["Walk"], written in early March 1924:

Schon ist mein Blick am Hügel, dem besonnten,
dem Wege, den ich kaum Begann, voran.
So faßt uns das, was wir nicht fassen konnten,
voller Erscheinung, aus der Ferne an—

und wandelt uns, auch wenn wirs nicht erreichen,
in jenes, das wir, kaum es ahnend, sind;
ein Zeichen weht, erwidernd unserm Zeichen . . .
Wir aber spüren nur den Gegenwind.

My gaze has already passed beyond the hill, sun-illumined,
Beyond the path I've scarce begun.
Thus, full of appearance, does what we could not grasp grasp us from afar—

and transform us, even though we don't attain it,
into that which we, scarcely suspecting, are;
A signal beckons in answer to our signal . . .
but we feel only the adverse wind.

I find our present and future situation described in this poem. If we take the path we have set for ourselves, then we are not alone, we are aided by what is distant, past, mythic, by what transcends the present day: thus do the things we could not grasp grasp us. And this alters us. We are not something fixed, dogmatic, closed off in ourselves, finished. "Was sich ins Bleiben verschließt, schon *ists* das Erstarrte" ["Whatever confines itself in permanence already *is* rigidity"], as Rilke wrote in *Sonette an Orpheus* (part 2, number 12). Sometimes we perceive a signal, but often we do not feel the alteration; we feel only the adverse wind, that which prevents us from entering into relations with another. Our hope, however, is expressed in the fact that it is not only words that rhyme but their content as well: "Wind" [wind] and "sind" [are] and, above all, "Zeichen" [signal] and "er-reichen" [attain].

In a superb letter (March 13, 1922), Rilke—in answer to a young man's questionings, summarizes once more what *art* is for him. He describes how young people should deal with the difficulties of the present, not by escaping into the external world but by turning toward deeper realms; how they should make the attempt "to weigh things with the carat of the heart." And then he explains to his young correspondent that

> it is not the ultimate intention of art to create more artists. It does not intend to call anyone to its ranks; indeed, it has always been my suspicion that art is not interested in having any effect at all. But insofar as its creations, emerging irrepressibly from an inexhaustible source, exist in their strangely silent and surpassable way among other objects, it could happen that involuntarily they somehow become exemplary for *every* human activity by virtue of their innate unselfishness, freedom, and intensity.[31]

Unselfishness, freedom, and intensity—an impressive triad that strikes us as a distant echo of that other one of freedom, equality, fraternity. Today freedom is a firm guarantee of our country's constitution; equality, a complicated problem, must be given further thought; the question of fraternity has not really been pursued. Is Rilke pointing out to us a path for the future when he speaks of unselfishness, freedom, and intensity?

Robert Walser
and His Publishers

I am not developing; perhaps I shall never put forth branches
and boughs. Some day a fragrance will emanate from my being
and my beginnings.

Robert Walser, Jakob von Gunten

THE SOLITARY

Few people are surprised when I give lectures on topics such as "Hesse and His Publishers," "Rilke and His
Publishers," "Bertolt Brecht and His Publishers." I
hope the public's curiosity will be aroused, on the other
hand, by the unfamiliarity of the topic, "Robert Walser
and His Publishers." For years now—for two decades,
to be exact—at the point in my lectures when I am
discussing what it is that motivates a writer to write, I
always quote the statement of one particular author,
prefacing it with the observation that the man who made
it is the greatest unknown author in the German language in this century. This statement was made by
Robert Walser and it reads: "It will be all over for me
the moment I stop writing."[1] We shall come back to this
statement, for it is essential to our topic.

The question immediately arises, who was this Robert
Walser? and the answer is a complicated one. In any
case, I am very fond of this author for whom the German language has created the special title *Dichter* (poet

or imaginative writer). After trying in vain for a long time, I finally obtained the rights to publish his works at Suhrkamp Verlag in 1976. The following anecdote is about my earliest attempt.

The first time I was in Switzerland after Peter Suhrkamp's death in March 1959, I wanted to call on Carl Seelig, the guardian of Robert Walser, who had died approximately two years previously in the sanitarium at Herisau. Seelig was Walser's literary executor as well, and I hoped to speak to him about the possibility of publishing Walser's works. But Seelig would not see me; he was annoyed with our firm because Peter Suhrkamp, like all the other German and Swiss publishers Seelig had turned to after 1945, had shied away from publishing Walser's works, regarding them as too great a risk. When I visited Hermann Hesse in Montagnola and told him that Seelig refused to see me, the Master exclaimed spontaneously, "He *has* to see you!" He got up, went to his study, and typed a letter to his friend Carl Seelig on his usual little sheet of stationery with its water-color illustration, requesting him in a friendly but very firm fashion to please see me, his publisher.

This meeting took place on my return trip to Germany. I can still see Carl Seelig, a clever and witty man of letters, with a mind of his own; a kind human being whose gentle and refined nature probably resembled that of Robert Walser, whom I never met in person. At that time I, too, joined the ranks of those publishers who made what was in a way the mistake of their lives. I made no promises that I would bring out Walser's complete works; I wasn't in a position to do so, for I was still too young and inexperienced a publisher to take on such a venture. Still, we did agree to a selection from Walser's works for which Walter Höllerer was to be responsible, and this volume appeared in 1960 in the

Bibliothek Suhrkamp. Three years later I again tried to get in touch with Seelig, but I received no answer; the good man had been fatally injured on February 15, 1962, when he fell while attempting to jump onto a moving streetcar at Bellevue Platz in Zurich. The question of the rights to Walser's works remained unresolved until the Carl Seelig Foundation was established; it then granted these rights to the Holle Verlag.

Who was this Robert Walser?

He was five years older than Franz Kafka, who admired those of Walser's writings that were known at the time. In an autobiographical sketch, Walser wrote: "Walser was born on April 15, 1878, in Biel in the Canton of Bern, the second youngest of eight children; he attended school until he was thirteen and thereafter learned the banking trade; left home at the age of seventeen, lived in Basel, where he worked for Von Speyer and Co., and in Stuttgart, where he found a job with the Union Deutsche Verlagsanstalt."

At the age of approximately fourteen he wrote the first piece we still possess, the scene "Der Teich" [The pond], which contains the statement, in Bern dialect: "I bi gärn elei. Do chöme eim d'Gedanken" [I like to be alone. That's when ideas come to you]. As a boy he read voraciously: "What I read took on the form of a species of nature for me. I began to read because life negated me whereas the books I read had the kindness to say yes to my inclinations, my character." *Someone who was always reading something.* He, "the most ardent of human beings inside," wanted to become an actor, but when he presented himself to Josef Kainz in Stuttgart, the great actor gave him no encouragement. When he was seventeen, he wrote to his sister, "The actor's profession is out . . . but, God willing, I shall become a great writer," and he did, over a span of thirty years. Then, in 1929, when he was fifty-one, he entered Waldau, the Cantonal mental hospital in Bern. Walser suffered the same fate as Friedrich Hölderlin, and what he wrote about Hölderlin is symptomatic and prophetic: "Hölderlin deemed it prudent, in other words, tactful, to lose his mind when he was thirty-nine." And again on the subject of Hölderlin: "Will the same thing happen to me?" It did, and he too was "tactful." In 1933 he was committed to the Herisau Sanitarium, where he remained until his death in 1956 and where he did no more writing. Carl Seelig recorded his conversations with Walser on the walks they took together; but *Wanderungen mit Robert Walser* [*Walks with Robert Walser*] is only now becoming recognized as a significant literary work displaying acute insights into the poet's craft and preserving conversations that in their intellectual scope recall those celebrated ones of Schiller, Goethe, Lessing, and Kleist.

Two statements by this man who wore the mask of a bourgeois, who was rich in modesty and a specialist in failure, give me food for thought: "No one is justified in acting toward me as if he knew me"; and, toward the end of his life, looking back: "There have always been conspiracies around me to fend off vermin like me. In a refined and arrogant fashion, people always warded off everything that didn't fit into their own world. I never dared to force myself into their world. I wouldn't even have had the courage to take a peek at it. And so I have lived my own life, on the periphery of bourgeois existence, and wasn't it best that way?"[2] This experience should give us something to think about, and not only in connection with the fate of Robert Walser.

Edited with loving care, the complete works—almost too weighty a label for Walser's delicate and gentle writing—were published in twelve good-sized volumes in 1976, and subsequently joined by a thirteenth containing the letters. The editor is Jochen Greven, the publishing house Kossodo Verlag AG (Anières/Geneva), and the project is financed by large Swiss foundations. This truly complete edition contains the turn-of-the-century novels—*Geschwister Tanner* [The Tanner children], *Jakob von Gunten,* and *Der Gehülfe* [*The Apprentice*]—as well as the tales, the stories, the prose phantasies, *Fritz Kochers Aufsätze* [Fritz Kocher's essays], the shorter works—*Poetenleben* [A poet's life], *Die Rose* [The rose], *Seeland;* masquerades, studies, sketches, dramolets, and poems. All of this has been provided with notes, commentaries, editorial annotations, detailed afterwords, careful indexes, and chronological biographical tables. The thirteen beautifully printed volumes, bound in expensive cloth, appeared in printings of from two to five thousand copies, at a retail price of between 35 and 40 Swiss francs. There is also an excellent biography of Walser written by a friend of Carl Seelig, Robert Mächler, who presents the poet's story with the help of first-hand documents. The works are thus finally here: enchanting, graceful, independent-minded, thought-provoking, often scurrilous, often serene in the face of disaster—these works with "their sudden eddies of irony and wit" that deal with the great topic of the lonely individual in the maelstrom of the masses, of the large cities, of technological civilization.

Robert Musil discusses Walser's *Geschichten* [Stories] in 1914, comparing them with Kafka's *Betrachtung* [Reflections] and *Heizer* [The stoker] and almost reproaching Kafka for having approximated Walser's tone too closely. "It seems to me," writes Musil, "that Walser's special style ought to remain just that and is not suited to stand at the forefront of a literary genre, and my discomfort with Kafka's first book, *Betrachtung,* is due to the fact that it gives the impression of being a special example of the type represented by Robert Walser in spite of having been written earlier than his *Geschichten.*" In 1929, Walter Benjamin admits him to the pantheon; Walser's characters, according to Benjamin, "are figures who have overcome madness. . . . If one wants to sum pu the heartening and uncanny element about them, one may say: they all are healed." Benjamin also produces *the* item of literary gossip about Walser when he states that "this apparently most playful of writers was a favorite author of the implacable Franz Kafka."[3] In our day, Walser's English translator, Christopher Middleton, compares him to the late Dylan Thomas; Martin Walser praises the unique qualities of this "gentle vagabond and great idler": "He brings himself into play in the gentlest manner, lets the world wash up against him and describes the resulting display of colors produced by the collision."[4]

His works are finally here, praised by great writers; it is rare for authors to praise one of their number with such unanimity. His works issue an invitation: take me and read. Why are there so few who do this? Why is Robert Walser not so well-known as the other great authors of the century—Kafka and Hesse and Rilke and Thomas Mann and Bertolt Brecht, a group to which he belongs? The lack of response to his work, the omissions of literary critics and the ignorance of literary scholars are certainly due in part to the special nature of this author's life. He was, in his own words, "the solitary," of whom he said, "It is uncertain whether he is sitting or standing." In any case, his popularity and impact depend upon the fate of his works, upon the history of their publication; it is this fact that confers significance on our topic, "Robert Walser and His Publishers."

''I BEGAN TO WRITE''

Walser's relation to the publishers of his day is an extremely interesting one. Only in good detective novels can the solution be divulged ahead of time. This principle permits us to summarize the case of Walser here: no other great twentieth-century writer in the German language had such varied contacts with the important publishers and publishing houses of his day as did this great neglected figure; no other author had, as did he, the misfortune that important publishers brought out one or two of his works and then dropped him from their lists: among them were Insel Verlag and Anton Kippenberg, Kurt Wolff, Bruno Cassirer, S. Fischer, and Ernst Rowohlt. It was also this experience that made Walser what he was: a great writer *and* an inmate of Herisau Sanitarium. Yet he could jest about his hopeless situation in 1926: in response to a survey made by the *Neue Zürcher Zeitung* he answered the question, "Are there neglected poets among us?" with "My publishers inform me that they are delighted with me."

Our investigation is based on five sources:

Robert Mächler's excellent and detailed biography, *Das Leben Robert Walsers* [Robert Walser's life]; the volume of 411 letters, edited by Jörg Schäfer with the assistance of Robert Mächler, that appeared in 1975 (this volume contains approximately four-fifths of those extant, but since we know that most of the letters have been lost or destroyed, the volume contains only a portion of Walser's correspondence); Carl Seelig's book, *Wanderungen mit Robert Walser;* the editorial annotations made by Jochen Greven in the appendixes of *Das Gesamtwerk* [The Complete Works]; and the Robert Walser Archive of the Carl Seelig Foundation in Zurich, i.e., the information supplied by Elio Fröhlich and the director of this archive, Katharina Kerr.[5]

On September 30, 1896, after stays in Biel, Basel, and Stuttgart, Walser arrived in Zurich, where—aside from trips to Berlin and Munich—he remained for ten years. He changed his residence seventeen times during this period, his job nine times: "For the pure enjoyment of quitting I have always quit jobs and official positions that, although they promised a career and the devil knows what else, would have killed me if I had stayed with them," he wrote in *Geschwister Tanner.* Toward the end of his Zurich years he worked in a special office (which had been opened in 1901 in the building "Zum Steinböcklin" on the Schipfe) where jobs were given to the unemployed. "Wherever I have been, I have soon moved on because I have not been content to let my youthful energies turn sour."

Mainly he worked as a "Commis," a clerk; this is the way he listed his employment on official documents. This position became the perennial object of his literary energies. Indeed, in describing the "Commis," Walser the writer was born; the figure of the clerk, whether conceived as a self-portrait or as the portrait of a colleague, appears repeatedly in his early books. *Fritz Kochers Aufsätze,* his first published book, contains variations on this figure. At that time, Walser began "to write little poems on small slips of paper": "I did this," we read in the essay "Ein junger Mensch" [A young person], "with an entirely calm, craftsman-like intention, but there was something secretive about it, and perhaps I began to write because I was poor and in need of a nice sideline so I could feel richer." And in the same work he continued, "Restlessness and uncertainty and the intimation of a strange fate may have led me to take up my pen in that situation to see if I could succeed in catching a reflection of myself." Here we have a very valuable example of an answer to that great question about the secret of creativity, about what it is that motivates the writer to write: restlessness, uncertainty, and the intimation of a strange fate—these are the distinguishing features in the psychography of this author.

He took his psychic make-up as seriously as he did his urge for expression. Writing was by no means an unconscious act for him; from the very beginning it was an act demanding the highest conscious concentration. We find a central and noteworthy piece of evidence for this in one of the four autobiographies he wrote in 1920, which are collected in the twelfth volume of the complete edition: "After the course of a year in Stuttgart, he wandered by way of Tübingen, Hechingen, Schaffhausen, etc. to Zurich, worked now in the insurance business, now in the banking business, lived in Außersihl as well as on the Zurichberg and wrote poems, in which connection it should be said *that he didn't do this on the side but for this purpose each time first quit his job, apparently in the belief that art is something great.*" With an attitude like this, with this intensity, Walser wrote his first poems, his lyrical prose, his lyrical dramolets. Writing was a kind of death for him; when he wrote, he had the overwhelming feeling that he was dying. The beauty of the stars, the moon, the night, the trees caused him pain. "My impressions," we read in the dramolet "Der Dichter" [The poet], which appeared in 1900 in *Die Insel,* "are arrows that wound me. My heart wishes to be wounded and my thoughts wish to be exhausted. I want to press the moon into a poem and the stars into one and mix myself among them. What should I do with feelings but let them twitch and die like fish in the sand of language? It will be all over for me the moment I stop writing, and I am glad of that. Good night!"

Between the ages of seventeen and twenty, Walser probably wrote approximately fifty poems and other lyrical works. After his twentieth birthday he wrote forty poems in a notebook and sent it to Josef Viktor

Widmann, the literary editor of the *Bund,* a Bern news-paper. Widmann was at that time the most highly re-garded literary critic in Switzerland. Since literary critics can seldom be said to foster new young talent, I am pleased to be able to cite this exceptional case: on May 8, 1898, Widmann published six poems by Robert Walser in the Sunday edition of the *Bund* under the heading "First Lyrics," but without mentioning the au-thor's name. He accompanied them with a friendly, slightly condescending introduction, expressing his joy that in Switzerland "happily quite frequently . . . new and original talents blossom," promising hope for the future. "For the twenty-year-old author, however, this early recognition is intended to be an incentive to de-velop his natural gifts to the level of masterful art through faithful work and diligence." The titles of these first six published poems are typical of Walser's work; they are "Helle" [Brightness], "Trüber Nachbar" [Sor-rowful neighbor], "Vor Schlafengehen" [Before going to sleep], "Ein Landschäftchen" [A little landscape], "Kein Ausweg" [No way out], and "Immer am Fenster" [Always at the window]. In these titles we can already see a foreshadowing of the themes and motifs of his later work: darkness and light, the sorrowful figure of his fellow man, the lover of landscapes, the dreamer and sleeper, the observer always standing at the window. And he who found no way out of his problematic life.

The publication of these poems had an important consequence. One of their readers was Franz Blei, the Austrian author, critic, essayist, and anthologist who was always so eager to discover new talent. He got the anonymous author's address from the *Bund* and paid him a visit. Blei and Walser have both described this meeting. Blei: "There was Walser: half traveling jour-neyman on the road, half page—a poet through and through." And Walser recalled his response to Blei's question, would he continue writing: "I shall scarcely have any other choice." Of course, Walser said, it would be a constant question of inspiration, and "isn't an apprentice clerk like me just as entitled to feel inspired as the next person?"

Walser also gave Blei a notebook containing some of his writings. Blei was a friend of Rudolf Alexander Schröder, Alfred Walter Heymel, and Otto Julius Bierbaum, who had been planning to start a periodical together since 1897; on September 1, 1899, the first issue of *Die Insel* came out, and in it were four poems by Walser. His prose pieces, dramolets, and additional poems kept appearing in subsequent issues in the company of other authors such as Schröder himself, Hugo von Hofmannsthal (who was also an early admirer of Walser's work), Scheerbart, Detlev von Liliencron, Richard Dehmel, Rainer Maria Rilke, Frank Wedekind, Max Dauthendey, and Henry van de Velde.

In his essay, *Aus den Münchner Anfängen des Insel Verlages*, Schröder had remarked on the great number of creative talents active around the turn of the century; among these new talents Schröder counted Jens Peter Jacobsen, Stefan George, Rilke, *and* Robert Walser, "who at that time, young like us, was a frequent guest in our group and in our journal." His poems, wrote Schröder, possessed "such density and daemonic quality and at the same time such delicacy and purity of expression that I don't know of anything in our language that measures up to them."[6] When Schröder wrote these words in 1935, he too was of the opinion that Robert Walser was a neglected author and that even in Switzerland, the Bern poet's native country, appropriate steps had not been taken to preserve his works. He quoted a poem by Walser in his essay (the only literary example he gives there) to call attention to this unknown and forgotten writer:

Und ging

Er schwenkte leise seinen Hut
Und ging, heißt es vom Wandersmann.
Er riß die Blätter vom dem Baum
Und ging, heißt es vom rauhen Herbst.
Sie teilte lächelnd Gnaden aus
Und ging, heißt's von der Majestät.
Es klopfte nächtlich an die Tür
Und ging, heißt es vom Herzeleid.
Er zeigte weinend auf sein Herz
Und ging, heißt es vom armen Mann.

And Went Away

He gently waved his hat
And went away, we hear of the wanderer.
It tore the leaves from the tree
And went away, we hear of the harsh autumn.
He smilingly distributed favors
And went away, we hear of His Majesty.
It knocked at the door in the night
And went away, we hear of heart's sorrow.
He pointed weeping to his heart
And went away, we hear of the poor man.

Die Insel was soon forced to cease publication for
financial reasons; in the last issue (September 1902),
however, there were two more stories by Walser: "Das
Genie" [The Genius], who proclaims at the queen's
banquet that he is "of a mind to overturn the world
tomorrow or the next day," and "Welt" [World], in
which total emancipation takes place: schoolchildren ar-
rest their teachers and girls force themselves on boys.
But then it all comes to nothing, and "with nothing we
too are no longer in a position to write something."

Walser stated in a letter (December 12, 1912, to

Rowohlt Verlag) that Schröder and Bierbaum had recommended him to Insel; Schröder had placed him in
contact with the man who was then head of that publishing house, Rudolf von Poellnitz.

INSEL: ROBERT WALSER'S
FIRST PUBLISHER

Among Walser's earliest letters is one dated January 6,
1902, from Berlin-Charlottenburg to "Dear Herr von
Poellnitz": "I am respectfully confirming my letter of
yesterday and am inquiring of you herewith in regard to
it whether you could give me a modest sum of money
(200 marks) in return for the delivery of my complete
literary works to date (dramas, prose, poems). At the
moment I am unfortunately in rather awkward financial
straits, which will certainly not last much longer."

This letter, Walser's first to a publisher, was characteristic. He offered his entire work up to that time,
asking a sum of money not that small in those days, and
mentioned his "awkward financial straits," which were
to accompany him for a lifetime. Poellnitz turned down
the request. This first rejection by a publisher affected
him deeply and immediately elicited a characteristic reaction: he picked up stakes, leaving Berlin and traveling
to Täuffelen, on the Lake of Biel, where his sister was a
teacher. He was very close to her all his life; *Geschwister
Tanner* provides eloquent testimony of this.

From the Lake of Biel he wrote to Widmann at the
Bund: "I would like to live in this area, that is, have the
means to live here. Couldn't you give me something to
write now, I mean a writing job, copying, etc. . . . In
Berlin, which I just left, my hopes of earning something
with my literary works were completely shattered."

We do not know how Widmann replied, but it can be
assumed that he encouraged Walser to continue writing
and said that he would be glad to publish additional

pieces in the *Bund*. Walser returned to Zurich to his lodgings on 23 Spiegelgasse, that famous street where Johann Caspar Lavater wrote the *Physiognomische Fragmente* [Physiognomic fragments] that so impressed Goethe, where Georg Büchner suffered and died, where Lenin later made plans for his revolution, and where the Cabaret Voltaire gave birth to the Dada movement in 1916. On March 23, 1902, a series of prose pieces that Walser had assembled, had "composed," began to appear in the *Bund*. In his introductory comments we read, "The boy who wrote these essays died shortly after leaving school."

Once again it was Franz Blei who gave encouragement to Walser, writing on November 3, 1903, "Why don't you send a collection of your finest poems, prose pieces, and your two verse dramas to Insel Verlag in Leipzig, 20 Lindenstraße, for a book?" Walser followed this advice, sending Poellnitz "a selection of works I find suitable for possible publication with Insel." He included the dramas "Die Knaben" [The boys], "Dichter" [Poets], "Aschenbrödel" [Cinderella], "Schneewittchen" [Snow White], a group of thirty to forty poems, and the prose work *Fritz Kochers Aufsätze*. Walser called Poellnitz's attention to this latter work in particular, calling it his "best prose." A short time later, in January 1904, Walser tried to convince Poellnitz to assign his brother, the artist Karl Walser, to illustrate the work; but Poellnitz did not reply, and again Blei intervened, advising Walser to turn to Heymel at Insel. Again Walser recommended *Fritz Kochers Aufsätze* and his brother, who would be glad to illustrate these "prose pieces" with "great love." Heymel sent this letter along to Poellnitz with the note, "am strongly in favor of a Walser book." That was the decisive factor. In May 1904, Walser received word from Insel that *Fritz Kochers Aufsätze* had been accepted for publication, and he immediately reacted like an author who knows exactly how his book should look.

A rapid succession of letters describes his wishes. "I find, moreover, that the larger and, consequently, the more opulent the book is when it appears in the world's marketplace, the more success it will have." The work, Walser's first published book and today a sought-after rarity, came out in November. On the left-hand side of the double title page we read: "Inhalt des Buches: Fritz Kochers Aufsätze: Der Commis: Der Maler: Der Wald: Elf Zeichnungen von Karl Walser" [Table of Contents: Fritz Kocher's Essays: The Clerk: The Painter: The Forest: Eleven Drawings by Karl Walser]; on the right-hand side: "Fritz Kochers Aufsätze: Mitgeteilt von Robert Walser: Bei Breitkopf & Härtel in Leipzig gedruckt (...compiled by Robert Walser: Printed by Breitkopf & Härtel in Leipzig). Karl Walser's eleven drawings are model illustrations of literary texts.

The book received two important reviews. One was the immediate response of Widmann:

Two years ago, when the extremely young Swiss poet named Robert Walser published his sketches in our Sunday paper, imitating the style of a gifted secondary-school pupil and pretending that they were the posthumous essays of a boy who had died at an early age, many readers shook their heads in disbelief and managed to forgive the editor for printing these pieces only by assuming that he himself believed in the existence of a "Fritz Kocher," who had died at an early age, and that he had perhaps considered it his pious duty not to withhold these jottings of a "certainly gifted boy" since they were pedagogically and psychologically interesting documents. But Robert Walser followed up *Fritz Kochers Aufsätze*—also in our Sunday paper—with individual sketches entitled

"Der Commis," "Der Maler," and "Der Wald," which he admitted being the author of and which closely resembled, in the studied simplicity of their diction, those fictitious essays. And the shaking of heads increased, those with fair curls and those with bristles like a toothbrush as well as those completely bald. But many readers were annoyed because, even though they found them 'absurd,' they couldn't help reading them to the end. There was something suggestive in Walser's way of letting his unusual thoughts roll without haste or emphasis, almost like gently gliding billiard balls on green felt. And a dreamlike magic enveloped the reader with an intimation of something beautiful that had just brushed past.[7]

A second reviewer of a special sort appeared on the scene, one who would accompany Robert Walser from then on: Hermann Hesse.[8] He wrote in the Sunday edition of the *Basler Nachrichten* (September 5, 1909), about Walser's "first slim volume, a coquettishly elegant thing with amusing drawings by his brother, Karl Walser":

At the time I bought it for its pretty, original appearance and read it on a little trip. . . . At first these remarkable, half-boyish essays seemed to be playful sketches and exercises in style by a rhetorically inclined young ironist. What was striking and fascinating about them was their studiedly careless, flowing tone, the delight in putting down light, pretty, charming sentences and clauses such as are found astonishingly seldom in German writers. There were also some observations on language in them, for example in a very amusing essay about the "Commis" the lines: "When he raises his pen, an efficient 'Commis' hesitates a few moments, as though to col-

lect his thoughts properly or as though to take aim
like a competent hunter. Then he lets fire, and the
letters, words, sentences fly as though across a
paradisical field, and each sentence has the graceful
quality of usually expressing a great deal. In matters
of correspondence the 'Commis' is a veritable rogue.
At a rapid pace he invents constructions that might
well astonish many learned professors."—In addition
to this coquettishness and loquaciousness, this playing with words and light irony, there emanates from
this first slim volume an occasional flash of love for all
objects, a flash of a true, beautiful human and artistic
love for all that exists, casting the warm, intimate light
of genuine poetry upon light, cool, bright pages of
eloquent prose.

One would think that such a strong reaction, such a
spontaneous reception, would pave the way for this
book's success: a favorable review by the most highly
regarded Swiss literary critic and the designation of
"genuine poetry" by the young author whose *Peter
Camenzind,* praised by Walther Rathenau, was a great
success and whose *Unterm Rad* [*Beneath the Wheel*] had
again made him a topic of discussion after Theodor
Heuss had acclaimed the novel for its demand that
youth have a right to youth. But how did things really
stand? How successful was this book, which contained
all the important features of Walser's later work: the
reflection of the author's inner world in *Fritz Kochers
Aufsätze,* the social perspective in "Der Commis," the
realm of art in "Der Maler," and Walser's hope, Nature,
in "Der Wald"? There was a first printing of 1,300
copies. Walser received an advance of 250 marks; his
brother refused to accept a share. A year later, Walser
learned the fate of his book: in response to a letter
(April 13, 1905) requesting an additional payment of

100 marks as agreed upon in the contract, the publisher answered that "only forty-seven copies have been sold so far!" Walser later reported, to the author of *Wanderungen,* that he never received this payment.

In the summer of 1905, Anton Kippenberg took over the firm. He was a man who had difficulty with contemporary literature and particularly with the writings of Robert Walser. Although Insel was supposed to follow up the first book with a second one containing poems and dramas, Kippenberg was not prepared to honor this part of the contract. He soon had Walser's first book remaindered; on one of their walks, Walser told Seelig that he had come upon such clearance copies in the Berlin department store Kaufhaus des Westens. Unfortunately, Insel Verlag was just one example of the way people around him were always, in Walser's words, "hatching plots" against him. The Swabian playwright Karl Vollmöller, born the same year as Walser and a protegé of Max Reinhardt, actively intrigued against Walser at Insel after the publication of *Fritz Kochers Aufsätze;* he once said to Walser, "You began as a 'Commis' and you'll always be a 'Commis.'"

The story of Walser's first association with a highly regarded publishing house is typical, one might even say "uncannily" typical. The author was received with initial enthusiasm, then the publisher was disenchanted when the book did not sell well; first the publisher had desired a connection, then he dropped it like a hot potato and was not even willing to honor his contract. In this first example of Walser's connections with a publisher, we can see how much a book's failure (especially a first book's) lowers the author in the publisher's opinion and how the impaired relationship between author and publisher cripples the author's productivity. As late as March 21, 1941, Walser—according to Seelig's reports in the *Wanderungen*—was still returning to this theme.

Walser told Seelig that Bruno Cassirer had urged him to write novellas "like Gottfried Keller," at which Walser broke out into peals of laughter. Then Walser said, "It is a real misfortune when, as happened to me, an author doesn't win recognition right away with his first book. Then every publisher feels entitled to dispense advice on how the author can become a success as quickly as possible. This seductive counsel has already *ruined* many a frail nature."[9] Walser did not allow himself to be seduced by such counsel, but his was indeed one of those frail natures that was ruined by lack of recognition.

BRUNO CASSIRER: "MY DEAR PUBLISHER"

In the spring of 1905, Walser went to Berlin for a third time. Now, in the wake of what he believed was the success of his first publication, he felt encouraged to embark on the experiment of being a free-lance writer. In the story "Zwei Männer" [Two men], he wrote:

> One day he fled a safe although insignificant position in life to devote himself completely to writing and its consequences. What he did was daring, if not foolhardy. An adventurous, bold, in a certain sense life-threatening act was being performed here. . . . Timidly enough he entered the dark, winding, dimly lighted, dubious street of artists and gypsies, sparsely populated with wandering minstrels; promising little that was good but much that was bad, it led to the realm of free-lance writing or independent poethood. . . . The spirit meant everything to him, material existence nothing any more. He could suddenly have laughed aloud, shouted with pure delight, run up and down with joy. How ardently, how passionately he loved the life that he was risking and placing in the balance. Involuntarily he

assumed a determined bearing, and with a happy expression and lively steps he continued along his way.

Walser did not yet suspect the failure of his first book and the consequences at Insel. In Berlin he lived with his brother Karl, who had three rooms, including a studio, on Kaiser-Friedrich-Straße in Charlottenburg. During this time, Karl Walser was winning more and more fame as an artist, illustrating works by Cervantes, Kleist, Hauff, E. T. A. Hoffmann, and—among contemporary authors—Hermann Hesse, Hugo von Hofmannsthal, and Christian Morgenstern. He frequently designed stage sets for Max Reinhardt and did frescos for the houses of the future foreign minister Walther Rathenau, the publisher Samuel Fischer, and the art dealer Paul Cassirer. (Walser described his brother's activities in one of his works, "Leben eines Malers" [Life of a painter], which Karl did not like at all.)

Geschwister Tanner

It was through his brother that Walser came into contact with the publisher Bruno Cassirer, a cousin of the art dealer Paul Cassirer. The correspondence with this publishing house is no longer extant; we must rely on double conjecture here. Karl Walser had told Bruno Cassirer about his brother and given him the manuscript of *Geschwister Tanner;* Cassirer handed it on to Christian Morgenstern, who had been an editor at Cassirer Verlag since 1903. Morgenstern didn't like the beginning of the story, but he was impressed by its concise form. He wrote a detailed and critical report, and at the conclusion of this "perhaps partly unwelcome letter" he wanted to say something positive as well, "that I have high, even the highest expectations of you as far as language is concerned." There is an extensive correspondence between Morgenstern and Walser; the two got along well together.

In the spring of 1907, Walser's first novel *Geschwister Tanner* was published by Bruno Cassirer. Again it was Hermann Hesse who called attention to this book in a review:

> This time I read Walser with a feeling of warm sympathy, no longer merely out of stylistic interest but fascinated by the nature of the poet himself, which at one moment seemed to flame up from the soul with one rapid stroke and then to be concealed half intentionally by cool gestures. Again I enjoyed the gentle, natural flow of the prose, of the sort usually held in such low regard by German writers; again I found delightfully amusing things and passionately moving ones side by side, and again I was intensely annoyed by a certain carelessness and rudeness. . . . I became so fond of the book that I had to ponder long upon its virtues and failings.

Walser remained in Berlin until September 1905. He stayed in Upper Silesia from October 1905 until January 1906; we shall come back to these four months later. In early January he was back in Berlin, where disappointment awaited him at Insel. Once again, after the relatively good reception given *Geschwister Tanner,* Heymel approached him and asked him to submit another manuscript to Insel. On February 1, 1908, he again received a rejection, this time dictated by Kippenberg. It was a collection of stories and fairy tales that Kippenberg wrote him about: "But then I also consider the things too uneven in quality to advise you to publish them together in book form. The short sketches in particular—those that have appeared in *Die Insel* as well as the new ones—are in part too lightweight." This judgment, which must be described as a classic lack of understanding, accompanied Walser from then on.

Although Heymel had also advocated the publication

of Walser's poems (Walser described the S. Fischer Almanac to Heymel in a letter of March 1907 as a model for a book of verse), Kippenberg's view prevailed at Insel. In the fall of 1906, Walser wrote a second novel, which was never published and whose manuscript no longer exists. In January 1907 there were reports of plans for additional novels that never materialized.

Der Gehülfe [The apprentice]

In June and July of 1907, however, within the space of six weeks, he wrote a novel that was to bear the title *Der Gehülfe.* In the meantime he had left his brother and moved into a place of his own; in the late prose work, "Eine Art Novelle" [A kind of novella], we read:

> At that time I had rented an apartment, which may not have been very expensive but nevertheless was relatively very pleasant and attractive, in order to attempt to write a book. In the beginning I had a hard time with my attempts. After approximately a month had gone by, certain circumstances put me in the right frame of mind so that, in quite a short time, a novel flowed from my pen that one publisher turned down but that another one took up into the framework of his business enterprise, seemingly with the greatest pleasure.

We know the story of these two publishing firms from remarks recorded by Carl Seelig in *Wanderungen.* The Scherl Verlag in Berlin—publishers of the family periodical *Die Woche* and, after 1904, of *Gartenlaube*—had invited Walser to take part in a novel-writing competition. This had given him the impetus to write his novel quickly, and he submitted it along with the audacious demand for payment of 8,000 marks. The manuscript was sent back to him by return mail with no ac-

companying letter, whereupon Walser went to the publisher's office and asked for an explanation. The head of
the firm mentioned the impossibility of the sum involved whereupon he was told that he was "a camel" and
didn't understand anything about literature.

Two episodes in Walser's life provided material for
Der Gehülfe. In late July 1903, he took a job as apprentice in Wädenwil near Zurich. His employer was a
thirty-two-year-old mechanical engineer by the name of
Dubler who had his inventions patented by the Swiss
government and ended up in bankruptcy. Since Dubler
allegedly never paid Walser any wages, the writer left
Wädenswil in early 1904 and returned to Zurich.

The second incident goes back to those four months
in the year 1905 mentioned earlier. It was then that
Walser took a course for domestic servants and accepted
employment as a footman in Dambrau Castle in Upper
Silesia. In the tale "Tobold" and in the prose piece "Ein
Lakei" [A footman] he describes "Monsieur Robert,"
who had to serve at table in a dress coat with gleaming
gold buttons and in patent-leather pumps. The castle
itself is described like something out of a fairy tale: "All
the rooms were like magic rooms, the park was a magic
park, and I myself, with my soft, cautious, and discreet
lamplight, felt like Aladdin with his magic or miraculous
lamp." But Monsieur Robert also knew that "the
ridiculous thing was that, along with being a footman, he
was writing on the side." Of course Walser tried to con-
ceal his literary activity from the people in the castle; he
asked Insel Verlag to use plain envelopes for the letters
they sent him there.

In his biography, Robert Mächler reproduced a letter
from Walser dated December 14, 1920, in which he
describes an accompanying photograph of a turreted
building set in a garden: "Here you see the 'Villa zum
Abendstern' as it still exists today in Wädenswil on the

Lake of Zurich. I once entered the household as a servant, and this is where the Tobler family lived and this is where that modest novel published by Bruno Cassirer, which really isn't a novel at all but only a scene from every-day Swiss life, takes place."[10] Walser relates that he based *Der Gehülfe* completely on real life, embellishing it with very few fictitious or imaginary details. "*Der Gehülfe* is a realistic novel through and through. I had to invent almost nothing. Life took care of that for me."[11] But here, too, the artistic process was decisive, for—as he later reported in the prose piece "Walser über Walser" [Walser on Walser]—he had no idea, when he was actually Dubler's apprentice, "that out of this bit of experience a 'realistic novel' would come into being—in other words, that an actual activity would lead to a literary one."

The manuscript of the novel, consisting of 197 oversized sheets completely covered with writing, has been preserved, thanks to fortunate circumstances. It shows that this novel was indeed written at one stroke; compared with other works of Walser, it contains remarkably few and only minor corrections and excisions.

Der Gehülfe appeared in May 1908 with a drawing in color by Karl Walser on the cover. "And then the cover for *Der Gehülfe:* this garden wall made of amusing, ironic bricks, this wall that I believed I personally ought to help to draw, possessed something of a smiling, all-too-smiling nature. The figure of the apprentice with an umbrella held over his head and hat looked almost comical. Perhaps it would have been better if I had never laid a hand on such immaculate bricks. Perhaps it was in punishment that the good book, otherwise certainly quite attractive, had no success, and I feel downright sorry for my dear publisher in retrospect when I think of how he became more and more taciturn toward me and toward himself."[12]

It is hard to understand why Walser stressed failure in this particular case, for of all his books this novel was the most successful: Bruno Cassirer issued three printings (the second one still in 1908, the third in 1909), each consisting of a thousand copies. The book was reprinted in 1936 by the Schweizer Bücherfreunde [Swiss book lovers] of St. Gallen, in 1953 in Carl Seelig's volume of selections, *Dichtungen in Prosa* [Poems in prose], and subsequently by a book club and in a paperback edition.

Nor was there any lack of a highly positive reception. Josef Viktor Widmann compared "Robert Walser's Swiss novel" with the works of Gottfried Keller. One of the characteristics of the book, according to Widmann, "is the secret laughter of its author as he circles around his characters, their domesticity, and at the same time around the reader." Later, Hermann Hesse wrote in the *Neue Zürcher Zeitung* (August 9, 1936):

> Although it is full of the atmosphere of the beginning of the century, this tale immediately wins us over with the timeless grace of its tone, with the delicately and spontaneously playful magic with which it transports everyday life into the sphere of enchantment and mystery. . . . *Der Gehülfe*, like all of Walser's work, is not free of frivolity. . . . This frivolity, this taking delight in the aesthetic even when it becomes ethically problematic, is not only a comfortable avoidance of moral issues, however; it is also a modest and warm-hearted refusal to pass judgment or to sermonize; here and there, behind the appearance of frivolity an aestheticism becomes visible which is no longer playful but genuine, an attitude which affirms life in its totality because as a drama it is splendid and beautiful as soon as we regard it without passion.

Another Swiss writer, Albin Zollinger, saw things

differently: "I have found that for me Walser's indescribable magic derives in the last analysis from his pedantic integrity in seeing and saying." He speaks of a certain "verism" in Walser's case:

> A fanaticism for truth in the depths of the dream world. With somnambulistic directness and assurance, an atmospheric landscape is created; in its psychological aspects we recognize ourselves, in its geography our native land—the novel describes the slow decline of a bourgeois family; the way Walser treats this process is—like, by the way, his skill in characterization as well—nothing short of masterful. . . . With the most economical symbolic means he knows how to intensify the mood of misfortune to the point that it becomes demonic. And at the same time: what a conscious technique of parallelism, of repetition, of motion in a circle—or more correctly expressed, motion in a spiral! . . . The apprehensive reader always thinks he knows what is going to happen, but the author always surprises him, and it always turns out that the author's plot is more in accordance with probability.

More and more, I myself see in this apprentice Joseph Marti a figure of our times. The novel's quality of a Swiss idyll strikes me as being only superficial and at bottom ominous. Upheavals are foreshadowed in the book: "All in all it was a picture of the twentieth century," as we read in the novel. That hits the mark, for as the author himself said, he was a "detector of decline" who recognized the signs of disintegration of this society. His book only appears on the surface to be artless; in reality, forms are dissolved as they are in Kafka, in James Joyce. Werner Weber has correctly observed that "the openness of the form" corresponds to the open, homeless nature of the atmosphere and factual details of the novel. At that time the reader was not yet in a position to recognize the "seismographic character" of this work, for indeed *Der Gehülfe* does have this character, pointing to what was, what is, and what one day will be. Walser expresses it in these words: "Yes, poets often have incredibly long snouts with which they feel out the future. They scent coming events the way pigs do mushrooms." Or: "World history is prophetically announced from the mouth of the poet of genius."[13] We are experiencing in our day the fulfillment of Walser's predictions seventy years after they were made.

Jakob von Gunten

Probably inspired by the three small printings of *Der Gehülfe,* Bruno Cassirer brought out a volume of poems by Walser before the third novel, which appeared later in that same year. It was a beautiful edition, for bibliophiles, of three hundred numbered copies bound in handmade paper and illustrated with sixteen etchings by Karl Walser. We have no information as to how this volume, sold at a subscription price of 30 marks, was received by the public.

The third novel, *Jakob von Gunten,* was written in 1908 and published by Cassirer in the spring of 1909. We know nothing about the circumstances of its composition, for there are no letters or documents from this period, and the manuscript has disappeared. The fact that *Der Gehülfe* had had three printings and that short pieces by Walser were appearing in the leading German periodicals gave cause to hope for the success of this fifth book. But the expected success did not occur. The first printing sold very slowly; thereafter the book was unavailable for over thirty years. It was not reprinted until 1950.

Reaction to *Jakob von Gunten* was mixed, even among Walser's friends. It was later learned that Kafka called it "a good book," and Max Brod always claimed that it had been Kafka's favorite book. Hermann Hesse again had praise for Walser:

> Walser's new book, *Jakob von Gunten,* has just arrived. It tells the old story: Jakob is Kocher, is Tanner, is the apprentice Marti, is Robert Walser himself. The tone, too, is the same. Again this sly delight in the fact that one can observe the world contemplatively and at the same time perceive the unnecessary and luxurious aspects of this activity.... The diary form reflects the need for confession of this poet, who often reminds us of Knut Hamsun in the way he repeatedly circles around the dark places in his own nature, almost like a criminal. What should actually be taken for granted in a poet but usually can't be, originality of expression and candor in his personal demeanor—this Walser has.

But Hesse's was the only positive voice. The critical reactions multiplied: even his mentor, Josef Viktor Widmann, was baffled by the novel. And Josef Hofmiller polemicized vehemently: "I could make even less of Robert Walser's latest novel than I could of last year's. Such effete and insipid scribbling at random is unendurable."[14]

Jakob von Gunten turned out to be a great disappointment for its author, alienating him from his friends. The book disappeared from the bookstores, receiving no attention either from the public or the literati—and to think of all the things there were to discover in it! Marthe Robert, the French translator of the novel, points out its fairy-tale structure: she sees Jakob as the prince, who, disguised or enchanted, must travel far and wide and undergo various trials. And the Benjamenta Institute, described in the novel as the scene of these trials, takes on mythical qualities. One could also trace the biblical motifs, e.g., the rich youth who becomes the helper of the poor. This novel in diary form is also a Bildungsroman, the Benjamenta Institute a kind of "Pedagogical Province." Robert Mächler mentions a high-school student (the future writer Albert Steffen) who visited Walser on October 30, 1907: "A large old-fashioned copy of Goethe's *Wilhelm Meister* lay on the table." It was open and quite obviously much used. "Walser spoke about Goethe's style, and I gathered that he was studying *Wilhelm Meisters Wanderjahre* [*Wilhelm Meister's Travels*], not only for its content but also for its form. It served him as a model that he referred to again and again." The reference to *Wilhelm Meister* is instructive; like Goethe in that work, Walser was ahead of his time in lamenting the modern world's sterile mechanization, commercialization, and decline in spiritual values. Today we can well understand his reference to his Institute as "the ante-chamber of life."

Walser's relationship with the two Cassirers inevitably suffered as a result of the fate of his novel. In 1907, Bruno Cassirer had wanted to pay for a trip to India, but Walser turned the offer down. Later it was S. Fischer who asked him "to go to Poland and write a book about it," but this offer was turned down as well. Fischer persevered and this time offered him a trip to Turkey, whereupon Walser responded, "Why do writers have to travel as long as they have imagination?" In one of his prose pieces Walser wondered, "Does Nature go abroad?" He told Seelig, "Yes, only the journey to oneself is important!" Another time, Paul Cassirer invited him on a balloon trip from Berlin to Königsberg (Walser described the trip in an essay and to Seelig). But then relations between the two broke off. (Walser had also had a falling out with Christian Morgenstern because of the latter's criticism of his book.) In 1912, Bruno Cassirer refused to advance 300 marks that Walser had requested for some new stories; this was followed by a further rebuff: Max Slevogt, someone who really had no cause, once made fun of Walser when they were sitting together at a table with Count Kalckreuth and Paul Cassirer, saying that his books were all failures and all of them a bore to the public. And he advised Walser to become a "Stendhalien." What was he to answer? Walser wondered in retrospect: "There I sat in all my failure and had to agree with him."[15]

There is very little documentation of the period between 1909 and November 1912. We must deduce Walser's condition and the events of his life in Berlin from the few reports of his friends, from his reflections and poetic works, and from his later conversations with Seelig. It was a period of increasing distress for him: he was described as "destitute" by Fega Frisch, who visited him. He had no money, but for two years "a kind woman" looked after him. He was especially offended by suggestions from publishers and editors that he write like Gottfried Keller. Relations with his brother were strained and reached their lowest point when Karl's wife advised him to write a suitable love story. Nothing came of his efforts to establish new connections with publishers. An example of this was his contact with Georg Müller in Munich: at Müller's request, Walser sent him his *Kleine Dichtungen* [Short poetic works] and received an advance of 300 marks, but then Müller decided not to publish the work after all. Walser later wrote to Rowohlt Verlag (December 10, 1922): "Müller didn't show any real desire to pursue the matter, which strikes me as a great wrong." Later, in 1925, he wrote, in a reflection entitled "Über eine Art Duell" [On a duel of sorts], that he had written six novels in Berlin, "three of which I felt it necessary to tear up." Morgenstern must have known at least one of these novels and spoken critically of it. Mächler remarks, "According to his brother, the reason for these destructive acts was not so much self-criticism as the unsuccessful search for a publisher." Anyone who understands Robert Walser's psychology will take his brother's testimony seriously.

He described the mood of the last days in Berlin in his reflection entitled "Heimkehr im Schnee" [Coming home in the snow, 1917]: he had made mistakes, we read there, he had wanted a great deal that could not be attained. "Weakness and exhaustion set in: . . . futile exertion made me more or less ill." But there were also people who encouraged him to return to "the lighted stage" and to seek "satisfaction in joyful, extravagant creativity." Walser decided to return to Switzerland: "I was optimistic about the future as never before, although I was engaged in a humiliating retreat. I did not consider myself defeated in any way, however; rather, I had the bright idea of calling myself a conquerer."

After a short side trip to his sister Lisa's that was to bear fruit later—there he met his future friend, Frieda Mermet—he returned in March of 1913 to Biel, where he was to spend the next seven years.

ERNST ROWOHLT AND KURT WOLFF

It was when he was still in Berlin, during the second half of 1912, that Walser must have met the publisher Ernst Rowohlt through his brother Karl and arranged for the publication of the essays and reflections he had written there. Those who know Rowohlt's first publications will be surprised at this arrangement; the prose Walser had written during his difficult Berlin period could not have been to Rowohlt's taste. There is no longer any documentation of this initial contact, for Walser's extant letters don't begin until after Rowohlt had left the firm.

Ernst Rowohlt, a native of Bremen, had founded the

E. Rowohlt Verlag Paris-Leipzig in 1908, but in the beginning the firm existed more in the publisher's imagination than in reality. It wasn't registered until June 30, 1910, and with an important addition: a silent partner by the name of Kurt Wolff, who probably contributed financially to the enterprise. The alliance between the vital, highly dynamic, inventive bon vivant Ernst Rowohlt and the sensitive, reserved, cultivated aesthete Kurt Wolff could not last, and their plan to have the one, Kurt Wolff, think about literature and the other about business was doomed to failure, since a publisher's responsibility is ultimately indivisible. The last of their disputes, stretching over a period of three years, concerned Franz Werfel's manuscript "Der Weltfreund" [The world's friend], which Rowohlt wanted to publish and Wolff to reject. The rift was such a deep one that their lawyer always had to speak with each partner separately. Wolff, man of the world and more accomplished, was the stronger of the two, and on November 1, 1912, Rowohlt was forced to leave the firm that bore his name with a settlement of 15,000 marks. Rowohlt Verlag had had a meteoric rise that came to an end when Wolff officially registered the Kurt Wolff Verlag on February 15, 1913.

These events led to another bitter disappointment for Walser: he had found a publisher who made him promises, and when he tried to collect on these promises, only the firm remained—the publisher himself was gone. The first letters Walser sent to Rowohlt Verlag while he was still in Berlin-Charlottenburg have a brusque tone: "Dear Sir: The letters you write me are quite remarkable, and they sound full of scorn and mockery to me. You cannot expect me to acknowledge the receipt of a sum of money I have not received. I don't know what I am to think. In any case, I find it necessary to point out to you that not one penny from you has

reached me to date. Meanwhile I remain respectfully. . . ."—7 November, 1912.

Later that month, Rowohlt Verlag sent him samples
of type for a volume of essays, asking him at the same
time to make as few corrections as possible in the
proofs. Walser again expressed himself in no uncertain
manner:

> I am in complete agreement with your letter of yes-
> terday insofar as I will not make stylistic corrections,
> which is something I wanted to tell you earlier. The
> text can therefore be printed as it stands. The pieces
> can be arranged in the order given in the table of
> contents I sent you. I find the type specimen you
> kindly sent me quite good. It strikes me, however, as
> a little too heavy and large. I would prefer to have the
> letters smaller and lighter. . . . I agree to the gothic
> type, only I like to imagine its appearance as airier,
> softer! Perhaps you would be kind enough to prepare
> another sample."—26 November 1912

On December 10, Walser offered Rowohlt two
books: *Kleine Geschichten* [Little stories], with illustrations by Karl Walser, and two comedies in verse,
Aschenbrödel" and "Schneewittchen," also designed by
Karl Walser. The author requested 1,500 marks for his
brother and a 600-mark advance for himself, half of
which was to go to the publisher Georg Müller, who had
advanced 300 marks for *Kleine Geschichten*. Rowohlt
agreed and was willing to publish these two volumes in
addition to the essays.

For a short time, Georg Müller caused problems:

> His letters to me are a mixture of irascibility and
> abjectness. He is a little furious, and we can be flat-
> tered by that. He's worked up, but he obviously feels
> himself in the wrong. Right is where the contract is.

The belated advance of 300 marks he rushed to me I have returned to him, i.e., to his representative in Leipzig; please make a note of this. To throw money at someone who doesn't ask for it is stupid and cruel. Müller's behavior in this matter is really low. I don't like the man and I am glad to be free of him.—Walser to Rowohlt, 22 December 1912.

In a postscript to this letter, Walser referred to the advance again: "These 300 marks are ridiculous and absolutely do not in any way affect the contractual agreement we have reached. This money says: Müller has a crass way of doing business."

I have cited these passages so extensively because they are characteristic of Walser. On the one hand he is constantly in financial straits and needs money; on the other hand, his need to have a book published is more important than the payment of advances.

For the rest, we see as always his careful attention to the format and design of the book. He again asked for the longish format that he had referred to in a pencilled note in which he said he found "that the longer form looks more elegant, more distinguished." And the paper: he and his brother were in favor of a "relatively thin and smooth one. Perhaps you would be kind enough to send us samples." He devoted a great deal of attention to the plans for the three books Rowohlt had agreed to publish; he didn't want to submit any more contributions to newspapers or periodicals. From Biel, he wrote to Wilhelm Schäfer (March 1914): "In this way I am breaking off all connections with newspapers for a while for political and professional as well as economic and artistic reasons and am again writing quietly and, I might say, modestly for my secret desk drawer. I must also strive to attain something great again. . . . I mean, from time to time the poet must have his head completely in darkness, in the realm of mystery."

The realm of mystery: Walser felt inwardly ill; he had returned to Biel without any real feeling of confidence, for he felt hostile and alienated from his surroundings. Now, he wrote in his prose piece "Flaubert," he was again living where his life had begun, he was feeling at home there once more because he had felt that way before, and it pleased him that this was happening; the renewal of something that used to be was like reentering a house. Thus, Walser felt himself recovering in Biel, where he lived with his eighty-year-old father until the latter's death on February 9, 1914. In August, after World War I broke out, Walser had to join the army and was assigned to a battalion of militia on border duty in the Jura mountains and in Valais. His prose sketches "Der Soldat" [The soldier] and "Beim Militär" [In the service] bear a resemblance to the book Max Frisch wrote while a soldier: "How much does a soldier have to think about all day long? In order for the thing called militarism to work, he is to think about absolutely nothing at all or else purposely little."

Meanwhile, Walser lived in Biel on its Lake. "Every day for eight years I sat myself down at the same place and for that same length of time refused to be an agreeable citizen." In November 1912, Walser sent Rowohlt the manuscript of his essays, assembled from copies of the original printings (Franz Blei probably had a hand in these renewed negotiations with the firm), and the book appeared in the spring of 1913 under the imprimatur of Kurt Wolff. Walser had not been informed of the changes the firm had undergone. *Geschichten,* which appeared in 1914, was also published under the imprint Kurt Wolff.

Walser's next book was *Kleine Dichtungen,* a collection of lovely prose pieces whose themes are drawn from his Biel surroundings; here the world is presented in idyllic terms, but it is an idyll that keeps leading to the abyss.

The collection was originally put together for Wilhelm Schäfer, who presented it to the Frauenbund zur Ehrung rheinländischer Dichter [Women's league honoring Rheinland poets]; with the recommendations of Wilhelm Schäfer and Hermann Hesse, Walser received the League's award. The head of the Frauenbund was Ida Schöller, a leading art collector and the wife of a Düren manufacturer. Carl Seelig mentions that Walser kept the money from the award—which was the only prize for literature he received until 1955, when he won the Award of the Schweizerische Schillerstiftung [Swiss Schiller Institute]—in the Düren bank, where it was later eaten up by inflation. The first edition of around one thousand copies of *Kleine Dichtungen* was printed for the Frauenbund by Kurt Wolff; the author had to autograph each of the thousand copies, as did Karl Walser, who contributed drawings for the cover and title page of the first edition. In 1915, the first Kurt Wolff edition, described as the second edition, appeared.

Walser's association with Wolff was never a very active one. Kurt Pinthus, Wolff's literary adviser for many years, had a high regard for *Kleine Dichtungen,* it is true, for he wrote: "Here everything that is heavy and tragic and problematical has disappeared from life; perfection and exuberance, poverty and revelry merge into a sweet harmony undisturbed by ugliness or fanfares."[16] But the book was not a success, and although it had not been particularly costly for Wolff (the plates had been paid for by the Frauenbund), he could not be persuaded to bring out any more books by Walser. On May 10, 1918, Walser again wrote to Kurt Wolff Verlag:

I have just completed a new book of prose, "Kammermusik" [Chamber music], in which I have woven twenty-seven pieces together with great care. . . . I believe I can say that the book presents a compact, rounded, and pleasing whole . . . . I flatter myself that I can very seriously offer you "Kammermusik" for publication, for I consider the book to be one of my best. . . . These twenty-seven pieces deal with matters of the mind, with humanity, humor, education, visionary concerns, and I am led to hope that each individual work has its own visible, completely self-contained form and its own special nature. The condition I set is that the firm, if it should want to publish the book, pay the author 500 marks when the contract is signed.

The offer was not accepted, nor does the firms published correspondence reveal any further communication. Neither Wolff nor the later historians of Kurt Wolff Verlag recognized Robert Walser as a significant figure: Bernhard Zeller, for instance, surveying the firm's list, wrote that Kafka, Heym, Trakl, Stadler, Werfel, Ernst Blass, Sternheim, Schickele, Heinrich Mann, and Karl Kraus were "roughly the authors of Kurt Wolff Verlag who are still of importance today."[17] The fact that Rober Walser was missing from this 1966 list is as regrettable as it is characteristic.

THE PRODUCTIVE PERIOD IN BIEL

Walser's years in Biel had really been a time of recovery for him although his financial situation wasn't very cheering. He sent an application for a loan to the Schweizerische Hülfs- und Creditorengenossenschaft für Rußland [Swiss Assistance and Creditors' Union for Russia] in Geneva, which was supposed to give financial support to Swiss citizens abroad when possible. Walser explained that he needed money not only because he wanted to finish a book but also because he wanted to put his "entire poetic production into proper order." He had the impression that he had written his best works during the period around 1920. In April 1921 he wrote to Frieda Mermet: "Last summer I . . . wrote far and away my best things, I hope to be able to publish them this year. I will never regret having spent such a long time in Biel. First of all, it was a splendid place to live, and secondly, it has been for me a way-station in my professional and human development."

Two unusual aspects of this period should be mentioned. A friend of his, the writer Emil Schibli, wrote, in "Erinnerungen an Robert Walser" [Reminiscences of Robert Walser] that in order to provide Walser with more income, he arranged for Walser to give a reading at the Hottingen Reading Club in November 1920. Walser went from Biel to Zurich on foot for the event. On the day of the reading, the president of the Club, Hans Bodmer, asked him to read a sample piece, whereupon Bodmer found that Walser couldn't read aloud at all and asked the editor of the *Neue Zürcher Zeitung,* Franz Trog, to read in Walser's place, which he did. An announcement was made to the audience that evening that Robert Walser was ill. How humiliating for the writer sitting in the first row!

Up until the Biel period, Walser had always submitted his first drafts for publication without making any corrections in them. Then he developed a new method, which he described in the reflection "Bleistiftskizze" [Pencil sketch]:

> You see, one day I found that it made me nervous to start right in with pen; to reassure myself, I started using pencil, which of course meant a roundabout way, an added effort. Since for me, however, this effort appeared to a certain extent like pleasure, it seemed to me I became healthy in the process. Each time a smile of contentment entered my soul and also something like a smile of cozy self-derision because I could see myself proceeding with my writing in such a carefully circumspect way. It seemed to me, among

other things, that I was able to work more in a dreamlike state, more peacefully, comfortably, thoughtfully with the pencil; I believed the way of working just described was developing into a strange kind of happiness for me.

Carl Seelig spoke of more than 500 pages of extant specimens of this "pencil system"; these pages are covered with tiny, seemingly illegible lines of handwriting. In editing the complete edition, Jochen Greven worked with this minute script in an exemplary manner, discovering that it was not written in code after all but in an ingeniously run-together German handwriting, a kind of private shorthand. With the adoption of this method, Walser also changed the way he worked on his manuscripts; before submitting his next books for publication, he thoroughly revised and reworked his texts.

In late August of 1916, Rascher Verlag in Zurich approached Walser for a contribution to a series of booklets entitled Schriften für Schweizer Art und Kunst [Writings in Swiss culture and art]. The publisher wanted a novella. On August 30, Walser replied that he would be delighted to write something suitable for the series; "it will of course be something that has not been printed before." Then he stated the fee he wanted: 50 francs per sheet, with a small type page; he expected the work to run to three to four sheets. On October 5 he seemed to be in sight of the "pleasant possibility" and sent Rascher an eighteen-page work with the title *Prosastücke* [Prose pieces]. He wanted to have these pieces treated with care and above all published as quickly as possible. He was especially concerned about the faithful reproduction of his texts:

In my opinion the little book will make a good impression in general, and the contents will not fail to make an impact. I can say with firm conviction that I consider this present work I am entrusting to you to be good, which is the reason I am offering it to you with full confidence. Each individual piece has been written with great diligence and with the most painstaking care, and I have gone to great effort to produce something of superior value for you. The pieces are partly serious, partly humorous in nature; they are all of a decidedly high level of quality, I am convinced. (*Briefe* [Geneva, 1975], p. 96)

Karl Walser again designed the cover of the booklet, which appeared in November 1916.

Rascher Verlag had special hopes for its series, Schriften für Schweizer Art und Kunst: "With this title the undersigned firm is publishing a collection of writings in paper or hard-back form that treat primarily those national questions arousing the greatest interest today." Only in a very loose sense did Walser's pieces fit in here. For the author himself they had another significance anyway, because it was the first collection of prose pieces that were newly written and not previously published. The selection includes a number of Walser's different themes and motifs and an especially large variety of the typical Walser forms: the anecdote, the moralizing tale, the linguistically playful humoresque, fairy-tale-like parables, reminiscences, and fantasies. We have to agree with the author, who felt he had produced something of superior value and had also attained a decidedly high level of quality in all the pieces.

A year later (April 1917), a work completed in September 1916, *Der Spaziergang [The Walk]* was published by Verlag Huber & Co. in Frauenfeld. This, too, was a collection, and it bore the subtitle *Studien und Novellen* (Studies and novellas). In his accompanying letter (March 3), Walser used words already familiar to us: "What I am offering your firm herewith is to have the title *Studien und Novellen* and represents—I may be so bold as to say—a fine and faithful piece of diligence and patience." He went on to tell Huber Verlag that he had sent A. Francke Verlag in Bern another selection of short prose, but it was not to appear until Easter "so that there might be sufficient time between the two publications." On the contrary, this was a very short space of time indeed.

It is not possible to reconstruct the story behind the third collection (written during this time, it appeared in April 1917), because all the correspondence with Francke has been lost. The prose pieces of this period resemble one another; they all reveal the delicacy of touch typical of Walser, who fashioned his playful poetry from a random allusion, from an insignificant motif.

THE LAST BOOK PUBLICATIONS
PRIOR TO 1933

Walser's last three prose collections (out of a total of nine) comprised works from the years 1915 to 1924. The first of these, *Poetenleben,* appeared in November 1917 with the imprint "1918 im Verlag von Huber & Co., Frauenfeld und Leipzig"; the second collection, *Seeland,* with the imprint "1919 erst 1920 im Rascher Verlag Zürich"; the third, Walser's last book, *Die Rose,* was published by Wolff in 1925.

Poetenleben

Huber Verlag had selected only the longish prose piece "Der Spaziergang" from the manuscript bearing the same title; it was impossible to reach an agreement about the other studies and novellas referred to in the subtitle. Walser withdrew them but wrote to the publisher from Biel on May 28, 1917: "Very honored Sir" (this form of address is used in all the letters to Huber Verlag that have been preserved. "Highly honored Sir" was used just once, but no name was ever mentioned, which indicates that there was no personal contact with a member of the firm):

> I have just finished writing a new, tightly constructed book, fifty-five pages of manuscript, twenty-five individual prose pieces, among them "Maria." The book has the title *Poetenleben,* is in my opinion the best, the cheeriest, the richest in poetry of all my books so far and with a small, elegant type page will come to approximately 200 printed pages. I was careful to select only narrative pieces about poets, which is why the whole thing reads like a romantic story. All the pieces have been rewritten in order to give you the most compact form as well as the most pleasing language possible. I am prepared to give you the book for a fee of 500 francs for the first printing. Payment as soon as it appears. Publication as soon as possible, that is, of course, this year. Are you interested? And if yes, are you willing to decide upon acceptance or the opposite within ten days?

In conclusion, Walser mentioned again that this book was "especially dear in personal terms." For this reason the *Studien* should come later. "The *Studien* will perhaps have more significance, *Poetenleben* will probably have more charm." Huber Verlag reacted positively, accepted the book, and said it would like to publish it that same year, with the *Studien* to appear the following spring. Again Walser requested "type specimens," i.e., samples of print and paper. He agreed to the choice of paper but not the typeface suggested; the book would elicit his "displeasure" with such type. He indicated that he did not want roman type, suggesting "a *plain, old-fashioned, respectable, simple, decent, unreformed gothic reminiscent of school readers,* completely in keeping with the *traditional; warm and above all round.*" He did not want anything suggestive of the reformers—for example, of Peter Behrens. Nothing sharp and hard, but rather graceful and soft. The typeface should, he thought, look soft, round, modest, warm, and decent. "The book should look as though it had been printed in the year 1850 if possible. In other words, my very eager, heartfelt wish in this regard is: unmodernity!" And he continued: "Under no circumstances do we want to imitate what has been produced in the book trade of the German Reich in recent years in the way of tasteful tastelessness or tasteless taste. May I ask you to send me *one, two, three different* samples?" There followed further comments about superfluous ornamentation, initial letters, and page numbers, which must be placed in the middle of the page. Moreover, the print should be darker and have "somewhat more force." On June 23, 1917, the publisher responded to the author's insistent, concrete wishes concerning the smallest details in what I think is a very pleasant way: "I hope I can interpret the marked solicitude I perceive in the personal interest you are taking in your charming little book as a sign that you are beginning to place your confidence in our firm. We shall make every effort not to disappoint you."

Walser's correspondence with Huber Verlag in July indicates that they reached an agreement on matters of format. Walser received the promised advance of 500 francs, and Karl Walser was invited to design the cover. Walser read proof while he was serving with the border patrol; the book came out in November 1917, in advance of the 1918 date on the title page.

Most of the twenty-five pieces in the volume had already appeared in German and Swiss newspapers and periodicals, but Walser had reworked them more or less thoroughly for book form, although his claim that "all the pieces have been rewritten" was probably exaggerated. The arrangement of the pieces reflects Walser's own biography since almost all of them deal with a poet or artist. In the second story, we read: "We two, you the poet probably no less than I the painter, need patience, courage, strength, and perseverance." One selection bears the title "Widmann" and thus is dedicated to his "discoverer." The story "Die Künstler" [The artists] begins: "The author of these lines wrote once years ago a kind of comedy that unfortunately, due to the fact that he tore it up into a thousand little pieces, has been lost to the stage forever. An irreplaceable loss!" And then he recounts the story of this comedy, the report of his journey from Munich to Würzburg on foot.

In the story "Marie," Walser describes one of the many places where he lived in Biel, and he describes his landlady Frau Ackeret, who appears in this tale as Frau Bandi: "There was something calm and refined about Frau Bandi, but I admit that the way she talked was almost a little too clever for me. She read a great deal. Her favorite writers . . . were not mine, however." When she reproached him for his "disreputable vagabond existence," he wrote her messages, letters, and notes and dropped them into her mailbox.

In "Aus Tobolds Leben" [From Tobold's life], Walser tells about the time he "entered service in a castle belonging to a count." Then, in "Der neue Roman" [The new novel], he describes his annoyance, his embarrassment, his dread at always being asked in company and on the street, "When is your powerful new novel going to appear?" This passage follows: "For my publisher, an estimable man in every regard, I had by this time become the target of large-caliber concern. Whenever I went to see him, he always used to look at me very sadly and utterly downcast, as though I were an enfant terrible in his eyes. Anyone can easily understand that this infuriated me." He reproduces his conversation with the publisher, who says to him: "If you don't bring me a successful new novel, then there is little or no point in your coming to me. The sight of a novelist who always only promises to deliver his big new novel instead of actually delivering it is painful to me, and therefore I should like to ask you to avoid visiting me until you are able to lay your good new novel on my desk." Thus, the "I" of the story became familiar with "the misery...that a novelist comes to experience...who holds out the prospect of his novel more than he writes it." He sums up: *"I was shattered."*

The next story is entitled "Das Talent" [The talent]: a talent is assisted and supported and gradually claims a right to fat advances and payments on a regular basis; this talent turns into a very comfortable gentleman, who discovers, however, that no one is obliged to assist him, and so he pulls himself together and becomes honest and brave, and this elevates the talent and "for this reason alone" he doesn't go to "piteous ruin."

In the story "Das Zimmerstück" [The chamber piece], a writer searches in vain for an inspiration and finally "gets the ludicrous idea of arranging a voyage of discovery under his bed. The result, however, as anyone could have told him in advance, was exactly zero!" Out of this "zero" Walser makes his chamber piece. One day the writer comes home despairing, restless, weary from the battlefield of the day, where weaknesses and defects are revealed; he then sees the stove, that coward bursting with strength, and gives a "Rede an einen Ofen" [Address to a stove], which ends: "Know that reputation is of less concern to me than my task, which appears more important to me than the vulgar fame connected with never having erred. He who has never erred has probably never done anything good either." In the next piece he gives a "Rede an einen Knopf" [Address to a button]. While sewing on a button, he had been struck by the button's serviceable strength and by the fact that he had never expressed his thanks to it: "You are fortunate, for modesty is its own reward and fidelity feels at home in its own skin."

"Der Arbeiter" [The worker], a pure self-portrait, is a splendid piece:

> He was a delicate, noble person in his way.... His low station permitted him to go around in simple clothes. No one paid any attention to him, no one took any notice of him. That was fine with him, he was glad of it.... A book meant weeks, often months, of simple pleasure for him. Spirits and thoughts befriended him, almost like kind-hearted women. He lived more in the spirit than in the world; he lived a double life.

Then comes a description of a day in this worker's life: "As silent as a soldier, he lived less for himself than for something else. In the evening thoughts came to him. With time his mind became keener and keener.... As far as political opinions were concerned, he was too solitary to be able to have anything of the sort.... He loved everything that was beautiful. He loved women.... Thus he lived, thus he loved." The story continues: "a certain nobility was in him. On one occasion he wrote the following 'Two Short Prose Pieces.'" He imagines a conversation that Friedrich Hölderlin had with his housekeeper, and the conversation is similar to those he must have with his own landladies: "'But it's impossible, Hölderlin,' the lady of the house said to him, 'what you want is inconceivable.'" The story ends with the sentences: "This is the way she talked to him. Hölderlin then left the house, wandered around in the world for a while, and then became incurably mad."

In the last selection, "Poetenleben," which gives the volume its title, the author pursues the question of how one becomes a poet. It's a matter of external conditions: one has to earn money, and thus the "person in question" soon becomes an "apprentice clerk." "Of course, on the side he seems to have begun very early to write poems on little scraps of paper." Why did he do this? This too is examined. It is also mentioned that an unusually frequent change in occupation as well as location took place in this poet's life. That too is understandable, for "a young soul who feels the call to become a poet [has need of] freedom and mobility." It seemed impossible to him to develop as a writer without freedom. Slenderness is becoming to a poet as well: "Writing doesn't mean getting fat, it means fasting and going without." He cannot live an opulent life, his expenditures are astonishingly small; tailors and doctors don't make any money on him, but shoemakers do: they keep having to repair and restore his worn-out shoes with their many holes. The poet grew according to his own lights. In this "poet's proletarian life, as we might call it," there are all kinds of work involved, but there is also the following: "Freedom as well as captivity, liberty as well as chains; privation, want, frugality as well as opulent, impudent, gleeful lavishness and costly, luxurious pleasures; hard bitter work as well as good-for-nothing, lazy, hit-or-miss, haphazard, living, breathing life; strict fulfillment of duty as well as pleasurable, reddish, bluish, or greenish sauntering, walking, and tramping about!"

The book's immediate impact could not have been great, for it was wartime, followed by the equally inauspicious postwar period. But two reactions should be noted that again stem not from literary critics but from writers, from poets. One was Oskar Loerke, who won the Kleist Prize for his poems in November 1913. S. Fischer published a volume of his poems in 1916, and, on October 1, 1917, he entered S. Fischer Verlag as an editor while

Moritz Heimann was still there. Loerke wrote in a review of *Poetenleben* that Walser

> invented storytelling per se, as it were, without an object.... Walser discovers the anonymous poetry of man and his times and surroundings. He can dispense with putting characters together, for every hour, every forest, every room, every journey, every visit is a character for him, and his hero, who characterizes everything with his eye so sharply, amiably, courageously, subtly, indulgently, modestly, lightheartedly, gently, saucily, enthusiastically—ah, how much is needed for such a glance—his hero, the poet, stands among these things almost as if he were only a blank space.... Walser pins down facts with words, but at the same time nothing but the psychic content of their factuality is present. Sometimes he is loquacious simply in order not to tire, in short, not to be hurried, aware but irresolute, determined but not ostentatious, bright but not glaring. Apparently chattering without point or purpose, he is in control down to the last syllable. A naiveté of so strong a nature that, even after being battered by consciousness, it presents itself with such certainty and completeness as though it were nature itself.[18]

Here Loerke has succeeded in giving an accurate characterization of these prose pieces, of this description of the life of a poet, of Robert Walser's psychography.

In connection with the second reaction to Walser's book I would like to inject a personal note. After Hermann Hesse's death, his widow permitted me to select a book from his library as a memento, and I chose the first edition of *Poetenleben*. The volume contains the dedication, "For Hermann Hesse with friendly greetings, Robert Walser." Inside the book I found the handwritten draft of a review Hesse wrote, which begins with the sentence, "Robert Walser is the most endearing Swiss poet of my generation." Also in the book was Hesse's review in the *Neue Zürcher Zeitung* of November 25, 1918 (Greven mistakenly dates it a year earlier). In it Hesse compares *Poetenleben* with Eichendorff's *Aus dem Leben eines Taugenichts* [*Memoirs of a Good-for-Nothing*]:

> If I merely say of an author and his book that here and there his words remind me of Eichendorff and *Taugenichts,* then that is a great deal, an uncommonly great deal. But since one is continuously mis-understood, it can easily arouse false impressions. Thus, when I compare the charming little book *Poetenleben* by Robert Walser with *Taugenichts,* I do not mean that Robert Walser is a romantic or "neo-romantic" who, with talent and good luck, re-uses old poetic formulas. Rather, it simply means: this Robert Walser, who has already played so much fine chamber music sounds even purer, even sweeter, even more soaring in this new little book than in the earlier ones.

This too is a clear characterization of Walser's man-ner. Hesse concludes his observations with some very typical insights: "If poets like Walser were among the 'leading spirits,' then there would be no wars. If he had a hundred thousand readers, the world would be a better place. As it is, it is justified by the fact that there are people like Walser in it and pretty, dear things like his *Poetenleben.*"

Two letters written by Walser to Hesse in 1917 have been preserved. The first is dated November 15, during the time when Hesse was doing relief work for pris-oners of war; he had probably mentioned to Walser that, in times like those, writers should play an active role and do something for the common good. Walser wrote in response: "It has been bruited about that Robert Walser

is leading a life of luxury, idleness, and bourgeois com-
placency instead of 'fighting.' The politicians are dissatisfied with me. But what do people really want? And
what great good can be accomplished by articles in
newspapers and periodicals? When the world is out of
joint, then the efforts of twenty thousand mad Hamlets
are of little or no use." He could be sure that Hesse,
who expressed very similar thoughts, would understand
him. Then, on December 3, he wrote:

> Dear Hermann Hesse: I have just returned from
> hiking in the snow in the Jura Mountains and am still
> full of very beautiful impressions and the warmth of
> exercise. Last week I read your brief, very beautiful,
> noble comments in the *Neue Zürcher Zeitung* about
> *Poetenleben.* Many people have surely already told you
> that you have an uncommonly good way of reviewing
> a book. By the way, I too am convinced of the in-
> credibly great value of Eichendorff's *Taugenichts.*
> What a German and what a graceful book! But be-
> cause a simple, good fellow is the main figure in this
> masterpiece, because everything in it is pure and
> quite natural—with no undercurrents or side cur-
> rents, nothing frightening, Strindbergian, nothing
> twisted or sick, villainous, treacherous, and hor-
> rifying—the reader is simply embarrassed, so to
> speak. I thank you sincerely and send most respectful
> and friendly greetings from my European chamber of
> war and diplomacy, that is to say, chamber of dep-
> uties.

I have gone into so much detail about *Poetenleben* because at the time, except for these two important voices,
the book found no great response. Both voices point
out "the beauty" in Walser's works; at the same time,
however, his works deal with extremely up-to-date
problems. The individual, in this case an artist, is at war

with his surroundings, but Walser makes no attempt to reconcile his artist with society (as earlier authors such as Goethe had done); on the contrary, his every line bespeaks alienation. Jochen Greven can rightly say that Walser's narrative tone is ironic and full of reflective questions when he deals with concrete social matters. If he appears to be naive as a narrator and to draw directly from his experiences and his memory, in reality his narrative style is artificial, a finely stylized projection of inwardness.

Seeland

Immediately after the publication of *Poetenleben,* Walser approaches Huber Verlag in Frauenfeld again. In the spring of 1917, an agreement was reached that, after *Poetenleben,* six long works from among his papers should be published. Again his accompanying letter is interesting and characteristic: "I consider the title [Seeland] suitable in every regard because it sounds simple and astute as well as sensuous and earthy. It strikes me as being as realistic as it is colorful and attractive. It describes in brief what the book is about, namely, a region. Besides, the word has something of a magical ring to it. I hope you will agree to it." He presses for an early decision because he is supposed to enter military service on February 18, 1918. And then he presents Huber with a steep bill. He has taken great pains with every sentence in the book, he has gone over them all carefully and has made considerable improvements in form and content compared with previously printed versions. For a month and a half he has labored "strenuously on just this one thing," and for this reason he is requesting a fee of 800 francs for the new book. But he is also being magnanimous: he will not approach any other publisher. In addition, he would like to consider future things with Huber and discuss his

next book, "a longish narrative whole (a novel)," right
now.

On March 28, 1918, he lodges an urgent protest with
Huber, stating that it is difficult for an author to deal
with a publisher who does not respond to a suggestion
made to him; as a general rule publishing houses need
only two to three weeks to make a decision regarding a
manuscript. As a sign of his good will, however, he will
leave the manuscript with Huber a little while longer,
but he insists that *Seeland* "must somehow and somewhere find a safe haven." Huber's delay is getting on his
nerves:

> You are acting just as if *Seeland* were of no im-
> portance to me. This matter is very close to my heart,
> and although I am quite composed, I absolutely
> will not and cannot let things slide in this fashion.
> From all this you can see that I value my association
> with you. You may express yourself quite calmly: re-
> jection or acceptance. My affairs and earnings are not
> a house of cards. If I don't receive an answer within a
> reasonable period, however, I will feel compelled to
> request you to return the book. Very respectfully and
> cordially. . . .

Huber reacted immediately by rejecting the manuscript. On the very next day, April 1, Walser submitted
Seeland to Rascher Verlag, stating that the book would
be from 200 to 300 printed pages long and that it contained "the six most significant prose works to date from
my period of productivity here in Biel." Once again he
elucidated the title, calling it sensuous and simple "and,
I should like to say, European or purely of this world.
Seeland can be in Switzerland or anywhere, in Australia,
in Holland, or wherever." He set forth explicit conditions: two weeks for examination; then a decision regarding acceptance or rejection; a fee of 800 francs,

payable upon signing the contract; and a percentage of the profits.

More than forty letters and postcards written by Walser to Rascher Verlag have been preserved. I didn't find one of them addressed personally to Max Rascher: the stereotyped salutation was always "Very honored Sir." But these letters are most interesting in one respect, for whereas Walser's composure vis-à-vis publishers was certainly simulated, on the other hand he had self-assurance and great confidence in his own works. It is amazing how businesslike he is in these letters.

Rascher accepted the manuscript, but it also had certain commercial considerations in mind. Karl Walser was a more successful artist than his brother was a writer, and the firm suggested that Karl Walser contribute some drawings for the book; this would be a strong selling point for collectors. Robert Walser reluctantly agreed. On April 17, 1918, he wrote: "Frankly speaking, I am still convinced that *Seeland* in particular either doesn't lend itself to illustration at all or only to a slight, i.e., to an all-too-slight, degree because the author leaves too few blank spaces here, in other words, because the poet *himself* is here *painting and illustrating* with his pen, with his words." He therefore thought it better for *Seeland,* because it was a book having to do with spiritual matters, to remain unillustrated. He also doubts whether his brother would be satisfied with the sum mentioned by the publisher, going on to suggest that the book appear unillustrated in Rascher's series Sammlung europäischer Bücher [Collection of European books]. Once again he warns against its being illustrated: "This would strike the professional and the artist as too—what shall I say—familial and private."

The correspondence went back and forth. At times Walser became ill-tempered and quoted a very high price for his brother, alluding to the fact that Karl

Walser was a master in the field of book illustration and recognized as such, especially abroad. He also pointed out that his brother did not like much of what he, Robert, wrote. *Seeland* in particular wasn't "in Karl's line," and Robert did not want to bring any pressure to bear on his brother. It would work only if the latter wanted to do it of his own free will and "on the basis of a good business arrangement you presented." Karl accepted Rascher's offer and did five etchings, which, however—Robert had been right about this—were not based on themes from the text but merely depicted scenes from Biel and its surroundings.

Walser didn't want the roman type chosen by the publisher, but the publisher prevailed. Then production of the book was delayed when Karl Walser fell ill: although the imprint indicated 1919 as the date of publication, the book did not appear until the autumn of 1920. It was a "luxury edition" of 600 numbered copies meant for connoisseurs, and each volume was signed— but, significantly, by the illustrator, not the author. Walser had to keep after Rascher for the payments due him from the book; a letter of May 8, 1919, reads: "If I can manage to sustain myself as a writer for the rest of this year, I will be glad to bear no one any ill will and then to leave the scene. In other words, take a job and disappear in the crowd. In the six years I have lived here, I have done all that is humanly possible in the way of frugality. I wish anyone who wants to imitate me in this much success."

During this period, Walser also wrote a novel with the title "Tobold," based on his Zurich experiences. He sent the manuscript to Rascher, praising it as a "Swiss work, i.e., a work Swiss in its nature." Rascher seems to have returned the manuscript and Walser to have lost or destroyed it. His biographer notes that the manuscript for a book entitled "Mäuschen" [Little mouse], which

Walser sent to Rascher, was also lost. On December 13, 1919, he sent Hermann Meister Verlag a "miniature book": "Liebe kleine Schwalbe" [Dear little swallow], "in the pleasant expectation that you might like to let it fly out into the world."

The last years in Biel were a time of personal crisis for Walser. On November 17, 1916, his brother Ernst, who suffered from schizophrenia, died in Waldau Sanitarium in Bern. On May 1, 1919, his second brother, Hermann, a professor of geography who had been unable to pursue his profession because of mental illness, also died. Surely the fate of his two brothers affected him deeply, and he realized that he too would one day probably be "put away." Perhaps this was why he attempted to marry during this period, although he didn't really try very hard. In the sketch "Belgische Kunstausstellung" [Belgian art exhibit] we find a sentence characterizing his efforts: "In matters of love all lack of success is almost a blessing."

Thus, he had to continue to rely on himself, on himself and his work. Biel was "a way-station in his professional and human development," but poverty and the fear that the region no longer offered him any creative stimulation began to overshadow this positive response. When Carl Seelig asked him why he had left Biel, he answered: "I was very poor in those days. Also, the motifs and details I derived from Biel and its environs were gradually beginning to run out." When he was offered a position that had just become available as second librarian in the State Archives in Bern, he leapt at the opportunity and moved to Bern in January 1921. "I came to Bern as poor as a churchmouse, since the few thousand marks I had deposited in a bank had gone down the drain due to the inflation. Yes, my life there was rather lonely and I moved from rented room to rented room. Certainly more than a dozen times."[19] We

245

know today of fourteen different addresses. "The few thousand marks" he refers to were the 5,000 marks the Frauenbund had awarded him.

He wasn't able to stand his job as librarian for long; he made a remark that offended his superior and was let go after six months. Again he was a free lance, unattached, poor, and yet productive, writing a series of prose pieces. "Now, under the influence of the sturdy, vital city, I began to write less like a country boy, in a more virile and international manner than in Biel, where I had used an affected style." "Theodor" and "Liebespaare" [Couples] were the titles of two works produced during this period. Nothing is known of the latter, a collection, although a prose piece with this title appeared in the July 1921 issue of *Weltbühne*.

On March 8, 1922, Walser gave a reading in Zurich from the manuscript of his novel "Theodor." Robert Mächler describes the occasion: "Walser stopped frequently during this reading to take a swallow of red wine, which elicited smirks from the audience. At the end there was very warm applause." But publishers did not share in this applause. We don't know all the firms to which Walser submitted his manuscript; in any case, he did send it to Rascher, which immediately rejected it. He then turned to the Schweizer Schriftstellerverein [Swiss Writers' Union]:

> Very honored Sir: The undersigned takes the liberty of inquiring whether you would be inclined to advance me a loan from your loan fund on the basis of the two enclosed manuscripts or of one of them. I do not have a publisher for them as yet. I assume that you are familiar with my previously published books. A group of shorter prose pieces would probably be less suitable as the basis for a loan, since it is difficult to find a publisher for such things.

The Schriftstellerverein reacted favorably: they immediately sent him 1,500 francs from the loan fund established a year previously; another thousand were to follow when either Walser or the Verein secured a contract with a publisher, which would then enable the author to repay this loan by consigning all the income he received from the work to the Verein until it had been repaid. The Verein also directed Walser to ask Cassirer to return the rights to his first three novels. Walser wrote to Cassirer in this vein in the spring of 1924 but there is no record of a reply. In the meantime, thanks to the good offices of the Verein, a new publisher had expressed interest, Verlag Gretlein in Zurich, but the head of the firm, Consul Hauschild, could not reach an agreement with Walser himself, so this attempt also failed.

Then Max Rychner, the Swiss editor and critic, printed twenty pages from Walser's manuscript in his periodical *Wissen und Leben,* whereupon the Verein asserted its claim to the fee in accordance with its agreement with Walser. This was too much for Walser; to be sure, the Verein was within its legal rights, but its bureaucratic pettiness offended him. He wrote to them (July 22, 1924), "Very honored Sir: After careful consideration I announce herewith my withdrawal from your Verein and remain very respectfully. . . ."

Walser again attempted to find a publisher for "Theodor." Franz Blei probably once more established a contact with Ernst Rowohlt, to whom, in any case, Walser submitted his novel—without success. The manuscript disappeared and has never been found, but we have a general idea of its contents from a report written by the author Lisa Wenger for the Schriftstellerverein. Walser himself wrote to Otto Pick on May 17, 1927, "A few years ago I wrote a flawed novel on the basis of which an association of Swiss writers located in

Zurich gave me a very nice loan, and due to the fact that since then I have not written a powerful new novel but numerous rather lively, happy, completely unbiased articles instead, the people in Zurich consider themselves justified in loudly announcing to the whole world that Walser is lazy." This he certainly was not, for he wrote a great many short prose pieces and tried repeatedly to place them in periodicals. In this way he became a "fee-hungry submitter of novellas."

An amusing example of this is found in Walser's recently discovered letter of December 27, 1926, to the Schünemann Verlag in Bremen:

> Very honored Sir: In return for an advance of 100 marks, I would be delighted to send you a contribution for your magazine. I am very trusting by nature. Here in Bern you get 100 francs for a song. There are reviews that are not averse to simply "keeping" contributions. Ricarda Huch [a prominent author on that publisher's list] enjoys my respect, but what kind of guarantee is that? If you are not offended by these lines, then Robert Walser is glad.

There is no record of an answer; Walser's card was found in a portfolio marked "Editorial Curiosities" among the posthumous papers of the writer Alma Rogger, who at the time was editor-in-chief of the journal *Niedersachsen.*

Die Rose

Finally, five years after *Seeland,* another book by Walser appeared, *Die Rose,* which turned out to be the last one he himself had published. We do not know how this manuscript got to Rowohlt; indeed, the whole history of the publication of the book is obscure.

In a letter to Max Brod in May 1925, Walser mentioned that Ernst Rowohlt was coming to Bern soon, and he asked Brod to speak to Franz Blei, who—because he was acquainted with Rowohlt—could establish a connection for Walser; but neither the correspondence between Walser and Rowohlt nor the manuscript has been preserved. Walser probably thought highly of Rowohlt from earlier days, for it was he who had wanted to publish Walser in his, and later Kurt Wolff's, house after things had fallen through with Insel. Rowohlt had left the firm and Walser's rights had remained with the Kurt Wolff Verlag. Thus, Rowohlt was really the only publisher never to have sent him a rejection! That is why Walser, apparently in the spring of 1924, sent him a manuscript with new prose pieces and dialogs, none of which had appeared previously. Rowohlt accepted the manuscript, and it was printed by Jakob Hegner in Hellerau; the illustration on the dust jacket was again done by Karl Walser. But this publication with Rowohlt was not successful, either.

Nor did Walser have any success with Orell Füssli in Zurich, whom he offered a book of prose with the title "Aquarelle" [Water colors]. In December 1925, he wrote Therese Breitbach: "I wrote some remarkable and perhaps even rather rude letters to very sensitive, delicate people, and the newspapers are printing me whereas messieurs les editeurs or Herren Publishers-in-Chief don't want any part of me because they are anxious, sullen, depressed, pessimistic. My colleagues have already taken so much money from the publishers that they now have none left for Walser." In January 1926, Walser wrote Otto Pick: "Several literature firms in Germany aren't paying me anything for my work, for example, Rowohlt. . . . My little book *Die Rose* seems to have been ostracized. Rowohlt is behaving like a true Teuton and treating me with every conceivable discourtesy because the book has been a failure."

We can read the pieces in the collection *Die Rose* as

the author's attempt to defend himself against a feeling of failure, to preserve his balance, to affirm his existence as a loner. But at the same time these selections also betray the master: the personal plight they reflect becomes unimportant because—thanks to his language and playfulness of form—the author succeeds in constructing another world beyond the real one; he is here, as Jean Paul once said, "the creator of a second world within the existing one."

"THE FURIOUS, DANGEROUS SERPENT OF FAILURE"

In January 1926, Paul Cassirer, the cousin of the publisher Bruno Cassirer, shot himself. Walser's memories of Paul, which he expressed to Therese Breitbach in a letter of January 15, 1926, were memories only of his own failure. One evening, he recalled, Cassirer had called him "a joker." *Geschwister Tanner,* according to Cassirer, had been "a colossal success and at the same time a colossal failure." Still, in Walser's view, Paul Cassirer understood more about literature than about art, from which he had made his livelihood. And Walser could never forget that, in 1913, Bruno Cassirer had refused to publish his essays and advance the 300 marks he had requested.

Walser was certainly not unproductive in Bern, writing one short prose piece after another, as the volumes of the recent complete edition demonstrate. But he was no longer able to find a publisher, and the journals also turned him down more often than not. He seemed condemned to fail.

Sensing that his feeling of failure was beginning to cripple him, Walser struggled on: "I am concerned about my survival as a writer and an artist," he wrote Otto Pick on May 14, 1926. He learned that Professor

Walter Muschg was an editor at Orell Füssli, and so he turned to him, only to discover that Muschg had recently left the firm. Again a hope was thwarted. On April 13, 1926, he noted that in the German Reich "as a matter of principle" no verses of his were being printed, as opposed to Czechoslovakia, where his friends Otto Pick and Max Brod were. The situation worsened. On May 30, 1927, he wrote Therese Breitbach: "At the moment I feel rather rotten. That is, fair to middling, since something approaching a crisis seems to have occurred in my career as a writer—something I have always expected, by the way. One enjoys a certain reputation, is considered accomplished and so forth, and all of a sudden one is dropped, as the expression goes, in artistic and other circles."

He complained about the unreliability of publishers: "For example, you send a batch of manuscripts to a publisher, i.e., to a person who at first acts like one, whereupon he stops communicating with you." In May 1927, after having been published at least twenty-seven times in the *Berliner Tageblatt,* he received, as he reported, "a blow that sent me reeling. No opportunities seem to be blossoming for me any more in Germany." In Austria, too, he seemed to have lost out, in fair Vienna, "where there must be countesses who amuse themselves by treading upon my manuscripts with their pretty little shoes. A certain 'Spiegelverlag,' which if anything seems to be running a carefully concealed brothel instead of seriously concerning itself with literature, invited me to submit some of my work, and now it's as if it had dropped out of existence; I have heard nothing more from Vienna."[20] From then on, "publisher" became more and more of a term of abuse for him. Otto Pick and Max Brod tried to interest the publisher Zsolnay in bringing out Walser's poems. Walser sent strong words to Brod:

Zsolnay is simply a vile editor of novels who runs off like a rabbit at the thought of publishing—that is, printing—poetry. Anyway, I would be delighted, i.e., in agreement, if you get the chance to recommend me to that rascal, who—like every other snotty publisher—trembles at the sight of a poem . . . if you write to the no-good s.o.b., then please make it very brief, serious, lofty—better to be arrogant than in any way beseeching. Writers, who are a pack of scoundrels in publishers' eyes, should deal with the latter as if they were mangy swine. In matters relating to me, be proud, refined, casual, high-flown with the cultural operator from Vienna. At present I wouldn't offer this numbskull any material for fear he would just sink into his stinking arrogance. But in my opinion a lot depends on how you treat them. And then I find the idea of publishing a book fine and interesting as long as it hasn't happened. Every book that has been printed is after all a grave for its author, isn't it?

Can a writer make a more devastating statement than this concerning the function of a book? Yet, didn't Walser have to come to this conclusion when manuscripts he sent to publishers kept disappearing? And now when Zsolnay, also, rejected his poems? When the volume "Neue Gedichte" [New poems], announced in the Bloch Erben catalog as part of an anthology *(Saat und Ernte* [Seeds and harvest]), didn't appear? And when he saw his last publication "ostracized"? He suffered depressing humiliations at the hands of editors of periodicals as well. He told Carl Seelig about them:

Imagine my horror when, one day, I received a letter from the literary editor of the *Berliner Tageblatt* advising me not to write anything for six months! I was in despair. Yes, it was true, I was totally written out. Burned out like a stove. I did try hard to keep on writing in spite of this warning. But they were ridiculous things that I painfully forced out. I have always had luck only with what quietly grew out of me and what I had somehow experienced. At that time I made a few clumsy attempts to take my own life. But I couldn't even make a proper noose.[21]

Hermann Hesse also experienced and described this "crisis of the man around fifty"; today, everyone speaks of what is called "the midlife crisis."

Is it any wonder that Walser had "states of severe anxiety" and that he "heard voices mocking him"? Two elderly ladies reported his depressions to his sister. She came and took her brother to the psychiatrist Dr. Walter Morgenthaler, who on the very same day, January 24, 1929, arranged for Walser's admission to Waldau Sanitarium near Bern. There are only six sentences in the so-called examination report, two of which follow: "I found Herr Walser decidedly depressed and suffering from severe torpor. He was aware that he was ill, complained about his inability to work, about periodic anxiety." The patient was aware that he was ill, and this illness had a double aspect: he suffered from anxiety and he was unable to work any longer as a writer. The striking thing is that Walser, being "aware," entered the sanitarium voluntarily. The director's diagnosis of schizophrenia was established from the very beginning, but it is impossible for someone with any familiarity with psychopathology to get a clear picture of his psychic condition from the reports made available thus far.

The case history is in error when it speaks of "the patient's complete creative sterility from the moment of his committal," in the words of Dr. Müller, the director. Walser did go on working in the sanitarium. Jochen Greven notes, in a report published in 1970, that during this period no fewer than eighty-three prose pieces and seventy-eight poems were written and that they were "even 'more normal' than certain earlier works," show-ing "for example a less mannered style and fewer of the erratic associations that had irritated many critics in the prose Walser had written in Bern."[22] Mächler correctly points out, in his thorough biography, that Walser's unimpaired perception of himself as a writer, reflected in the works written in Waldau, is "difficult to reconcile with the diagnosis of 'schizophrenia.'"[23] In April 1933, Walser had the satisfaction of being able to arrange a new printing of *Geschwister Tanner* with Rascher Verlag in Zurich. The previous month, the director of Waldau, with whom Walser had been on good terms, had retired and his successor, a certain Prof. Dr. Jakob Klaesi, re-organized the sanitarium. He wanted to have Walser taken to an institution for more severe cases. He found it suspicious that the patient wanted to remain at Wal-dau, or, barring this, preferred to be released rather than transferred to another institution, since—as Walser contended—an author can write only in a situation he himself has freely chosen. The following entry in his case history on February 24, 1929, touches upon this subject: "Today he expressed the desire to be released as soon as possible for economic reasons, saying that he had to earn some money and that he was afraid of being spoiled here because he had it so good. He thinks he should get back to work, to his career as a writer; he says he won't be able to work here, he has to be free, has to be on the outside."[24]

Under its new management, Waldau didn't want to keep Walser. This led to conflicts within the Walser family: his brother Karl opposed the transfer to Herisau Sanitarium, but Lisa, his favorite sister, saw to it that the move took place. Once again, in mid-1933, Walser pro-tested his transfer to Herisau: "After everything had been arranged, he suddenly refused to leave, stating that he didn't see any reason for going to another institution, he could decide for himself what he wanted, what he wished was to be released altogether, in any case he didn't want to change institutions." How reasonably and rationally this "mental patient" reacted! If one had gone along with him, we would have witnessed the further development of a poet. The irresponsible—indeed, scandalous—aspect of Walser's story is not mentioned by Mächler; we learn it from a letter of Müller's to Carl Seelig: "He finally had to be transferred more or less by force."

On June 19, 1933, Walser was admitted to Herisau Sanitarium in his native canton of Bern. Just a few days earlier, he had submitted some prose pieces from his early period to a journal, but this date marked the end of his life as a writer; he never wrote another line. He said to Seelig: "It is nonsensical and cruel to expect me to continue writing in this institution. The only soil on which a poet can produce is freedom."[25]

It is not my intention here to attempt to set down a psychography of Robert Walser, although this is something that must be done some day. Since, however, the factors leading to his crisis and his particular illness are, I believe, closely connected with our topic, I should like to make some conjectures in five general areas: Walser's pervasive anxiety; his alienation from his fellow human beings and from society; his relationship with publishers; his relationship with fellow writers; and, finally, his lethal lack of success.

Walser's Pervasive Anxiety

A careful reader of Walser, Elias Canetti, has the following view of Walser's anxiety:

> Robert Walser's peculiarity as poet lies in the fact that he never expresses his motives. He is the most secretive of all poets. He is always fine, he is always delighted with everything. But his enthusiasm is cold, since it leaves out a part of his personality, and

therefore it is also uncanny. Everything is *external* nature for him, and he denies what is its essential, innermost element—anxiety—all his life. Only later do the voices materialize that avenge themselves on him for all he has concealed. His works represent an unceasing attempt to silence his anxiety.[26]

Walser's anxiety can be traced in many, if not all, of his works. It can be seen, for example, in his attempt at bold disguise in *Jakob von Gunten:* "I enjoy nothing more than giving a false picture of myself to people I have taken into my heart. This is perhaps unjust, but it is bold, therefore fitting." In the story "Fidelio" we read: "today I am egoistic, but no, I don't want to deny my nature too severely. I take the word back, declaring it to be unsuitable. It's just that I have never found an appropriate occasion for self-surrender." In "Bildnis eines Mannes" [Portrait of a man], which can certainly be regarded as a self-portrait, we find the lines:

The conscientious, faithful, honest people are always those who are most strongly guarded from within, as are those who are truly knowledgeable, compassionate. Had he been more indifferent, he would have been able to appear friendlier, happier, and it would have been easy for him to give the appearance of being a warm-hearted person. But being as he was, he was what he didn't want to appear to be and often appeared to be what he wasn't.

At the end of "Helblings Geschichte" [Helbling's story], we find an extremely clear expression of Walser's anxiety: "I really should be all alone in the world, I, Helbling, and besides me, no other living creature. No sun, no culture, I naked on a high rock, no storm, not even a wave, no water, no wind, no streets, no banks, no money, no time, and no breath. Then at least I would no longer experience anxiety. No anxiety and no questions." Walser is plainly revealing his own anxiety here. We read in the same story: "Am I really ill? There is so much I am lacking, actually I don't have anything. Should I be an unhappy man?" He is and always will be a solitary individualist, and he accepts his lack of ties. In his last book, *Die Rose,* there is an inconspicuous dialog that I find most significant, entitled "Der Liebende und die Unbekannte" [The lover and the unknown girl]. The two characters pass each other, they stop—it would have seemed "unnatural" to him to pass her by. The girl asks him if he is always alone. He answers:

> It is true, I am harmless as far as girls are concerned. I don't belong to myself, never walk alone, am fettered and at the same time too happy to be able to do anything wrong. There is someone who is with me all the time but who pays me no heed. What she is and the way she is hover about me. She speaks with me, sometimes serenely, that is, I allow her to talk only seriously with me. I have her just the way I most like to think of her, do what I want with her presence, often chase her away, never need to fear I might lose her. If she knew how dear she is to me, how I deal with her, she would be indignant, but can she stop me from thinking? Every smallest thought connected with her strengthens me.

Here the poet is speaking not of his muse but of the power of poetry, of poetry as his actual partner. For him this relationship is real, although it must seem unreal to the rest of the world. Even more than Walser's sketches, his letters reveal the playful paradox that was his strong point; for example, he addresses his correspondents "from the heights of my unutterably humble self," closes a letter to Max Rychner with "your solicitous sovereign, your high-born servant," closes another with "respectfully and graciously with the faithful good will of a servant, in other words, in perfect friendliness." His exaggerations, his mockery, his scorn, his distortions, his scurrility, even his occasional untruths are shields against his anxiety. Once, when he was walking with Carl Seelig in 1949, they came to a monastery; a young priest was looking out, and Walser remarked, "He is homesick for the outside, we for the inside."[27]

His Alienation from His Fellow Human Beings and from Society

Closely associated with the foregoing is Walser's difficulty in relating to his fellow human beings. Mistrust was a basic characteristic of his nature; it determined his course from the beginning. "There have always been conspiracies around me to fend off vermin like me." Or: "Reserve is the only weapon I possess that is appropriate for me in my lowly position." The solitary individualist and seeker of the absolute knows that he cannot establish ties with society. In the prose piece "Kutsch," written in 1907, we are told that Kutsch has three unfinished dramas in his closet, that he is a kind of lofty person: "he is mistrustful and perhaps he has cause to be, for he is striving for the highest, and all those who strive for something very high cannot be really intimate with their fellow human beings. . . . Kutsch is so poor, so forsaken by the world. . . . He is not a human being like other human beings, just as most human beings are not human beings like other human beings." This passage is also revealing. Most human beings are alienated from their fellows, and Walser suffers from this. This is the source of his despair, expressed as follows by Mächler in his biography, "It is true that he found society sick, and probably because he was healthy, he became sick as a result."[28]

His distance from society was strikingly evident. Walser even required a "strained relationship with human society" on the part of artists. If that is missing, they will soon slacken in their efforts. They must not let themselves be pampered by society, "because then they would feel obligated to go along with conditions as they are." This is a significant sentence: Walser—like Gottfried Keller—was of the opinion that writers must hold a mirror up to the public and must detect "coming events." "Never," he confided to Carl Seelig, "not even in periods of extreme poverty would I let myself be bought by [society]. My personal freedom was always more important to me."[29]

This refusal to let himself be bought was also a basic characteristic, a form of protest. The payments he requested were carefully considered, measured, appropriate, but he would rather remain unpublished than accept an inappropriate fee. Once, he gave in to the Swiss Radio, but not without making some sharp remarks: "At present, as far as literature is concerned there is still simply a system of exploitation everywhere. There is *still* no possibility of combatting this."[30]

Walser wrote to Adolf Schaer-Ris, the president of the Kunstgesellschaft Thun [Thun Art Society], on October 4, 1926, saying that he found himself struggling for survival:

> If I had money, if I were rich, then I would be assured of being treated with respect. But since this is not the case, since in addition I am still one of those questionable bachelors whom people are so eager to attack on moral grounds, I am afraid of being regarded as a *poverer diabel*. You know yourself how, especially today, so much weight is placed on externals, how a person is judged solely on that basis. . . . I must call to your attention the fact that my name is definitely not associated with any coat of arms, any imposing house, any castle . . . as far as the material side of our negotiations is concerned, my bourgeois opponents, who

seem about to take me for a beggar (and slander is a powerful thing in this world), lead me to disclose to you that I was afraid of offending propriety if I requested a fee of less than 200 francs for my reading in your esteemed city. Indeed, several years ago in Bern, where I have been living since that time, my very status as writer was attacked in a simply shattering way in one of the leading local newspapers.

When Seelig told him, in May 1944, that he had started a collection for the German emigré dramatist Georg Kaiser, who was in dire need of money, Walser expressed the view that one should, as a matter of principle, accept only large sums. "Small contributions invite mockery and derogation. I personally prefer to live in squalor than to have to say 'merci' to stingy contributors. To perform services oneself is always better than to be their recipient." Walser had his standards; when he was once asked how much he would need to be able to live as a writer, he answered that he could manage on 1,800 francs a year. But he also studied the standards of other writers, such as Gottfried Keller and Conrad Ferdinand Meyer, "two democrats and storytellers such as this country hasn't seen the likes of before or since." "Just read your Goethe and Mörike some time! There you will learn to smile mockingly at yourself," he told Seelig on September 10, 1940. Indeed, he kept going back to Goethe, whom he especially admired in one respect: "There was really something quite splendid about Goethe's social instincts and his genius for conjuring up appropriate areas of endeavor for all the periods of his life. There is nothing to equal it. When he got tired of writing, he found refreshment in the areas of geology and botany, in civic and theatrical pursuits. He always discovered new sources of rejuvenation."[31]

His Relationships with Publishers

Our investigation has been devoted to Walser's "deplorable experiences with *messieurs les éditeurs.*" We recall that he described the advice of publishers who wanted to make a successful author out of him, establish him in his career, and impose models upon him as "seductive counsel" that "has already *ruined* many a frail nature." He complained that in dealings with publishers there prevailed "a pathological unreliability that resembled an illness of epidemic proportions." Everywhere, one got caught in "mouse or wolf traps" set by publishers, manuscripts disappeared, or one was deceived. Publishers "who want things from me," he wrote in 1927, "are stupid jackasses, because they won't get anything, *since their intentions toward me are dishonorable.*" Zsolnay was a "vile editor of novels," Rowohlt—because of his "discourtesy"—a "true Teuton." Most publishers didn't understand anything about literature anyway: that is one side of Robert Walser—the productive, creative, easily offended, disappointed, despairing side.

His other side, no longer involved in the creative process, was capable of giving publishers their just due. In that conversation of September 10, 1940, already cited, we find one of the most impressive passages in Seelig's *Wanderungen mit Robert Walser:* Walser recalled events of the distant past distinctly, dozens of names and details from the lives of Frederick the Great, Napoleon, Goethe, Keller, and many others; and then he asked:

> Have you ever noticed how every publisher flourishes only in a particular epoch? The printing houses of Frobenius and Froschauer in the Middle Ages; Cotta at the time of the rise of the bourgeoisie, the Cassirers in the *dulci jubilo* of the pre-war years; Sami Fischer in the early days of a Germany just

freeing itself from emperor and empire; the adventurous Ernst Rowohlt in the hectic postwar years. Each one finds the atmosphere he needs for his enterprise and in which he makes a handsome profit."[32]

Seldom has an author so accurately described this secret of publishing success. The publisher is dependent upon his time and its authors. If he has set up his firm correctly, then its history will parallel the literary history of the epoch. Walser's insight is striking and—especially after the experiences he had with publishers all his life as a writer—astonishing. Is this the insight of a sick man, of a man who is mentally deranged? This same entry has a startling conclusion. Seelig and Walser were discussing why exclusively unmarried people were in the sanitarium. Does repressed sexuality have a negative effect on the brain? "But perhaps you are right," Walser said to Seelig and then continued, "Without love the human being is lost." On this evening, Walser returned, as always, to the sanitarium.

HIS RELATIONSHIPS WITH HIS FELLOW WRITERS

The writer who gave Walser the most support, who spoke out in public about him the most frequently and in the most glowing terms was Hermann Hesse; yet Hesse was the most frequent target of Walser's scorn. But he was just as blunt about other authors; for example, he ridiculed the "poet" Hans Mühlenstein, this "genius," whose wealthy wife pays for trips that provide material for his writing and who confides his "elevated" thoughts to a dictaphone. Nor was Albin Zollinger, who praised him in an early review, spared his scorn. Even Carl Spitteler was criticized, the "great man" and "model" (who, however, made some very

negative remarks about Walser in a letter to Cassirer).
Walser wrote ironically about the "hygiene" of Thomas
Mann's success:

> Thomas Mann had everything from the very begin-
> ning: bourgeois tranquillity, security, a happy family
> life, recognition. Not even emigration could throw
> him off balance. On foreign soil he went on writing
> like an industrious office clerk, witness the Joseph
> novels, which give a dry and labored impression, by
> far not as good as his marvellous early works. Some-
> how his later things betray the stuffy air of the study,
> and that's the way the man who produced them looks:
> like someone who has always sat industriously behind
> his desk and his account books. But there is some-
> thing that commands respect in his bourgeois order-
> liness and his almost scientific effort to put every de-
> tail in the right place.

The motives behind Walser's attitude toward Thomas
Mann were transparent: he admired him, envied him,
but he didn't want to be like him—and yet here was
someone who had made it, who found success. Directly
following his remarks on Mann we read, "How many *are
sent to an early grave by lack of success!*"

At Christmastime 1952, Seelig and Walser exchanged
views about "Anna Koch, the murderess of Gonten."
She did not act under the influence of base emotions,
and yet she was executed. Walser said he strongly opposed the death penalty; he found it an effrontery that
he abhorred. Then, during the midday meal, as he was
cutting his sole, he asked, "Who is a murderer
anyway?—Can you tell me that?" Seelig answered, "No,
the boundaries are much too indistinct!" Walser, after a
long pause: "Isn't *a successful writer a murderer* in his own
way too?"[33] It is not clear from the passage whom

Walser might have had in mind, but we can guess which successful writer he regarded as his "murderer," who brought him, the unsuccessful one, to "an early grave."

His feelings of aggression toward Hesse were most pronounced. In 1904, both *Peter Camenzind* and *Fritz Kochers Aufsätze* appeared. Whereas Hesse's novel broadcast his name "throughout Germany with one stroke," as Hugo Ball reported, and Hesse "now was where he belonged: in a forum where he could be heard from far and wide," *Fritz Kochers Aufsätze* was a a total failure. Yet Hesse wrote, "if poets like Walser were among the 'leading spirits,' then there would be no wars. If he had a hundred thousand readers, the world would be a better place." But Walser did not find these hundred thousand readers, and somehow or other we get the impression, reading his remarks about Hesse, that he held Hesse's success responsible for his own failure. In May 1943, he spoke his mind about the "people of Zurich": "[they] took no notice at all of my poems. In those days they were all carried away by their enthusiasm for Hesse. In their hullaballoo over Hesse I was drowned in silence."

These words leave no doubt about Walser's hostile feelings toward Hesse. And because his hostility was misdirected, such outbursts reveal more about their originator than they do about their target. But Walser felt more than scorn for Hesse, and his remarks betray more than mere malice. On a day in June 1937, Seelig and Walser had lunch together in a restaurant, Zum steinernen Tisch [The stone table], from whose windows they had a broad view of that region of Lake Constance where Hesse had lived decades earlier. The sight of this landscape awoke associations in Walser's imagination that led him to ask the despairing question, "Do you know what *my misfortune* is?" And he went on to answer his own question with great seriousness:

Mark my words! All the dear people who think they can order me around and criticize me are fanatic followers of Hermann Hesse. They have no confidence in me. For them there is only an Either-Or: "Either you write like Hesse or you are and always will be a loser." With such extremism do they judge me. They have no confidence in my work. *And that is why I landed in the sanitarium. . . .* It's just that I have always lacked a halo. Without one you can't get anywhere in literature. A nimbus of heroism, of martyrdom, and the like, and you're on the ladder to success. . . . People simply see me mercilessly, just as I am. That is why no one takes me quite seriously.

This day, too, as recorded by Seelig, ended with an important observation. Lack of success was Walser's misfortune, but it could also be a source of productivity. "Good fortune is not good material for poets. It is too self-satisfied. It needs no commentary. It can sleep rolled up in a ball like a hedgehog. Suffering, tragedy, and comedy, on the other hand—they are loaded with explosive forces. You just have to know how to ignite them at the right moment. Then they shoot up into the sky like rockets and illuminate the whole region."[34] In the space of two pages of the *Wanderungen,* misfortune and suffering are described as abysmal failure, as the reason "why I landed in the sanitarium" but also as the bearers of explosive forces that, ignited at the right moment, can light up the world.

His Lethal Lack of Success

Walser's last book, *Die Rose,* contains a piece entitled "Kurt" whose titular character is a boor, or is at least considered such. He betters himself and becomes a snob. He happens to hear about a review in which only married people can publish. Then he meets a girl named

Kunigunde in a café and immediately becomes convinced that "my spirit will celebrate its resurrection in the marriage bed." One day he receives a letter admonishing him not to follow the bad example of Gottfried Keller (who was a bachelor). Kurt reacts quickly by considering marriage to a voluptuous village girl he has met. Producing a partner in marriage would be for him like producing a work of art. Then we read, "The best thing will be to beget a child and offer the product to a publisher, who can hardly reject it: what a promising future!"

An unwanted marriage, just for the sake of being married; begetting a child so he can send it to a publisher who can hardly reject it. What Walser felt to be his fate—constant and inevitable failure, rejection by publishers—can scarcely find more trenchant expression than in these images. But his ironic bitterness at his lack of success was still under control: "We know a young man," we read in the prose piece "Die Ruine" [The ruins, summer 1925], "who gave up his career as a businessman for a poetic one. Heaven and human society punished him severely for this. He became a writer and, as such, remained exceedingly unsuccessful."

He knew how to withstand the attacks of professional critics. On July 17, 1946, he made the following remark about literary criticism: "Laugh and be silent, that is the best one can do in such a case. You also have to be able to put up with a little stench." And yet critics were a threat: "Like a boa constrictor conscious of its own power, they wrap themselves around authors, squeezing and suffocating them when and how they will."[35]

On one point Walser was especially sensitive—criticism of his language. Perhaps, to understand and appreciate this language, readers first had to experience the modern art of this century. How wounding it must have been when an actress to whom he had given one of his books returned it with the words, "First learn German before you try to write stories." And even in the sanitarium he had to endure the insults of his "worshipful" head doctor, Hinrichsen; this man, who thought he was a writer of note himself, reproached Walser in a seemingly tactful way because of the language in *Geschwister Tanner:* he found the first pages good, the rest "impossible." Thus, Walser was still dogged by his lack of success, even in the sanitarium. The conclusion he drew for Carl Seelig was a justifiable one: "Yes, failure is a furious, dangerous serpent. It tries without mercy to choke what is genuine and original in the artist."[36]

Here we come to the heart of the matter. The fate of Robert Walser—the failure, the man who was ruined by "seductive counsel"—was determined by his furious and dangerous serpent, who finally succeeded in smothering what was genuine and original in him. When the world completely deprived him of his freedom and forcibly committed him to the second institution, Walser stopped writing altogether: "It will be all over for me the moment I stop writing, and I am glad of that. Good night."

Walser did stop writing when he was admitted to Herisau, where he remained for twenty-three years. He died on December 25, 1956, while taking a walk.

FROM HIS FIRST DEATH UNTIL HIS SECOND ONE: ROBERT WALSER'S LIFE FROM 1933 TO 1956

It is to the credit of one man that Robert Walser's work remained alive after the author had given up writing and had withdrawn from the world. Carl Seelig, who admired Walser's books, learned of the author's fate and decided to come to his aid and to the aid of his work. As early as their first walk together, he brought up the idea of publishing an edition of selections from the author's works, but Walser turned the suggestion down, claiming that the time for his books was past and he did not want to have anything further to do with the literary rat race.

Later he gave in, and subsequently, in the fall of 1937, *Große kleine Welt: Eine Auswahl* [Large little world: a selection] was published by Eugen Rentsch Verlag in Zurich under Seelig's editorship. Walser took no notice of it; he only asked Seelig once, with dry irony in his voice, whether he had "made a killing" with the Rentsch selection. In 1940, a collection of Walser's works was published by Sauerländer Verlag in Aarau. In 1944, *Stille Freuden* [Quiet delights] appeared as a publication of the Oltener Bücherfreunde [Olten book lovers], edited by Seelig, and in the same year *Vom Glück des Unglücks und der Armut* [On the good fortune of misfortune and poverty] was published by Schwabe in Basel, again with Seelig's editorship.

In the conversations recorded in *Wanderungen* that stretch from July 26, 1937—the day on which his first meeting with the fifty-eight-year-old poet took place—till Walser's death, Seelig has drawn a remarkable likeness of the writer, a portrait of the artist as a sage hiding behind the mask of insanity. Without these records, which have been cited over and over again in these pages because they offer such authentic testimony about the author and his poetics, the picture we have of Robert Walser today would be incomplete; indeed, without them he might really have gone down in literary history simply as the inmate of a mental institution. If Seelig hadn't invited him on these walks, he could not have gotten Walser to express himself as he did. How circumspectly Seelig treated his friend's illness, how easy he made it for Walser to talk about it.

One of the most intriguing things about this book is

how alert the mind of this mental patient was, how independent and accurate his political judgments were. His views about his Swiss compatriots, about the Germans, about the rise of National Socialism, and about Stalin are very impressive. For example: "Completely surrounded by servility, [Stalin] finally became an idol who was no longer able to live like a normal human being. Maybe there was an element of genius in him. But it is better for nations to be governed by mediocre natures. In the genius there almost always lurk evil traits that must be paid for by nations with pain, blood, and degradation."[37]

How full of praise he still was, of love and respect: "You don't have to try to get to the bottom of every secret"; how much he delighted in food and drink (Seelig's book is also a kind of gastronomical report; approximately seventy times in its 163 pages there is mention of the pleasures of the table). But the end of a walk, the end of a day, always brings them back to the madhouse.

When Walser was admitted to Herisau, he had inherited assets amounting to 6,296 Swiss francs, which would have financed seven years in the institution. Seelig initiated collections and tried to obtain literary prizes for Walser. He appealed to the Schweizer Schriftstellerverein to make an annual award to the author, but this request was refused, even though Hermann Hesse supported it by pointing out that this annual award would "guarantee Walser a secure place in the history of literature and of the German language," for this writer had "enlarged the scope of Swiss writing and added to it nuances practically unknown in this country heretofore."

In his conversations with Walser, Seelig repeatedly made cautious attempts—against the advice of the doctors—to encourage him to leave the institution. But

Walser no longer wanted to. The world had taken a stand against him at the time of his compulsory transfer from Waldau to Herisau, and now he would no longer have anything to do with that world. It is thanks to Carl Seelig that his expenses in the institution were met. Walser's sister Lisa, who must have had a guilty conscience, assigned the administration of her brother's literary rights to Seelig, and later, on May 26, 1944, Seelig became Walser's legal guardian.

In the summer of 1953, when Walser was seventy-three, Seelig took an important step on the author's behalf that unfortunately made no impression on Walser. Seelig found, in Ulrich Riemerschmitt of Holle Verlag (Geneva and Darmstadt), an editor who was an enthusiastic admirer of Walser's and signed a contract with this firm for a complete edition of the prose works. The owner of Holle Verlag was Helmut Kossodo, who was to give the firm his own name in 1956 and who purchased the publishing rights for a complete edition of Walser's works. The first volume of *Dichtungen in Prosa* appeared in 1953; the second (containing the unpublished works rescued by Seelig), in 1954; and, a year later, a reprint of *Der Gehülfe* became the third volume. Volumes 4 and 5 appeared in 1959 and 1961. Royalties began to come in, although sparingly. In addition, money accumulated in the form of tributes to the writer, including an award from the Schweizerische Schillerstiftung in 1955 and, finally, through Seelig's initiative, an old-age pension as well. Thus, the last years of this insecure man were spent in relative security.

In the last walk he recorded, Seelig provided—no doubt unintentionally—a characteristic illustration of our thesis: it was Christmas 1955 and a dreary, rainy day. They had a detailed discussion about Kleist, during which Walser recalled that, when he was an apprentice in a bookstore in Stuttgart, he had seen a performance of Kleist's *Der Prinz von Homburg* [*The Prince of Hom-*

burg]. Then the conversation turned to prizes for beginning writers. If young writers "are spoiled at an early age, they will remain eternal schoolboys," the seventy-seven-year-old Walser contended. "In order to become a man, suffering, lack of recognition, struggle are necessary. The state must not play nursemaid to poets." A striking statement! True, in most cases: in Walser's case, however, any kind of support that expressed confidence in him would have been of the utmost help.

Seelig then reported that Walser was "extremely amused" by the behavior of the Icelandic writer Halldór Laxness, winner of the Nobel Prize for Literature in 1955. Although he had never read anything by Laxness, he had seen a picture of him in a magazine that he thought must be characteristic; he still had to laugh at "the audacity with which Laxness had whirled the Swedish princess around at a ball during the celebrations in Stockholm. On a woodland path, Walser demonstrated how Laxness, clad in tails but acting like a peasant, spun her around as if he wanted to proclaim triumphantly: 'Now I have the West as well as the East in my grasp!' for, shortly before, Laxness had also received an award from the Soviet Union."[38] Once again, in the last months of Walser's life—a year later he was dead—the specter of his failure rose to the surface, reflected in his jealousy, and once again the successful were, for him, also the corrupt: they throw themselves into the arms of both East and West!

On December 25, 1956, Walser took his walk alone, without his companion of long years. Seelig gives a moving description of Walser's death: "The dead man found lying on the snowy hillside is a poet who took delight in winter with the light, cheerful dance of its snowflakes—a genuine poet who yearned like a child for a world of tranquillity, purity, and love."[39] In his breast pocket were three letters and a postcard that led to the writer's identification. Seelig's modesty prevented him from noting that, along with these letters and card (addressed to his sister and his friend Frieda Mermet), there were also receipts for royalty payments Seelig had sent his friend, his ward, and the author who had entrusted him with his unpublished works.

Werner Weber wrote the following comment on Walser's death in the *Neue Zürcher Zeitung* of December 29, 1956: "That was a piece of news that bewildered us; we had lived with the works of this writer and had thought of the man himself as already departed from this world."

WALSER AND THE ROBERT WALSER ARCHIVE

After Carl Seelig's accidental death on February 15, 1962, the ownership of the rights to Walser's works was vague and unclear. Elio Fröhlich, a lawyer, established the Carl Seelig Foundation in Zurich and personally set up the Robert Walser Archive. In 1966, the thirteen volumes of the complete works began to appear, one by one, under the imprint of Kossodo Verlag. This edition, completed in the year 1976, is a model of careful editing; we have the Carl Seelig Foundation and the efforts of Elio Fröhlich to thank for it. In addition, the financial as well as personal efforts of Martha Düssel on behalf of Walser's work deserve recognition; Kossodo Verlag would not have been able to carry out the project of publishing the complete works without her, for when the firm was having difficulties she purchased its stock.

As the result of an agreement with Kossodo Verlag, *Geschwister Tanner, Der Gehülfe,* and *Jakob von Gunten* appeared in the series Bibliothek Suhrkamp in 1975 and 1976. A contract with the Carl Seelig Foundation led to the publication of *Wanderungen mit Robert Walser* as volume 554 in this same series.

The director of the Robert Walser Archive, Katharina

Kerr, prepared a report on Walser's reception since his death.[40] She believed she could detect a "significant upsurge" of interest in Walser. This is undoubtedly true, to a certain extent. Literary critics, scholars, and interested readers can now refer to a carefully edited edition. Katharina Kerr established the fact that "since 1956 there have been thirteen published and unpublished dissertations, monographs, and authorized works, one habilitation thesis and one documented biography, and a series of lengthy essays about Walser and his work along with many reviews and critiques." Is this what one would call a "significant upsurge"?

A genuine upsurge may now well be in sight, however. The following lines were written specifically for publication here (the author of these pages, being himself the publisher and thus closely involved with the printing of his book, can insert a last-minute bit of news): in Zurich, on November 24, 1977, Fröhlich, on behalf of the Carl Seelig Foundation, signed a contract granting Suhrkamp Verlag in Zurich the rights to Walser's works after having regained them from Martha Düssel of Kossodo Verlag. In 1978, the one-hundredth anniversary of Walser's birth, Suhrkamp published a popular pocketbook edition of Walser's complete works in twelve volumes. It has been a long road since our first publication of a volume of his selected works in 1960!

Walser will now be available to a large segment of the reading public in a reasonably priced edition. Hereafter, his name will no longer be a well-kept secret of the few but will belong, as a matter of course, among the great authors of this century. Let us end with the words cited from *Jakob von Gunten* at the beginning of this chapter: "Some day a fragrance will emanate from my being and my beginnings."

Notes

The Responsibilities of a Literary Publisher

1. In the military court's verdict against Palm, we read:
   "These men were charged with being authors, printers,
   and distributors of libelous works directed against His
   Majesty the Emperor and King and His armies and written with the intent of subverting the minds of the resi-
   dents of southern Germany by inciting to mutiny, in-
   surrection, and assassination against the French troops,
   indeed, even of trying to lure the latter to disobedience
   and neglect of their duties toward their lawful superiors"
   (Hans Widmann, ed., *Der deutsche Buchhandel in Urkun-
   den und Quellen* [The German book trade in documents
   and sources] [Hamburg, 1965], 1:294 ff.).

2. See the chapter, "Der Selbstverlag" [The private press],
   in Ernst Kund, *Lessing und der Buchhandel* [Lessing and
   the book trade] (Heidelberg, 1907), pp. 41 ff., and Otto
   Reiner, "Lessing als Verleger" [Lessing as publisher], *Imprimatur* vol. 1, 26 January 1930.

3. Widmann, 1:419.

4. See the chapter, "Verlagsbemühungen" [Attempts to
   start a publishing house] in Bert Andreas-Wolfgang
   Mönke, *Neue Daten zur "Deutschen Ideologie"* [New data
   on *The German Ideology*], Archiv für Sozialgeschichte
   [Archives for social history] (Hanover, 1968), 8:37 ff.

5. Quoted from *Schriftsteller, Verleger und Publikum: Eine
   Rundfrage* [Writers, publishers, and the public: a ques-
   tionnaire] Zehn-Jahres-Katalog Georg Müller (Munich,
   1913), p. 23.

6. The passages from Ralf Dahrendorf and Peter Meyer-Dohm appear in Meyer-Dohm's "Verlegerische Berufsideale und Leitmaximen" [Ideals and guiding maxims in publishing] in *Das Buch in der dynamischen Gesellschaft: Festschrift für Wolfgang Strauß zum 60. Geburtstag* [The book in a dynamic society: festschrift for Wolfgang Strauß on his sixtieth birthday] (Trier, 1970), pp. 133 ff.

7. *Die Zeit,* 15 November 1968.

8. Hans-J. Liese, "Verlage im Strukturwandel" [The changing structure of publishing houses], *Börsenblatt für den Deutschen Buchhandel,* 8 January 1971.

9. See *Der Groß-Verlag: Seine gesellschaftliche Bedeutung und Verantwortung* [The giant publishing house: its social significance and responsibility], special issue of *Bertelsmann-Briefe,* n.d. [1973]. In 1973, there also appeared a brochure about the Klett Verlag in Stuttgart: *Grundsätze der Firma Ernst Klett* [Principles of the Ernst Klett verlag]. In its eleven pages, which otherwise present the history and responsibilities of the firm in an extremely winning manner, the matter of the author is mentioned only once.

10. See Peter de Mendelssohn, *S. Fischer und sein Verlag* [S. Fischer and his publishing house] (Frankfurt, 1970).

11. Mendelssohn, p. 1,028. The description originated with the Germanist, Philipp Witkop. Thomas Mann wrote: "And 'the Cotta of naturalism' is a very good phrase." Cotta was the publisher of the classical German authors Goethe, Schiller, et al.

12. Mendelssohn, p. 40.

13. Mendelssohn, p. 47.

14. Uwe Johnson and this author have written down their recollection of this conversation; both accounts appear in *Die Begegnung: Jahresgruß 1965–66 der Buchhandlung Elwert & Meurer* [The encounter: annual greetings 1965/66 from the booksellers Elwert & Meurer] (Berlin, 1965).

15. Frisch, *Öffentlichkeit als Partner* [The public as partner], edition suhrkamp, vol. 209 (Frankfurt, 1967), p. 56.

16. Martin Walser, *Erfahrungen und Leseerfahrungen* [Experi-

ences in living and reading], edition suhrkamp, vol. 109 (Frankfurt, 1965), p. 98.

17. Hans Erich Nossack (Frankfurt, 1972), pp. 247, 249.

18. James Joyce, *Briefe*, ed Richard Ellmann, trans. Kurt Heinrich Hansen, 3 vols.

19. Richard Ellmann, ed., *Selected Letters of James Joyce* (New York, 1975), p. 83.

20. Holthusen, "Die Literatur der Verbrannten Erde: James Joyce in seinen Briefen" [The literature of the scorched earth: James Joyce in his letters], *Merkur*, January 1974.

21. *Ulysses* (London: Penguin Books, 1969), p. 704.

22. Ellmann, p. 285.

23. von Horváth, *Gesammelte Werke* [Collected works] (Frankfurt, 1971), vol. 4.

24. Erich Heller and Jürgen Born, eds., *Franz Kafka: Briefe an Felice und andere Korrespondenz aus der Verlobungszeit* [Letters to Felice and other correspondence from the period of his engagement] (Frankfurt, 1967), pp. 97, 115.

25. Kurt Wolff, *Briefwechsel eines Verlegers 1911–1963* [The correspondence of a publisher: 1911–1963], ed. Bernhard Zeller and Ellen Otten (Frankfurt, 1966), p. xxi.

26. Franz Kafka, *Briefe: 1902–1924*, [Letters: 1902–1924] ed. Max Brod (Frankfurt, n.d.), ed. authorized by Schocken (New York, 1958), p. 96.

27. Wolff, p. 25.

28. Wolff, pp. 25 f.

29. Wolff, p. 43.

30. Wolff, p. 54.

31. Wolff, p. 60.

32. On the question of the appropriateness of format, I would like to call attention to a book written after the present chapter was completed, that deals with this question in detail: Siegfried Unseld, *Der Marienbader Korb: Über die Buchgestaltung im Suhrkamp Verlag: Willy Fleckhaus zu ehren* [The Marienbad basket: on book design at Suhrkamp Verlag: in honor of Willy Fleckhaus] (Hamburg, 1976).

33. Walter Jens had the following to say in an article entitled "Ein Meister, der die Welt nicht mehr verstand" [A mas-

ter who no longer understood the world] in the Literary Supplement of the *Frankfurter Allgemeine Zeitung,* 2 February 1974: "Hofmannsthal's guardians of the grail! For years and years now they have been talking about a critical edition that would include all the variants—an absurdity considering the way Hofmannsthal worked! This would be an edition so complete that by the year 2074 everything would be published that carries the seal of approval 'autos epha': he himself said it. And this at a moment when everything depends on publishing, in the first place, a practical and affordable Werkausgabe à la Suhrkamp and, in the second place, the most important sketches and fragments as quickly as possible!"

34. Fascinating reading on this topic is provided in Alexander Mitscherlich, ed., *Psychopathographien 1: Schriftsteller und Psychoanalyse* [Psychopathographies 1: writers and psychoanalysis] (Frankfurt, 1972). The contributions to this volume attempt to get to the root of the "secret of creative accomplishment." The book is significant because of Mitscherlich's introduction, which sheds light on much of the "madness" in an author's nature.

35. Bernhard, *Midland in Stilfs,* Bibliothek Suhrkamp, vol. 272 (Frankfurt, 1971), pp. 93 f.

36. Thomas Bernhard to Siegfried Unseld, 15 December 1972, Suhrkamp Archives.

37. Paul Nizon to Siegfried Unseld, 15 November 1972, Suhrkamp Archives.

38. Karl Scheffler, "Berufsidealismus," *Navigare necesse est: eine Festgabe zum 50. Geburtstag von Anton Kippenberg* [. . . In commemoration of Anton Kippenberg's fiftieth birthday] (Leipzig, 1924), p. 44.

39. Hermann Hesse to Siegfried Unseld, April 1959, in *Hermann Hesse–Peter Suhrkamp: Briefwechsel 1945–1959* [. . . Correspondence . . .] (Frankfurt, 1969), p. 406.

40. Mitscherlich, Bibliothek Suhrkamp, vol. 246 (Frankfurt, 1970), p. 22.

41. Peter Handke, *Ich bin ein Bewohner des Elfenbeinturms* [I am an inhabitant of the ivory tower], suhrkamp taschenbuch, vol. 56 (Frankfurt, 1972), pp. 39 ff.

42. Bertolt Brecht, *Tagebücher 1920–1922* (Frankfurt, 1975), p. 131.
43. Theodor Adorno, *Gesammelte Schriften* (Frankfurt, 1970), 7:259 ff.

Hermann Hesse and His Publishers

1. Brecht is quoted in Hans Mayer, *Bertolt Brecht und die Tradition* (Pfullingen, 1961), p. 13; Samuel Fischer, "Reden, Schriften, Gespräche," in *In memoriam S. Fischer*, ed. Brigitte and Gottfried B. Fischer (Frankfurt, 1960), p. 23; Karl Korn, "Peter Suhrkamp," in Siegfried Unseld, ed., *In memoriam Peter Suhrkamp* (Frankfurt, 1959), p. 46; Hermann Hesse, "Freund Peter," ibid., pp. 27 f.
2. I told this story once before in Siegfried Unseld, *Erste Lese-Erlebnisse* [First reading impressions], suhrkamp taschenbuch, vol. 250. As a token of appreciation, a reader sent me the book after I had delivered the lecture reprinted here; thus, I can check my recollection. *Der Löwe von St. Markus: Erzählung aus Venedigs Vergangenheit* [. . . A tale from Venice's past], by G. A. Henty, is adapted from the English by E. Osius, with colored illustrations based on originals by M. Wulff (Berlin, n.d.). The foreword notes that "G. A. Henty is at present the most popular children's author in England." Well, he was mine, too.
3. Hesse, *Gesammelte Werke* [Collected works], 12 vols. (Frankfurt: Werkausgabe edition suhrkamp, 1970), 11:244; also cited in Horst Kliemann, ed., *Stundenbuch für Letternfreunde* [Book of hours for lovers of lettering] (Frankfurt, 1954), p. 22. In it, Kliemann also printed Hesse's poem "Bücher" [Books] (Hesse, *Werke*, 1:63) in a special typeface:

Alle Bücher dieser Welt
Bringen dir kein Glück,
Doch sie weisen dich geheim
In dich selbst zurück.

Dort ist alles, was du brauchst,

Sonne, Stern und Mond,
Denn das Licht, danach du frugst,
In dir selber wohnt.

Weisheit, die du lang gesucht
In den Büchereien,
Leuchtet jetzt aus jedem Blatt—
Denn nun ist sie dein.

All the books in this wide world
Won't bring you to your goal,
Yet they point the secret way
Back to your own soul.

There lies everything you need,
Sun, moon, and star,
For the light that you've been looking for
Is glowing where you are.

The wisdom that you long have sought
In myriad bookstores
Now shines forth from every page
For now at last it's yours.

4. Hermann Hesse—Helene Voigt, *Zwei Autorenporträte in Briefen 1897 bis 1900* [Portraits of two authors in letters from 1897 to 1900] with an introduction by Eugen Zeller (Düsseldorf, 1971), p. 124.

5. *Gesammelte Briefe: Erster Band 1895–1921* [Collected letters, vol. 1 . . .], ed. Ursula and Völker Michels, in cooperation with Heiner Hesse (Frankfurt, 1973), p. 38.

6. Hesse, *Werke*, 11:17 ff.

7. Hesse, *Briefe 1*, [Letters, vol. 1] pp. 53, 55.

8. Cited in Siegfried Unseld, *Hermann Hesse: Eine Werkgeschichte*, [. . . A history of his publications] suhrkamp taschenbuch, vol. 143 (Frankfurt, 1973), p. 13.

9. Hesse, *Briefe 1*, p. 53.

10. Ibid., pp. 57 f.

11. Hesse, *Werke*, 11:19.

12. Hesse, *Briefe 1*, p. 78.

13. Ibid., p. 81.

14. Ibid., p. 78.
15. Hesse, *Werke,* 11:298.
16. Cited in Peter de Mendelssohn, *S. Fischer und sein Verlag* [S. Fischer and his publishing house] (Frankfurt, 1970), p. 380, an uncommonly informative book, interesting not only in terms of publishing and literary history but also as a document of the culture of the twenties. Everyone concerned with the history of publishing should read it; it is certainly required reading for every budding publisher.
17. Ibid., p. 381.
18. S. Fischer's letters are cited from the firm's correspondence, which I possess in photocopy, and also from Mendelssohn.
19. Hermann Hesse, *Eigensinn: Autobiographische Schriften* [Self-reliance: autobiographical writings], selected and with an afterword by Siegfried Unseld, Bibliothek Suhrkamp, vol. 353 (Frankfurt, 1972), p. 22.
20. Hugo Ball, *Hermann Hesse: Sein Leben und sein Werk* [. . . His life and his work], Bibliothek Suhrkamp, vol. 34 (Frankfurt, 1956 [written in 1927]), p. 99.
21. I have photocopies of the 1903 contract and the two supplements (1 February 1908 and 31 March 1912).
22. Hesse, *Briefe 1,* pp. 167 f.
23. Hesse, *Werke* 11:301 ff.
24. Ibid.
25. Mendelssohn, p. 1,024.
26. Hesse, *Werke,* 11:292. Someone should treat in detail Hesse's relationship with Albert Langen, especially his staff work for *Simplicissimus* and *März.* It was the humor magazine *Simplicissimus* that made out of Hesse, who was basically apolitical, a critic, indeed, a "revolutionary." The series of drawings by Th. Th. Heine entitled "Durch das dunkelste Deutschland" [Through darkest Germany] stirred him; the French spirit of the magazine, its combination of art and politics, fascinated him. In 1905, in Langen's offices, Hesse participated in the discussions about the founding of the periodical *März.* This journal, too, was viewed as a challenge to the "arbitrary regime of Wilhelm II, to the subaltern spirit of the society, and to

justice based on the class system"—Hesse, *Politik des Gewissens: Die politischen Schriften* [The politics of conscience: political writings] (Frankfurt, 1977), p. 401.

27. Ibid.

28. I have this detail from Mendelssohn's book. In the chapter "Exkurs über Orden und Ehrendoktoren" [A digression about awards and honorary doctorates], he describes Thomas Mann's vain efforts at the Universities of Freiburg, Berlin, Leipzig, and Heidelberg to obtain an honorary doctorate for Fischer on the occasion of the fortieth anniversary (October 22, 1926) of the founding of the firm: "It would be great fun if one could give the old man this undoubtedly delightful satisfaction for the anniversary." In his correspondence with Mann, the Freiburg Germanist Philipp Witkop described Fischer as "the Cotta of naturalism," which Mann found to be a "very good phrase"—Mendelssohn, pp. 1,026 ff.

29. Hesse, *Werke,* 11:297 ff.

30. Hesse, *Eigensinn,* p. 29.

31. *Schriften zur Literatur 2: Eine Literaturgeschichte in Rezensionen und Aufsätzen* [Writings on literature 2: A history of literature in reviews and essays], ed. Volker Michels, separate ed. (Frankfurt, 1972). This collection also appears in Hesse, *Werke,* vol. 12. "Hesse's *Schriften zur Literatur* are guides to literature (they contain characterizations of unforgettable accuracy)—but they are at least as important as sources of information about Hesse himself"—Werner Weber, *Neue Zürcher Zeitung,* 26 July 1970.

32. Siegfried Unseld, *Hermann Hesse: Eine Werkgeschichte,* expanded ed. (Frankfurt, 1973), pp. 303–6.

33. Hesse, "Deutsche Erzähler," *Neue Rundschau* 25 (1914): 425, idem, *Werke,* 11:163 ff.

34. Hesse, "Georg Müller," *Neue Zürcher Zeitung,* 10 January 1918.

35. Siegfried Unseld, (University of Tübingen, 1951). Jean Paul's conviction that "poetry is a *second* world within this one" was central to Hesse. What he wrote in his afterword to *Siebenkäs* applies to himself as well as to Jean

Paul: "Every true work of literature is affirmation, arises from love, has as its basis and source gratitude toward life, is praise of God and his creation"—Quoted in my diss., p. 110.

36. Thomas Mann described Hesse's literary activities as: "service, homage, selection, revision, rediscovery, writing of intelligent introductions—sufficient to fill the life of many a learned *literatus*"—quoted in Mendelssohn, p. 1,024.

37. Hesse, *Briefe 1*, p. 226.

38. Hesse to Carl Busse in Hesse, *Briefe 1*, p. 86. After reading *Romantische Lieder* [Romantic songs], Busse invited Hesse to submit a new volume of verse for his series, Neue deutsche Lyriker, published by the Grote Verlagsbuchhandlung in Berlin. Hesse's second volume of poetry, *Gedichte* [Poems], was published by Grote in 1902 with an introduction by Carl Busse.

39. *Neue Zürcher Zeitung,* 20 June 1954.

40. Hesse, *Werke,* 11:300.

41. Hesse's unpublished note, written on the back of the original letter from the *Kölnische Zeitung* of 30 August 1930, reads: "For a long time the *Kölnische* was the last German newspaper to pay its contributors relatively well. Now their payments have also sunk to a minimum. One more sign of the esteem that intellect enjoys in Germany." The original is in the Suhrkamp Archives.

42. Hesse, *Briefe* [Letters], expanded ed. (Frankfurt, 1964), pp. 229 ff.

43. *Weltwoche,* 25 June 1954.

44. From an unpublished letter to Dr. Hubert Steiner (probably August 1938) in Hesse's posthumous papers. In another connection, Hesse accepted current practice in capitalization and rejected the uniform noncapitalization of German nouns (cited in the essay "Großschreibung oder kleinschreibung" [Capitalization or noncapitalization] by Siegfried Unseld).

45. Hesse, *Werke,* 11:7 ff.

46. Hesse's report on the problem associated with Unger Fraktur and roman type in his books appears in *Bericht an*

die Freunde [A report to my friends], written in 1959, privately printed in 1960.

47. Hesse to Fischer, in Hesse's posthumous papers.

48. There is a thorough and informative treatment of the function and influence of the *Neue Rundschau* from 1933 on in Falk Schwarz, *Literarisches Zeitgespräch im Dritten Reich, dargestellet an der Zeitschrift "Nue Rundschau"* [Literary discussion in the Third Reich, illustrated by the periodical *Neue Rundschau*], reprint from the Archiv für die Geschichte des Buchwesens [Archives for the history of the book trade], vol. 12 (Frankfurt, 1972).

49. Hermann Hesse—Peter Suhrkamp, *Briefwechsel: 1945–1959* [Correspondence: 1949–1959], ed. Siegfried Unseld, with notes and a detailed afterword as well as an appendix, "Dokumente der Trennung zwischen Peter Suhrkamp und Gottfried Bermann Fischer" [Documents relating to the break between . . .] (Frankfurt, 1969).

50. Volker Michels, ed., *Materialien zu Hermann Hesses "Das Glasperlenspiel"* (Frankfurt, 1973). This volume contains all Hesse's important statements on this novel: "Vom Wesen und von der Herkunft des *Glasperlenspiels*" [On the nature and origin of *The Glass Bead Game*]; "*Das Glasperlenspiel* in Briefen, Selbstzeugnissen und Dokumenten" [*The Glass Bead Game* in letters, the author's own remarks, and documents]; "Texte zum *Glasperlenspiel,* Entwürfe, Fragmente, Notizen" [Texts relating to *The Glass Bead Game,* sketches, fragments, notes]; and a biographical chronicle, "Die Entstehungsjahre des *Glasperlenspiels*" [The years spent working on *The Glass Bead Game*].

51. Hermann Hesse, *Neue deutsche Bücher: Literaturberichte für Bonniers Litterära Magasin 1935–1936* [New German books: reports on literature for . . .], ed. Eugen Zeller (Marbach, 1965).

52. Hesse devoted two major pieces to Suhrkamp that I quote frequently here: "Glückwunsch für Peter Suhrkamp zum 28. März 1951" [Congratulations to Peter Suhrkamp on 28 March 1951] in *Briefe.* expanded ed.,

pp. 370–75, and "Freund Peter" in *In memoriam Peter Suhrkamp,* pp. 25–33.

53. Hesse to Kurt Kläber, December 1936; Hesse to Fritz Gundert, 5 April 1937; and Hesse to Kläber, July 1938. All in Hesse's posthumous papers.

54. Hesse to Bermann Fischer, June 1938, in Hesse's posthumous papers.

55. The two extracts dealing with Hesse's relationship with his publishers during the Third Reich were taken from letters unpublished at the time I wrote this lecture. Hesse's political writings, in which these quotations appear, subsequently came out in two volumes. In the afterword to this edition, Volker Michels—on the basis of new documents—once again describes in detail Hesse's attitude toward the possibility of publication of his works during the Nazi years: Hermann Hesse, *Politik des Gewissens: Die politischen Schriften* [The politics of conscience: the political writings] 2 vols. (1914–1932 and 1932–1962), foreword by Robert Jungk, ed. and with an afterword by Volker Michels (Frankfurt, 1977). See Michels' description of this relationship, pp. 931–37.

56. Hermann Hesse—R. J. Humm, *Briefwechsel* [Correspondence], ed. Ursula and Volker Michels (Frankfurt, 1977), p. 64.

57. See the chapter, "Ende einer Freundschaft" [The end of a friendship], pp. 318–24, in Gottfried Bermann Fischer, *Bedroht—Bewahrt: Wege eines Verlegers* [Threatened—saved: paths of a publisher] (Frankfurt, 1967). My own account appears in Hesse—Suhrkamp, *Briefwechsel,* pp. 441 ff.

58. Adorno, "Dank an Peter Suhrkamp," in *In memoriam Peter Suhrkamp,* pp. 16 f.

59. Hesse to Unseld, in Hesse—Suhrkamp, *Briefwechsel,* p. 406.

60. I have described my relationship with Hesse in detail in *Begegnungen mit Hermann Hesse* [Encounters with Hermann Hesse], suhrkamp taschenbuch, vol. 218 (Frankfurt, 1975).

61. This is not meant as a criticism of Frau Hesse's work; she was influenced by friends who declared that Hesse was "untranslatable." In my obituary notice for Ninon Hesse I called attention to the great credit due her for the way she handled Hesse's posthumous papers: "Ninon Hesse zum Gedächtnis" [In memory of Ninon Hesse], *Frankfurter Allgemeine Zeitung,* 7 October 1966. This article also appears in *Begegnungen mit Hermann Hesse,* pp. 166 ff.

   For Hesse's impact in the United States, see Unseld, *Werkgeschichte,* p. 235. We cannot and do not wish to imagine what would have happened if Frau Hesse had not returned the rights to us at that time and we had not been in a position to encourage and approve new translations in the United States.

62. This story is told in detail in Siegfried Unseld, *Der Marienbader Korb . . . ,* pp. 7 f.

63. Hesse to Unseld, Suhrkamp Archives.

Bertolt Brecht and His Publishers

1. Herzfelde knew this only too well. He was the first publisher to attempt a complete edition, and this under the difficult conditions of exile. He has given two accounts of his professional relationship with Brecht: "Über Bertolt Brecht" [On Bertolt Brecht], written in 1956, in *In memoriam Brecht* (Leipzig, 1964) pp. 129 ff. (the sentence cited here appears on p. 136), and "Wieland Herzfelde über den Malik Verlag," *Der Malik-Verlag: 1916–1947,* catalog of the exhibition, ed. Academy of Arts in Berlin (Berlin, 1966), pp. 5–70.

2. See *"Baal": Der böse "Baal," der asoziale: Texte, Varianten, Materialien* [*Baal:* Evil, asocial *Baal:* texts, variants, documents], critically ed. and with a commentary by Dieter Schmidt, edition suhrkamp, vol. 248 (Frankfurt, 1968). Dieter Schmidt refers to the following versions: two carbon copies of the missing original, a printing by Georg Müller in 1920, the first printing by Kiepenheuer in

1922, the second printing by Kiepenheuer in 1922, the first printing by Suhrkamp in 1953, and the printing by Aufbau-Verlag in 1955. In addition to these manuscripts and printings, there were countless revised versions used for stage productions.

3. *Brecht in Augsburg,* suhrkamp taschenbuch, vol. 297 (Frankfurt, 1976). Another important source for his Augsburg years is Hans Otto Münsterer, *Bert Brecht: Erinnerungen aus den Jahren 1917 bis 1922* [... Reminiscences from the years 1917 to 1922] (Zurich, 1963).

4. Hermann Kasack, *Rückblick auf mein Leben* [My life in retrospect], 1966, cited in Wolfgang Kasack, comp., *Leben und Werk von Hermann Kasack: Ein Brevier* [Life and works of Hermann Kasack: a reader] (Frankfurt, 1966), p. 27.

5. Ibid., p. 29.

6. The three Kiepenheuer publications were: *Baal* (Potsdam, 1922), *Leben Eduards des Zweiten* [*The Life of Edward II*] (Potsdam, 1924), and *Bertolt Brechts Taschenpostille* (1926).

7. Elisabeth Hauptmann to Siegfried Unseld, 12 August 1964, Suhrkamp Archives. I had asked her about Brecht's first relations with publishers; she described to me at length "this long story ... whose details I remember distinctly because it occurred at the beginning of my acquaintance with Brecht."

8. Brecht to Herzfelde, printed in facsimile in *Der Malik-Verlag,* p. 155.

9. Herzfelde, "Über Brecht," p. 132.

10. Herzfelde writes, "In this way the money for the trip back was obtained and my activity as a publisher was over." This can't be quite correct. In the Malik catalog, Aufbau-Verlag announces an Aurora Series; the editors were the same authors as in New York, i.e., Brecht was one of them. Herzfelde is not mentioned. According to the catalog, "the Aufbau-Verlag, Berlin, has obtained the *rights* to all publications of the New York firm and is issuing them as the Aurora Series." Herzfelde cannot have given up his publishing activity entirely, for Brecht

wrote to Suhrkamp that he was keeping his word to W. H. regarding the complete edition. In 1951, Aufbau published Brecht's *Hundert Gedichte* [One hundred poems]. We know that Herzfelde made the selection together with Brecht; he also wrote a signed afterword, although he is not mentioned as compiler or editor.

11. Brecht, *Arbeitsjournal: 1938–1955,* ed. Werner Hecht, 3 vols. (Frankfurt, 1973), 2:740.

12. Brecht to Suhrkamp, October 1945, Suhrkamp Archives. Suhrkamp's letter has not been preserved. Suhrkamp did not write to Brecht during the Third Reich in order to avoid trouble with the authorities. It is significant that, in this letter to Suhrkamp, Brecht recalls that the publisher had helped him to escape. Then he recapitulated his exile. "Of course I've done a lot of writing." The "of course" is also significant; it shows the importance of productivity for Brecht. We can "go through some of it together": he turns to Suhrkamp as a co-worker and partner. And then the remark, "Everything needs to be revised": not a single play could be performed the way he wrote it.

The rest of the letter is also interesting. He asks about his friends Caspar Neher, Hesse-Burri, and Müller-Eisert. Then, at the end, he notes, "Heinrich Mann, Feuchtwanger, Leonhard Frank, Kortner, Eisler are still living here." Added in handwriting, "Döblin is leaving for France—he is a French citizen." Not a word about Thomas Mann.

13. All quotations are taken from the correspondence between Brecht and Suhrkamp in the Suhrkamp Archives.

14. Brecht to Horst Baerensprung, 8 November 1946: "In due course I signed two contracts with Bloch Erben, first a contract for *Die Dreigroschenoper* (according to which Elisabeth Hauptmann and Kurt Weill were to share in the royalties) and after that another contract guaranteeing me an income for seven years on the basis of my dramatic production during those seven years. According to this second contract, my earnings from *Die Dreigroschenoper* could under no circumstances be deducted from this new

income. When the reactionaries became stronger in Germany, Herr von Wreede, who was beginning to have doubts about the financial success of my future productions, tried to persuade me to let him deduct my earnings from *Die Dreigroschenoper* from the income payments stipulated in the second contract; only under these circumstances was he willing to continue with the payments. We did not reach an agreement. The publisher discontinued the payments even before Hitler seized power and thus unilaterally broke the second contract with me. Under Hitler, the publisher withheld all my earnings from *Die Dreigroschenoper,* in part on the grounds that, according to the second contract, I owed him money. It is now my position that the publisher never had the slightest right to withhold my *Dreigroschenoper* earnings and that he also no longer has any claim to the income already paid me, since he broke the second contract even before Hitler came to power. Only if the publisher recognizes this am I prepared to enter into a new contract for *Die Dreigroschenoper.*"

15. I have referred to the year 1947 in another connection in Siegfried Unseld, "Kein weißer Elefant" [Not a white elephant], in *Helene Weigel zum 70. Geburtstag* [For Helene Weigel's seventieth birthday] (Berlin, 1970), pp. 47 ff.

16. Announced in *Neue Bücher im Suhrkamp Verlag 1952* [New books with Suhrkamp Verlag 1952], Suhrkamp Archives.

17. There is still much to be written about Elisabeth Hauptmann as Brecht's collaborator. Brecht wrote a kind of testimonial for her in 1935, which was meant to be helpful when she applied for work: "She possesses extraordinary linguistic gifts and has assisted me in an active and critical way with all my dramatic works; she has herself written novellas."

Until her death on April 20, 1973, she was the definitive editor of Brecht's works, not only for the 1953 ff. edition but also for that of 1967. Werner Hecht edited the theoretical writings for both of these editions, but

Hauptmann did all the others. She edited the dramas almost completely, and the fragments selectively. She had some difficulty with the poems: on the one hand, she slavishly followed the arrangement of the original volumes of verse; on the other, she shied away from lines that she found too daring and assigned many poems to the category of fragments, which were supposed to be published at a later date. Hauptmann was a collaborator of the highest rank. No one else served Brecht so well as she during those years.

18. Brecht, *Gesammelte Werke* [Collected Works], ed. Suhrkamp Verlag in collaboration with Elisabeth Hauptmann (Frankfurt am Main, 1967), 7: 948. This is a double edition: 8 vols. in cloth and 20 vols. in soft cover with identical pagination.

19. Brecht, *Werke,* 7:1,015.

20. Feuchtwanger, "Bertolt Brecht," *Sinn und Form,* 2d special issue devoted to Brecht (Berlin, 1957), p. 105.

21. *Versuche 1–3* (Berlin, 1930), p. 1.

22. Brecht, *Werke,* 8:554.

23. Herzfelde, "Über Brecht" [On Brecht], *Neue Deutsche Literatur* (October 1956), pp. 11 ff. "If a visitor came," Bernhard Reich wrote, "Brecht saw in this an event favorable to his work—he read him an especially troublesome passage, testing the quality of his work on the visitor or going over it with him."—"Erinnerungen an den jungen Brecht" [Memories of the young Brecht], *Sinn und Form,* pp. 434 f.

24. The most important collaborators: Karl von Appen, W. H. Auden, Eric Bentley, Ruth Berlau, Benno Besson, Arnolt Bronnen, Paul Dessau, Slatan Dudow, Hanns Eisler, Erich Engel, Lion Feuchtwanger, Jakob Geis, Elisabeth Hauptmann, Emil Hesse-Burri, Wieland Herzfelde, Christopher Isherwood, Karl Korsch, Charles Laughton, Peter Lorre, Egon Monk, Otto Müller-Eisert, Caspar Neher, Peter Palitzsch, Georg Pfanzelt, Vladimir Pozner, Bernhard Reich, Käthe Rülicke, Margarete Steffin, Erwin Strittmatter, Peter Suhrkamp, Bernhard

Viertel, Helene Weigel, Kurt Weill, Günther Weisen-
born, Manfred Wekwerth, and Hella Wuolijoki.

25. See Brecht, *Arbeitsjournal,* 2:597 f.

26. In Brecht's writings on literature, Joyce is mentioned in-
frequently and always as seen by others. In response to a
questionnaire "concerning the best books of the year
[1928]" he writes, "The novel *Ulysses* by James Joyce,
because in Döblin's opinion it has changed the situation
of the novel and as a collection of various methods of
observation (introduction of the interior monologue and
so forth) represents an indispensable reference work for
writers" (*Werke,* 8:65). Thereafter, Joyce always appears
only in connection with the controversy with Lukács: "I
have heard Joyce's book [*Ulysses*] praised for its realism
by very intelligent readers. . . . Not that they praised the
style as such (some spoke of mannerism), but it seemed
to them to be realistic in subject matter. Probably I will
be called a compromiser when I confess that I laughed
over *Ulysses* almost as much as over *Schweyk,* and someone like me usually laughs only at realistic satires"
(*Werke,* 8:293).

27. Although Brecht characterized Kafka as "a truly serious
phenomenon," he also said it was to the credit of the times
"that the times candidly admit they are not in favor of
phenomena like Kafka" (*Werke,* 8:61). Later, in 1938, he
placed Kafka in the category of "modern Czechoslova-
kian literature," which he preferred to all other bourgeois
literatures: "I am thinking here of the names Hašek,
Kafka, and Bezruč. . . . bourgeois democracies have fas-
cist dictatorship in their bones, so to speak, and Kafka
described with remarkable imagination the future concentration camps, the future unreliability of the legal
system, the future absolute state, the apathetic state of
many isolated individuals whose lives are governed by
inaccessible forces. . . . German writers will definitely
have to read these works, as difficult as that is, since the
mood of futility is very strong and a key is needed for
everything, just as though it were written in code. I see

that I have enumerated many negative points in these few sentences that were intended as homage, and indeed I am very far from suggesting a model here" (*Werke* 8:447).

28. Hanns Eisler, "Bertolt Brecht und die Musik," *Sinn und Form,* pp. 440 ff. Heinrich Strobel (*Paul Hindemith* [Mainz, 1948], p. 52), wrote: "This was the only time that Hindemith collaborated with a really significant poet: with Bert Brecht. People thought at the time that this was the beginning of a long cooperative effort, but this hope was not fulfilled. Brecht's ideas concerning a new, politically didactic art and Hindemith's musical tendencies could not be reconciled in the long run."

29. Brecht to Döblin, 1938, Walter Benjamin's posthumous papers, Archives of the German Academy of Arts, Berlin.

30. See Brecht's statement on the writing of *Galilei* in *Materialien zu Brechts "Leben des Galilei"* [Documents relating to Brecht's *Galileo*], edition suhrkamp, vol. 44 (Frankfurt, 1963).

31. To mention some examples of such materials in addition to the most familiar case, John Gay's *Beggar's Opera* (trans. Elisabeth Hauptmann), which became Brecht's most popular play (the name *Dreigroschenoper,* by the way, originated with Feuchtwanger): he wrote the poem "Kohlen für Mike" ["Coals for Mike"] in 1926 after reading the novel *Poor White* by Sherwood Anderson; "Die Ballade von der Billigung der Welt" ["The Ballad of the World's Approbation"] was based on an emergency decree by Chancellor Brüning; the occasion for the poem "Die Teppichweber von Kujan-Baluk ehren Lenin" ["The Rug Weavers of Kujan-Baluk Honor Lenin"] was an anonymous report, "Ein Denkmal für Lenin" [A monument to Lenin] in the *Frankfurter Zeitung* of 30 October 1929 (this newspaper clipping with Brecht's underlining is preserved in the Brecht Archive); the play *Die Tage der Commune* [*The Days of the Commune*] was written in 1948–49 as a kind of counterscheme after reading Nordahl Grieg's drama *Niederlage* [Defeat]; *Der kaukasische Kreidekreis* was a commissioned work and probably goes back to Klabund's version of Li Hsing

Tao's *Kreidekreis;* and the "folk play" *Herr Puntila und sein Knecht Matti* owed its creation to a competition—it was based on stories and the outline for a play by the Finnish writer Hella Wuolijoki.

32. Feuchtwanger, p. 103.
33. The typescript is among Elisabeth Hauptmann's papers, Berlin Academy of Arts.
34. Bunge, "Vorbemerkungen zu einer Historisch-kritischen Ausgabe der Schriften Bertolt Brechts" [Prefatory remarks to a historical-critical edition of Brecht's writings], *Spectrum* (Berlin, 1958), p. 25.
35. We have already mentioned that Peter Suhrkamp's correspondence with Helene Weigel contains an "application for duty exemption" for the luggage the Brecht family intended to take along from the United States to Switzerland and from there to Germany. She described the luggage as consisting of thirteen pieces: five trunks with clothes, a basket with linens and dishes, a trunk with a sewing machine and book-binding material, a trunk with photographic equipment, two boxes of books, two trunks with books, a chair" (see Unseld, "Kein weißer Elefant," p. 47 ff.).
36. Hertha Ramthun, *Bertolt Brecht-Archiv: Bestandsverzeichnis des literarischen Nachlasses,* vol. 1, Plays (Berlin, 1969).
37. Quoted by Hans Mayer, *Bertolt Brecht und die Tradition* [Brecht and tradition] (Pfullingen, 1971), p. 20.
38. See Karl Schlechta, *Der Fall Nietzsche* [The case of Nietzsche] (Munich, 1959), p. 128, and Günther Müller, "Goethe-Literatur seit 1945," *Deutsche Vierteljahresschrift* (1952), pp. 377–410.
39. The quotations from Schiller and Wieland are in Viscount Goschen, *The Life and Times of Georg Joachim Goschen, Publisher and Printer of Leipzig, 1752–1828,* 2 vols. (New York: G. P. Putnam's Sons/London: John Murray, 1903). Especially relevant are chapters 16, 17, and 19; the latter begins: "I now approach a very sad episode in my grandfather's life—a long estrangement from his most distinguished and most beloved author-friend." See also

chapter 20, "The Great Undertaking," in which the history of the Wieland edition is recounted.

40. When the periodical *Die Dame* questioned Brecht (on 1 October 1928) about his "most vivid [literary] impression," he replied, "You'll laugh: the Bible."

41. Brecht scholars have attested to the publisher's "exemplary thoroughness and lucid arrangement" (Urs Jenny, *Süddeutsche Zeitung,* 16 January 1967). "The most complete, reliable, best arranged Brecht edition there is, the easiest to use by virtue of its index and notes" (Günter Schloz, South German Radio, 19 October 1967); "All in all, this publishing venture is probably the most meritorious in recent decades" (Peter Hamm, *Stuttgarter Zeitung,* 15 November 1967).

42. *Bibliographie Bertolt Brecht: Titelverzeichnis Band 1: Deutschsprachige Veröffentlichungen aus den Jahren 1913–1972: Werke von Brecht: Sammlungen: Dramatik* [. . . Index of titles: vol. 1: Publications in German from the years 1913–1972: works by Brecht: collections: dramas] (Berlin and Weimar: Academy of Art of the German Democratic Republic, 1975), p. v.

43. Mayer, *Brecht in der Geschichte: Drei Versuche* [Brecht in History: three essays], Bibliothek Suhrkamp, vol. 284 (Frankfurt, 1971).

44. Baxandall, "The Americanization of Bert Brecht," in *Brecht heute: Jahrbuch der internationalen Brecht Gesellschaft* [Brecht today: yearbook of the international Brecht society], ed. John Fuegi, 1 (1971): 150 ff. Baxandall's article ends with the words, "To conclude briefly, in result of the emergence of a thoroughly critical outlook among a considerable and growing number of Americans, Brecht has gained a positive Americanization to an extent not to be thought possible a few years ago. Our poet has even become a ponderable political factor—I do not think it exaggerated to say so. His life work has passed the barrier of its national and political culture. With admitted difficulties and divergencies of reception, we now have it—the lighted torch of a sensuous consciousness with its imaginative productions, which in Brecht's case are so

precious that we may in no wise neglect the further
transmission."

45. Karasek wrote, in part: "Brecht has been dead for over
twenty years. But our memory, intent upon rank and
Olympian consecrations, considers him the greatest
dramatist of the twentieth century, whose work endures.
Really?

"Giorgio Strehler, whom a stubborn rumor wants to
make into the most significant director and man of the
theater of our day, is considered Brecht's prophet. Ivan
Nagel, director of the Hamburger Schauspielhaus,
brought mountain and prophet together, uniting them for
the season's premiere in *Der gute Mensch von Sezuan*—the
mountain labored and brought forth a 'theatrical event.'
But things don't always turn out as expected. The combination of Strehler's straining for effects and Brecht's
simulated naiveté resulted at best in a 'beautiful
corpse.' . . . Just as a scarcity of game necessitates a closed
season, so too grass must be allowed to grow for a while
over plays that have nearly been trampled to death.
Brecht would be spared if we were spared such performances."

46. Kesting, *Bertolt Brecht in Selbstzeugnissen und Dokumenten*
[. . . A self-portrait with documents] (Hamburg, 1959).

47. *Bertolt Brechts Gedichte und Lieder,* [Poems and Songs]
Bibliothek Suhrkamp, vol. 33 (Frankfurt, 1958), p. 6. In
the same foreword, Suhrkamp speaks about Brecht's
"political" aspects: "I do not—it must be said—share the
opinion expressed by some that Brecht's talent suffered
from politics; I am more inclined to think that political
dogma saved him from the anarchy and cynical nihilism of
his early period. . . . Songs that a poet intends to be used
for political purposes are always lapidary and plebian—
that is the nature of the genre. (Kleist's 'Kriegslied der
Deutschen' [War song of the Germans] or his 'An die
Königin von Preußen' [To the Queen of Prussia] are not
pure works of art, either.)"

48. Wekwerth, *Notate* [Notations], edition suhrkamp, vol.
219 (Frankfurt, 1967), p. 12.

49. Quoted in Mayer, *Brecht in der Geschichte,* p. 116. Now we know that this was one of Brecht's jokes and that he by no means had such good grades in Latin, which does not mean, however, that his style was not Latinate.

50. Brecht, *Werke,* 4:656.

51. Brecht, *Werke,* 8:496.

52. Brecht, *Werke,* 5:564.

53. Brecht, *Werke,* 7:57 f.

54. Quoted by Mayer, *Brecht in der Geschichte,* p. 17.

55. Herzfelde, "Über Bertolt Brecht," p. 134.

56. Brecht, *Werke,* 7:725.

57. Mayer, *Brecht in der Geschichte,* pp. 24 f.

58. Brecht, *Werke* 7:1276. Brecht's essay "Einschüchterung durch Klassizität [Intimidation by classicism], from which this quotation is taken, was occasioned by his work on a production of Goethe's *Urfaust* (premiere, 23 April 1952).

59. Brecht, *Werke,* 10:1,014.

60. Brecht, *Werke,* 7:952.

Rainer Maria Rilke and His Publishers

1. Rilke, *Briefe an Seinen Verleger: 1906–1926* [Letters to his publisher . . .], new expanded ed., 2 vols. (Wiesbaden, 1949), 2:519.

2. This and succeeding extracts are from Hartmut Engelhardt, ed., *Materialien zu Rainer Maria Rilke Die Aufzeichnungen des Malte Laurids Brigge* [Documents relating to Rainer Maria Rilke's *Notebooks of Malte Laurids Brigge*], suhrkamp taschenbuch, vol. 174 (Frankfurt, 1974), pp. 11 ff.

3. Ingeborg Schnack, *Rainer Maria Rilke: Chronik seins Lebens und seines Werkes* [. . . A chronicle of his life and work], 2 vols. (Frankfurt, 1975), p. 19.

4. Ibid., pp. 23 f.

5. Reported by Anton Kippenberg in *Reden und Schriften* [Speeches and writings] (Wiesbaden, 1952), p. 104.

6. Engelhardt, *Materialien,* p. 15.

7. Schröder, *Gesammelte Werke in 8 Bänden* [Collected works, 8 vols.] (Frankfurt, 1952–1965), 3:945 ff.

8. Ibid., 3:959–60.

9. Ibid., 3:965.

10. Kippenberg, p. 38.

11. Rilke, *Briefe an seinen Verleger,* 1:15.

12. Ibid., p. 16.

13. Ibid., p. 18.

14. Kippenberg, p. 33.

15. The history of Rilke's attitude toward Goethe is presented in my book, *"Das Tagebuch" Goethes und Rilkes "Sieben Gedichte"* [Goethe's "The Diary" and Rilke's "Seven poems"], Insel-Bücherei, vol. 1,000 (Frankfurt, 1978).

16. Schnack, p. 272.

17. Mendelssohn, *S. Fischer und sein Verlag* [S. Fischer and his publishing house] (Frankfurt, 1970), p. 465.

18. Rilke, *Briefe,* 1:35–41.

19. Schnack, p. 302.

20. Rilke, *Briefe,* 1:78.

21. In the original, this is a play on words: *Hühnchen* (chicken) can be read as a homonym of the diminutive of *Hühne* (giant).—Translators' note.

22. Rilke, *Briefe* 1:176.

23. Ibid., p. 177.

24. Engelhardt, *Materialien,* p. 121.

25. Kippenberg, p. 108.

26. Rainer Maria Rilke–Katharina Kippenberg, *Briefwechsel 1910–1926* [Correspondence], ed. Bettina von Bomhard (Wiesbaden, 1954), p. 594.

27. Hesse, *Werkausgabe,* 12: 442–44.

28. Kippenberg, p. 109.

29. Walter Benjamin, *Briefe,* ed. and annotated by Theodor W. Adorno and Gershom Scholem, 2 vols. (Frankfurt, 1966).

30. Rilke, *Briefe,* ed. Karl Altheim and the Rilke Archive in Weimar in cooperation with Ruth Sieber-Rilke (Wiesbaden, 1950).

31. Ibid., pp. 760 f.

Robert Walser and His Publishers

1. Robert Walser, *Das Gesamtwerk,* [The Complete Works], ed. Jochen Greven, 13 vols. (Geneva and Hamburg: Helmut Kossodo, 1972 ff.), 11:51. All quotations from Walser's works are from this edition.

2. Carl Seelig, *Wanderungen mit Robert Walser* [Walks with Robert Walser], Bibliothek Suhrkamp, vol. 554 (Frankfurt, 1977), p. 37.

3. Benjamin, "Robert Walser," in *Schriften* [Writings], ed. Theodor W. and Gretel Adorno with the cooperation of Friedrich Podszus (Frankfurt, 1955), 2:151.

4. Martin Walser, *Erfahrungen und Leseerfahrungen* [Experiences and experiences in reading], edition suhrkamp, vol. 109 (Frankfurt, 1965). I particularly recommend this book; the second part contains three significant essays, "Hölderlin auf dem Dachboden" [Hölderlin in the attic], "Leseerfahrungen mit Marcel Proust" [The experience of reading Marcel Proust], and "Arbeit am Beispiel: Über Franz Kafka" [Work on the example: on Franz Kafka], and then a study that is especially illuminating for me, "Alleinstehender Dichter: Über Robert Walser" [A poet alone: on Robert Walser].

5. Additional sources are contained in Elio Fröhlich and Robert Mächler, eds., *Robert Walser zum Gedenken: Aus Anlaß seines 20. Todestages am 25. Dezember 1976: Im Auftrag des Robert Walser-Archivs der Carl Seelig-Stiftung Zürich* [In memory of Robert Walser: commemorating the twentieth anniversary of his death, December 25, 1976: Commissioned by the Robert Walser Archive of the Carl Seelig Foundation in Zurich] (Zurich and Frankfurt, 1977). Other relevant literature: Paul Mayer, ed., *Ernst Rowohlt: In Selbstzeugnissen und Bilddokumenten* [. . . A self-portrait in words and pictures] (Hamburg, 1967); Peter de Mendelssohn, *S. Fischer und sein Verlag* [S. Fischer and his publishing house] (Frankfurt, 1970).

6. Schröder, *Gesammelte Werke in 8 Bänden* [Collected works, 8 vols.] (Frankfurt, 1952 ff.), 3:945 ff.

7. Widmann, *Bund* (Bern), no. 344 (9 December 1904).

8. I acknowledge with great gratitude that it was Hesse who called my attention to Walser's work. I refer to Hesse's writings on Walser repeatedly in this chapter.

9. Seelig, pp. 31 ff.

10. Robert Mächler, *Das Leben Robert Walsers: Eine dokumentarische Biographie* [Robert Walser's life: a documented biography] (Geneva and Darmstadt, 1966).

11. Seelig, p. 59.

12. Walser, "Abhandlung" [An essay], 8:183.

13. Seelig, pp. 62, 78.

14. Hofmiller, *Süddeutsche Monatshefte,* 2 (1909): 253.

15. Seelig, pp. 89 f., 90, 59 f., 102.

16. Kurt Pinthus, *Zeitschrift für Bücherfreunde,* n.s. 7 (1915): col. 196.

17. Kurt Wolff, *Briefwechsel eines Verlegers 1911–1963* [Correspondence of a publisher . . .], ed. Bernhard Zeller and Ellen Otten (Frankfurt, 1966).

18. Loerke, *Neue Rundschau,* 2 (1918): 253.

19. Seelig, pp. 21, 77.

20. Walser to Max Rychner, 31 May 1927.

21. Seelig, p. 26.

22. Jochen Greven, "Robert Walser-Forschungen: Bericht über die Edition des Gesamtwerks und der Bearbeitung des Nachlasses, mit Hinweisen auf Walser-Studien der letzten Jahre" [Research on Robert Walser: a report on the edition of the complete works and the handling of the posthumous papers, with reference to Walser studies of recent years], *Euphorion* 64 (March 1970).

23. Mächler, p. 251.

24. Quoted in a letter from Müller to Seelig, 14 May 1957.

25. Seelig, p. 26.

26. Elias Canetti, *Die Provinz des Menschen: Aufzeichnungen 1942–1972* [*The Human Province*], Fischer taschenbuch (Frankfurt, 1976).

27. Seelig, p. 122.

28. Mächler, p. 231.

29. Seelig, p. 126.

30. Mächler, p. 193.

31. Seelig, pp. 81, 96, 30, 36 f.

32. Ibid., p. 29.
33. Ibid., p. 135.
34. Ibid., pp. 17 f.
35. Ibid., pp. 107, 102.
36. Ibid., pp. 117, 66.
37. Ibid., p. 147.
38. Ibid., pp. 168 f.
39. Ibid., p. 175.
40. Kerr, *Die Aufnahme von Robert Walsers Werk seit seinem Tod 1956* [The reception of Robert Walser's work since his death in 1956]. This report was later published in *Robert Walser zum Gedenken.*